PRAISE FOR THE CALL

"Featuring a well-paced plot and an engaging protagonist, Mills's new series launch is a solid . . . suspense title."
Library Journal

"Mills kicks off the Call of Duty series with a novel jam-packed with twists that will leave readers breathless. Intriguing characters, a crisis of faith, and the element of surprise make this novel a must-read for any avid suspense reader."
Romantic Times, 4½-star review

"Once again, Mills has crafted an engaging page-turner with intriguing characters facing difficult choices."
CBA Retailers + Resources

"A fast-paced, character-driven thriller. . . . Readers who enjoy the works of Dee Henderson, especially her O'Malley series, will love *Breach of Trust*."
Midwest Book Review

"Mills has spun an action-packed tale of romance, deception, redemption, and trials. Recommended to anyone who enjoys a little romance and a lot of adventure."
Church Libraries

"DiAnn Mills has written an excellent suspense novel. . . . highly recommended."
ChristianBookPreviews.com

"If you have been waiting for a story to match Dee Henderson's O'Malley series or Susan May Warren's Team Hope, look no further than *Breach of Trust*, the first in the Call of Duty series."
TitleTrakk.com

SWORN to PROTECT

DiAnn Mills

Tyndale House Publishers, Inc.
Carol Stream, Illinois

Visit Tyndale's exciting Web site at www.tyndale.com.

Visit DiAnn Mills at www.diannmills.com.

TYNDALE and Tyndale's quill logo are registered trademarks of Tyndale House Publishers, Inc.

Sworn to Protect

Designed by Jessie McGrath

Edited by Kathryn S. Olson

Published in association with the literary agency of Janet Kobobel Grant, Books & Such, Inc., 4788 Carissa Avenue, Santa Rosa, CA 95405.

Library of Congress Cataloging-in-Publication Data

Mills, DiAnn.
  Sworn to protect / DiAnn Mills.
    p. cm. — (Call of duty ; 2)
    ISBN 978-1-4143-2051-9 (pbk.)
    1. Border patrol agents—Fiction. I. Title.
  PS3613.I567S96 2010
  813'.6—dc22   2009032537

Printed in the United States of America

16 15 14 13 12 11 10
 7   6   5   4   3   2   1

This book is dedicated to the courageous men and women of the Border Patrol, who protect our country's borders.

★

Don't copy the behavior and customs of this world, but let God transform you into a new person by changing the way you think. Then you will learn to know God's will for you, which is good and pleasing and perfect.

ROMANS 12:2

★

Many thanks to all who made this book possible: Carol Cox;
Richard Mabry, MD; Kathy Roeth; and Debbie Gail Smith.

★

CHAPTER 1

We are truly a nation of immigrants.
But we are also a nation of laws.
BRENT ASHABRANNER

McAllen, Texas

THE RIO GRANDE was not just murky. It was toxic. Danika Morales respected the river's temperament—lazy and rushing, crystal and muddy, breathtaking and devastating. To many illegal immigrants, its flowing water signified hope and an opportunity for a better tomorrow, while others viewed the river crossing as a means of smuggling drugs or spreading terrorism. But for Danika, the depths meant death, and it didn't discriminate among its victims. That was why she chose a Border Patrol badge and carried a gun.

Shortly after the 8 a.m. muster, Danika snatched up the keys to the Tahoe assigned to her for the next ten hours and checked out an M4. A hum of voices, most with Hispanic accents and clipped with occasional laughter, swirled around the station. A labyrinth of sights and sounds had succeeded in disorienting her. A daze.

She took a sip of the steaming coffee in hopes no one saw how the day's date affected her. Her hands shook. The twelfth of July. The second anniversary of Toby's murder. She thought she could handle it better than this, but the raw ache still seared her heart.

"Tough day for me too," Jacob whispered beside her. "We can get through this together." The familiar tone of voice, as in many times before, nearly paralyzed her. Jacob sounded so much like his brother.

She stood shoulder to shoulder with her brother-in-law and glanced at his muscular frame and the silver streaks in his closely cropped hair, everything about him oddly different from Toby. Gone were the gentleness, the patience, and the outstretched arms of love.

"Thanks. But I'm all right."

He frowned, a typical expression. "Well, I'm not, and you shouldn't be either."

She was in no mood to rile him today. "I miss Toby every minute of the day, but we have to move on. He would have wanted it that way."

"Not till his murderer is found." Jacob's jaw tightened. "I'm disappointed in you."

Danika took another sip of the hot coffee, burning her tongue. Caustic words threatened to surface and add one more brick to the wall dividing them. "I want the killer found too. I'm committed to it. I think about him every day and mourn for our daughter, who will never know her daddy. But I choose not to spend my time harboring hate and vengeance."

"You must not have really loved my brother."

The words cut deep, as Jacob must have known they would. No woman could have loved Toby like she did. "I refuse to be browbeaten by you anymore. Your hate is going to explode in your own backyard one day." She stopped herself before she lit a match to his temper. Actually, she'd rather have been dropped in the bush for the next ten hours with a shotgun and a can of OFF! than argue with him. But the time had come to distance herself from Jacob.

"Hey, Danika," an agent called, "do these belong to you?"

She turned to see wiry Felipe Chavez carrying a vase with a huge bouquet of roses. *They remembered.* She swallowed a chunk of life. "Oh, guys, you didn't have to do this."

Felipe made his way toward her. The other agents hushed; then one of them started to clap. She smiled through the tears as he handed her the clear glass vase. The sweet fragrance no longer reminded her of death, but of life and her resolve to live each day in a way that commemorated Toby's devotion to her and their little daughter. Perhaps this was what the two-year marker meant.

She took the roses and studied the small crowd of agents. Good men, all of them—even Jacob.

"We cared about what happened to Toby too," Felipe said with a grim smile.

Danika brushed her finger around one of the delicate petals and formed her words. Memories had stalked her like a demon since last night. "Don't know what to say except thank you. Toby was a soldier for his own cause, and he spent his life doing what he believed in. Just like all of us."

One agent shook his head, frowned, and left the room. Far too many explanations for his disapproval raced through her mind. But Danika needed to put the ugliness behind her.

She set the flowers on the long table in front of her. "Today is the second anniversary of Toby's death. All of you have looked after me and my daughter, especially during holidays and special occasions. His death is why I'm more dedicated than ever to help protect the border." She paused, sensing her emotions rushing into chaos. "I appreciate your remembering him and the sacrifice he made, especially since his beliefs were controversial." Enough said.

She took a deep, cleansing breath. "I brought doughnuts."

And they were buttermilk, Toby's favorite.

She glanced at Jacob, hoping to end the tension between

them. How Barbara could stay married to him was beyond her comprehension. He treated her and their four kids like yesterday's trash.

Danika wound through the crowd of agents, greeting those who offered condolences and others who offered a good-morning.

The field operations supervisor, Agent Oden Herrera, stood in front of the flags—the U.S., Homeland Security, and the Border Patrol. Pushing the emotions of regret and grief about Toby aside, Danika captured the supervisor's attention. "During the muster you said intel had picked up a cocaine drop last night?"

Herrera walked to a wall map and pointed. "Like I said earlier: arrested seven men and two women right along here, your area. A kid had a small bag of cocaine on him. Most likely a deterrent. The drug smuggler either hid it before being apprehended, or he's still waiting for someone to pick him up. Dogs have been out there most of the night, but Barnett and Fire-Eater are headed that way in a few minutes."

Danika finished her coffee and made her way into the stifling heat and stopped by Jon Barnett's truck. As Fire-Eater's handler, he had everyone's admiration, and the Belgian sheepdog had a reputation for being the best of the K-9s. Barnett snapped on the dog's leash and waved.

"I hear we're working the same area today." Danika refrained from patting Fire-Eater. Some days he wasn't people friendly. After seeing the dog in action a few times when he'd found drug runners, she sometimes felt sorry for those he brought down.

Barnett grinned and wiped the sweat already beading on his face. "He's a good dog, Morales. Just needs a little help with his people skills." He laughed, his freckles deepening in the intense sun. "And he's great with the wife and kids. Like another member of the family." He pulled out his keys. "Do you want to talk? We have a few minutes."

All she really wanted was for the day to be over. Talking

increased the chances of liquid emotion—which was more lethal than the river flowing between the U.S. and Mexico. "No thanks. I'm fine."

"Do you *need* to talk?"

"It's been two years." Therapeutic or not, she would not open up, even to a sweet guy like Barnett. She'd spent hours building a reputation as a tough agent, and she wasn't about to take a nosedive now.

"Right, and the sooner you admit that today has crept up on you worse than a case of food poisoning, the better you'll feel."

She had to agree. "Have you turned psychologist?"

"Fire-Eater and five kids taught me all I know."

"I had a dog when I was a kid," she said, looking for any subject except Toby. "Gentle, sensed my moods, smart. My best friend. Sure missed him when he was gone." Danika blinked back a tear, despising her reaction. She stared at Fire-Eater rather than look into Barnett's face.

"I bet he slept at the foot of your bed."

Fire-Eater climbed into the backseat of the double-cab truck.

"Sometimes in it. We even shared meals. I didn't like meat, and he'd eat it for me."

"Who's your best friend now?"

She swallowed the ever-increasing lump in her throat. "Toby's gone, and I have a tough time in church."

"Confession is a beginning. Any family?"

"Toby's family has been good to me." *Never mind Jacob.* "My folks never approved of my marriage." She sucked in a breath. It hissed like the poisonous snakes she feared. "Well-meaning friends do this to me."

"Do you feel any better?"

Sneak. "Yeah, thanks, doc. You—"

Fire-Eater barked. No doubt anxious to get moving. The animal and Jacob had similar personalities, but today she'd rather be with the dog.

Danika turned off Old Military Road and bounced along a narrow dirt and gravel path, bordered by tall, thick grass and brush and laden with prickly pears on the Rio Grande side and more thick brush on the other. Jon had radioed ahead and reported signs from last night, but nothing new. Every agent was on alert. Trouble brewed along the entire two-thousand-mile border between Mexico and the United States. Drug cartels were slaughtering innocent people in the streets, and those on the U.S. side feared it was only a matter of time before the fighting spilled over the line. Not on her watch.

She drove slowly past the few houses perched on the right side of the road, most of which had been stash houses at one time or another, havens for illegal aliens and drug smugglers. She stopped the truck beside a well-worn trail to look for recent signs in the dirt. After a generous spray of mosquito repellent on her uniform and hands, she stepped into the stifling ninety-degree heat and bent to study the hours-old footprints indicating where the illegals had gained access into Texas before being apprehended. Most of them only wanted an opportunity to better themselves, but others had a darker agenda. At least she hoped the footprints had been accounted for.

A breeze from the north fanned her face and offered a brief reprieve from the unrelenting sun. The tall grass with its thick growth waved as though mocking her commitment to the Border Patrol.

Fifteen minutes later, Barnett radioed a call for assistance.

"Spotted a man wearing a backpack near the 112 sensor. He headed into the *carrizo*."

Danika ran back to the truck and raced her vehicle toward Barnett's location. She wanted to tell him to wait for backup and not search through the thick grass alone, but she knew Barnett and Fire-Eater were a team and stayed on the traffic. The smuggler probably hid on a rattler's nest.

She was the first to respond to Barnett's request. Pulling in behind his truck, she unclipped her HK from her belt while radioing her arrival. She grabbed her cell phone and dialed his number.

"Barnett, I'm here," she said. "Tell me you're not in the middle of the *carrizo*."

He chuckled. "Fire-Eater's after him. I'm skirting it. Neither one of us is coming out until we have our man."

She pocketed her cell phone and followed the agent's footprints on the dusty road until they disappeared into the thicket. Hot as it was, the Kevlar vest felt good, even if it was worthless against a stab wound or a shotgun blast.

Fire-Eater barked, snapping Danika's attention toward the riverbank. The dog growled from somewhere in the depths of the overgrowth.

Gunfire cracked in the still morning air. Alert to the danger, she pulled her weapon.

"This is the United States Border Patrol! Come out with your hands up!" Barnett's voice roared.

Another shot fired. Fire-Eater yelped.

Blood pumping, Danika yanked out her radio. "Shots fired. Shots fired. Agent or K-9 may be down."

Two more shots pierced the air.

When Barnett didn't respond, she clicked the radio in place on her belt. "Barnett," she yelled, "tell me you're all right."

Nothing.

A dark-haired man emerged from the right side of the road

7

several yards away, wearing a backpack that no doubt contained drugs. His attention scattered in different directions.

"*Alto, o disparo,*" she said.

The man turned and fired at her before racing across the road. The bullet angled to her left. Danika returned the fire and sank a bullet into his thigh. He fell, and she raced toward him.

"Drop the gun, or I'll be forced to shoot again."

He kept his fingers wrapped around it. She wrestled with the rage that always seemed to lie below the surface of her control. If she killed him, she could claim self-defense. But her job title meant self-control.

"I said drop the gun." She fired above him and kept running in his direction.

He lifted his hand and aimed. Instinctively she pumped a bullet into his hand. His wound caused a burst of blood to splatter the ground and the quiet air to echo with obscenities. Still he refused to release the hold on his gun.

"Do you want your whole hand blown off?" She stood over him and clamped her booted foot over his injured hand.

He screamed, and she pointed her firearm at his face. Danika trembled. She wasn't a murderer, but anger did struggle to rule her emotions.

"You'll pay for this," the man said. "I know who you are, and there's a contract out for you."

"You aren't the first or the last to threaten me." She picked up the man's gun, an older model Beretta. With his leg and hand bleeding, he wasn't going anywhere. She slipped the handcuffs from her belt and clamped them on his wrists. Rolling him over, she brushed his bleeding leg against the hard ground, and he moaned. Where was backup? *Please, let Barnett be okay. Five kids. A respected agent.*

"The drug cartels will destroy the Border Patrol."

"Big talk for a man in handcuffs."

"You wait and see who wins." He spit on her boot. "You'll never find out who killed your husband."

She smothered the gasp that nearly stole her breath. How did the man know her? know about Toby's death? He clearly had inside information—information that couldn't have been obtained easily. Unless Toby's murder was related to something bigger than she had imagined.

Focus. Now was not the time to weigh the shooter's words. Later she'd look into it.

Her gaze searched the area. An outstretched arm poked through the overgrowth where the downed man had attempted to cross the road. She hurried, gun raised, eyes taking in every inch of the brush. As she grew closer, she saw the rest of Barnett's body sprawled on the trodden grass. Blood soaked the ground, creating a small puddle of red against the vibrant green. Danika bent to his side.

Barnett moaned. "He shot Fire-Eater," he whispered. "Get him."

"I have him cuffed. Hold on. Help's coming." She pulled out the radio. "Need EMS. Agent down."

She hadn't been there for Toby, but she could be there for Barnett.

CHAPTER 2

Think like a man of action; act like a man of thought.
HENRI LOUIS BERGSON

DR. ALEX PRICE leaned forward in his chair and massaged the rock-hard knots in his shoulder and neck muscles. In the bright fluorescent lights, he allowed himself the luxury of closing his eyes for a few moments. The air-conditioning in the ER treatment area should have wakened him, but too little sleep and too many hours had taken its toll.

A child cried behind one of the pulled curtains, and an old man moaned. The sounds of his chosen profession. During the past nineteen hours, one patient after another had entered ER, and 90 percent of them couldn't speak English—and he'd bet his next paycheck that none of them were documented.

But healing was his game, and he didn't ask questions except, "Where does it hurt?" and "When was the last time you had something to eat?"

In response, Alex's stomach growled, reminding him that in order for his brain to function, it needed fuel. And the rotgut, ulcer-generating coffee didn't cut it.

He scooted back from the circular counter that separated the doctors and nurses from the patients. "I'm taking a break. Heading to the cafeteria."

"Haven't you been here over eighteen hours?"

Alex chuckled at the nurse's question. "And your point is?"

Elaine's dark eyes glanced over the top of her computer screen.

"We don't have any extra beds." Her response sounded in his ears as a garbled mixture of Spanish and English. He must really be tired.

"Depends on how picky I am." He yawned. "I'll go home after I make sure the little guy who had the appendectomy is okay."

"And the woman who delivered the twins. And then you'll try to find out more about the girl who slipped out of ER after you treated her."

Alex stood and inhaled deeply. "Elaine, it's scary how you can read my mind like that. See you in a little bit." No matter how hard he tried to suppress the hospital sights and sounds, some cases haunted him. The girl last night was one of those.

He momentarily tuned out the hospital noises and walked down the hall to the cafeteria. Breathing in the smells of eggs and bacon, his insides churned at the prospect of filling his empty stomach. Tired of the strong coffee, he filled a glass with ice and sweet tea—and plenty of it. The moment he spooned the first bite of scrambled eggs into his mouth, his mind spun again with the memories of the young woman who'd entered the ER shortly after 2 a.m. Knife wound to the chest. And as soon as she'd been stitched up, someone had snatched her out of the hospital. Her eyes had been swollen shut, and her body looked like a punching bag. Tender kidneys, too. She told him in Spanish that she'd fallen. Fat chance of that. More like she'd fallen into some jerk's fists . . . and his knife.

What bothered him the most was the rash of beaten young women flooding the ER. They were routinely dropped off at the edge of the parking lot, where the injured woman pressed a solar-powered ER button for help. To date, the women had refused to name their abusers, and all were undocumented immigrants. Alex toyed with the unlimited possibilities. After treatment, they simply walked out of the hospital.

"Mind if I join you?"

Alex recognized the voice without looking up—the chief patrol agent of the McAllen Border Patrol Operation, Edwardo Jimenez. "Sure, Ed. But I don't have a thing to report other than what I already told you—and the McAllen police."

The big man noisily pulled out the chair and lowered his muscular frame. "We found a woman's body dumped right outside the sector office gate shortly after four o'clock this morning." His soft voice didn't match his impressive stature.

"That doesn't mean she was involved in the same human trafficking outfit."

"Doesn't mean she wasn't, either." Lines ridged Ed's forehead like a plowed field in early spring. "Look, day after day we process women who would do anything to stay on this side of the border. If they have to smuggle a few drugs, sell their bodies, or allow some jerk to beat them up, then that's what they'll do. Desperation takes a lot of forms."

Alex wanted the butchers caught too, for more reasons than he had the energy to list. But cooperating with an investigation of the local Border Patrol office while treating undocumented immigrants didn't settle well, until he realized it was a part of the same commitment to healing. "So do you still think you have a rogue agent?"

Ed nodded. "Without a doubt."

Alex bit into what he'd hoped would be a crispy slice of bacon, but it was greasy and chewy. Didn't he have enough to do? "Some of the agents have family on both sides of the river."

"That doesn't mean they're breaking laws to get them here or smuggling drugs or involved in terrorists' activities or human trafficking. I know those agents, and believe me, they're dependable. Which makes this thing more of a mess. But someone is supplying our list of sensors and where they're located." Ed leaned in close and swore in Spanish. "Have you forgotten the woman sliced up like a tomato? I need your help to get this stopped. Frankly I don't care if McAllen's finest arrest who's doing this or the BP finds him stumbling over the border. I want it stopped."

Weariness tugged at Alex's eyelids, and he remembered the mountain of work left to do before he drove home to sleep a few hours and it started all over again. So why was he sitting across from Ed, debating the probability of ever learning the identity of the trafficker working in McAllen? Because every time he treated one of these women, he grew angrier.

"I'll do my best." Alex took a swallow of tea, its sweetness and caffeine pouring life into his veins like a glucose IV. "The girl from last night slipped away before I could question her."

"How? You said she was in bad shape."

"She had to have help. And no one saw a thing."

Ed scowled. "Maybe you have a leak here."

Alex had repeatedly considered the same thing. But his staff was capable and committed to healing, not sending a patient back to the same abuse. Still, human nature was strongly attracted to money.

"You must be thinking the same thing, or we'd be in a shouting match by now."

Alex picked up a piece of cold wheat toast and tried to spread hard butter over it. "We've been friends too long, and you know me too well. I'm on it."

"Good. This is just between us, and it's dangerous. I will notify Homeland Security since they're all over the problems down here."

"I understand. And for the record, I—" Alex's pager sprung to life. He glanced at the code and then his half-eaten brunch. "Gotta run."

★ ★ ★

Danika knelt at Barnett's side. The calloused veteran agent had a bullet in his stomach. He refused an ambulance or a ride to the hospital until she promised to search through the brush for Fire-Eater. Once an SUV and a truck arrived with three agents to handle the drug smuggler and tend to Barnett, she found a towel in the truck and thrashed through a barricade of prickly pears in search of the dog.

Not sure whether she wanted to find an animal tormented in pain or to face the mental thrashing of losing a good friend, Danika continued to whack through the dense growth. In less than ten minutes she spotted Fire-Eater, still breathing despite the loss of blood from his neck. Her heart ached for the animal and his handler. Did anyone ever realize the sacrifice agents and good dogs made to protect the border?

Fire-Eater attempted to lift his head, but the effort seemed too much. Danika knelt and softly soothed him before laying the towel over his head. She needed to carry him out without getting bitten.

"I have him," she called. The time spent in the gym had strengthened her arms, but it hadn't toughened her heart. Perhaps her emotions were on overload because of Barnett's serious wound, the suffering dog, the shooter's mention of her husband's murder, or the anniversary of Toby's death. Or all of it.

She loaded the dog into the caged area of another agent's truck, and the driver sped down the narrow dirt road to the vet's.

"Thanks for taking care of him." Barnett held his breath and tried to turn over. Groaning, he stared at his own blood spilled like an offering beside him. One of the agents had bandaged him, but he needed immediate medical attention. "Let me call my wife." His face had grown ashen, his breathing labored. "I don't want her to hear about Fire-Eater or me from anyone else."

"You need to get to the hospital," Danika said. "The ambulance will be here any minute."

"You drive me . . . in my own truck." Barnett closed his eyes. "Where's the shooter?"

Danika glanced across the road. "Like you, he's waiting for an ambulance. And he did have cocaine in his backpack underneath cans of Red Bull." She considered Barnett's dedication to keeping lawbreakers out of the United States.

"How much?"

"Better than ten pounds. We also confiscated his Nextel."

Barnett attempted a crooked smile. They both knew the phone had connectivity on both sides of the border and would provide the numbers of those who were involved with the drugs. "Get me in my truck. He'd better not get treated before me. The dirty . . ."

"Then let's go."

Danika glanced at the other two agents. The three of them carried Barnett to his truck and laid him awkwardly across the seat. She slid into the driver's seat and grimaced at the stinging in her legs from the tiny, often invisible barbs of the prickly pears. Later she'd yank them out with tweezers.

The other two agents hurried back to the drug smuggler. In the distance, the whine of an ambulance grew closer.

"Step on it, Morales."

How did he have the strength to bark orders? Any other time, she'd have whipped sarcasm back at him, but not today.

A cloud of dirt billowed in every direction as she raced toward the highway and McAllen Medical Center, determined to get Barnett help before the drug smuggler who'd shot him.

"The phone," Barnett whispered.

"I'll call her."

"No way."

She handed him his cell, knowing the futility of arguing. He could barely talk. Would she ever be this tough—or brave?

"Hey, Livi," Barnett said in a futile attempt at sounding light. "You might want to meet me at the medical center." His words seemed to steal his last bit of energy. "Got a little matter to take care of."

★ ★ ★

Danika sat beside Livi Barnett in the surgical waiting area of McAllen Medical Center while doctors patched up the bullet-torn body of her husband. The crowded room spoke of the many friends who had gathered to support Livi and Jon, several of whom were Border Patrol agents. That was the way of agents; they were family. However, Barnett's petite wife appeared as strong as her husband. Rumor was Barnett had plenty of scars, so Livi must have had plenty of practice.

Livi turned a stoic look Danika's way. "Are you married?"

She recalled the shooter's words. "Widow."

"I'm sorry. Are you Danika Morales?"

Danika nodded.

"Jon speaks highly of you. You have a little girl, right?"

"A four-year-old."

"Don't know what is worse, the constant dread of what might happen or facing a death call head-on."

Danika didn't have an answer. "How can a woman be prepared?"

"I'm not ready to be a widow."

"Neither was I." No woman was ever ready to bury her heart.

They sat in silence while Danika tossed around what she could say to pass the time and hopefully relieve some of Livi's concerns. But the day had brought all the memories to the forefront, and try as she might, Danika couldn't seem to get past her own ghosts. But she must. As soon as Barnett was out of danger, she'd find out about the shooter's record.

"Do you know the doctor?" Danika said.

"Alex Price? Fine man. He's stitched up Jon a few times and has taken care of the kids."

Danika braved forward. "Confidence in the doctor is always good."

"And he prays for his patients."

Toby was always praying for someone. Must life always come back to him?

Livi sucked in a breath and quickly stood. "There's Alex now." She hurried to the doctor, stepping over feet and children, and Danika followed her.

The doctor's eyes were cavernous pits indicating an extreme sleep deficit. "Livi, he's going to be all right. I removed the bullet and stopped the internal bleeding. Lucky for Jon that none of his organs are permanently damaged."

"Praise God." For the first time Livi whisked a drop of wetness from her face and attempted a shaky smile. "Thanks, Alex." She swung her attention to Danika. "This is the agent who brought him in, Danika Morales."

Danika shook his hand. He had a kind face and a firm grasp. Toby always said a man's character was in his handshake.

"My pleasure," Alex said. "Far too many people fail to appreciate the work of the Border Patrol."

She sensed someone at her side who was out of breath. Whirling around, she saw Jacob. His ashen face and the fiery gleam in his eyes alarmed her.

"Couldn't you have had the decency to call me?"

CHAPTER 3

No act of kindness, no matter how small, is ever wasted.
AESOP

ALEX THOUGHT he'd stepped into a hornet's nest when the angry border agent confronted Agent Danika Morales in the surgical waiting area, but he had no intentions of getting stung. Perhaps the other agent was a good friend of Jon Barnett's, and he was nervous and concerned about the man's condition. They all should be. Barnett had nearly passed from this life to the next and was still in critical condition.

"Jacob, I haven't had time to call you," Danika said.

The wide-shouldered agent bristled. "My guess is you've been in the waiting room with Livi."

"Precisely." Danika remained amazingly calm. Maybe Jacob was more than a coworker—a relative . . . or a boyfriend.

"Alex, this is Jacob Morales," Livi said. "Another agent from the McAllen sector."

Oh, a husband worried about his wife. "Mr. and Mrs. Morales, glad to meet you."

"They're brother- and sister-in-law," Livi quickly added. "Not husband and wife."

Alex should have kept his mouth shut and stuck to healing his patients. "I'm sorry. Been a long night and day."

Danika smiled her understanding. *Quite an attractive lady.* Intense blue-gray eyes penetrated into his very soul. That rarely happened. He quickly noted she didn't wear a ring, but he knew many agents who didn't wear them for safety purposes. Hazardous working conditions meant the possibility of losing a finger in the day-to-day operations of protecting the country's border or having their families threatened by those who didn't value or respect the Border Patrol.

"Jon made it through the surgery and is resting in recovery," Alex said to Jacob. "From there, I want to keep a close watch on him in ICU. He's a tough guy, and I'm optimistic about his recovery."

Jacob reached out and shook Alex's hand. "Thanks. He's a good agent." He glanced at Danika. "Can we have a word outside?"

For about one tenth of a second, a flash of animosity creased her features. "I suppose so."

Alex studied Jacob Morales long enough to realize he strongly resembled the late Toby Morales. Perhaps they'd been brothers. Could Danika be Toby's widow?

The two walked outside the ER into the afternoon heat. He could read body language well enough to tell Jacob was perturbed about something.

Alex turned to Livi. "You doing okay?"

"For a close call, I guess so."

"Anything I can do?"

"Keep that stubborn, daredevil husband of mine alive."

"I'm doing my best." Alex had seen Livi's ability to hold up in times of stress on previous occasions when Jon had been injured.

"When can I see him?"

"Soon. I'll have a nurse notify you when he's awake."

"Waiting is not my best trait." Livi glanced at her watch.

"I don't think it's anyone's shining point. Have you called your pastor?"

A thin-lipped smile met him. "I was too busy praying to call."

Alex touched her arm. "That's not a bad thing. I'm sure Jon

felt them, because he fought hard. Why don't you get some coffee and relax a few more minutes?"

Livi nodded.

Danika appeared and wrapped her arm around the woman's shoulders. Alex hadn't seen her return, and Jacob was nowhere in sight.

"I'll wait with you until Jon's out of recovery," Danika said and peered into Alex's face. "On behalf of the Border Patrol, thank you for taking good care of Agent Barnett. One of our supervisors will be here any moment."

"You're welcome." Alex excused himself to get back to work. He heard Danika ask Livi about the kids getting home from school and offer to have someone meet them there. Alex blinked back the weariness. He could use someone to greet him at the door when he got home from the hospital, but first he'd have to find the time to establish a relationship.

He let his mind linger on Danika for a moment longer. Curiosity about the possibility of her being Toby's widow marched across his mind. Before his death, Toby often spoke about his wife and how much he cared for her and their daughter, but he'd never mentioned her name.

Alex shook his head. Getting involved with a Border Patrol agent was asking for trouble, especially when he knew they'd have conflicting views about the immigration problem. *Ah . . . maybe not that different.*

Back to work. Then a nap on the cot in his office.

The best time of the day was when Danika returned home from work and opened the front door. Tiana would rush to greet her, and all of the stress and problems of the day disappeared. Danika used to wonder how her precious, hearing-impaired little daughter could sense the exact moment when her mommy arrived home; then she learned Tiana could feel the vibrations. Today's reception was no different.

Danika hugged her daughter and signed, "I love you."

The four-year-old responded and reached for Danika's hand en route to the little girl's bedroom, their normal evening routine. Tiana's sign-language vocabulary was the same as any four-year-old who could hear. Sometimes the words were those understood only by Danika and Tiana's nanny, Sandra. Yet their communication was typical and vivid.

Once in the child's disorganized sanctuary, Tiana pulled out Candy Land and placed the game on a small table for the two to play together.

"*Buenas tardes,*" Sandra called from the kitchen.

Danika drank in the familiar aromas wafting down the hallway. "I smell the coffee. Do you know how much I appreciate you?" More of the normal routine. Home. How she treasured the times with Tiana and sweet Sandra. Especially after today.

"What game are you playing?" Sandra appeared in Tiana's doorway with a fresh cup of decaf coffee for Danika and a glass of soy milk for the little girl. "Peppermint?" Sandra's Hispanic accent and her occasional English mix-ups added one more delicious part to the homecoming.

"Candy Land." Danika gave her dear friend a quick kiss on the cheek. "Did our little girl behave herself today?"

Sandra's clear brown eyes widened, and she stared lovingly at the child who looked more like her daughter, with her dark hair and olive skin, than Danika's. The child did not have a single trait of her mother's except that she was left-handed.

Tiana grinned as though she understood every word. Lip-reading would come later, but right now signing was Tiana's best source of communication.

"We worked on school lessons." Sandra signed each word

carefully. From the moment she had come to live with Danika nearly two years ago, the woman had worked hard to master sign language.

"Wonderful," Danika signed. She took the coffee and handed Tiana her milk.

The little girl obediently signed, "Thank you."

"Oh, Sandra, we didn't have to prompt her."

"She's a good girl."

Danika chose not to mention that Tiana's preschool teacher last year had said that the child had a behavior problem.

"I prayed for you all day," Sandra said.

Danika nodded. "Thanks. Tough day. The man who shot Barnett knew me and also claimed I'd never find Toby's killer." She chose not to worry Sandra about the contract on her life.

Alarm crested Sandra's eyes. "What did you learn from his arrest?"

"Nothing. No previous arrests. No gang markings."

"You'll find whoever did this to your family."

Danika had just about given up, but the shooter's words had given her new resolve. Perhaps later tonight she'd look through her notes for any new leads. Problem was she'd exhausted her search.

"We can talk if you like."

Sweet, dear Sandra. "I'm okay. When we finish here, I need to use the oven, unless you're in the middle of baking something." Danika clung to her policy of leaving work outside the confines of her home. "I need to whip up a dessert. Remember we're all invited to Jacob and Barbara's tonight."

"I'll have a headache."

Danika refused to give up that easily. "Won't you reconsider and go with us?"

Sandra narrowed her brows.

"I hate to beg," Danika continued. "But you know how uncomfortable it is for me there. And you're my rock."

Sandra crossed her arms over her small chest and shook her head, her black ponytail accentuating her response. "God is your rock, not your nanny. Besides, Lucy will be there."

"I know seeing your employer at a social outing can be awkward, but do you detest her that badly?"

Sandra lifted her chin. "You're my boss. Lucy just writes me a check."

"I understand, really I do. Sorry I pressed you." Danika didn't want to spend an evening at the Morales home either. Jacob's temperament had steadily declined since Toby had died, and to make matters worse, he was highly critical of Barbara and their children. The way he treated them was appalling. Add to that his overprotectiveness of Danika and Tiana, and it made for an unpleasant evening. Tiana steered clear of him, and she couldn't hear a word her uncle said. In this case, her daughter's deafness was a blessing. But Tiana must sense the animosity in the home. Whenever the agents were together, Jacob huddled over her, breathing down her neck like a dragon as if he were her guardian.

The other agents laughed at his domineering attitude, but not Danika. She'd earned a reputation of being a good agent by clawing her way to prove herself in a mostly male-dominated role. Repeatedly she'd told him to back off. She could do her job and converse with the other agents without his permission. Toby had been his brother, but that didn't give Jacob the right to supervise her life.

While waiting with Livi at the hospital, Danika realized she wasn't any closer to solving Toby's murder. Or was she? She suspected today's shooter probably knew more about Toby's killer than she did, and that frustrated her. Tomorrow she'd do a little more investigating—read the reports one more time and look for a lead.

An hour later, Danika lifted a fresh blueberry cobbler from the oven and scooted it into an insulated bag. She pulled a huge platter of avocados and tomatoes from the fridge and grabbed a bunch of green onions and jalapeños. She set the vegetables on the table to free her hands.

"Ready?" she signed to Tiana.

Tiana looked around and signed for Sandra.

Danika shook her head. "She's staying home. Just you and Mommy are going to the barbecue at Uncle Jacob and Aunt Barbara's."

Although Danika was certain Tiana understood, the child appeared perplexed.

Danika bent to her level. "You'll have fun with your cousins."

Tiana frowned and signed, "No."

Another member of the family who didn't want to make an appearance at Jacob and Barbara's. Danika hid her exasperation. Couldn't really blame Tiana or Sandra. But Jacob and Barbara were family, all the family either of them had—at least the ones who acknowledged them.

"I'll go," Sandra said, walking toward them from her room.

Danika released her appreciation in a soft sigh. "Thanks so much. We'll make it a short night."

"That's my condition. The last time nearly did me in."

"Jacob or Lucy?"

"Both."

"Once Tiana starts reading lips, we're going to have to watch what we say."

Sandra picked up the plate of fresh vegetables. "She already knows too much. Remember what you told me? Most of our communication is body language."

Danika stifled a laugh and stared at her precious little girl, then glanced back at Sandra. "Okay. If the heat rises, we're out of there."

"My kind of woman." Sandra always amazed her with something she said or read.

"Let's make a deal. If Lucy corners you—and I know she likes to talk—I'll come to your rescue. And if Jacob starts in on one of his tirades, then—"

"No worry. I've got the drill." Sandra winked at Tiana.

Danika felt the tension the moment she stepped into the ranch house in the north part of town. The home had Jacob's touch throughout. He had a gift for building with his hands, and he'd customized cabinetry, furniture, and trim throughout. Since Toby's death, he hadn't picked up a hammer, except to pound his family with demands.

She didn't hear the lively sounds of Nadine, Kaitlyn, Amber, or Jake Jr. Neither did she detect Jacob's favorite country and western music. The house sparkled from Lucy's routine cleaning, and the enticing smells of dinner permeated inside and out. The beans, simmering with peppers and onions, were a sweet reminder of Barbara's ability to prepare truly authentic Mexican food. But the quiet brought a bitter chill, urging Danika to take her daughter and Sandra back home.

Danika had come this far, and for Barbara and the children, she'd venture closer. Through the kitchen window, Danika viewed Jacob flipping burgers on the patio grill, and inside, Barbara scurried about setting the table, but her face and neck were redder than the tomatoes. What wasn't said shouted louder than the silence. The two younger daughters helped Barbara set the table. Danika saw Jake Jr. standing beside his dad. But where was their oldest daughter?

"Where's Nadine?" Danika asked, dumping a bag of nacho chips into a bowl.

"Don't ask," Barbara said.

As Danika suspected, discord had sung its song before they arrived. She was determined not to get involved in family problems, but the lines deepening around Barbara's dark brown eyes revealed the burden on her heart.

"Hey, kids, I'm here to help Mom. Why don't you play until dinner's ready?" Danika captured Sandra's attention and silently reaffirmed their earlier commitment.

The nanny escorted Tiana from the kitchen in the direction of her youngest cousin.

Alone, Danika turned to her sister-in-law. "Do you want to talk?"

Barbara's eyes watered. She shook her head and lifted the lid on the bean pot. Steam rose and clouded the glass lid. "I don't want to take advantage of our relationship. Lately, Lucy seems to be right there when I need to talk." She reached for a tissue. "Thanks for coming tonight. It helps. It really does."

"I'm here if you need another listening ear."

Barbara washed her hands before stirring the pot's contents. Must have been a huge argument. "Nadine is in her room."

Was it choice or had she been banished? Even though she was seventeen, Jacob refused to allow her to date, and he restricted her girlfriends as well—just like he ruled the rest of his household. Toby had never been abusive. He'd been kind, caring, encouraging Danika to reach out to others . . . No wonder the two men argued.

"Can I talk to her?" Danika asked.

Barbara placed the lid back on the beans. "Lucy is with her." She shrugged. "Praise God my dear friend has a way of calming her, or . . . I don't know what I'd do."

"I'm so sorry." At least the girl wasn't alone. Danika had no idea why Sandra didn't like Lucy when she was always there for Barbara. The woman had a successful maid and nanny service, and she was intelligent and attractive. But then again, Danika didn't work for her.

"Jacob's getting worse." Barbara drew in a breath. "Nothing any of us can do is right."

"Is he still meeting with Father Cornell?" Danika placed her arm around Barbara's waist.

"He quit several months ago. Said he couldn't fit it in with work and family responsibilities. And he's spending a lot of time away from home. I have no idea what he's doing." She didn't have to say how his family suffered. Barbara peered out the kitchen window to where Jacob stood with Jake Jr. He was telling the boy something. He pointed his finger in Jake's face. The boy stepped back. "Please, Jacob," Barbara called to him. "I can't stand by and do nothing while you browbeat our children."

Jacob's shoulders fell. He bent to the boy's level and held him close and then kissed the top of his head.

"That's my Jacob, not this strange man who is angry all the time." Barbara's words seemed more like her most intimate thoughts.

"He's not happy with me right now about some work matters," Danika said. "I'll go talk to him." She had no intentions of apologizing to Jacob for this morning, but she'd explain to him again what happened with Barnett. Shouldn't his concerns be about a wounded agent?

Opening the door leading to the patio, she stepped into the heat. "How are the burgers coming?"

Jacob rose from talking to Jake and grabbed a large shaker of seasoned salt. "A few more minutes. Of course, you're the one who eats the bun with cheese and the fixin's without the meat. Jake, would you go get Nadine for me?"

"Sure, Dad."

Maybe this was a step in the right direction. "About this morning, I—"

"I thought you'd been shot too."

Now she better understood his fiery reaction at the hospital.

"I'm sorry you were worried. But I had my hands full with the situation."

"As I said earlier, I deserved a call."

She inwardly groaned. "Jacob, when I'm working, my thoughts are on the job and what is required of me. Barnett didn't look like he'd make it, and Livi needed my full attention."

He pressed his lips together. "You are my brother's wife, a member of the family. I have a responsibility for your welfare."

"I'm perfectly capable of taking care of myself."

"Not if you're dead."

Danika heard his pain, the grief that he wore like a crimson bandage. "It's not your fault Toby was killed."

"I should have been able to protect my brother, to warn him about the dangers of keeping company with illegals."

A mixture of pity and frustration whirled, sickening her with the memories of a life lost. Jacob needed to get some help instead of making life miserable for those around him.

"The whole Border Patrol can't stop all of the illegals from infiltrating U.S. soil. So where do you get that Toby's death was your fault?"

"It's there, Danika. It sticks in my throat like a rock."

"Didn't your priest offer any help?"

He shook his head and lifted a burger onto the platter. The burgers and hot dogs smelled wonderful, even if she didn't often like the taste of red meat. Danika waited for Jacob to reply, something she'd learned from her own counselor.

He blew out an exasperated breath. "You gave up on trying to talk it out, too."

"I decided today to start again. It was foolish for me to stop, and my counselor really helped me cope with the pain and bitterness."

"I'll think about it."

"Good. I love you and Barbara. You are all the family Tiana and I have. But Toby is in heaven, and—"

The door opened and Nadine walked out alone. A pretty girl, slim and tiny with full lips and big eyes. Time for Danika to exit, and hopefully father and daughter could patch up whatever damage had been done before Danika arrived.

"Hi, Nadine. I'll see what I can do to help your mom."

The girl lifted her head, and it took only one glance for Danika to see she was high.

CHAPTER 4

There's more to the truth than just the facts.
AUTHOR UNKNOWN

IN THE GAME ROOM, Sandra listened to the Morales children fuss over which DVD to watch. Tiana was as noisy as the other three, voicing her opinion in little-girl squeals and pointing to her favorite movie. The closed captioning didn't help a child who couldn't read, but she no doubt followed the movie.

The youngest daughter, Amber, selected a Disney feature. Kaitlyn and Jake protested with all the vehemence of a fourteen- and a twelve-year-old.

"It's only a few minutes until dinner," Sandra said from her position on the sofa.

Their voices rose.

"Of course if your father hears the roar, a couple of kids may go to bed hungry, and those burgers smell real good."

That did it, and the combination of her warning and the movie quieted all of them.

"Smart move," Lucy said.

Sandra didn't reply. She detested the woman who now stood in the doorway, even if she had fronted the money for Sandra to get across the border. For three years, she'd worked as a maid for free until Lucy decided the money had been paid in full. Shortly after Toby's death, Lucy found her a job with Danika and Tiana. But the woman who owned a maid and nanny service cared only about herself and what went into her bank account.

Lucy sat on the sofa beside Sandra. "Are you and Danika still more friends than employer and employee?"

Sandra's stomach nearly revolted. "My personal relationship with my employer is none of your business."

"Where's the respect I deserve for taking good care of you?"

"I spent it on toilet paper."

Lucy gripped Sandra's arm and leaned close. "I thought you liked your job, living in a nice house like you were a real person."

Sandra pried Lucy's fingers from her flesh. "Go ahead and fire me. Danika will keep me on."

"Not if she learns you're illegal."

Sandra took a deep breath. She'd tolerated Lucy's condescension long enough, feared what she could do, and avoided being alone with her. Sandra's realization of what the law would do to Lucy changed things. "You don't want to know the trouble I can cause. Think about it."

Sandra stood and walked from the room. Her legs barely held her frame, and heat flooded her face. For three years, she had worked like a dog for free. She'd paid her dues and didn't owe Lucy a thing.

Shocked to see the truth glazing over Nadine's eyes, Danika gave her niece a hug and left her alone with Jacob.

The sound of ice chinking into glasses didn't block the bellowing revelation slamming against Danika's head. Where had Nadine gotten drugs? How did she pay for them? Was that the cause of the argument between father and daughter? Did the teen think she could hide drug abuse from her parents? The questions bombarded her senses, and Danika couldn't pose a single one of them to Barbara and Jacob. Maybe Danika had misread the signs. . . .

Barbara lined the ice-filled glasses on the kitchen counter. A frosty pitcher of iced tea sat nearby. "Thanks for going out there. I could see Jacob's face soften, and Jake said he asked for Nadine."

"So they argued earlier?"

Barbara hesitated before pressing the button on the refrigerator for more ice. "She wanted to go out with friends tonight, and Jacob wanted to know if any of them were boys. Nadine said it was none of his business, and it went from bad to shouting from there."

Danika watched Barbara fill three more glasses. She couldn't allow the truth to go unchecked. After eight years as a Border Patrol agent, she knew what high looked like, but so did Jacob. Barbara couldn't possibly be that naive either. Danika wanted to be wrong, so very wrong.

"Has she been sick?" Danika reached into the fridge for a pitcher of lemonade.

"A little. Allergies, I think." Barbara stole a glance out the window to where Jacob and Nadine were talking. "She's been a bit pale lately and not eating, but I think that's from the constant quarreling with her father. Maybe I should take her to the doctor. She may have a summer cold with her runny nose and hacking cough."

The more Barbara talked, the more the evidence stacked up against Nadine. "A checkup is always a good idea," Danika said. "She shouldn't have to suffer through not feeling well on her summer vacation."

"I agree." Barbara sounded better.

What a dysfunctional mess. If this weren't Danika's family, she'd stay away. But this *was* her family. "Hard to believe she's going to be a senior this year."

Barbara studied one of the many photos taped on her fridge. She touched Nadine's second-grade picture. The cute little girl's mouthful of missing teeth hadn't stopped her from smiling at the camera. "Where have the years gone? Praise God Nadine and I get along fine. Jacob is the problem, and I'm afraid he's going to destroy his relationship with all of his children."

Danika's cell phone rang, and she excused herself to the corner of the kitchen while pulling the phone from her jeans pocket. The caller ID showed Felipe. "Hey, what's going on?"

"Wanted to let you know that Fire-Eater pulled through the surgery and recovery time. The vet says he's stable—one lucky dog."

"Both he and Barnett are lucky," Danika said. "Thanks for letting me know." She slipped the phone back into her pocket. "Fire-Eater pulled through."

Barbara folded her arms over her chest, her face a mass of worry lines. "For a moment I forgot how terrible your day was, and then you walked into this mess. Jacob will want to know the dog's okay."

The back door opened, and Jacob carried in a tray of hot dogs and hamburgers. Danika studied his face, waiting for the big thermostat to set the temp for dinner.

"Thanks, Daddy," Nadine said.

Danika seized the opportunity to study the girl's eyes again. No mistake. Pupils were dilated. Nadine picked up a couple of miniature chocolate bars and smiled at her mom.

"Make sure you get permission," Jacob said. A heavy moment passed before he rested his dark eyes on Barbara. "I told her she could spend the night with Lucy, but to ask her first. In case she has plans."

The final word. Barbara couldn't have objected if she'd wanted to. Danika didn't approve of the way Jacob ruled his household, but thank goodness she wasn't married to him.

"Naddie, would you tell the others it's time for dinner?" Barbara said.

Before the night was over, Danika planned to confront the teen about drug abuse. What was this family thinking? Jacob, Barbara, and Lucy . . . and none of them mentioned the apparent drug abuse signs of one teenage girl. This was like tracking down a dozen illegals carrying stuffed backpacks, and a rookie agent asking them what they were carrying.

After dinner, Lucy helped with cleanup while Nadine scurried away to pack for her overnight trip. Danika gave the teen a few moments before trailing after her. Nadine had a clean pair of jeans and a T-shirt on the bed, along with a cosmetic bag. Could that be where she kept her drugs? *This has to be a mistake.*

"Got a minute?" Danika plopped herself onto the other twin bed, where Kaitlyn slept. All the training in the world hadn't prepared her for confronting her niece. She toyed with what to say while studying the colors of the bedroom. One side of the room was orange and yellow with huge butterflies on the walls; Nadine's side was turquoise and brown.

"I'm kinda in a hurry," Nadine said, tossing a hairbrush onto the mix. *Distant* didn't begin to label her attitude.

"Are you okay?"

Irritation cemented the teen's gaze. "I'm fine. What are you talking about?"

Danika hated what she was about to do. "You look tired. Your mom says you haven't been feeling well."

She smirked. "Are you going to diagnose me?"

"Why don't you tell me?"

"I'm too old for games."

"I agree. So tell me why your pupils are dilated, you're pale, and your mother says you haven't been eating. She says your nose is running constantly, and she suspects a cold with your hoarse cough."

Defiance flowed from every pore of Nadine's face. "She's my mother. That's what she does. So what's your problem?"

"I'm concerned you might be sick."

"Oh, please. I'm fine, just sick to death with all of the archaic rules around here. Daddy won't let me breathe."

"Nadine, I care about you. If you need help, I—"

"What I do is none of your business." Nadine sealed her guilt.

Danika wanted to shake her, but she wasn't a child. "Is it worth what you're doing to your own health and those who love you?"

"You sound like a TV ad for vitamins. Leave me alone, Danika. You and your brat are here eating our food because your loser husband got himself killed doing something stupid."

Heat anchored the ire in Danika's face. Insulting her was one thing, but referring to Tiana and Toby with contempt made her furious. When had Nadine changed from a considerate and lovable young woman to such a . . . She refused to let the descriptor roll around her head. "You and I have always been close. I don't understand why you're pushing me away. This doesn't make sense."

"Makes as much sense as you sticking your nose in my life. If I need to talk to someone, it'll be Lucy."

"What gives you the right to upset my daughter?" Jacob's voice bounced off the walls of the bedroom, dumping a hollow emptiness into Danika's resolve to support her family.

With her ears ringing, Danika slowly crossed the room to face Jacob. "The right? Guess I don't have one."

Alex checked on Jon Barnett before leaving the hospital for the day, or rather the night. Jon slept comfortably while Livi rested in a vinyl chair beside him. She alternated her focus between her husband's ashen face and the monitors hooked up to his wounded body. He drifted in and out of consciousness and was still in critical condition, but his vitals were good. Alex felt confident of the man's recovery. Jon lived life hard—worked hard and played hard—and today he fought hard against the damage inflicted on his body.

Border Patrol agents filtered in and out of the hospital offering support, not just with statements but by putting their words into action. Livi said an agent and his wife offered to stay with the children for the night. Another agent handed Livi a list of families who would be bringing food for the next week. And another agent and his wife planned to spend the night at the hospital. Some volunteers attended the Barnetts' church, but most of the support came from the Border Patrol family. BPs always rallied together when needed. Alex had learned that most agents stepped into their roles with a desire to serve their country and its citizens. Only after they'd been on active duty for a while did they realize the danger and understand the toll their careers could take on their families.

"I'll be calling in to check on Jon," Alex said. "He's a fighter."

Livi lifted her gaze from the monitors. "So many people have been praying for him and for you. Thanks, Alex."

He bent and squeezed her shoulders. "I'll be here early in the morning." The few hours' rest on the cot in his office wasn't the same as eight solid ones in his own bed. Exhaustion had attacked him in full force, and his body and brain needed downtime to function.

He rode the elevator to the lobby and spotted Danika Morales entering through the hospital's double doors. Catching her attention, he waved. "Good evening, Agent Morales."

She smiled, and in jeans and a T-shirt, she looked more like a soccer mom than a BP agent. Curly hair hung almost to her shoulders, loose and free. The color reminded him of dark honey.

"Danika, please," she said. "Hey, you've put in a long day."

"Comes with the territory."

"I understand. I'm sure Livi is overwhelmed with all of this, and I wanted to check on her before I went home."

What a sweet gesture. "She's a soldier, just like Jon."

"Well, I'm going to see about the Barnett boot camp. Have a good evening, Dr. Price."

"Alex."

"Okay, Alex." Danika tossed another quick smile and strolled past him.

I'm an idiot. He didn't have a single intellectual, stimulating, witty, bachelor-like thing to say. He'd been married to the medical profession far too long. Next time he'd be prepared.

Wait a minute! Hadn't he decided that pursuing a BP agent invited a troubled relationship?

I need sleep.

CHAPTER 5

Give justice to the poor and the orphan; uphold the
rights of the oppressed and the destitute.
PSALM 82:3

On Thursday morning, Danika sped down Old Military Highway in the Tahoe assigned to her for the day. Felipe kicked up dirt in his jeep ahead of her, and Jacob followed behind her. Another truck with two more agents led the convoy. They'd gotten a call from an informer about a safe house filled with illegals and drugs. The caller, a man with a thick Hispanic accent, gave the location and hung up. Later the supes at the station would analyze the voice, but the agents' job was to make arrests and confiscate the drugs.

She thought about the illegal who had shot Barnett. She'd dug into the shooter's records and questioned the other agents who had brought him in for medical treatment. One more time, she'd hit a dead end. Except his knowledge about Toby's death was in his database. He refused to give his name, but she wouldn't forget his face or his claim.

Within seconds, all four vehicles swung in front of a dilapidated one-story house, penning in a ten-year-old van with a dented-in passenger side. Two large dogs, a shepherd and black Lab mix, snarled their reception at the agents. Both animals were lean enough to eat an agent for lunch.

Danika lived for this excitement—the thrill of danger—in the landscape of her being. Five years ago, she would head into a field of sugar cane for one illegal, but after she got pregnant, she took a few more precautions. After Toby's death, she curtailed the daredevil tricks.

Danika opened the door of her Tahoe and gulped in stifling heat to mix with the adrenaline pumping through her body. She doubted if many of the American public understood the danger BP agents faced the moment they buttoned up their uniforms. Sometimes an illegal fought back, and a good agent had to be prepared. When she was fresh out of the academy, an illegal had swung his fist at her, nearly breaking her arm. Jacob had been with her that day and took action. The two became friends, and Jacob had introduced her to Toby, a high school math teacher and track coach. She often wondered if Jacob regretted his matchmaking.

Most of the illegals were simply hardworking people who risked all for a better way of life. She knew many of them were driven by desperation, believing they had no other options to provide for their families' basic needs. When apprehended, they wore the cloak of defeat and misery. Some cried. Some swore. Others were silent and fingered a cross or a rosary. The cost of entering the U.S. ranged from two thousand to four thousand dollars, life savings from family and friends. And for what purpose? To be returned with nothing to show for the financial sacrifices of others?

Guides and drug smugglers were more dangerous. They carried weapons and had no intention of letting a future behind bars jeopardize their current lifestyle. Adrenaline surged through their veins too, but their motivation was pure and simple greed.

She drew her weapon and approached the parked cargo van. It was locked but empty. Later the agents would check inside. Drugs could be concealed in the floorboard, doors, ceiling, tires, gas tank, or specially constructed compartments. She walked up the driveway with Felipe while other agents spread out to surround the house. All had their handguns drawn. Ready.

A door thudded shut in the back, and she raced with several other agents toward the sound.

"Patrulla Fronteriza," an agent shouted. *"Alto."*

Nine men raced from the rear of the house toward the thick brush of spindly trees and tall grass. Odd, no women or children were with them. Three agents took off after the obvious illegals, while Danika and Felipe made their way to the back door, where the men had exited.

"Patrulla Fronteriza. Salgan con las manos arriba," Danika said.

No response. The two dogs had tired of following the other agents and the illegals and growled at Danika and Felipe. Were they about to be attacked by those possibly still inside the house or by angry dogs?

"Get out of here," Felipe said to the mangy animals, but the dogs inched closer. He stepped inside the house, and Danika trailed him, shutting the door behind her.

The house smelled of unwashed bodies, stale cigarettes, and rancid food. Quiet. Eerie. As though trouble was a wound jackin-the-box ready to pop.

All around the carpenter's bench.

Empty bags from Burger King sat on a kitchen table. Chairs were overturned. A beer can on its side dripped its amber contents from the table to the floor. Opened soda cans with frosty sides sat on the counter.

Felipe's voice filled the house. "There's no place to hide. Come out peacefully."

The monkey chased the weasel.

Felipe kicked in a closed door on the left. Danika entered a room on the right where a radio blared Hispanic music.

That's the way the money goes.

Bundles of marijuana and cocaine were stacked tightly in a corner beside six cases of Pampers. The diapers were used to wrap the bundles and deter the checkpoint's K-9s.

Pop goes the weasel!

"Felipe, I found a stash in here," she called, keeping her eyes on one last room and its closed door. "Looks to be at least a million dollars—maybe more."

He appeared in an instant. "Plenty of sleeping bags in there. Two of them are still warm."

"I didn't see any women with the group that raced out of here."

"Neither did I."

She nodded at another closed door and motioned a silent message for Felipe to cover her. She turned the knob and flung open the door into a shadowed room. Two women huddled together, one holding a toddler, and another woman lay unmoving on the floor. The stench of what had gone on in this room churned her stomach. One woman's T-shirt had been ripped from her neck to her abdomen. These women had been abused and left behind. Sobs rose like a bubbling pot.

Compassion surfaced Danika's sympathies. "U.S. Border Patrol. No need to be afraid." Her gaze swept over each woman's face. Bruises and hollow eyes met her. They were young, too young to be involved with this. A prostitution ring or an isolated incident? "Who did this to you?"

Nothing.

"Would you like some water?" Danika knelt at their side. "Are you hungry?"

"*Sí,*" came the reply.

"These women need medical help." Felipe pointed to a young woman in the corner. "She's not moving."

"What's wrong with her?" Danika asked the others. "Is she sick?"

No one responded. The women trembled; one of them started to cry. No doubt they had heard the Border Patrol were monsters, instead of people who revered human dignity more than those who had taken their money and, in this case, ravished their bodies.

Danika swallowed the acid inching up her throat. Whoever had done this deserved to rot in jail—or worse.

Felipe walked across the small room and felt the pulse point of the still young woman. "She's alive." He yanked his radio from his belt. "Need an ambulance at our location on Old Military Road. Apprehended illegal women in bad shape."

Jacob watched the ambulance speed away in a flurry of dust and dirt with its siren alerting all to clear the road. Three injured young women and Danika were inside the vehicle. The one in critical condition could not speak from the beating someone had given her. They looked to be about the same age as Nadine. He'd kill a man who ever attempted to hurt his daughter. And those girls' fathers weren't even around to protect them.

Nadine . . . what had happened to his precious little girl? All he ever wanted was her happiness and to keep her safe from those who would break her heart. But in the last several months, she'd changed. His eldest daughter had become sullen, rude, and preferred being in her room to time with her family. Barbara had caused this, spoiled her by allowing her to spend nights with girlfriends and attend parties. He'd have to talk to his wife—set her straight on who ruled his house.

Jacob watched the young man in front of him. He looked to be around sixteen or so. He'd lagged behind the others and spit obscenities at the agents. None of the illegals had admitted it, but this smart-mouthed kid with the cell phone was most likely the guide. Because of his underage status, he'd be escorted back across the border only to lead another group across the Rio Grande tomorrow. They'd kept the other illegals outside of the trucks and jeeps until the ambulance left in hopes one of the men might comment on the injured women. The illegals huddled together, docile, as was usually the case.

Most of the men had been drinking, and three were drunk. Surprising that none of them drowned last night crossing the river with that much alcohol in their systems. All of the men claimed not to have any idea about the maltreatment going on in the back bedroom. One man expressed visible emotion at the sight, and another appeared angry. Not all of the men who claimed they wanted work to take care of their families were hardworking illegals; two wore gang colors—Zetas. Those men were searched and cuffed.

"I'm an honorable person," a man, about forty-five, said. "I want to work in the U.S., not hurt anyone."

Jacob believed him. He understood an empty belly and poverty moved a man to do what he could for his family.

Another curse came from the youth's mouth. Ire twisted through Jacob. All he could think about was the condition of the young women on their way to the medical center. He grabbed the kid by the shoulder and swung him around. This was the kind of derelict that needed to stay away from Nadine.

"Go ahead and punch me," the kid said.

"Shut up and keep up with the others." Jacob raised his fist.

"Jacob!" Quin, one of the other agents, called. "Let him go. This isn't worth getting fired."

Jacob heard him, and his grip on the kid loosened.

"I'll escort him," Quin continued. "Come on, man. Give it a rest."

Jacob dampened his lips and stiffened. *Back off.* He released the kid and shoved him toward the others in custody. Running his fingers through his hair, he inhaled and exhaled to gain control. "Thanks, Quin. All I could think about were those young women . . . and my daughter."

Quin, a tall Caucasian who'd served in the Marines like about 25 percent of the Border Patrol, clamped his hand on Jacob's shoulder. "We're all shook up. Only animals could have treated those girls like that."

Alex knew the Border Patrol's protocol for bringing undocumented Mexicans to the medical center for treatment. Agent Danika Morales would stay with the women until he gave them clearance to travel back across the border, unless one of them had a record. In that event, they were handled by ICE. During her ten-hour shift, she'd guard them from anyone who might intend harm or aid in escaping the jurisdiction of the agents.

Two of the young women—actually they looked more like kids—were treated and released into the custody of another agent for processing. They'd looked worse than their injuries had indicated.

The third was a different story. She had five stitches on her left temple, and he'd set her left arm. But her nonresponsive attitude and tender internal organs alerted him to more extensive injuries. Alex guessed her age at around fourteen—probably frightened and all alone.

Danika held the young woman's hand and smiled. She spoke softly to her in Spanish, offering the same reassurance that Alex had done. He'd conducted a little investigation of his own about Danika. She was Toby's widow. His old friend used to bring undocumented workers who needed medical attention to the hospital, but Alex chose not to reveal that information to Danika. He had no idea how much she knew about her husband's work as an immigration activist. Alex realized now why Toby had never invited him to his home, refused e-mail contact, and asked him to use Toby's cell phone only. Certainly with his wife a BP agent, their controversial views about immigration must have been an issue in their marriage.

"Better call your supervisor," Alex said, writing out his orders. "I need to keep this young woman at least overnight for observation and additional testing. Don't suppose she gave you her name?"

Danika stared at her bruised face. "I couldn't get her to say anything. In fact, I wondered if she could speak at all."

"She's in shock and afraid. No wonder, considering she's been sexually assaulted."

Danika shook her head. "Two of the illegals were gang members. Although they denied abusing her, my guess is it was them. One of them claimed it was the guide."

"Perhaps she'll tell us when she's not so frightened." He thought back over the number of abused women he'd treated during the past few months. Could this poor girl be a link to the brutal beatings of late?

"I'll do my best." Danika bent to the girl's face and smoothed back her black hair. *"Pequeña, ¿cómo te llamas?"*

Tears formed in the girl's eyes. Yet she didn't utter a sound.

"Perhaps I can earn her confidence while I'm with her," Danika said.

Many times Alex had seen compassion and pity in Border Patrol agents, and Danika appeared to genuinely grieve the abuse of the young woman. "She had a picture of Saint Toribio in her back pocket."

The saint who was supposed to help Mexicans cross the border safely.

Most of the undocumented immigrants only wanted to work and were afraid of the Border Patrol. Which was why he believed the U.S. immigration laws needed reform. Those who needed U.S. jobs to feed their families deserved an opportunity to better themselves. However, he had no solution. Did anyone? What he despised were the drug smugglers. The gang leaders and cartels were in the news daily—often with gruesome pictures of those they'd killed. Lately they'd begun to exploit their cruelty via the Internet. Those lowlifes deserved all they received.

"I have a niece about her age. Protecting our border is not all I do." Danika patted the young woman's arm. *"Me quedaré contigo por ahora,"* she said, then looked at Alex. "I'm thankful this hospital treats those who need care—without question."

"Which is why I'm here. I have a few minutes. Could I bring you some coffee or something? Cafeteria coffee is not Starbucks, but it's not too bad when it's fresh." Alex sensed the same attraction that he'd felt before, not so much the physical as a sincere desire to establish a friendship.

Danika blinked. Had he said something stupid—again? "That would be nice."

"I'll get us both a cup and be right back. It will take a little while for admitting to complete the paperwork and locate a bed."

"And a bath," Danika said. "Sorry. I can be a little blunt."

He smiled. "No problem. And you're right. I've already noted it on the orders."

"Now I'm really embarrassed. I didn't mean to tell you how to do your job."

"No need to apologize." He glanced at the girl, who trembled and most likely wished she knew what Alex and Danika were saying. He explained to her about being admitted to the hospital and assured her that no one would hurt her. "I'll be right back."

Alex noted Jacob Morales in the hallway of the ER. He stood wide-legged with his thumbs stuck in his belt, reminding Alex of a cowboy. Even the crusty exterior seemed in character. "How's the girl Agent Morales brought in?"

"I'm admitting her."

Jacob frowned. "Sorry to hear that."

Did his disapproval come from not being able to process her and get her back across the bridge or because of her injuries? Alex chose not to ask. "She's been badly beaten and sexually assaulted. I'm concerned about internal injuries as well as a concussion."

"What were her parents thinking to allow her to cross the border? She's still a kid." Jacob shook his head. "I know what they were thinking. This was a chance for their daughter to have a better life."

"They all take chances and hope for the best."

"This one probably scarred her for life." He glanced at the curtained partition where Danika waited.

"I have the same concerns. We weren't able to get her name."

Jacob cleared his throat. "I did. One of the other women called her Rita."

Relieved, Alex stuck out his hand. "Thanks."

Jacob's brows narrowed, and his right hand did not budge. "It's my job."

Did this guy ever relax? The man was a heart attack in the making—probably popped antacids like Life Savers. "I'm going after coffee for Danika. Would you like a cup?"

"That's Agent Morales to you, Dr. Price. And no thanks to the coffee. My advice to you is not to attempt to get friendly with Agent Morales."

That remark hit Alex's anger spot. "And what is the repercussion if I do?"

Jacob offered a tight smile. "You two aren't compatible; that's all."

Alex tucked his hands inside the pockets of his white jacket and headed to the cafeteria. Was the agent simply playing a protective role for his widowed sister-in-law, or did Agent Jacob Morales have another motive?

CHAPTER 6

The Promised Land always lies on the other side of a Wilderness.
HAVELOCK ELLIS

"How long have you been seeing Alex Price?" Jacob's voice grated against Danika's nerves. If he raised his voice even the slightest, the medical staff in the ER area would hear him. Didn't he have a life of his own without interfering in hers? They hadn't talked since he'd berated her for asking Nadine questions about her health. At one time, she'd looked up to Jacob—his loyalty to the Border Patrol and the way he loved his family.

"What are you talking about?"

"He called you by your first name."

"My conversations with Dr. Price are none of your business."

"He's bad news, Danika." Jacob gestured around the small curtained area. "Look at what he stands for! He's on staff at a hospital that treats illegals for free. Where do you think his loyalties lie?"

"I have no idea, and neither is it any of my concern. Compassion and human dignity happen to be a part of who we are too." Danika hadn't addressed his accusations last Friday night or voiced her suspicions about Nadine to him or Barbara. But they were on the tip of her tongue. "And for the record, you can browbeat your wife and children, but not me. Tiana and I are separating ourselves from you until you calm down."

"You were out of line in questioning Nadine about her cold."

He'd pushed her buttons for the last time. "You've got to be kidding. Don't tell me you didn't see her eyes or note the other symptoms."

"Are you insinuating my daughter is using drugs?"

You have to know. "I care about Nadine, and I see a troubled teenager. I'm saying she has enough of the symptoms for you to look into the possibility."

"You're a liar. I know my daughter." Anger flushed his cheeks. "Maybe you *do* need to distance yourself from us. I can't have anyone around my family who insults our integrity or my parenting skills."

"Wake up, Jacob, before it's too late."

The curtain swished open, and Alex stood with two mugs of steaming coffee in one hand. She hoped he hadn't overheard the heated discussion. "Took a few minutes for the cafeteria to brew a fresh pot."

"Thanks." This was just what she needed to get something besides fury to energize her. "Smells wonderful."

"I'm checking on Barnett before heading back to the station." Jacob's angry glare troubled her. He seemed to wear his state of mind on his face, just like he'd done for the past two years.

"I plan to do the same while I'm here."

"I'll call Barbara and let her know about our new arrangement."

Danika frowned. What had happened to the once-congenial man who laughed and teased? Now all he did was scowl. "I'll call her before the day is over."

"Not necessary. In fact, I prefer you don't." Jacob opened his mouth as if to say more but instead he whirled around and left.

Danika glanced back at the young woman, battered and frightened. Her eyes were closed, either from the medication Alex had ordered for her or because the tone of Danika and Jacob's conversation alarmed her.

"I'm sorry about my brother-in-law's attitude," Danika said.
"Is he always this friendly?"

"Always." She hesitated. She didn't even know the man before her. "His brother, my husband, was killed two years ago, and he's had a tough time dealing with it."

"I'm sorry. You handling it okay?"

"By the book. Toby was murdered, and the crime has never been solved." Awkwardness rippled through her. She'd said too much to a stranger.

She took a sip of the coffee. Alex must have bribed the cafeteria personnel because the coffee was excellent. At her first break, she'd contact Barbara.

A warning flashed across her mind. That wasn't a good idea since Barbara and Jacob's relationship had suffered of late. Turning wife against husband and creating more chaos in the household went against everything Danika believed in. She'd wait to talk to Barbara, and maybe the situation at their home would mellow.

A nurse interrupted her thoughts. "Dr. Price, we have a room ready for your patient. A wheelchair is waiting."

"Let's move her on a gurney, and I've learned her name is Rita."

The young woman opened her eyes, probably in recognition of her name. Alex used her native language to explain that she would be transported to her own room. Fear, like that of a cornered animal, flashed across her eyes.

Danika took her hand. "We won't allow anyone to hurt you."

Rita's eyes clouded. Distrust. And she couldn't blame the girl.

"How long will you be here today?" Alex said.

"Until somewhere between five thirty and six o'clock. Depends on the agent who takes over for me and how long it takes for me to summarize the situation here."

"I understand. I'll be back before I leave my shift to check on our friend. Maybe we'll have time to talk."

So Danika had read the signs correctly. Dr. Alex Price had more than a passing interest in her. But Jacob may have been right about one thing: she and Alex probably had polar opposite opinions about the immigration laws. To her, it seemed impossible for anyone to work at this hospital and not have conflicting views with the Border Patrol regarding the immigration laws. However, his viewpoint, like many other doctors' and nurses', could revolve around his dedication to healing. Alex had a nice smile and didn't appear pretentious. A friendship would be nice . . . but nothing more. Someone to talk to or accompany her to a movie.

Reality punched her in the stomach. In addition to a possible conflict of interest with Alex, she had Tiana to consider. Her precious daughter needed lots of mommy time.

Danika watched the nurse assist Rita onto the gurney. The young woman winced. The man who did this was an animal. As soon as Rita was well enough to travel, she'd be taken to the station for processing. Her name and fingerprints would be entered in the computer database and a criminal check conducted. If she had a clean record, she'd be escorted across the Hidalgo Bridge to the life she'd forsaken. If she returned and was apprehended again, she'd be spending time in jail. That was the law, and Danika had sworn to uphold it.

Rita slept all afternoon, which gave the girl's bludgeoned flesh time to heal. She was so young, and so many dreams had been shattered because she'd made a poor decision. Before the agent arrived who would relieve her, Danika received a call from the station and learned a different agent had been assigned to her day shift tomorrow. According to procedure, an agent who apprehended an illegal who required medical care was supposed to spend his or her shifts at the hospital until the doctor signed the patient's release. Why the veering away from policy? But who was she to question the chief? Still, the change in protocol was odd.

Danika seized the opportunity to phone Sandra about arriving late that evening because of the day's events and the need to complete paperwork at the station. She explained to Sandra about what happened to Rita.

"Poor girl," Sandra said. "She sounds much too young to attempt crossing the border without a parent or relative."

"It's illegal," Danika said. "Age has nothing to do with it, except she's been thrown into an adult role and doesn't appear equipped to handle it."

"*Sí.*" Sandra paused. "Perhaps she has family here."

"Or she has an uncle or a brother who is involved with drugs."

"Do you really think that?"

Danika massaged her neck. "I know a mere girl is asleep on the bed beside me because she attempted to gain access to our country illegally and someone beat and raped her. I don't know why she came alone or what she planned for the future. All I know is she could have been killed."

"Our Tiana took a long nap this afternoon."

Danika appreciated the change in conversation. "What's she doing now?"

"Drawing pictures."

Danika smiled, wishing as she so often did for a way to communicate audibly with her daughter. The doctors indicated she could be taught to talk in a few years, and that would help. "Add her artwork to the mounting collection on the fridge."

"I will. Do you smell dinner?"

"I wish. I skipped lunch, and my stomach's growling. What are you cooking?"

"Cilantro and pepper meatloaf."

"Yum. You sure make my life easier."

"Have you thought about hiring me from Lucy?"

"I made the request, but she's not willing to release you from your contract. Don't worry. I'll take care of it. Give my girl a hug, and I'll see you later."

"Oh, I nearly forgot. Becca phoned."

"Thanks. I'll call her later." Danika slipped her phone back into her purse. Sandra . . . what a blessing. And Danika did plan to call her attorney about the legal ramifications of breaking the employment contract between Lucy's Nanny and Maid Service and Sandra. Sure would make life easier.

Becca called. She'd phone her best friend after Tiana went to bed and invite her over for late coffee. So much had happened, and she needed a listening ear. Unfortunately so much of how she filled her hours could not be repeated.

Sandra set the phone back on the cradle and turned to watch Tiana color. Such a beautiful child. The silence in which she lived seemed like a blessing when so much of the world shouted defiance. And Sandra was one of the rebellious ones. She lived a lie. Each time she took up for an immigrant who had been discovered, she questioned the logic. Danika must never learn the truth about Sandra's falsified work documents or all would be lost. She'd be escorted back to Mexico, and her friendship with Danika would be destroyed.

Guilt rippled through her. And yet she had no choice. She remembered reading somewhere that the end justified the means. Although Sandra didn't think God agreed with that philosophy, it made sense. To admit the truth would mean her parents no longer had the added income to help with medical bills. And dear Tiana . . . Sandra loved her as her own.

Once Tiana no longer needed her, Sandra planned to take her savings back to Mexico and purchase her own chicken farm. She'd learned much about running a business from books and TV programs, and as a young girl she'd worked long hours on a chicken farm. With the current economy problems in the U.S., and with the Border Patrol and ICE enforcing the immigration laws, she simply wanted to live safe and take care of her parents. Maybe by then the Mexican government would give aid to those who wanted to make a decent living. Until then, she believed God would watch over her.

She stole a peek at the little girl at play and signed, "Would you like strawberries or a banana as a snack before dinner?"

Tiana held up an imaginary banana and pretended to peel it. She took a bite and rubbed her tummy. Like Sandra's forged documents, the illusion was nearly as good as the real thing.

CHAPTER 7

To fear love is to fear life, and those who fear
life are already three parts dead.
BERTRAND RUSSELL

ALEX KICKED UP the volume of Beethoven's Fifth a notch,
just like he kicked his chicken pasta dish up a notch by adding
a dash more of Tabasco sauce. A chunk of whole-grain bread
sprouting with bits of vegetables and raisins warmed in the oven,
and a wedge of lettuce dripping in blue cheese dressing and real
bacon pieces called his name. He ran his finger around the salad
bowl and popped a generous dollop of dressing into his mouth.
Ah, a bit of cracked pepper would top this nicely.

Cooking helped Alex unwind and work through stress and
problems. Tonight his mind spun with the idea of pursuing
Danika Morales. *Make that Border Patrol Agent Danika Morales.*
Combine that with his commitment to Ed—chief patrol agent
at the McAllen Border Patrol Operation—to help put an end to
the flood of recent crimes supposedly due to a rogue agent, and
Alex had a fine mix of flammable relationships. Made him wonder if his recent lack of sleep had affected his good judgment.
More like he'd met a woman who was not only drop-dead gorgeous but had values and priorities that lined up with how he
felt about life. Respect and admiration for the way she'd tended
to the beaten young woman today had attracted him to her even
more. Getting to know Danika could be a challenge with her

brother-in-law following her like a stalker and the fact that Alex and Toby had been friends. But she no doubt could handle herself, or she wouldn't be an agent. Toby had said his wife had the moral fiber of three men.

Alex shook his head. Danika Morales was definitely a matter of prayer. And putting his heart out on a limb again for all the flaming arrows to take aim gave him a twinge of doubt. Renee had left him five years ago for a banker in San Antonio. She claimed he had less demanding hours and didn't prefer his work over her. That accusation stung. Alex admitted to being devoted to his patients, but Renee had always come first in his heart. Stack up her discontent and unfaithfulness with his desire for children, and that equaled a heartbreaking divorce. Did he want to risk another heartbreak?

After he'd checked on Rita during the late afternoon, he'd had but ten minutes to chat with Danika. Her replacement had walked in and needed to be briefed on the situation.

Later, Alex joined her on the elevator and walked her to the parking lot. "Is home close by?" he'd asked.

"Just a few minutes, but I need to drive back to the station and file my report."

She looked tired, and he didn't want to detain her. Not much of an exciting beginning, but he'd take it.

He lifted a glass of water, heavy on the lemon, to his lips and took a long drink. *I should tell her about knowing Toby.* But when?

Alex spooned pasta onto his plate and added the chicken and spicy marinara sauce. Glancing at the clock, he calculated how long before his cell phone alerted him to a critical hospital situation. Not that his self-worth had anything to do with his profession. He just believed in his calling.

His cell phone rang on the second bite of his salad.

★ ★ ★

Danika set a plate of chocolate chip cookies on her kitchen table and shoved them Becca's way. "Sandra baked these just for you, and they have extra macadamia nuts."

Becca swirled her spoon through her coffee laced with sugar and half-and-half. She leaned over the freshly baked cookies and inhaled. "Oh, I've died and gone to cookie heaven. One of these days, Sandra's baking is going to catch up with my thighs."

"It will give you character." Danika laughed and poured a second cup of decaf for herself.

"Redheads do not wear potato sack thighs with distinction."

"Worry about it when it happens." Danika reached for a cookie, extra-large as usual.

"Sounds like a plan." And Becca reached for two. "So what's going on in your world of arrests and protecting the border?" All traces of girlish fun disappeared. "Don't tell me how many times you were in danger."

"Sweetie, that's a fact of BP life." Danika twirled a loose strand of hair at her earlobe. Tonight she needed a break from the pressures of work—and family problems. Should she talk about Jacob or the poor girl in the hospital or possibly Alex or—

"You've met somebody." A smile lifted the corners of Becca's mouth.

"Sort of." Danika wasn't sure she should discuss Alex, certain her best friend would advise her to stay clear of a man who obviously had conflicting views about the border problem.

"Another agent? I know it's Felipe Chavez, the cute guy with the big eyes and dimples."

"I'd never date Felipe when you have a serious crush on him."

Becca laid her spoon across the saucer. "Thank you. Now tell me about this guy."

What had she gotten herself into? "I have to think about it."

"What's there to think about? Spill it. You know I won't let up until you give me all the yummy details."

"Okay. His name is Alex, and he's a doctor."

"Woo-hoo, girl! I like him already. How many dates?"

Danika should not have opened up, because Becca would never let it rest. "None. We're just talking."

"Where did you meet?"

"At the hospital."

"Duh. I should have figured where. McAllen Medical Center?"

Danika nodded. "First it was for Jon Barnett when he got shot."

Becca raised a brow. "How is he?"

"He's doing fine. Going home tomorrow. Anyway I talked to Alex twice during that time and then today when I brought in a young girl who needed medical attention."

"What's he look like?"

Honestly, she should recognize the inner qualities of a person before assessing his potential for *GQ*. "Becca, other things are more important than looks."

"I know, but it's a good starting point."

Danika laughed. She and Becca both appreciated a good-looking man. "His eyes are blue, very blue, like they've been outlined with black pencil."

Becca sighed. "I'm about to get a dissertation."

Danika wrinkled her nose. "Okay, so here's the skinny. He has blond hair, a little taller than me, a wide smile, and beautiful teeth." An image of Alex flashed across her mind. Over ten years had passed since a man had affected her this way. Perhaps two years after Toby's death wasn't long enough.

"What about the stuff that counts?"

"From what I've seen, he's dedicated and compassionate with a sweet sense of humor." Danika thought back to the first time she met him when Jon Barnett was shot. Alex had comforted Livi and told her in easy-to-understand language about Barnett's condition. And today, he'd been so tender with Rita.

"Ah, while you have that dreamy look on your face, tell me if he has a brother."

"And disappoint Felipe?" Danika pushed the plate of cookies a little closer to Becca. "We have half a pot of decaf coffee to drink yet, so tell me what I should do about Alex."

"Any smoke signals?"

Danika rested her chin on her fists. She didn't want to ruminate about Toby. As much as she'd loved him, he did have secrets. "Nothing other than he works at a hospital where illegals receive free treatment."

"Does he wear a sign that says 'activist'?"

Danika nearly choked on her coffee. "No."

"Then let him know you're interested," Becca said. "Enough time has passed for you to consider seeking friendships with men. Toby would not have wanted you to stay single."

"I've been thinking about other things too. What about the practical things like Tiana, our careers, and faith?"

Becca's eyes widened. "I advise you to talk to God about the serious issues. I'm your good-time friend who wants your life to be like Cinderella."

Danika sobered. "You and I know Prince Charming always has a bag of toads."

"But if you know about the warts first, they have a way of working out."

CHAPTER 8

Rather than love, than money, than fame, give me truth.
HENRY DAVID THOREAU

"EIGHT HITS AT SENSOR 114," the radio blared.

Danika shoved her jeep into gear and whipped it around to head back down the narrow road toward the sensor location. Typical Friday. Never an easy day. But this beat sitting in the hospital waiting for Rita to heal. Thank goodness another agent had taken her place, although she didn't know why. She'd noted an unusual amount of tension at the station, but again she didn't know why. If she'd done something wrong, wouldn't the chief have called her into his office? Perhaps she should simply ask him.

In the distance, she saw a funnel of dirt bringing another agent toward the point. Usually illegals crossed over during the night, but lately they'd gotten braver, or their guides had convinced them the Border Patrol wouldn't stop them. By the time she reached number 114, two other vehicles were there.

Felipe led the way on foot down a well-worn path to the river and disappeared behind a clump of spindly trees. Known for his speed and agility, Felipe seldom allowed an illegal to slip past him, and he could read a trail like an Indian scout.

She yanked out the truck keys and jogged after Felipe over the trodden grass. Already the sun baked the earth and stole the breath of man and animals, causing the locusts to protest in an earsplitting discord of voices.

Over the morning air, Felipe shouted out the familiar calling card of the Border Patrol. Ten people, some still wearing muddy clothes and shoes from crossing the river, stood about twenty feet from the riverbank. Why had they attempted this in the middle of the day? Made no sense.

Danika heard a cry, the distinct wail of a newborn. Her gaze flew to the women, but none of the four in the group was holding a baby. She searched the ground around them but saw nothing.

"Dónde está el bebé?" Danika studied the faces of the women again. "Do you want your baby to die in this heat?"

A man stepped forward and lifted an infant from inside his jacket, causing an otherwise-protruding stomach to look flat. Danika gasped. The baby looked to be about two weeks old. The man handed her the crying child, who was clad in only a soggy diaper. She didn't want to think about the toxic river.

"Is the mother here?" She cradled the crying infant and studied the women's faces.

When no one acknowledged the baby, Danika turned back to the man and handed him the infant. "Your little one could have drowned."

He said nothing but pulled a capped bottle of milk from his pocket. *Oh, the germs.* The enormous sacrifices these people paid to get to the U.S. proved their desperation.

A flash of metal caught her attention. A man wielded a knife in Felipe's direction.

"Felipe!"

But the wiry agent had already detected the danger and quickly had the man pinned on the ground. Felipe tied the illegal's hands.

"Soy ciudadano estadounidense," the man claimed.

"Then why did you pull a knife on me?" Felipe jerked him to his feet.

"I was afraid."

The other agent searched his overstuffed backpack and found

approximately twelve pounds of cocaine, his cell phone, and two cans of Red Bull.

"Was that supposed to give you courage?" Felipe hoisted the backpack over his own shoulder.

Danika immediately recognized the tattooed markings of the Zeta gang. For the past two years, Mexican police had been working to bring an end to this highly organized drug gang. But now the open fighting had the White House's attention and every Border Patrol agent on alert.

The man, around eighteen years old, sneered at her and spat on Felipe's uniform. "You'll pay for this."

She curtailed her emotional restraint. "You got it wrong. You'll be in jail for a long time."

He narrowed his gaze. "Contract is already out on you, lady. Big reward for pretty, blonde woman agent. Might have some fun first, huh?"

Twice she'd heard this. The energy it took to keep calm would take its toll later. "From whom?"

He laughed. "You'll find out soon enough. Maybe from me. All the gangs know about you and the reward. You better keep looking over your shoulder."

Hours later, Danika pored over the police report from Toby's killing for the hundredth time. His body had been found in a field near the Highway 281 checkpoint, an area noted for illegals attempting to slip by en route to Houston, San Antonio, or Austin. Agents knew to look for bodies when vultures swarmed the area—sometimes lack of water and food or exhaustion killed the illegal.

But not Toby. He had a hole in his head from a 9 mm semi-automatic pistol—execution style—and no one knew why. She dealt with facts, and she didn't have enough to lead her or the authorities to the killer.

★ ★ ★

Jacob listened to the last snippet of sports on the late night news before reaching for the remote and powering off the TV. He'd checked on the kids during the last commercial, and they were asleep.

"We need to talk," he said.

Barbara moved the newspaper from the front of her face and stared at him with a familiar frown. "What about?"

"I'd rather have this discussion in our bedroom."

"Right here, Jacob. Right now." Her voice started to escalate.

"Hush. Do you want to wake the kids?"

"They hear it all anyway. Why is this any different?"

"Things are bad between us. Can't we talk civilly like two adults?" Jacob reached over and snatched the paper from her hands.

She started and her face reddened. "You could have asked before you grabbed the paper." She sighed. "What do you suggest?"

"My concern is for the children."

A tear slipped from her eye. Good, she needed remorse. "They worry about their parents fussing all of the time."

"Whose fault is that?" Jacob would not allow her to turn this around. He'd prepared for this discussion.

Barbara stiffened. "Not all mine."

"They're afraid of me." He hadn't thought he could get those words out, but in doing so, he'd found the strength to say what must be stated.

"You are constantly criticizing them," she said softly and leaned toward him. "You seldom play with them anymore or encourage them in their interests. Meeting with Father Cornell helped before. This time I'll go with you. We can do this together."

Jacob clenched his fists. "The kids are afraid because you're poisoning their minds against me."

Her eyes flared. "What are you talking about? I've never dis-credited you in front of our children. That's insane."

"But true." He lowered his voice and attempted to keep him-self in control. "I'm warning you, Barb. If you value our family, do not turn my children against me."

She stood and faced him. Her lips quivered. "If you value our marriage, then you will seek help before you lose your whole family. Toby is gone. You can't bring him back. And where are you spending your time when you aren't at work?" She opened her mouth as if to say more, but instead she walked away and left him sitting in his favorite chair with regret ringing in his ears.

Never had he known such frustration with Barbara. Like a splinter under his fingernail, the discontent needed to be yanked from his home.

CHAPTER 9

The truth does not change according to our ability to stomach it.
FLANNERY O'CONNOR

DANIKA FINISHED BRUSHING Tiana's thick black hair into a ponytail. Her daughter's dark eyes danced in anticipation of the station picnic. Today the off-duty Border Patrol agents and their families would gather for a picnic at Cascade Park. Luckily, Danika had a rare Saturday off. Despite the broiling temperatures guaranteed for this Saturday, heat would not stop the fun and games—including softball and volleyball—and all the good eats. Danika could almost smell the barbecue and taste the mounds of food that she didn't have to prepare.

What a great bunch of people. Block parties and church picnics were okay, but Border Patrol functions allowed her to be herself with no pretense. Most of her neighbors had no idea she worked for the Border Patrol. She changed into her uniform at the station and back into street clothes before she drove home. Many agents did the same. They strove to protect their spouses and children from disgruntled illegals or pro-immigration activists or drug smugglers. Their children were not told what they did when "at work," and spouses kept the information to themselves. No point advertising their controversial position in a community largely Hispanic.

Danika kissed her precious olive-skinned little daughter. They'd be worn-out this evening, but today would be a memory maker. She snatched up the ice chest and her softball glove and handed Tiana the sunscreen and mosquito spray. They were off for the day. Sandra chose to stay home for a little rest and time alone, which she highly deserved. She always seemed to notice when Danika and Tiana needed special mommy-daughter time.

As soon as Danika and Tiana arrived at the picnic site, Danika spotted Barbara and Nadine. She wanted to at least be cordial, but she and Jacob hadn't spoken since their last blowup. How would he feel if he found her talking to his wife and daughter? Nadine's suspected drug abuse drove Danika to see for herself, to look into her niece's eyes and hope they were clear and bright, sparkling brown pools of youth and vitality. Danika saw the effects every day—strung out users who thought they had control over their habit. The thought of Nadine ending up in the same viper pit made her physically ill.

Holding firmly to Tiana's hand, Danika strolled toward Barbara and Nadine, who were sitting in lounge chairs under a huge live oak. Danika didn't pray as much as she should, especially since Toby was murdered. But Jacob and Barbara's family were in desperate need of strong intervention.

Barbara looked her way and smiled. Danika relaxed slightly and waved. She had missed talking to her sister-in-law this week and finding out what those sweet kids had been doing. Between ball practice, swimming lessons, and whatever else Barbara arranged for their summer fun, Danika was always eager to listen. Her own growing-up days had been spent in a rigid environment filled with dos and do-nots. This way she vicariously relived what she'd missed.

Tiana released Danika's hand and ran toward her aunt. Taking a deep breath, Danika turned her gaze to Nadine. *Please, sweetie. Be clean.* The closer she walked, the bigger Nadine's frown, until Danika stood face-to-face with the two. Stomach twisting, Danika swung her attention to her niece.

Glazed eyes. Dilated pupils.

She was high.

"Isn't this a beautiful day?" Danika said.

Tiana hugged her aunt, then reached for Nadine. But the teen's interest had been snatched by something going on in another direction.

"Naddie." Barbara's voice lowered.

The teen rolled her eyes and offered a light tap to Tiana's shoulders. "I'm going to see what the girls are doing."

"Don't leave the grounds." Barbara raised her chin.

Something had happened, but what? A hundred scenarios rolled through Danika's mind. None good.

Barbara watched Nadine walk away. Tears filled the woman's eyes, and she clamped down on her lower lip.

"What's wrong?" Danika asked.

"What isn't?" Barbara brushed a mosquito from her leg.

"Do you want to talk?"

"I hate to bother you when you have your own life."

"I'm here and I'm listening." Danika took the empty chair where Nadine had sat and pulled Tiana into her lap.

"It's hard to know where to begin." Barbara avoided eye contact. "This morning I told Jacob I suspected Nadine of drug abuse." She took a deep breath, and Danika took her hand. "He called me a liar. I dared him to search her room, never thinking he'd actually do it. Nadine witnessed the whole thing. He tore her room apart, dumped out drawers, everything. Anyway, he found pills under her mattress, ones she called oxycotton. She admitted using them to cope with 'life.' He wanted to know where she got them, and she refused to say. I don't need to tell you about the shouting that followed."

Danika wanted to ask if Jacob and Barbara had discussed help for their daughter, but knowing Jacob, he wasn't finished with his lecture and ensuing punishment. He'd demand to handle it his way. "I'm so sorry. What can I do?"

Barbara reached into her purse and pulled out a tissue. "Prayer is the best thing you can do for this family. You were right when you questioned my Naddie, and I should have spoken up sooner. I suspected she was using something for a few months, but I couldn't bring myself to approach her. Where does a teen find street drugs? She goes so few places. I still find it incredible to believe."

"Why—"

Barbara shook her head. "Don't berate me. I get enough criticism from Jacob."

"Oh, honey, I don't want to upset you." Danika felt her throat tighten, and she reached for Barbara's hand. "Jacob's hurting from finding out about Nadine."

"According to Nadine, he pushed her into using. She's repeatedly cried to me about how he won't let her have friends or go places. My goodness, she'll be a senior this fall, and he wants her playing Barbies. I purchased her a cell phone, but Jacob doesn't know about it. I thought that concession would help. It did for a short while, but she's miserable. And so are the other kids." Barbara glanced to where Jacob was practicing softball before the game. "He accused me of turning the kids against him."

Danika believed every word. Jacob made life intolerable for those he loved at home and his peers at the station. She wanted so much for her brother-in-law, but he had to make the first step.

"I can't take much more. What he's doing to the children is forcing me to make a decision."

Divorce. Barbara didn't need to say the word. Danika had feared the split for several months. "Can I have Nadine's number? Maybe I can call or text-message her." She reached into her purse and wrapped her fingers around her phone to input the information. Barbara gave her the number with a reminder that Jacob could not find out about it. "Thanks. What about help for Nadine's problem?"

"I've been sitting here thinking about the services offered by the Border Patrol, church, and the community. Not sure which option would be the best. I'd like for the counselor to be Christian."

"My counselor prays for her patients."

Barbara tilted her head. "I thought you stopped going."

"I did, but this week I scheduled an appointment for Tuesday night. She sees patients as late as nine o'clock, which allows me to get Tiana to bed."

"Would you write down the name and number?"

Danika reached back inside her purse and pulled out a small notebook to jot down Shannon Perry's information. "You'll like her. She listens with her heart, and her method is to help the patient find their own solutions to their problems, not give orders."

"Nadine is stubborn. She'd butt heads with someone else telling her what to do."

Like her father. "This sounds like a good fit and definitely worth a try."

Barbara gasped. "Jacob is heading this way."

"Great. I'm out of here." Danika stood. For a moment she thought she'd stay and have a face-off with her brother-in-law, but that meant Barbara would take the brunt of his temper. "Please call me." She took Tiana's hand and strolled toward the snow cone machine for a treat before the softball game.

Her little angel sensed where they were going and quickly signed "snow cone" and "blueberry."

Danika stopped and bent to the little girl's side. She held her close and let the tears flow freely.

"Mommy cry," Tiana signed. Confusion etched her delicate features.

"Just sad."

"Aunt Barbara?"

The little girl's perception did not surprise Danika. "We'll pray for Aunt Barbara and all of her family," Danika signed. Her spirit ached for Jacob's family and where the turmoil would lead if he refused to get help along with his daughter. Danika prayed Tiana would be able to withstand the pressures of a sometimes-cruel world.

★ ★ ★

Sandra's cell phone woke her from a rare Saturday afternoon nap. With her eyes still closed, she reached for the phone and pressed it against her ear.

"Sandra, this is Lucy."

She should have looked at the caller ID before answering.

"Did you think about what I need you to do?"

"No thinking about it. The answer is still no."

"I can make it worth your trouble."

Sandra had enough to do without adding more work from a woman she detested. "I'm not interested."

"You used to want your family here. I can make it happen—no cost."

Lucy's sweet voice—as artificial as a politician's promise—grated against her nerves. "So my nieces can clean toilets for free until you write off your investment? Or my nephews run drugs? What about my seventy-year-old mother? What would she do for you? Forget it, Lucy. My loyalty is to Danika and Tiana. And remember, whatever you threaten, I can make it worse for you."

"You're nothing but a poor maid and babysitter to Danika. She could easily replace you. I'm offering to help you rise above the status of an illegal wetback."

"My status is my choice." Sandra disconnected the call. She closed her eyes with the intent of going back to sleep, but her mind raced with Lucy's interference in her life.

She may be illegal, and her conscience may attack her on a daily basis for deceiving Danika, but she no longer had to bow to Queen Lucy.

CHAPTER 10

They do not fear bad news; they confidently
trust the Lord to care for them.
PSALM 112:7

DANIKA SLOWLY SWUNG her legs over the bed to get ready
for work. She ached all over from the softball and volleyball
games the afternoon before, and she spent five days a week at
the gym. Her body simply could not handle all of the twisting
and turning—and falling—anymore.

Sunday.

When she was better in church attendance, the Sunday shifts
depressed her. The high point of her week had been worshiping
with her husband and their baby. Then Toby died, and if she
was scheduled to work on Sunday, it didn't really matter. God
as a priority fluctuated depending on the critical issues in her
life. She still believed. She prayed. She talked the walk, and yet
she held back from trust. Sad, but true. Yesterday's conversation
with Barbara had been one of those times when she'd asked God
to intervene in her sister- and brother-in-law's lives in hopes He
would smile favorably on them, unlike He'd done with Toby.

A phone call to Nadine had gone unanswered, as well as a text
message. Danika empathized with the girl's heartbreak over a
father who couldn't seem to grasp the importance of a relationship with his daughter.

At the station, Danika changed into her uniform and grabbed
some coffee before muster. Those who had been at the picnic

looked tired, but the laughing and teasing about the games and the fun indicated how much the agents appreciated family time together.

"You missed me winning the horseshoe championship." Felipe's dimple deepened. No wonder Becca drooled at the sight of him.

"Didn't want to take your trophy."

"Trophy? I won a dinner for two at Chili's."

Revenge time. "How sweet. You're asking me out, aren't you? When did you want to go?" Danika swallowed her laughter.

His reddened face was priceless. "Uh, I'm not sure. What I wondered—"

"My free nights?" Danika was getting even for all of his merciless teasing. He'd laughed the hardest when she ate dirt sliding into third base yesterday. "This week or next?"

"Well, my point is—"

"A movie too? I'd love it, Felipe. You're such a sweetheart to think of me."

"Could you slow down a minute?"

"Sure. I'm just excited about a real date." She shrugged. "I've known you were interested in me for a long time."

His jaw had fallen to his boots—more like a little boy who'd just dropped his ice cream cone. "I'll think about a movie . . . and get back with you later in the week." He headed for a couple of his buds.

"Felipe?"

He slowly turned. "Yeah."

"I'll e-mail Becca's phone number when I get home."

He gave a thumbs-up and grinned—generously. "I had that coming, but you did look real good grabbing for third base." He started to walk away, then whipped around, his face devoid of any humor. "Did you hear the latest?"

She knew exactly what Felipe referred to. "You mean about the cartel possibly having FBI and DEA bulletproof vests?"

He nodded. "They have the money to get whatever they want. How do you tell the good guys from the bad?"

"Same way you tell the corrupt police from the cartel."

He leaned against the lockers. "Right. Ever wonder when it will spill onto our side?"

"Every day." She studied him a little closer. "What's the news on your cousin?"

"He's back across the border where he belongs. And my great-uncle disowned me." He shook his head. "I told Chief Jimenez about it this morning."

Danika offered a grim smile. "Is that what happened to your windshield?"

Her cell phone rang.

"Better answer it," he said.

She wrestled with letting it go to voice mail, but Felipe pointed to her phone and walked away. Not recognizing the number, Danika almost opted for the caller to leave a message, but it could be Nadine or Barbara calling from a different phone.

"Danika, this is Alex Price, the doctor at McAllen Medical."

A delicious tingling spread through her. "Hi. What can I do for you, Doctor?"

"Alex."

"Okay, Alex." She caught herself in the middle of a giggle. How stupid. Utterly stupid, like a junior high girl.

"I was wondering if you'd like to meet for coffee or lunch or something this week. Maybe breakfast." He sounded as nervous as she did.

"I suppose that would be all right." Her heart thumped. She had Tuesday and Wednesday off.

But before she could suggest a day, guilt for laying aside her widow's clothes assaulted her. Toby had been gone only two years.

Was she betraying him? Was she even ready for this? "I'm sorry, but I don't think that's a good idea. Finding the time to socialize with the demands of my job and my daughter is tough."

"I understand."

"Thanks, though, and I appreciate the call." Danika clipped her phone back onto her belt. Too soon to wade in up to her neck. Maybe next year or the year after.

The clock showed five minutes to eight. She spotted Felipe talking to a couple of other agents and waved. Perhaps they'd have time to talk later.

Agents took their seats at the rectangular tables while the supervisor, Agent Oden Herrera, took his place at the front of the room. The buzz of conversations softened to a low hum. Jacob sat at a table on the left side, his usual spot. She prayed again that he and Barbara were able to have a sensible conversation after the picnic and make concrete plans to help Nadine.

"Apprehended nearly fifty illegals last night." Herrera crossed his arms over his chest. "One of them was another Zeta. Not sure what's going on with the gangs, but keep an eye out. Our sources say retaliation against the Border Patrol is imminent. Thanks to the Border Patrol along the Rio Grande, the tricks used by the smugglers are falling by the wayside." He took a sip of his coffee and pointed to the wall map. "Right here, near sensor 215, we found a man and woman shot in the head. Most likely drugs. No identification."

Jacob couldn't concentrate on muster with the truth about Nadine ringing in his head. The horrible accusations they had thrown at each other kept repeating like an obnoxious mockingbird, and the other kids had heard every word. He'd tried to sleep on the family room sofa, but his racing thoughts barred any rest. The idea of lying next to Barbara, who had betrayed him to his children, made him want to stay as far away from her as possible.

Memories of Nadine filled his mind all night. He remembered when he learned Barbara was pregnant and that their first child would be a girl. They didn't have a cent in the bank, but he had his job as a Border Patrol agent and plenty of dreams to last a lifetime. As the weeks went by, Barbara urged him to touch her bulging stomach so he could feel his baby girl move. When Nadine chose to enter the world, he was there to welcome her. Barely six pounds, she struggled to breathe. Within an hour, the doctors had rushed her to surgery for a damaged heart. He and Barbara had prayed until there were no more words or tears left. But little Nadine Marie Morales fought to live.

Jacob had promised Barbara and Nadine that he'd always be there to protect them. Later his promise extended to Kaitlyn, Amber, and Jake Jr. He'd done a good job until two years ago. That was before he became disillusioned with the politics and policies of the Border Patrol. Or maybe his disillusionment was due to the inept police who couldn't find his brother's killer.

What had happened to Nadine? Seventeen years later, his little girl despised him and used prescription drugs to balance her problematic life. His Naddie had chosen to escape reality instead of confronting life with the same fight that had carried her when she was a few hours old.

Barbara was someone he no longer recognized. She barely tolerated him, and his children fled to other parts of the house when he entered a room. No wonder his doctor had upped his blood pressure medication.

Shaking off the lack of sleep, Jacob snatched up his keys and headed to his assigned vehicle for the day. He didn't talk to any of the other agents, and the last person he wanted to see was Danika. She and Barbara were in this thing together to discredit him to his family and peers. But he'd prevail. He wasn't a loser. Not yet, anyway.

The morning wore on with the signs leading nowhere. His mood plummeted.

His cell phone rang, and when he saw it was Barbara, anger surfaced again. He'd have given both arms for it to have been Nadine.

"Jacob, we have a problem." Her voice trembled.

"What's wrong? Out of bread and milk?"

"Keep your sarcasm for another day," she said. "Nadine has run away. She's taken her clothes and left a note."

This had to be a ploy on Barbara's part. His daughter would not leave home. Would she? "What did the note say?"

"You're not going to like this. But since you asked, I'll read it to you: 'Mom, I can't live with Daddy any longer. I'm tired of waiting for him to change, and he just gets meaner. I tried to be patient and be strong for Kaitlyn, Amber, and Jake. But I can't. I'm sorry.'"

"Did you put her up to it?"

"Why do you say such cruel things?"

He heard the belligerence, the disrespect. He should be used to it by now.

"Sensor tripped at 210," the radio blared.

"I have to go." He disconnected his phone and responded to his radio. "I'm on it."

Jacob sped up his truck. He didn't want any backup. What he needed was to sink his teeth into his job and forget the stacked-up garbage at home. He'd call Barbara as soon as this situation was handled. Perhaps they could discuss the whereabouts of their daughter without a fight.

A Border Patrol truck raced behind him.

Jacob cursed. "Go chase your own illegals," he muttered.

"These are mine." He knew his attitude was wrong. That wasn't the way the BP worked together; they were a team.

A woman stepped out from the brush, saw his truck, and disappeared into the thicket on the opposite side of the road. Jacob slid the truck to a stop. Grabbing only his keys, he took out after her. He caught sight of a man who grasped the hand of the woman. Together they ran, shoving aside tall grass and brush in an effort to lose the BP. If there were more illegals, they were well hidden. Adrenaline flowed, pumping through his veins more powerfully than the anger that had nipped at his heels all morning.

Jacob shouted the canned phrase for them to stop, hoping it would bring them to a halt.

The woman dropped a plastic bag. No doubt containing all of her personal belongings.

He closed the distance between him and the couple. With his chest heaving, Jacob allowed all his frustration to propel him a few more feet. He reached out and batted the woman's shoulder, throwing the couple off balance and tumbling into the brush.

Jacob seized the man by the shoulders and sank his fingers into the thin flesh of both of the man's arms. He yelped and tried to shake off Jacob's hold. The woman screamed.

Jacob yanked the man to his feet and slammed a fist into his jaw. The sound of flesh grinding flesh should have alerted him. He knew better. He knew to stop. But he seemed to be fueled by the blood streaming from the man's face and his own knuckles. Shouts from the two agents behind him startled him, but Jacob tuned them out and swung another punch into the man's abdomen.

The agents seized Jacob's arms and dragged him from the man's body. Jacob struggled, curses falling from his mouth like an old man's dribble.

"What are you thinking?" Bud said, a veteran agent who had attended the academy with Jacob. "Look at his face."

Jacob's gaze flew to the blood-covered man. Horror over what he'd done swept through him. In the sweltering heat, he shivered. What had happened to him? His record had once been impeccable—until two years ago.

"I'll take him to the hospital," Jacob managed. He watched Bud help the illegal to his feet. The woman clung to the beaten man and wept.

"Don't think so," Bud said. "We're driving back to the station to report this."

Realizing he'd beaten a defenseless man sent an acid cocktail to the pit of Jacob's stomach. He'd violated this man's rights as a human being. And his fit of rage may have destroyed his hope for salvaging his career. His failure to control his temper would slip right into place with his inability to lead his family.

"Nadine has run away."

Jacob forced his attention on the distraught woman. She glared at him as though he were a rabid animal. Her dark eyes seemed to penetrate his soul. If he still had one.

CHAPTER 11

Whoever gives to the poor will lack nothing, but those who close their eyes to poverty will be cursed.
PROVERBS 28:27

ALEX SQUEEZED HIS TRUCK into the elementary school parking lot's last available slot labeled Visitors. This morning he'd be a part of a community project offering free medical checkups and vaccinations to all those elementary-age kids entering school in approximately one month. A number of free clinics in the city offered the same services, but his understanding was that here some of the teachers would be on hand to meet the kids and talk to parents. Other professionals had volunteered their time to administer dental exams and free hearing and vision screenings, and a local TV station was giving away backpacks filled with school supplies. Already the school's entrance swarmed with kids and parents. The white Channel 5 TV van sat next to the curb, its microwave antenna raised high in the clear sky and pointed toward the station.

He smiled at the gray-haired woman sitting beside him in his truck, a retired nurse who worked harder as a volunteer than she had done for a paycheck. With her hair brushed back into a ponytail and tied with a red scarf, she looked like a picture of nostalgia, complete with a white blouse and turned-up pant legs on her jeans.

"We'll work our tails off today, Nancy."

"It's not work when you're helping families stay healthy." She opened the passenger door and stepped down. "Get your stuff, Doc. We have a schedule to follow."

He laughed and exited his side of the truck. "Have you thought about hitting the road with a motivational speaking tour?"

"Couldn't pay me enough." Nancy hoisted a shoulder bag and reached into the rear seat of the truck. She grabbed a plastic container that held the required forms, a blood pressure cuff, an otoscope, tongue depressors, a stethoscope, plenty of sharpened pencils, and a good supply of yellow smiley-face stickers. "I hope you have more balloons than the last time," she said, then took off down the sidewalk at a fast clip without him, her typical pace.

He lifted an insulated refrigeration chest filled with vaccinations from the other side of the seat. Supporting that in one hand, he wrapped his fingers around the plastic box containing the all-in-one needles and syringes, prepackaged alcohol swabs, a red plastic container to hold used syringes, *and* additional balloons to please Nurse Nancy.

Balancing his supplies with both arms, Alex made his way up the sidewalk to the entrance. He focused on a woman and a little dark-haired girl who waited with the others to enter the school. She turned his way, and he saw it was Danika Morales—Agent Danika Morales, as Jacob had so pointedly corrected. Dare he try again to be friendly? Her rejection early Sunday morning had burst his balloon. Yet he wasn't a quitter; he simply failed a lot when he approached women. Perhaps this time his devilish good looks and irresistible charm would persuade her to ask *him* out.

She waved, and he returned the gesture. That was a good sign. The closer he walked toward her, the bigger her smile. At least he thought so. She wore a light blue knit top and earrings to match. He had no clue why Danika Morales held him captive with just one look, but everything he'd seen in the way she handled herself and treated others spoke of integrity. When he and Toby used to talk, he bragged about his gorgeous wife and all the things she did for their family. Toby used to worry about the danger, especially when she worked nights. He should have worried about himself.

"Good morning," she said. "Are you our resident doctor?"

"Sure am. I'm armed with disposable shots and little vials of medicine." He glanced down at the little girl. "Oops, I shouldn't have mentioned those."

Danika placed an arm around the little girl's shoulder. "She's hearing-impaired and doesn't read lips yet, so you're safe."

Odd. Toby had never mentioned this. He set the boxes on the pavement and bent to the little girl's level. After taking a moment to give himself a refresher in sign language, he signed, "Hello. What is your name?"

She raised her gaze to her mother.

"It's all right," Danika signed.

The little girl signed, "Tiana."

"Beautiful child." Beautiful mommy too. Alex met Danika's gaze. He saw a spark of something that didn't look like rejection to him. "The lines should go fairly fast."

"She's up-to-date on her shots. I'm volunteering for the morning."

Alex stood. "What area?"

"Assisting moms to complete the school forms. Tiana is going to help me."

"Have her come by my section when she's finished being your assistant, and I'll make sure she gets a balloon and a sticker."

Danika smiled, and he felt his knees weaken. "Go ahead and tell her yourself. Looks like your signing is pretty good."

He bent again to Tiana's side and told her about seeing him later. The little girl's fingers rapidly conveyed her enthusiasm.

As much as he'd have liked to stay and talk, he needed to set up inside. Standing to face Danika one more time, he reached for a handful of courage. "I'd like to get to know you, but I understand your hesitation." He handed her a business card. "My personal cell number is on the back. When you're ready, let me know. All of us need a friend."

She tilted her head, the highlights in her hair picking up the morning sunlight. "Thanks, Alex. I'll think about it."

Hope. What more could a man ask for?

Danika entered the two-story professional building where Dr. Shannon Perry met with her patients. The marquee read Christian Counselor, but Danika referred to her as "counselor extraordinaire." No sarcasm entered her thoughts. Shannon had dug deep into Danika's heart and pulled up emotional trash that should have been deposited into the dump years ago. Returning nightmares and the old feelings of poor self-worth indicated the separation from counseling had been premature.

The tall, thin woman, who wore a sprinkling of freckles across her nose and designer jeans like a runway model, greeted her with a hug. "Missed you. I'm looking forward to catching up."

Once seated, Danika took a deep breath. She began with Tiana's behavior problems and moved on to Jacob and Barbara's relationship and Nadine's disappearance, then ended with her attraction to Dr. Alex Price.

"What about your job at the Border Patrol?" Shannon's smile was meant to relax Danika, but nervousness had caused her stomach to roll.

"It's what keeps me sane. It's my purpose, my call of duty. I believe I'm good at what I do." Thoughts about Felipe and his family's immigration troubles had bothered her all day. Commitment to keeping the borders safe didn't come with ifs, but that didn't mean she lacked sympathy for the miserable lot of too many would-be immigrants.

Shannon smiled. "I'm breaking open a can of Diet Coke with that one." She slipped from her chair and opened a small refrigerator. Handing Danika a can, she studied her for a moment. "Counseling is not just for those who are having problems managing the stress in their lives. It's for the healthy too, a validation of how we can praise God through the good and challenging times."

"I'm journaling and keeping a list of God's blessings." Danika flipped the tab on the can. "However, my relationship with Him is not what it used to be."

"Still angry?"

Danika nodded. "Guess I need to get over it and move on." For over a year she'd attempted to put aside the many times she asked why He had to take Toby from her and Tiana. By the time she stood face-to-face with God, why Toby had betrayed her and been murdered wouldn't matter. At least that is what she kept telling herself.

Shannon leaned toward Danika. "Talk to me about your anger and grief. That's the only way you'll find the peace you so desperately crave."

Danika agreed, but it was so painful to discuss the feelings she'd shoved to a remote corner of her heart.

"I understand the difficulty in talking about these issues, and I want to help. The nightmares will continue to haunt you until you are able to let it go."

"And that's why I'm here." Danika heard the resolve in her own words and knew she must be transparent in order to heal. "I want to move on with my life." She shivered. "I'm ready to take the next step."

CHAPTER 12

*There is nothing—no circumstances, no trouble, no testing—that can
ever touch me until, first of all, it has come past God and Christ, right
through to me. If it has come that far, it has come with a great purpose.*
ALAN REDPATH

JACOB HAD TO GET BACK to work. The flu had kicked his
rear, and the drain on him physically and mentally only served
to depress him even more. By Thursday afternoon he decided
dying couldn't be any worse than sitting on the toilet and throwing up in a trash can. He forced himself out of bed and drove to
see the doctor. A prescription to stop the vomiting and a sleep
aid helped, but it didn't change what he had to face at the station
or the problems at home. As he lay in bed and watched the late
afternoon shadows creep across his walls, the situations crash-
ing against his brain started his stomach to rumble again. He
didn't feel like talking to his kids, and he dreaded Barbara coming home from work.

Where is Nadine?

The whole discipline process at the station triggered paralyz-
ing anxiety. Jacob refused to admit to fear. That was beneath
him. But a veteran of the Border Patrol shouldn't have to go
through such humiliation for a minor infraction. The illegal
man he'd punched had been interviewed, and the two agents
who witnessed the incident had given their testimony. So Jacob
had made a mistake. Write him up, stick it in the file, and let him
get back to work. Except his supes viewed the day's happenings

according to the rule book. Before Jacob was dismissed for the day, he'd been given a report that stated the Office of Inspector General, the Border Patrol Internal Affairs, and the Office of Professional Responsibility would receive immediate notice of the incident. The ultimatum at the station came from Chief Patrol Agent Ed Jimenez—mandatory counseling and administrative work until his supes decided his future with the Border Patrol. This was his second offense, according to them. It could be the end of his career and certainly the end to any hope of a supervisor position.

Jacob had been an agent for twenty years, and he'd seen a lot of changes. Some he liked, and some he despised. All the new blood exiting the academy as a result of the former presidential administration's request for more agents consisted of some kids filling a man's shoes. The Border Patrol was a paramilitary organization, not a place for little boys to play army. The mentoring program with seasoned agents was a start, but Jacob hadn't signed up to babysit. To keep the job he was so dissatisfied with meant going through a company counselor who wanted him to discuss his feelings. "Anger management" is what Jimenez called it. Jacob planned to fight it for as long as possible. He needed his spare hours to make extra money that would put Nadine through college, if she ever decided to come home.

The counseling aspect infuriated him the most. His wife needed counseling, not him. It was her fault his family and his job were falling apart. How ironic that his wife who had pledged her love to him nineteen years ago had forgotten her vows. She'd set out to destroy him ever since Toby had been killed, and now it looked like she was succeeding.

Jacob glanced at the time. Barbara would be home soon. Strange how he could once love a woman and now wish she was out of his life. He needed to get back to work—face the repercussions of his actions and get on with his life. But the doctor had given him written orders to stay home until Saturday. One more day stuck at home in bed and he'd need intense anger management.

CHAPTER 13

I have known sorrow and learned to aid the wretched.
VIRGIL

By Friday, Danika had serious concerns about Jacob, and Barbara hadn't called during the week. News about his abusing an illegal spread like a twenty-four-hour virus. He faced disciplinary action, and it wasn't the first time. Danika would not have been surprised if he'd been dismissed on the spot. She heard the murmurings, but she'd witnessed his slow progression into a bitter man. He'd alienated his old friends and hadn't attempted to make new ones. She realized the shock of learning about Nadine's drug problem could have pushed him over the edge, but it didn't justify beating a man. She wished she had free time during her shift to visit Barbara at the accounting firm, but that luxury was not for Border Patrol agents.

She punched in Barbara's cell phone number. "I'm worried sick about Jacob and Nadine," Danika said. "Not just them, but all of you."

"I should have called you Sunday, and here it is Friday. The problems keep escalating."

Solutions for Nadine must not have been found. Now they also faced Jacob's problems at work. Home life for Barbara must tug on all her emotion strings.

"What can I do to help? The last time we talked, you were going to try to find someone for Nadine to talk with."

"That's minor compared to what has happened." Barbara's

tone was flat, almost scary. Normally she bubbled with enthusiasm about life and all the happenings going on with her family—even while she lived in denial of Jacob's bullying.

"I'm confused. Maybe you could explain."

"Naddie ran away."

Fear seized Danika. Not since Toby's death had she sensed her world falling apart like this. "When? What do the police say?"

"Sometime Sunday night. The police haven't turned up a thing. It's as though she's disappeared."

"Oh, honey, you should have called. I'd have been right there."

"I wanted to tell you, wanted to every day, but Jacob . . ."

"I understand. No wonder he cracked at work."

Barbara gasped. "What do you mean? What happened at the station?" Hysteria crept into her voice. "He's been home since Tuesday afternoon. Said he was sick, and he's been vomiting. Hasn't been to the doctor that I know of, but we aren't really communicating."

"I'm not the one to tell you about the incident. Maybe you should call the station."

Sobs broke through the phone, and Danika blinked back her tears. This precious family had more burdens than they could bear. Her thoughts focused on the other children. Were they grieving and confused like Nadine? Children ultimately suffered the most in family turmoil. They needed sane outlets, just like adults.

"Have you or Jacob contacted a priest?"

"Jacob said he was too embarrassed, but I've talked to our priest twice this week."

Embarrassed? Full of pride more accurately described him. "So he's still blaming you?"

"I know it's not my fault she ran away, just like I know he's hurting. Both my Jacob and my little Naddie are in so much pain."

"Is there any place I can look for her?"

"Oh, Danika, you are so sweet." Barbara's voice broke with a sob. "I've talked to her friends and their parents, and no one has heard from her."

"What about the other children?"

"Scared. Upset tummies. Kaitlyn sleeps to avoid what is going on, while Jake isn't sleeping. Amber refuses to eat."

"I'm here for all of you," Danika said. "Oh, that sounds so lame. I want to do something."

"I know I can always depend on you, and I'll do better to keep you posted. Right now I need your prayers. One more thing. Jacob said not to tell you about Naddie's disappearance because your prayers didn't count—because you're not Catholic. I don't believe that, never have. And I should have spoken up for you at the time. He never got over Toby's . . . leaving the Catholic church." Barbara continued to ramble. The dear woman craved peace.

"Barbara," Danika interrupted. "It's all right. We can discuss our faith when your family settles down a bit. Let it be enough to say God hears the prayers of the believer, and He doesn't ask which church we attend." How long had it been since she'd practiced words of encouragement to a Christian sister?

"Thank you. I'll call tomorrow. Maybe Nadine will be home or call me by then." Barbara hung up, leaving Danika lost in a whirlwind of near panic and love for her family.

Her session with Shannon had proved how desperately she needed to work through the demons in her own life. The situation looked like God had deserted all of them. But then again who else was there to turn to?

Sandra pushed her cart through the grocery store. She loved her job and her adoptive family. Cooking for Danika and Tiana and keeping their home clean—her home—filled her with satisfaction. She no longer looked for a husband, and she'd wait for her own family until Danika no longer needed her. The troubles circling her life two years ago had faded into manageable chunks. Even Lucy was handled since she believed Danika's lawyer held the evidence implicating her traffic in illegal workers.

Danika had purchased a beautiful home right after Sandra had taken the job as Tiana's nanny. It was a split floor plan that allowed Sandra and Danika to have their own privacy within the same house. What more could she ask for?

Tiana pushed a small cart beside her. Inside were a bunch of bananas and a box of graham crackers. The little girl tugged on Sandra's shirt. "Cookie," she signed, and Sandra nodded her consent.

At the end of the next aisle, the bakery offered free cookies to children. And Tiana loved the sugared treats.

The delicious aroma of hot bread teased Sandra's nostrils, reminding her the hour moved quickly to noon. As a child, she'd often gone to bed hungry, and she made certain Tiana ate a balanced diet that ensured a healthy little girl. Sandra had pored over many books on nutrition especially for her Tiana. She did think of the little girl as her own. After all, she spent more waking hours with her than Danika. Sandra remembered how hard she'd labored to learn to read and write before accepting this job. Everything had paid off. Even Lucy's abuse.

She picked up a loaf of marble rye bread and tortillas and helped Tiana pick out a sugar cookie. Stopping at the fresh produce, she selected four red bell peppers. She'd roast them and make a cream soup for dinner with a huge spinach salad. Danika encouraged her to watch the Food Network and prepare other dishes besides traditional Mexican foods. Right from the start, Danika had made it clear that trust was the most important factor in their relationship, and she didn't question the food bill.

So Sandra budgeted her spending and tried new recipes, and Danika was pleased.

Then Sandra remembered the morning's call from Lucy, as if spiders were crawling inside her stomach and threatening to destroy her. The woman's demands had increased, and although Sandra refused to comply with any of them, the threats continued. Lucy had hardened over the years, grown greedier and bolder. She despised Danika, and Sandra thought she knew why, but she didn't want to speculate. The nagging suspicions about Lucy's depraved mind cropped up at unexpected times, suspicions Sandra dreaded to face. Even if true, even if Lucy were involved in other things besides an illegal maid and nanny service, Sandra didn't want to know. Lucy had means of securing falsified U.S. documents, which kept ICE off the woman's back.

"Do you know where Cira is?" Lucy had asked.

"Cira Ramos? She's been gone from McAllen for two years." Sandra hoped the young woman and her baby never returned to the area.

"That's not what I asked."

"I have no idea." Cira had fled to Houston, where she planned to raise her child without fear of Lucy forcing her to work for free.

"If you value your life, you'll do what I tell you," Lucy said. "I need to find Cira. And I need Border Patrol information."

"Forget it. As many threats as you toss my way, I have more. I'd get shipped back to Mexico, but you'd be sentenced to jail for a long time." Her words sounded brave, and they packed enough punch to stop Lucy from sending someone to change her mind, but Sandra understood how evil Lucy could be.

Sandra no longer needed to talk with the women who worked for Lucy to know the rumors—how many illegals worked seven days a week for nothing to pay back their indebtedness for bringing them to the United States. Sandra never understood why Lucy didn't want to let Cira go. The pretty young woman had been cornered repeatedly by Lucy's men until she turned up pregnant. That's when she ran.

During the time of her indebtedness, Sandra lived under Lucy's rules. The woman supplied toast and coffee for breakfast and beans and tortillas for dinner. The illegal workers alternated between a bed and a floor, often four to a room. The years became a monotonous blur in her memory. She'd been freer in Mexico, until Danika came to Lucy with a need for a live-in nanny. The position gradually developed into a cook and maid, not because Danika asked any more of her but because Sandra had quickly grown fond of the mother and daughter and wanted to do everything possible to help the widow and her deaf child. Everything but tell her the truth about her status within the U.S.

No matter what Lucy claimed she could do, Sandra would never change her mind and betray Danika unless . . . She didn't want to think about the letter she'd received yesterday about her aging parents needing urgent medical care. Sandra already sent them all she could spare from the last paycheck, but her mother insisted it wasn't enough. Next week, she'd send more. Her parents would receive what they needed, and Sandra's comfortable life would continue.

CHAPTER 14

**The Lord has comforted his people and will have
compassion on them in their suffering.**
ISAIAH 49:13

DANIKA ALWAYS SPENT the last two hours of her ten-hour shifts informing the agent taking over her watch of any leads, then driving back to the station to complete paperwork. Friday afternoon was no exception. As she labored over the report citing the half-dozen illegals discovered this morning, her thoughts repeated her conversation with Barbara earlier in the day. Her dear sister-in-law shared the agony of a runaway daughter and a husband who had intense emotional problems. Counseling would help them all and possibly save their marriage.

But Nadine's whereabouts scared Danika the most. A pretty teen who had chosen drugs to help her cope with life and disappeared so cleverly that the police hadn't been able to find her was nothing short of a tragedy.

Conscious of someone standing over her, she turned her attention to Chief Patrol Agent Edwardo Jimenez.

"I'd like to see you in my office before you leave, Morales," he said.

"Yes, sir." For sure this was about Jacob, and she dreaded it.

After she finished her daily report, Danika made her way to Jimenez's office. She could count on one hand how many times she'd been in his office, and none of them were ever good. He had an impressive reputation, starting with his record in the Marines as a crack shot.

She steadied herself. The last time she sat in this office was when he told her about agents finding Toby's body out in a field close to checkpoint 281. She stood in Chief Jimenez's doorway.

"Come on in and shut the door." He had one hand on an open file. "I have a few questions."

She eased into a chair. How she hated for Jacob to be involved in any more trouble. "What is this about?"

"Your husband."

Startled, Danika held her breath. If Toby's killer had been found, wouldn't that have come from the police? "What about him?"

"Two years ago you stated you were unaware of his activist involvement until the morning of his death."

"Yes, sir." The question made no sense. She'd been through this with him before.

"Exactly what happened the morning of your husband's death?"

A trickle of apprehension dripped into her veins. "I don't understand. It's all in my file."

"I'd like for you to tell me again."

Did he have any idea how it hurt to recall that day? And for what purpose? A hammering against her temples blurred her vision. "Why?"

He sat back in his chair and studied her face. She despised the emotionless look he gave her, as though she'd done something wrong. "We have strong reason to believe a rogue agent is at this station."

"Surely you don't suspect me?" Anger added to the pounding in her head.

"I don't, but I need this information again."

"Who else are you talking to?"

"I have a list. Every agent in this sector is under investigation. Someone is releasing sensor locations."

Danika considered refusing. After all, she had her rights, and the past was documented in her records. But if she cooperated, then he'd have no reason to suspect her. The drug cartels would pay well to have that information.

Okay, she'd dredge up every painful memory. "On the morning of his . . . death, I was running late in getting our toddler to day care. Halfway there, I realized I'd forgotten the diaper bag. I went back to the house, opened the garage door, and saw Toby arranging cases of water in the trunk of his car. When I got out to retrieve the diaper bag, I saw he also had small first aid kits and nonperishable food stacked near the car. I asked him what was going on. Honestly, I thought he might be involved in a summer school project at the high school. He taught there, you know. But he finally told me he planned to deliver the stuff to a safe house for illegals."

She paused as the betrayal against all she believed in washed over her again. She could remember the scene as if it had happened yesterday . . . the white T-shirt he wore with their church's softball team logo on it . . . the way his baseball cap sat on the left side of his head . . . the stifling heat in the garage . . .

"Give yourself a moment," Jimenez said. "I'll wait."

She nodded and let the flood of memories rush past her heart.

"I don't believe this. You can't help the illegals," she said. "What are you thinking? I put my life on the line every day to enforce our borders, and you're bringing water and supplies to the illegals? How many of those people are guides and drug smugglers?"

He sighed and pushed his cap back on his head. "Honey, I didn't want you to find out this way. I've been trying to figure out how to talk to you about what I'm doing. I don't see it quite the same way you do."

"What you're doing? As in, you've done this before?" Her chest felt as though someone had clamped a weight on her.

"I've helped many people over the past year. It's not a decision I made lightly. It took lots of prayer." Toby reached out to hold her, but she stepped back. *"God tells us to have compassion on the poor. All they want is a chance to provide for their families."*

"There are legal channels to allow them to enter the U.S."

"Danika, you know as well as I do that many of the immigrants we're dealing with here will never qualify for a visa. And even if they do, it takes years. The Mexican government is killing its own people."

"God also tells us to obey the law. And it's my job to enforce it."

The diaper bag. *She'd come for the diaper bag. Brushing past this man she was no longer sure she knew, let alone shared a life with, she opened the door to the kitchen and snatched the familiar pink and green bag with* Tiana *embroidered on it. The news was worse than if she'd learned Toby had been unfaithful. In a sense, he had been. He'd betrayed her and the Border Patrol.*

Danika slammed the door behind her. "When God gave you the green light to break the law, did He also say it was okay to deceive your wife?"

"Danika, let's talk about this."

His patronizing attitude was further fuel on the fire. She opened the car door and glanced back at Tiana, for once grateful her precious baby was deaf and couldn't hear the angry words passing between her parents. *"There's nothing to talk about! You've gone against everything I believe in!"*

"Don't you think I've thought about that? Let me explain."

"No! It's too late for that. I've watched agents get shot down while chasing drug dealers. I can't believe my own husband has been helping them. Chew on this, Toby: You make a choice. It's either Tiana and me . . . or your little crusade."

She backed the car out of the driveway, leaving him standing in front of his open trunk.

"That was the last time I saw Toby alive." She swallowed her tears. She was a professional, not a weepy widow. "That's it."

"And you had no idea of his views on immigration until then."

"No, sir. I assumed they were the same as mine."

"And you still expect me to believe that your husband could have been so involved in immigration activism without your knowing anything about it?"

Danika stiffened. "It's the truth. Look at my record, sir. It's impeccable. I've applied for a supervisor position because I want to help other agents work the border. Give me one incident indicating I'm not dedicated to the policies of the Border Patrol."

Jimenez slowly nodded. "All right, Agent Morales. You made your point. Thanks for repeating your story and not blowing up."

"One Morales with a temper problem is enough." She said it before thinking.

"Are you insinuating Jacob and Toby worked together?"

Her eyes widened. "Absolutely not. Jacob felt just as betrayed as I did after we found out what Toby was doing behind our backs."

"Something is not right about your husband's death—"

"*Murder*. Tell it like it is. It's never been solved, and no one knows why his body was dumped a mile from the road."

He folded his hands over her file. "I'll let you know if I have any more questions."

Maybe she'd answer them, and maybe she wouldn't.

★ ★ ★

Alex walked out of Rita's room. He'd discharge her in the morning, which meant she'd soon be on her way back to Mexico. After much persuasion, the young woman agreed to talk to the Border Patrol about who had raped and beaten her. With the name

Rita had given him, hopefully charges could be filed. Unless the assailant had already been processed and sent back home.

Glancing at the 6:10 reading on his watch, Alex took a chance that Ed would still be at the McAllen station. He stepped into his office and closed the door.

Ed answered on the second ring. "Recognized your number." His voice spoke of weariness.

"Long day?"

"Not until about forty-five minutes ago." Ed blew out a sigh, and Alex heard his chair squeak.

"I won't take up much of your time. The young woman brought into the hospital last week?"

"Abuse?"

"Yes. I'm discharging her in the morning. She had internal injuries and resulting surgery, but she's well enough to be transported back across the border."

"I remember Agent Morales brought her in. But another agent took over once I realized her name was at the top of the list as a suspected rogue."

"Danika?" Shock rippled through Alex. "Surely you don't suspect her."

"Not really, but it's possible."

Irritation replaced Alex's surprise. He'd been wrong about a woman before, but his heart told him Danika Morales was trustworthy. "I barely know her, but from all outward appearances, she seems dedicated to the Border Patrol and the agents."

"I think so too. Just contact me if anything unusual occurs."

Toby had never indicated that Danika agreed with his immigration views. "The girl asked to speak to Agent Morales."

Ed cleared his throat. "I'll have Morales pick her up in the morning. Let me know if you see or hear anything unusual about the agent, who she talks to and the like."

"I suppose."

"By the way, did your patient ever talk about who abused her?"

"She said it was the guide."

Ed swore. "Goes right with my day."

Alex sympathized with the burden of a heavy workload. "Has he already been released?"

"Worse. He's underage. First offense."

This time Alex wanted to swear. Instead, he swallowed his curses and dug for more information. "Nothing you can do?"

"I'll add the charges to his data and hope he's picked up again."

Furious by the news, Alex snapped his pencil in two. "I'm heading out of here in a few minutes. Want to meet for dinner?"

"Are you sure you want me for company?"

"I asked, didn't I?"

"The wife and kids are out of town visiting her mother. I'd planned to go home to the dog and TV, but I'd take a steak."

Whose mood would be worse? "Our favorite spot?"

"I'll be there in thirty minutes."

Alex dropped his cell into his jean pocket. Whatever was bothering Ed must have been a doozy. Normally he left work problems at the station, and even in their accountability times, Ed kept his emotions intact. Tonight Alex would encourage him to talk. The man carried twenty extra pounds in the middle—with all his stress, not a good recipe for health.

He lingered for a moment on the prospect of seeing Danika in the morning. He'd spend all night thinking up something clever to say, then forget it the moment she strolled into the hospital. Ah, those women in uniform.

Danika's patience had stretched to the snapping point. She had nearly given up trying to figure out what had happened to put

Tiana in such a foul mood. Her daughter's behavior reminded Danika of what the preschool teachers had reported last spring—uncontrollable anger. Tiana had refused dinner and thrown toys, and now she balked at her bath.

"What's wrong?" Danika signed.

"Why do Harper and Asher have a daddy and I don't?" Tiana wore her disappointment on her face and in her fingers.

"We saw them at the grocery with their dad," Sandra said, standing in the bathroom doorway. "She's been like this ever since." She patted Danika on the shoulder and left mother and daughter alone.

This was not the day to discuss Tiana's lack of a father, but Danika had no choice. Her daughter had never asked about Toby before, and Danika had thought that when the day ever came, she would somehow find the appropriate words. Now she wasn't so sure.

"Your daddy is in heaven with Jesus."

"Why?"

The question Danika had been pondering for the past two years. She turned the faucet to warm and added more water while she formed her words. "I don't know. I wish I did. Sometimes Mommy gets sad and misses Daddy too. But when I feel this way, I start to remember all the wonderful things about him that made me happy. Then I feel better."

Tiana stuck out her lower lip and began to sign. "Doesn't Jesus know I need my daddy?"

Danika reached into the warm bathwater and gathered up the little girl and pulled her into her arms. Wrapped in a towel, Tiana sat in her lap while Danika signed. "Jesus knows you miss your daddy, but he won't be back. He can't come back to us after going to live in heaven. We can only do what Daddy would want for us to do, and that is to be happy."

Tiana began to sob. "Can we go there?"

Danika kissed her forehead. "That's for Jesus to decide. Until then we do the best we can to make sure Daddy is proud of us. But it's okay for us to cry when we miss Daddy because we only cry for those we love."

"Is he mad because I can't hear or talk like other kids? Is that why he went away?"

A lump formed in Danika's throat. This was the most progress ever made in getting to the source of Tiana's bottled anger. "Oh no, honey. Daddy loved you just the way you are. You were his joy."

"Are you mad because I can't hear or talk?"

"Of course not. We talk in a special way."

"Are you going to heaven with Jesus and Daddy?"

"Someday, when Jesus decides it's time." Danika rocked her precious baby girl and continued to sign. "No one is mad at you. I love you. You are my precious little girl, a gift from God."

"And you won't leave me?"

She thought about Toby's murder and the problems at the station. "I'm doing my best to stay right here with you. I love being your mommy."

Tiana leaned against Danika's chest and relaxed. A breakthrough had been made, and for that Danika was pleased. But the agony in Tiana's eyes spoke volumes. Her daughter's anger had been unveiled—the issue of not understanding and blaming herself for her daddy's death. Danika learned a lot tonight. She and Tiana shared the same heartache.

CHAPTER 15

If God did not exist, it would be necessary to invent Him.
VOLTAIRE

FOR THE FIRST TIME in months, Danika slept through to her six o'clock alarm. She woke refreshed, feeling more positive than she'd been in a long time. Tiana was still sleeping when the clock read seven thirty and it was time for Danika to get to work. She'd miss her early morning workout, but her body would survive.

She grabbed her coffee in a to-go mug and brushed a kiss on Sandra's cheek. Her friend appeared preoccupied. "Are you okay?"

"Oh yes. Everything's fine. I'm thinking of what Tiana said to you last night."

Danika nodded, a mixture of bittersweet emotions looming over her. "I think we're on the right track to solving her behavior problems. At last, my baby is telling us how she feels. I'm going to talk to Shannon about how to proceed."

"Sounds like a good idea. I'll make sure Tiana knows she's special. I read that in one of your parent magazines, and I see her VeggieTales movies reinforce it too."

Danika set her coffee down on the counter to give Sandra a hug. "I love you, dear one. No amount of money could ever be placed on all you do for us, especially the love."

Sandra's lips quivered. "We are like sisters in our hearts."

"Mexico lost when you became a U.S. citizen. I look forward to the two of us being friends when our hair is gray and our teeth are gone."

Sandra smiled through tear-filled eyes. "Not me. I'll use Clairol, and I brush my teeth."

Danika laughed and hugged her. "Okay, Sandra. I'm off. You hold down the fort while I go fight the Indians."

"I thought you said the Indians were treated badly."

"I did. It's a saying."

Sandra waved her away. "You confuse me."

Once at the station and through muster, Danika was told she needed to pick up Rita at McAllen Medical Center. Odd, since the agent who spent the night with the patient could have provided the transportation. But after Danika's conversation with Jimenez yesterday afternoon, she wasn't questioning a single order. The confrontation had her biting her tongue and swallowing the cynicism. Being suspected as a rogue agent *did* make her angry enough to consider quitting, but why give Jimenez the pleasure?

Then a delicious thought shoved her superior from her mind: she might see Alex.

At the medical center, she replaced the agent in Rita's room and learned Rita had spent a restless night with the thought of returning home. After greeting the girl, Danika waited for Alex or the nurse to bring the discharge papers.

She took Rita's hand—a child who hadn't been ready for an adult world. "You look healthy and pretty."

"Dr. Price took good care of me." She smiled, her large nut-brown eyes sparkling like Danika had often seen Tiana's do.

"I see that. Are you in pain?"

"A little. Just worried about going home. My parents were afraid for me to make the trip, but they wanted a better future for me than in Mexico." A wistful look passed over the girl's face. "I did want to come here to work. I told them I could send them money so their life wouldn't be so hard."

Danika's emotions plummeted. But the laws protecting the

border were in place for a reason. "You had a worthy goal, but the U.S. has laws concerning how to gain access into our country."

"But it takes so many years."

"Wouldn't it be better to come here boldly and full of confidence than to go through the dangers of crossing the border illegally? I'd love to see you march across the bridge at Hidalgo with your visa in one hand and your suitcase in the other."

"It does sound good. Hiding from the Border Patrol was scary."

At least Danika had accomplished something. "Look at the amount of money it cost you and your family."

Rita propped herself on one elbow. "It was only half for me. I planned to work for a lady for free until the rest of my fee was paid."

Danika had choice words to describe that type of arrangement. Many young girls ended up as work-worn maids or prostitutes and were never able to repay the money owed. "What kind of work would you have been doing?"

"Cleaning houses."

"I see. Who would you be working for?"

Rita tilted her head. She reminded Danika of a younger Nadine. "I don't know her name. The guide was supposed to take me and two others to meet her." She frowned. "I hope a rattlesnake got him. But I'm afraid he might find me and kill me. Besides, he did lead some good men across."

"Were there any drug smugglers with you?"

Rita shook her head. "I cannot say. Many work with gangs, and I'd be killed as well as my family. It is very dangerous at home."

"I'm sorry."

Danika saw a shadow in the doorway. A young man with blue scrubs and auburn hair pushed a cart of medication into the room. "Agent Morales, Dr. Price would like to see you. He's at the nurse's station."

Danika released Rita's hand with a promise to quickly return. She ventured down the hall and around the corner, anticipating Alex to be standing there. If her life wasn't in such shambles, she'd accept a date. Right now her insides were doing flips at the thought of simply seeing him.

The nurses buzzed around the station like bees on honey. Maybe Alex sat in the middle. She nearly laughed at her own joke. When she didn't see him, she lingered in the hallway thinking he must be with a patient. Ten more minutes passed.

Danika glanced at her watch. "Excuse me, I was told to meet Dr. Price here," she said to a nurse behind the circular enclosure. "I'm to pick up discharge papers for a young woman."

The nurse shook her head. "Dr. Price is in emergency. He hasn't been up here for rounds this morning. However, I do have the papers."

Apprehension clutched Danika's chest. She raced back down the hall to Rita's room with one hand on her weapon. She flung open the partially closed door.

Blood stained the white sheets and puddled on the floor. Rita had been stabbed in the chest.

★ ★ ★

Jacob's stomach hadn't been this sore since he'd gotten over food poisoning at a crawfish festival. He patted his shirt pocket for his doctor's slip to give to his supe and walked toward the station's employee entrance. He was dreading today, actually despising the day. Everyone knew what happened. When disciplinary measures had been meted out, the news spread through the agents faster than rising water in a hurricane. They'd ignore him. Of course, he'd been avoided for quite some time, much the way Barbara and his kids treated him. The other agents used to look up to him—an icon of the McAllen Border Patrol sector. Those days faded into oblivion when Toby died. Everyone seemed to have forgotten his brother's murder. But not Jacob. He'd not give up until justice was served.

Inside the station, he changed into his uniform, minus his weapon, which had been confiscated when he'd been brought in for the abuse charges. He trailed down the hall to the field operations supervisor, Agent Oden Herrera, and presented the doctor's slip.

"You need to schedule your counseling appointment," Herrera said.

"Now? I just walked in." Jacob clenched, then unclenched, his fist. "It's Saturday. No one's open today."

"Jimenez's orders. The call's been made, and I have three appointments available." He pulled a folded piece of paper from his pocket. "Pick one."

Jacob looked at his options. All three interfered with other things. "Can't do any of those."

"You're not scheduled to work then."

"I have a life," Jacob snapped.

"That attitude is why you're seeing a counselor and why your job is on the line."

Jacob started to say he didn't need the job, but he did. He could agree to this counseling and still lose his job with the BP. He stiffened. "Is there an appointment available thirty minutes prior to the second one listed?"

"I'll look into it. Get back with me after your shift."

"All right."

Herrera leaned back in his chair. "Morales, we're on your side. Something is eating at you, and we're all in this together."

"Yeah. I've heard that."

Herrera stared at him. Disgust—or was it pity?—clouded his eyes.

CHAPTER 16

Only the brave know how to forgive.
LAURENCE STERNE

DANIKA CLASPED TIANA'S HAND firmly in hers and walked into the sanctuary of McAllen Community Church. The Saturday night service didn't draw near the worshipers Sunday morning did, but this uniquely scheduled time allowed people like her who worked on Sundays to honor God.

Tiana released Danika's hand. "Mommy, why are you shaking?"

Danika willed her body to relax and put aside the memory of Rita's limp and crimson form. Murdered. And for what purpose? Would the word *why* be permanently engraved in her heart for the deaths stalking her? She'd seen dead bodies before; it often came with the job. Except this time, Danika had formed a bond with a young woman who had trusted her. And Danika had failed her.

"I feel sad, and I need God to help me feel better."

"I'm sorry, Mommy. When I ask Jesus for a daddy, I'll ask Him to make you happy."

"Thank you." Right now she needed a few crimes solved, not another man in her life.

Danika's mind focused on this morning at the hospital. Fortunately a volunteer had seen the young man pushing the medicine cart down the hall—the same cart that was found abandoned in the hallway.

The police did not blame Danika. Neither did Jimenez find fault in the way Danika had followed directions to meet Dr. Price at the nurses' station. Danika, however, believed she should have been able to detect the killer. He ran loose while a family in Mexico no longer had a daughter. Danika remembered the young man's features, and an artist at the McAllen police station did a sketch from her description. Then a call came in to the McAllen Border Patrol station claiming Danika Morales would be next.

At least she wasn't under suspicion as a sold-out agent, but there wasn't much comfort in that knowledge. She refused to crouch and hide like a scared rabbit. If someone wanted her bad enough, they'd find her anywhere. Trusting God came to the forefront of her mind, which was why she and Tiana sought peace and refuge in His house.

Danika and Tiana slid into a pew beside Becca, and she hugged them both.

"I'm so sorry about today," she whispered. "And I'm glad you're here."

"About time I trusted God. My own way isn't working very well." Danika chose not to mention the threat on her life. No point in alarming her friend or anyone else. She'd faced the risks of her job before and held her ground.

Tiana stood with the praise songs and hymns, her tiny hand tapping the back of the pew in time with the vibrations. Once the pastor began his sermon, she opened her coloring book and crayons. The Sunday service had a college student who signed the Sunday school lesson for the hearing-impaired, but nothing was available for Saturday evening. Danika hoped her daughter kept her word to behave. Since the outburst about not having a daddy, she appeared to be much happier.

The back of Danika's neck chilled. Her desire to have Tiana with her tonight might not have been wise with someone out there seeking vengeance. Danika shook off the eerie sensation and concentrated on the pastor's words.

Thirty minutes later, tears streamed down her face. She was back where she belonged. Home. And the revelation came not in the sermon or in the Scripture reading but in a nudging in her spirit during an updated arrangement of the old hymn "It Is Well with My Soul." The confusion about Rita, Jacob and Barbara, Nadine, Toby, and her job had not disappeared, but the restlessness had ended, and in its wake was blissful peace. The stubbornness and bitterness plaguing her life for the past two years would still erupt, but she had the means to fight those moments of despair.

Danika closed her eyes and prayed for the road ahead to be an easier walk. Yet she understood life's challenges and the stalwart faith required to survive. Forgive she must, but that didn't mean she'd stop searching for Toby's killer or leave Jacob and Barbara alone to fight their own insurmountable problems.

"Have you had dinner?" Becca asked when the service was over.

"Not yet. Want to grab some chiles rellenos?"

Becca grimaced. "You've been working with men far too long."

"Thought we could add a little spice to your life."

Becca moaned and squeezed Danika's shoulders. "You look good."

"Long time coming. Thanks for not giving up on me."

"I could never hold down the type of job you have. The heartache and critical situations would give me a lot of sleepless nights, and the stress would give me a heart attack."

"It's who I am. Now, where are we going to eat?"

"Seafood?"

"Perfect. Tiana loves popcorn shrimp."

"One more question. Have you decided to take a chance and get to know your doctor friend?"

In truth, Danika pondered the same thing. Alex's kindness this morning when she discovered Rita's lifeless body demonstrated his integrity. He'd sat with her in his office until the police and Chief Jimenez arrived. It wasn't his words that had comforted her but his quiet presence. She'd heard enough clichés from well-meaning people who attempted to comfort her when Toby died, and the tears in Alex's eyes were exactly what she needed. She didn't want to hear Romans 8:28 again.

"Well, have you decided?"

Becca's sweet voice drew Danika back to the present. "I'm thinking about calling him. You know, take a leap."

"All right! And I want to know all the juicy details."

"Well, I haven't done it yet. Has Felipe called you?"

Becca shrugged. "We are going to dinner Tuesday night."

"At Chili's?" Danika stifled a laugh.

"Did he tell you?"

"In a way. Are you going to see a movie too?"

"As a matter of fact, we are."

Sandra finished putting the dishes into the cabinets and closed the dishwasher. With a little extra time on her hands this evening, she planned to watch a recorded history documentary. Learning had become a passion for her, everything from cooking shows to history.

The doorbell to the back door sounded. Hoping it wasn't Lucy, she glanced through the window portion of the door. Instead she saw a familiar face.

"Jose." What a surprise. She hurried to unlock the door and let the man inside. The moment she opened the door, he whisked her up into his arms and hugged her.

"*Sandra, eres cada vez más bonita.*" His dimpled grin made her tingle.

"You should come around more often."

His dark eyes danced. "Ah, I'm here now." He brushed a quick kiss across her lips. "And now I know what I've missed."

She sensed herself grow warm, but falling for Jose was out of the question. "Come in. Would you like a Coke or coffee? I have chicken enchiladas or brownies—"

He covered her mouth. "All of it and lots of you."

"You're making me blush."

He stepped back. "I meant talking time."

"Good. I thought I would have to put you in your place."

Jose laughed. "You are sounding more American all the time."

She lifted her chin. "Well, I am—sort of."

"On paper."

Sandra frowned. "I'll take those papers any way I can get them."

"At least you have them."

Oh, Jose, if you had the same papers, then we could be more than friends. She took his hand. "Come in, and let's talk. How did you know I was alone?"

"I took a chance."

How very nice. "Then let's make the most of our time together."

A few moments later, she set out a plate of warm enchiladas and another platter of brownies with a Coke for Jose.

He picked up a brownie. "You should be married with lots of *bebés.*"

Jose as a husband would be nice, but he never stayed with a woman very long. He liked them all.

"Someday. Right now I have Tiana to take care of and a dear friend in Danika."

"The Border Patrol agent?"

"Yes. I know it's dangerous, but Lucy does good work."

He shook his head. "If you can survive the first couple of years working for her."

"I'd do it again. It was worth it."

"Can you vote with those papers?"

Sandra remembered the last presidential election. "I didn't try." She'd lied to Danika about voting. Another lie among so many.

"I've never figured out why those of us who just want to work aren't allowed to cross the border. Americans don't want our jobs anyway. You cook and clean, and I mow yards and pull weeds."

Sandra nodded. "Even with a bad economy, they need us. Then they complain about too many Mexicans."

"Maybe things will change soon."

"I hope so. Sorry to hear about your sister."

His face clouded. "She was walking home from work when fighting broke out in the streets between the police and the Zetas. A policeman's bullet got her."

"Are your parents doing better?"

"Yes. I'd like for them to come here too, but I'm afraid they're too old to make it across the river."

Sandra toyed with a napkin. "Jose, why are you here? It's been months since I've seen you. The last I heard, you were living with Linda."

"She left me for a man who was a real citizen."

"What about your little girl?"

"Linda has my daughter and won't let me see her." He glanced away, then back to Sandra. "Please forgive me for hurting you. I thought Linda and I would be together forever."

Right now, looking at Jose and remembering the past . . . she'd like to have him back until he found another prettier woman. "Of course I forgive you. But I'm sure there's more to your visit."

"There is. I wouldn't lie to you. I need a favor."

She should have known. "What's that?"

"I really need more yard work. From the looks of your yard, I can tell someone is already doing it. But maybe if you put in a good word for me . . ."

Sandra reached across the table and touched his arm. "I would be happy to, but Danika checks everyone's papers."

He covered his face. "I really need the money to send back to my parents. After my sister's death, they have no one to help them with bills and medicine."

Sandra understood taking care of aging parents. "I wish I could help." A thought occurred to her. "Lucy might be able to help you. She's a wicked one, and you'd most likely be working for nothing for a while."

"I'll do anything."

"Then go see her and see if something can be worked out. Believe me, the deal will be in her favor. And she does handle the yard service here."

He smiled and stared into her face. Hope brightened his face. "If I worked here, we could see each other more often. And I'd have my documentation papers."

"That would be nice."

"God smiled on me when I came to see you tonight, Sandra. I'll never forget this. Never."

CHAPTER 17

Every action of our lives touches on some chord that will vibrate in eternity.
SEAN O'CASEY

DANIKA STARED at the phone in her kitchen. Tiana was asleep, and Sandra had retired to her room. Calling Alex had sounded like a terrific idea when she mentioned it to Becca last night. Yet, at eight thirty on a Sunday evening, the reservations had returned with reinforcements.

"Do it," she said to no one. Even if he was no longer interested, he'd be kind enough to bring her down graciously.

One more time, she stared at his business card. Plain and simple. No embossed lettering or high-dollar card stock, only the numbers to reach Dr. Alex Price, Family Medicine and Surgeon.

"You have no guts, Danika Morales," she whispered.

Breathing in to steady herself, she picked up the phone and quickly punched in Alex's personal cell phone number that he'd handwritten on the back of the card. Standing from the kitchen table with knees as weak as a newborn colt's, she paced the length of the room.

One ring.

Two rings.

Three rings.

"Hi, this is Alex. I'm bronc ridin' and unable to take your call. If you want to join me, leave a message. And don't forget your spurs. Wouldn't want you to miss out."

She laughed. "This is Danika Morales. I'm heading out to do a little skydiving. If you want to join me, call me back. And don't forget your parachute."

Taking a deep breath, she coaxed herself into gaining control of her schoolgirl feelings. Of all the things she should be wasting energy on, she doubted if taking the first step to get to know Alex was on the list.

A twinge of regret nibbled at her resolve, as though she hadn't considered the cards stacked against her and those she loved. Contacting Alex made no sense until Nadine was found and care taken to rehabilitate her physical and mental health. Add to that restoring Jacob and Barbara's suffering marriage and their relationship, removing the doubts about her loyalty at the Border Patrol, and finding the caller who had threatened her life. What a dumb move.

Remember: God is in control. She'd be reduced to pulling the covers over her head and taking on the characteristics of a coward if she hadn't rededicated her life to Him last night. For too long she'd been off the radar with God, but she was back. And she intended to stay. Tiana deserved a mommy who modeled a godly woman, one who was filled with love and strength.

Danika's cell phone rang, startling her like a gunshot to her ears. Where was all the courage when she needed it? Caller ID registered *Unknown.*

"This is Danika."

"I've got my parachute ready and a private plane fueled to take off at a moment's notice." Alex's strong voice rippled through her.

"And I'm wearing my favorite boots and spurs." She began the pacing again.

"Which will it be, planes or horses?"

"Not sure. I'm leaving it up to you." Her heart needed to slow down, or she'd be scheduling an appointment for a stress test. But she did want a chance to get to know him.

"Where do we start?"

"In the beginning."

"Ah, a woman who quotes Genesis. Okay, here goes. Hi, my name is Alex Price."

This was easier than she'd thought. "Danika Morales."

"I'm a doctor at McAllen Medical Center. Been there over seven years. I'm deeply committed to my job."

"I'm a Border Patrol agent at the McAllen station. Been there eight years, and I'm deeply committed to my job."

"I'm a Christian."

"Me too." She laughed a bit nervously. Definitely a trait she needed to work on.

"We're off to a good start."

She felt the warmth in his voice and envisioned his eyes and sun-drenched hair. "Hobbies?"

"You already know my passion—bronc riding."

Not at all what she expected. "I was serious."

"I am. The local rodeo happenings are filled with rugged cowboys and Wild West entertainment."

"I'm sure it's fantastic." She'd been called a cowgirl a few times in her life.

"Can I ask when you have your next days off?"

"Tuesday. Great, huh?"

"So are your ten-hour shifts."

She ceased pacing and slid into a chair. "You must know another Border Patrol agent."

"Chief Patrol Agent Edwardo Jimenez and I are accountability partners."

The thought of ending the conversation waved its banner. Until last week, Chief Jimenez had been a man she respected and emulated. Right now the jury was out about his redeemable qualities.

"I know his wife and kids." Had Alex picked up on the coldness?

"Great family. So how about dinner on Tuesday night?"

Uncertainty dug its claws into her heart—big-time.

"Don't chicken out on me."

She smiled through the phone. "Oh, you picked up on that."

"Somewhere around the mention of Ed's name. Let's delete that comment and go straight to dinner on Tuesday night."

Staring out into the dark backyard, she questioned her sanity. "Okay. Where do I meet you?"

"I'd like to pick you up. I've met Tiana, and I'd like to reassure her that Mommy will be home early."

Danika churned the thought in her mind. What happened if Tiana grew attached to Alex and then he was out of the picture?

"I'll tell your daughter we're going to talk about doctor things. And we will. Hard for me to have a conversation without discussing the hospital. One of my bad habits. Will that help your dilemma?"

She hesitated. Why had she put herself in this position?

"And if you decide you never want to see me again, then you never have to worry about me darkening your doorstep again."

"I guess this one time will be okay." She gave him her address and hoped the warning signals were false alarms. "What time and where are we going?"

"Seven o'clock and is Chili's okay? Lots of people there in case you feel uncomfortable."

She laughed at the thought of Felipe and Becca being there. "Perfect." The best prescription she could think of to put her woes on hold. At least he hadn't asked her to attend a movie.

Alex clapped his hands. Hallelujah. He'd done it. Danika had agreed to a date, a real date. A plush restaurant had topped his mind a few times, but she didn't come across as a woman who needed to be impressed with wealth and prestige. If he'd read her right, she'd be swayed his direction by truth and honesty. Instead of a black silk suit, he'd wear his jeans. Instead of a French menu, he'd opt for all-American. Come to think of it, did McAllen even have a restaurant printed in anything but Spanish and English?

Dating hadn't been on his BlackBerry since before medical school, and then blackberries were little black sweet berries, not a modern technological necessity. He sensed from Danika's nervousness that her dating schedule may go back a few years too. Even ground. If they both had trepidations about the relationship arena, then theirs could be rooted from the ground up. If one of them didn't scare the other into total isolation.

Conversation was another layer of the dating process. Maybe he should take a fast-track course in text messaging. He could answer *IDK* to those questions which were out of his comfort zone or *LOL* to her witty comments. Somehow he knew those tactics wouldn't work either.

Oh, the gut-wrenching agony of a first date.

After the dinner, he'd order flowers for Danika and a balloon bouquet for Tiana along with a singing telegram. Wow, what a guy. Too bad his confidence didn't measure up to his plans.

CHAPTER 18

Virtue can only flourish among equals.
MARY WOLLSTONECRAFT

DANIKA HAD FOUR outfits laid out on her bed in her dilemma to figure out what to wear for Tuesday night's dinner: blue jeans, white jeans, a sundress, or a white cotton skirt. The skirt won out, along with a short-sleeved red and white blouse. She slipped her feet into a pair of wedged sandals and examined herself in the mirror. If this was what dating meant, tonight would be her last. Oh, rats, she'd forgotten the matching dangly red and white earrings.

Seven o'clock came far too quickly. Sandra laughed, but Danika didn't find her anxiety amusing.

"Where are you going?" Tiana signed.

"To dinner with a doctor friend."

"Are you sick?"

I'm getting there. "No. We're going to talk about his job."

"Am I going?"

This may have been a huge mistake. She didn't want to upset her baby. "Not this time."

Tiana pursed her lips in a much-too-cute pout.

Danika reached down and pulled her into a big hug before freeing her arms to sign. "You know how you enjoy being with your friends without Mommy?"

Tiana nodded.

"This is a playtime for Mommy. I'll tell you all about tonight over breakfast in the morning."

Tiana had to think about it for a moment. She touched her finger to her chin as if deciding what to sign. "Can we go get doughnuts?"

Normally Danika frowned on those little delicacies filled with grease and sugar. And they'd eaten Sandra's cinnamon rolls on Sunday and Monday morning. "Okay. We can."

The doorbell rang, and Danika jumped. Alex had arrived. What had she been thinking? With a deep breath designed to make her feel vibrant and thoroughly accustomed to a gentleman caller, she made her way to the door. But her insides shouted she'd failed.

From the instant she opened the door, her pulse escalated into overdrive. Alex looked like he'd just stepped off a *GQ* runway. No wonder he was popular at the hospital. She nearly forgot to invite him inside. "Where are my manners? Come on in."

"Thanks. You look great." He walked inside, head up and amazingly confident. Her entrance never looked this good.

"Thanks." Now they needed another word.

Tiana peeked around her skirt.

Alex bent to one knee and signed his greeting. She giggled and asked if he'd brought a shot for his mommy.

Danika was mortified. "Tiana, would you find Sandra for me? I'd like for her to meet Dr. Price."

Sandra entered from the kitchen. She took one look at Alex and paled. What was wrong?

"Sandra, this is Dr. Alex Price."

Alex took a step forward and reached out to take her hand with both of his. "It's a pleasure."

"Yes . . . it's good to meet you too." Sandra trembled.

Danika wanted to know why her dear friend was nervous with Alex. And she wanted the answers before she left for the evening.

"Sandra, can we have a word in the kitchen?" Danika smiled at Alex. "I'll be right back."

"Sure. Tiana and I will get to know each other better."

In the kitchen, amid the leftover smells of Sandra and Tiana's hamburger and baked potato dinner, Danika faced her friend. "Is there something about Alex I should know?"

Sandra gave a tight-lipped smile, forced at best. "I've never met him before. He's quite handsome, and he knows how to sign."

Danika understood evasiveness. "We've lived together long enough for me to see that he bothers you. I can't go out with him until you tell me why."

Sandra took her hand. "Maybe I'm afraid you'll like him too much and replace me."

Sympathy poured into Danika's emotions. "I could never part company with you. In fact, I worry you will meet someone and not need us. And that is really selfish of me when you deserve happiness of your own."

"We are silly women." Sandra shooed Danika from the kitchen. "Go. Get to know the doctor. We all could use free medical care."

Danika hugged her and stepped into a new world, at least for tonight.

CHAPTER 19

Extreme fear can neither fight nor fly.
SHAKESPEARE

WEDNESDAY MIDMORNING, Danika bumped along in her truck down the back roads of the Las Palomas Wildlife Management Area. This morning at muster, Herrera had announced what they all knew—there was a traitor among them. Homeland Security had initiated an investigation and urged all agents to come forward with pertinent information or suspects.

"I don't want to think any of you might put your fellow agents in danger or betray your country. But until this problem is resolved, all of you are on alert. We've talked to some of you already, and the rest will be interviewed within the next week."

The fearful murmurings that followed showed how seriously each agent took his job and the anger resulting from knowing one of them was a traitor. Danika glanced at Felipe. His black eye indicated his family had found him last night and done more than shatter his windshield in retribution for his refusal to help his illegal cousin find safety in the States. Possibly the supes viewed his straightforwardness in a positive light. She hoped so.

"A former BP agent in Laredo was convicted of taking bribes from drug smugglers. He received fourteen years in prison," Herrera said. "No one suspected him either."

Danika inhaled deeply and attempted to relax. The Laredo agent's name was Morales. Did trouble come with the name? She'd undergone her interrogation and hopefully had passed.

But her concern was for Jacob. Life for him had spun out of control. Nothing about his future with the Border Patrol looked good.

Each day that passed without the authorities finding Nadine caused Danika to fear the teen had fled the McAllen area— or worse. Jacob had chosen not to alert the newspapers about his missing daughter due to the sensitive nature of his job. He claimed that if Nadine was hiding and the wrong person recognized her, her life could be in danger. Danika had mixed feelings about it. If Nadine's disappearance was simply the act of an angry teenager, running the story with her photo in the paper could help in locating her. Ever since she had learned about the girl's disappearance, Danika had text-messaged Nadine hoping for a response. And she'd continue to try to contact her niece for as long as it took.

She thought of Nadine, pretty, alone, and naive, thinking she could escape her problems with drugs and live life on her own. Danika lived with the danger of the area and what others could do to her, but not Nadine. Fear gripped Danika for what could happen to her niece. She had so much of life ahead of her—and so much to lose. What a nightmare for Barbara and Jacob. Usually tragedy brought a couple closer. However, this time a common sorrow had shattered any semblance of unity.

Guilt washed over her for having such a wonderful time on Tuesday night with Alex while misery clouded her family. She and Alex had talked during the appetizers and on through the molten chocolate cake for dessert. She liked him, but was it too soon? Was she betraying Toby?

Alex and Toby shared the same compassion for others, except Toby'd had a moody side. Alex knew how to laugh, and she cherished humor when her world carried such blackness. For now, she planned to ride it out, to see if Alex could prove to be a great friend.

★ ★ ★

Wednesday morning found Jacob knee-deep in paperwork. He hated it, relished the idea of lighting a match to the whole mess. Who cared about the consequences? Administrative duty, they called it. It was paperwork from the abyss. He'd chosen not to tell Barbara about the disciplinary actions here. She'd go straight to the kids and tell them. Lately he wondered if she knew where Nadine was hiding. Then he remembered Barbara's red, swollen eyes. No drama presentation there. Or was it?

This morning, he had phoned the police on the way to the station. The officer in charge of the investigation indicated they had no lead. Jacob needed to ask the question penetrating his waking and sleeping hours. Forming the words was even harder. "Have you checked the morgue?"

"Nothing, Mr. Morales."

"You're telling me a seventeen-year-old girl has disappeared, and you can't find her?"

"Yes, sir. But we haven't given up."

Neither had Jacob, but the chances of finding his daughter alive steadily diminished. "Put more men on it. Do you need a reward?"

"Sir, our officers do their job. An incentive is not required or appropriate. I have officers working overtime in an effort to find your daughter. And the FBI has been on this case since twenty-four hours after she turned up missing."

He well remembered the FBI questioning. He and Barbara as well as each of the children were interviewed privately. The girls were in tears, and Jake kept glancing between his parents. No one had any idea of Nadine's whereabouts. Unless Barbara was lying.

Afterward, Jacob phoned Barbara at work with this new grenade. "The FBI hasn't turned up a thing either."

"Where is our little girl?" She sobbed unlike he could ever remember. "Don't you think she would have contacted us by now?"

He needed for her to get past the emotion and on to a solution. "Are you sure you've thought of every place she could be?"

"There's nowhere else to look."

"Unless someone is lying."

Barbara blew her nose. "I've wondered if one of her friends could be hiding her."

"That's not what I meant."

"What, then?"

"You, Barbara." Jacob's discontent with his wife bubbled near the surface. "Do you know where Nadine is, and you're keeping it from me?"

She gasped. "Jacob, would I be this upset if I knew?"

He'd gone too far. Of course she had no idea. He took a few breaths to calm himself. "Look, we're both upset. I think we need to hire a private detective."

"I can make some calls—"

"I'm the head of this household. I'll handle it."

"Stop it, Jacob. I can't stand any more of your bullying. You criticize and accuse me of everything. Nadine's disappearance is your fault. Don't you get it? You are driving away your whole family. You say we can't put this in the newspaper, that it increases Nadine's danger. But I no longer agree with you. I want my daughter found. If something terrible has happened to Nadine, blame yourself. She ran away because of the way you treated her." She hung up on him. The first time ever.

Shoving aside his anger and Barbara's accusations, he reached for another stack of papers to file. At least with the administration demotion, he was able to leave the station a little earlier and get to the cabinet shop. The carpentry job was supposed to pay for Nadine's college so she could attend an Ivy League school. Her grades were top-notch and scholarships were available, and he wanted nothing to stand in the way of his little girl's having the best education.

At lunch, Jacob had no appetite. While inhaling some of the odors coming from the break room, his stomach wrenched again. Where was his little girl? His mind swept to Kaitlyn, Jake Jr., and Amber. He hadn't spoken to them in days. Tonight he'd make things different at home. No yelling. No threats about their behavior. He needed to feel their arms around his neck and to hear the sound of "daddy" on their lips.

Jacob glanced up to see Herrera in the doorway. Had Jimenez sent him to make life more unbearable? Herrera held a small package in his arms. "This came for you."

Confused, Jacob reached for it. "I have no idea what this could be." He examined it on all sides. Plain brown paper. Only his name and the station's address were on the top of the package. "Do you want me to open it?"

Herrera eyed him, then slowly nodded. "Probably so, since it doesn't have a return address."

"Did you have the bomb dogs sniff it?"

"I did."

Furious at the thought of Herrera suspecting the worst, Jacob ripped into the package to find a shoe box. He lifted the lid. The contents curdled his stomach, leaving a mixture of grief and repulsion swirling throughout his body. He turned his head and vomited.

It was a finger. Nadine's finger, wearing the opal birthstone ring that he'd given her on her sixteenth birthday.

CHAPTER 20

What wholly takes possession of the mind is said to fill it.
JOSEPH THAYER

ALEX WHISTLED his own version of "Zip-a-Dee-Doo-Dah" through his morning shower, the makings of his cheese omelet deluxe, his truck ride to the hospital, and on to pick up the charts on his patients. "My, oh my, what a wonderful date."

Dr. Sanderson, a bald pediatrician, peered up from his bifocals and his own patients' charts. "What's got you in such a great mood on a Wednesday morning?"

Alex grinned. "I had a fabulous evening."

Sanderson moaned. "Must be a woman. Take a word of advice from a man who's been down that road three times and hit all the potholes. Don't."

"I'm not thinking marriage after one date." Actually, the thought had crossed his mind, but he didn't want to admit it.

"Doctors keep crazy hours, and women want all that attention stuff. Oh, they like the money, which helps them deal with the pain of divorce and the settlement."

The cynical pediatrician. Alex hoped he had more optimism when dealing with his pint-size patients. "Her job is as busy as mine."

Sanderson offered a grim smile. "You might have a fighting chance. Two ships passing in the night have less opportunity to collide." He wagged a finger at Alex. "I've been through enough women and lawyers to know I'm never going to tie that noose around my neck again."

Alex sorted through his files to keep his mirth in check. "I'll keep your advice in mind." His failed marriage corroded last night's memories.

"From the look on your face, it's probably too late. Good luck, old man. Consider yourself warned. Experience has spoken."

As much as Alex was afraid to admit it, Sanderson was right. It was too late. Danika had made a huge dent in his heart. He liked her wit, her gorgeous blue-gray eyes, her guts, her laughter that was almost a giggle. Oh, he liked everything about her. She even liked stuffed jalapeños. Wow, they could share heartburn together.

Strange, though. Her housekeeper and nanny was an undocumented immigrant. He recognized Sandra as a woman Toby had brought into the hospital for treatment not long before his friend had been killed, and Toby only brought undocumented people for medical care. Alex was also aware of her connection with Cira Ramos. He was certain Danika would lose her job if the Border Patrol learned the truth about Sandra's status.

Alex glanced through his files, noting how each patient had spent the night and their response to hospital care and scheduled treatment. Another cup of coffee would be nice. He headed to the cafeteria and allowed his mind to drift back to last night. . . .

Driving Danika home, he hadn't been quite ready to let go of the evening.

"I'd like to see you again," he'd said. Bluntness had always been one of his headline characteristics. She'd admitted to the same when she'd brought in Rita.

"Before I respond, let me tell you about my schedule."

"Sure, go ahead." Alex had an idea from Toby, but he wanted to hear it from Danika. She'd mentioned it before, and it obviously was a concern to her. Besides, he hadn't decided when would be the opportune moment to tell her about how he knew Toby.

"You told me about your friendship with Chief Jimenez, but let me remind you I work ten-hour shifts five days a week. When I'm on days, it's not so bad. I'm home around six. But I'm a devoted mother. Tiana requires so much attention, not only because of her physical challenges but also because I'm the only parent."

"I understand the demands of your job and raising a daughter by yourself. I may not have a child to rear, but I can be called to the hospital at any time."

She nodded. "Weekends are not an option for me. Sometimes I get a Saturday or Sunday off, but rarely. Then every four to six months, my shift changes to either four to midnight or nights. During those months, what little time I have is filled with work, sleep, and being a mommy. Without Sandra, I'm lost."

"Ed's relayed the problems of crazy hours and the shift changes."

"I want you to understand I don't have a normal job."

"And neither do I." He stopped at a red light. "So is your answer a yes?"

She paused, and Alex counted the seconds. "I'd like to see you again too. I guess as long as we understand the demands of each other's careers and my love for Tiana, then we can arrange our schedules the best we can."

"Deal."

"One more thing. My neighbors don't know I'm a Border Patrol agent. I change into my uniform at the station and change back at the end of my shift. It's simply not smart, and those who have illegals in their families and friends would not appreciate what I do. Tiana or Sandra could be a target for their aversion toward the BP."

"I'll keep it to myself."

"Thanks." Again she paused, and again he counted the seconds. "I have a serious question. You're a doctor at a hospital that treats anyone and everyone, no questions asked. Are you a pro-immigration activist?"

Alex expected this, but not on the first date. "I'm committed to healing every person who is in need of medical attention. I am also a U.S. citizen and believe our laws are in place for a purpose—to be obeyed." He started to add he and Toby had been friends, and they had shared genuine sympathy and compassion for the hardworking undocumented immigrants, but they didn't always agree on the manner in which to help them. Alex opened his mouth to speak, then changed his mind. His and Toby's relationship could be discussed at another time. The discussion would take some time, especially the parts about his and Toby's differences.

"I respect your views."

"So, we can do this again?"

She lifted her chin and slowly nodded. "I believe we can."

And he'd been like a frog on a lily pad ever since.

Jacob shoved the trash can aside. Tears poured from his eyes while the vomit soaked the contents of the trash. His pulse pounded in his head and heat rose to his face. He wanted to wrap his hands around the neck of whoever had done this atrocity to his little girl. He'd kill them and enjoy every minute of it.

"What's in the box?" Herrera's voice echoed around him.

Jacob couldn't respond. Curses and vows took root, but the words rose and died in his throat, while the world around him spun in an eerie gyration.

"Oh no," Herrera whispered. "Morales, what do you know about this?"

Again, Jacob attempted to speak. He covered his face, willing the image of Nadine's finger to vanish. And for the first time in months, he wished Barbara were there to help him. *No, I wouldn't want to put her through this.* Yet he needed her. He couldn't bear facing this alone.

"It's my daughter."

Herrera slammed the door shut and scraped a chair close to Jacob. "Are you sure? Let's call her."

Jacob shook his head. "She's been missing for ten days."

"Have you received a ransom note?"

"No. She ran off. Police can't find her."

"I'm going after Jimenez."

Jacob's chest ached as though his heart would burst. He peered at Herrera. "Why?"

"You don't need to go through this alone, Morales. Not this." Herrera stood. "Stay right here." He glanced at the shoe box. "Let me take that."

"No!" Jacob's voice bounced off the walls of the small room. "It belongs to my little girl." For a moment, he thought he'd be sick again. A grown man was supposed to be in control. But the grounds for his demotion to filing papers were that he couldn't control himself.

Herrera leaned toward Jacob. "I'd want to kill someone too." He picked up the desk phone and punched in four digits, an interoffice number. "Sir, got a critical situation with Jacob Morales. Need you here."

"I'll kill whoever has done this," Jacob said. "I'll not rest until he's dead."

CHAPTER 21

A man cannot be too careful in the choice of his enemies.
OSCAR WILDE

"ARE YOU DOING BETTER NOW?" Jimenez sat across from Jacob.

"I think so." The box sat between them with the lid firmly affixed. He couldn't let it out of his sight. Rationality seemed to have left him. "I . . . apologize for—"

Jimenez waved his hand. "Don't worry about it. Your kids are fingerprinted, right?"

"You're thinking of tapping into the database for a positive ID?"

"You need to know for sure about this. What if this isn't your daughter?"

Numb with grief, Jacob grasped on to a lifeline of hope. "I don't know how it could not be hers. The ring is the one I gave her." He hadn't considered this as someone's revolting joke.

"Desperate people have desperate means to scare us. Let's walk this to the operations intelligence area and check it out."

Jacob listened, but he physically hurt. "You're right." He took a deep breath so he could stand. Cradling the box in his hand, he fought the dizziness to clear his head. "How will I ever tell Barbara?"

"Maybe you won't have to. We'll have the results in a matter of minutes. Are you sure you want to watch me do this?"

"I have to."

The minutes ticked by in Jimenez's office, slow and painful. Jacob couldn't see how the finger could not belong to Nadine. Even though Jimenez was discreet in running the fingerprint, the nightmare of opening the box repeated and clawed at his heart.

"Praise God," Jimenez whispered. He released the mouse and clenched his fist. He turned the computer screen for Jacob to see the results. "It's not your daughter, Jacob. There isn't a match for this fingerprint."

He ached with relief. But it was true. That horrible appendage did not belong to his Naddie. So whose daughter was minus a finger? And how did these people get his daughter's ring? A notion so evil, so horrible, swept through him. What kind of people held his Nadine? . . . Or who had she gotten mixed up with?

Thursday night Danika walked through her quiet house. Tiana and Sandra were asleep, and she had her home all to herself. Soft classical music played in the background, and she flitted here and there putting nondescript things in place: a book turned to look more appealing on the coffee table, a flipped sofa pillow. She inhaled the roses Alex had sent and admired the balloon and cookie bouquet delivered to Tiana . . . and she continued to think about all that had happened to her and her family.

She'd have a full agenda to discuss with Shannon.

Danika believed God was in control. Her rededication had cemented that, but the trials plaguing her and those she loved seemed insurmountable. In the days following his death, she'd been obsessed with the investigation. Then she realized being Tiana's mommy had to take precedence.

The problem with Jacob had only grown worse. His very career might soon disappear along with his wife and children. A buzz was astir at the station, and she wondered how long before the investigation for the rogue agent would be completed. She heard the murmurings; many suspected Jacob. The mere thought seemed incomprehensible. The other agents didn't know about Nadine, and she wasn't the one to tell them. Then again, would it make a difference?

Nadine. Where are you, honey? The girl needed to come home or, at the very minimum, contact her mother.

Danika's cell phone rang. She looked for the caller, but it read as a private ID. Odd, because she guarded her cell phone number and cautiously gave it to only a few people whom she could trust. Perhaps it was a random sales call. When it rang the third time, she answered it.

"Evening, Danika. Looks like it's quiet at your house. Everyone in bed?"

"Who is this?"

"A messenger. Do you want to know who the rogue agent is at the station?"

"Only a coward refuses to give his name."

He chuckled. "You play a good game."

"If you can't tell me who you are, I'm not interested."

"Sure you are. You're a curious woman."

"How did you get this number?" She paced the living room.

"I have my means."

"Forget it—"

"Ah, I wouldn't hang up if I were you. Your job's on the line, and you know it. So listen up. Jacob is selling you out. He's making big money working for the drug cartels and smuggling guns on both sides of the border."

"You're a liar." Danika searched through the archives of her mind to name the accuser, but the database was blank.

"Oh, am I? There's more. Jacob killed Toby. Your husband discovered what Jacob was doing and tried to stop him. Took a bullet to Toby's head to silence him. And it worked. Don't you agree?"

"You're sick, and I intend to report you."

"And what would you say? Who do you think is next on Jacob's list? He's furious with his demotion, and guess what? He can't give my people sensor numbers any longer. He blames you. He thinks you went to the supes with your suspicions about who may have killed Toby. He also thinks you're feeding information to Barbara—and that's why his marriage and family are falling apart. Maybe next time I'll tell you what happened to Naddie. You're next, Danika Kathleen Morales."

Danika disconnected the call. Trembling and trying to remember how to breathe, she stared at her cell phone. Where had the caller gotten his information? He sounded . . . as though he knew her intimately. As though he'd read her mind and knew her heart. Who could it be? No one had been privileged to her innermost fears, that Jacob could have sold out the Border Patrol. Barbara had mentioned he'd been depositing extra money into their savings account. He refused to tell her where it had come from, and Danika had no idea how much money was involved.

Jacob would not have killed Toby. Never. That was a lie, something she'd never contemplated. Jacob and Toby loved each other. They may have disagreed about politics, religion, and Border Patrol policies, but not enough to instigate murder. And what did happen to Nadine?

She attempted to swallow the lump in her throat. Threats on her life had happened before, but not by anyone who had access to her cell phone number or knew her middle name. Fear rippled through her with an icy chill. If this person had gone to the trouble of obtaining personal information, then he had her home address. Dare she phone Jimenez and relay the phone call? It meant implicating Jacob, and his career already teetered on extinction.

She allowed the germ of Jacob's involvement with Toby's death to take root in her again. Could Jacob have feigned being the caring brother-in-law out of guilt after Toby died? For the first time in her career, Danika wondered if resigning was the best solution.

Burying her face in her hands, she prayed for guidance. Sensing the presence of someone else, she glanced up at Tiana.

"I can't sleep, Mommy," she signed.

Danika opened her arms to the one human being she cherished the most. Tiana had lost her daddy, and Danika owed her child a future with a mommy. The little girl crawled up onto her lap.

"Mommy shaking?" Tiana did not experience the often-obtrusive sounds of the hearing world, but she could pick up on emotions and touch.

"Mommy is fine. Why don't you sit here on my lap until you can go back to sleep?"

Tiana lay her head on Danika's chest and closed her eyes. Holding her daughter tightly, she realized what must be done. She owed her daughter and the Border Patrol the knowledge of what had transpired, and with that realization, she punched in Jimenez's number. He answered on the second ring.

"This is Danika Morales. I just received a threatening phone call on my private cell phone, and I thought you should be told."

"I'm listening."

When she finished, she waited for his response.

"Have you talked to Jacob or his wife?"

"No, sir."

"I ask you to keep this information to yourself. Today, Jacob received a shoe box containing a human finger. He thought it was his daughter's finger because of a ring he'd given her."

Danika forced herself to breathe. Criminals did base things, but this went beyond sick. "You said 'thought.'"

"We did a fingerprint check and learned it was not Nadine Morales. But the fact remains she's missing, and someone obtained her ring."

She attempted to control her quivering body for the sake of Tiana curled up on her lap. What was happening to her family?

CHAPTER 22

Fear cannot be without hope nor hope without fear.
BENEDICT SPINOZA

SANDRA TIPTOED back to her room and closed the door. She leaned against it, hating herself and what she'd done. She knew Lucy was behind tonight's threatening call to Danika, but how had she gotten the cell number? Repeatedly, Lucy had asked Sandra for it, along with many other demands, but she'd refused. Neither Jacob nor Barbara would give the private number to anyone. Could Lucy have broken into the house and searched through Danika's desk? Or could the number be posted in Jacob and Barbara's house for easy reference—like on the refrigerator?

The implications of the call frightened her. Lucy meant business, deadly business. The woman had killed before. But Sandra had assumed Danika had immunity since she was a Border Patrol agent, and Lucy would never risk her position in the community. Stupid thought. No one escaped Lucy when she needed information or sought revenge.

This situation was heading into deeper, more dangerous waters.

"Either you help me, or those you love will be hurt," Lucy had said earlier. She'd stopped by to see Sandra and give her a monthly paycheck.

Sandra glanced at the check, hoping to gather her thoughts before responding. "You shorted me seventy-five dollars."

"You owed me association dues. It's a privilege to work for my services."

"I will not be bullied."

Lucy walked over to the coffeemaker and poured herself a cup. She reached into the refrigerator for the half-and-half and topped her cup with a generous portion. "Do you remember what happened to my parents?"

Sandra remembered the story. Lucy's parents were dead. They'd been killed when they refused to tell where their oldest son had stashed drugs. Lucy hooked up with one of the gang members who executed her parents. Rumors were she had killed a woman in El Paso and assumed her identity.

"No need to answer. A fire at night would be a sad thing for your parents."

Was this a bluff, or was Lucy capable of such a thing? "I have nothing to give you about Danika."

"I want her backpack searched to see if she keeps a list of the sensors."

Sandra was trapped. "I don't think I could get it."

"Let's start with something easy. What's her middle name?"

"I've never heard it, and I've heard her say she doesn't use it."

"It has to be written somewhere. Look around. What about Tiana's baby book? Or her Bible?"

Sandra could give one concession out of fear for her parents. What hurt was there in giving a middle name?

"Where is Tiana now?"

"She's playing in her room."

"Go check the baby book. I'll wait here."

Sandra complied. It was a small thing. Right? What damage could this information do?

But tonight she heard Danika tell her supervisor that the caller had used her middle name. Now, as Sandra glanced around the shadows of her tastefully decorated room, the bedroom Danika had redone according to Sandra's tastes, she despised her small role in the phone call. This was only a beginning for Lucy. The woman had Sandra right where she wanted her, and the next order would not be as simple. Sandra's parents had been targeted, and if they were gone, she'd come after Tiana. The little girl was like her own—*mi niña*. She'd do anything to protect her. God forbid such a thought, but Sandra would allow her parents' death before her Tiana . . . even Danika's death.

And she'd sent Jose to Lucy? Had she become as base as the evil woman? Sandra reached for the cross hanging around her neck and sobbed. How deep into this snake pit would she have to venture before this nightmare ended?

CHAPTER 23

The Christian ideal has not been tried and found wanting;
it has been found difficult and left untried.
G. K. CHESTERTON

FRIDAY MORNING at eight o'clock, the pre-weekend rush
of patients hit Alex with a full ER. He heard the crying babies
and the coughs over the hum of voices mixed with the TV. He
sighed. Long day ahead. An accident in the wee hours of the
morning had sent two to the morgue and four to the hospital.
Then a young Hispanic woman walked in with a missing finger.
She said she'd cut it off a few days ago while cutting frozen meat
and the knife slipped. That made no sense, but she refused to
change her story. She didn't have the finger, and he scolded her
for not having her hand treated before now. No wonder a doctor's life expectancy ranked near the bottom. Between the sleep
deprivation and the coffee that ripped their insides raw, their
hearts wore out faster than most people's.

"Got a minute?"

Alex glanced up from his perch behind the ER station. He
mentally noted the patient's medical history in the file before
him and closed it. "Ed, I sure hope you don't have patients for
me. It's going to be a while."

Ed scanned the waiting area. "Looks like illegal processing on
most mornings."

"Very funny. What can I do for you?"

"Is there someplace we can talk?"

Alex picked up on the seriousness. "For a couple of minutes. I'm sorry, but that's all I can give."

"My truck's outside. Will that work?" Obviously Ed didn't want the conversation overheard.

Alex followed him out the double doors and into the sultry air. Already he was dripping. Once inside the white Border Patrol truck, Ed cranked up the air-conditioning.

"What's happened? I saw the news last night. So someone told reporters about the investigation for the rogue agent."

"Media always has a field day with the Border Patrol. The only time we look good is when we apprehend significant criminal activity." He shook his head. "That's not true of late. With all the fighting in Mexico and the threat to our borders, we've garnered more appreciation. I have no idea who leaked the information. That's not why I'm here. I've got two agents named Morales, and they're eating my lunch."

"Pardon my bluntness, but Jacob has the personality of a junkyard dog. Danika is a woman of integrity."

"You've had one date with the woman, and you're ready to nominate her for sainthood. Problem is, I can't figure out Jacob. He's not the agent we once respected."

Alex needed to get back inside. Patients waited, and he didn't want to think about the woman who had stolen his breath as an agent on the take. "Just tell me what's going on."

"First of all, this is between you and me. Homeland Security is aware you're helping us nail whoever is leaking information." When Alex nodded, Ed continued. "Wednesday morning someone mailed a finger to Jacob, a human finger. On it was a ring that he'd given his daughter for her sixteenth birthday. That daughter has been missing for almost two weeks."

Alex moaned. No wonder the man had been in a bad mood. "I take back everything I've thought and said about him."

"The finger wasn't hers. But it means she had to give the ring to someone or someone took it from her."

"How old is his daughter?"

"Seventeen. Police haven't found a lead on her whereabouts. Seems real strange that she's missing, her ring shows up on a human finger, and we have a rogue on our hands."

Alex considered a connection. "Last night I treated a young Hispanic woman who had severed her finger. The odd part was the injury had been done a few days prior, and she didn't have the finger."

"Did she give a name?"

"Are you kidding? As soon as I treated the infection and stitched her up, she slipped out. Didn't wait for me to hand her a bottle of pain meds or antibiotics. Looks like the two incidents are related."

"Oh, I'm sure of it."

Alex's thoughts rolled back to Jacob. "Do you still think Jacob's selling Border Patrol info?"

"Maybe. Blackmail is responsible for a lot of crime." Ed tapped the steering wheel. "He's pretty torn up. I wanted to send him home, but he begged me to stay. Said he and his wife weren't getting along."

"No surprise there." Alex remembered his own marital problems and the exchange of emotions that propelled him into overdrive. "Is he riding the line?"

"The past few days he's been working administration."

Alex didn't ask what Jacob had done to deserve a desk job filing papers. A veteran Border Patrol agent stuck behind a desk doing menial tasks typically meant disciplinary action. "What about Danika?"

"Someone called and threatened her, which is why I'm here."

He barely knew her and Tiana, but he was ready to fight for her. "I'm listening."

"She's a good agent. Impeccable record. In fact, she's up for a supervisor role as soon as this mess is cleared up."

Good. A desk job would keep her inside and away from danger. "I knew her husband."

"I remember. Does she know it?"

A tweak of his conscience was supposed to be a good thing. "Ah, not yet."

Ed lifted a brow. "Go ahead and tell me it's none of my business, but she needs to know about your friendship with Toby. You know his killer was never found."

Alex nodded. "No motive, either."

"My personal opinion is his death is tied to what's going on with my agents, specifically the change in Jacob. I used to think grief ruled his temperament. But with the rogue investigation and his missing daughter, my mind is churning with other possibilities."

"As in you suspect Jacob was involved with Toby's death?"

"What do you think?"

"That I'm glad I'm not in your shoes. What do you want me to do?"

"Just what you've been doing—be my eyes and ears."

Alex understood exactly, and he didn't like the guilt accompanying it. "You want me to ask Danika questions and report back to you."

"Exactly."

"Ed, that's low and not my style. You already said she's being considered for a supervisor position. How can you suspect her?"

"I don't. My goal is to keep her alive. I can't go into all of my suspicions because that is all they are. Someone is out to kill her, and I want the jerk found. The more facts I uncover, the more I'll tell you."

So Ed believed Jacob had betrayed the Border Patrol. If Alex could be with Danika every minute of the day, he would. How noble he sounded. If the truth were laid bare, she possessed the skills to defend herself. But that didn't stop the fear embedded in his heart.

CHAPTER 24

**For everything there is a season, a time for
every activity under heaven.**
ECCLESIASTES 3:1

SATURDAY MORNING, Danika stumbled into the kitchen after
a restless night and made a strong pot of coffee. Alex had called
after she'd talked to Chief Jimenez, but she chose not to answer
her phone. He didn't need to be involved with the threats. If he
and Jimenez were as close as Alex indicated, he may have already
learned about the new problem.

"*Amiga querida.* Dear friend, did you not sleep last night?"
Sandra opened a cabinet door and reached for two cups. Her
hand trembled. Maybe she hadn't slept well either.

Danika forced a smile. She must really look bad for Sandra to
comment. "I had a lot on my mind."

Sandra frowned. "Worries add wrinkles to your pretty face."

"I may look seventy by the time I'm forty."

"Not funny. Anything I can do to help?"

Danika leaned against the kitchen counter. "Pray for wisdom and guidance." She hesitated, choosing her words carefully.
"Let's sit at the table for a few minutes. I need to discuss an
important matter."

Sandra added cream and sugar to her coffee and sat opposite
Danika.

"I've been threatened," Danika began. "It's happened before, but this time the caller had access to information that . . . well, he couldn't have gained easily."

Sandra's face paled, and she reached across the table, taking Danika's hand into hers. "I will take Tiana with me to Mass this afternoon and light candles for you."

"My sweet friend. You are so dear to me." With a sigh, she continued. "Be very careful when you are out with Tiana. Don't let her out of your sight for a moment."

Sandra squeezed Danika's hand. "I never do. Someone might know you are a Border Patrol agent."

Danika allowed her friend's touch to soothe her weary spirit. "Don't open the door to any strangers. I understand these are precautions you take every day; just be more careful. And if someone calls and starts asking questions, hang up. If a situation alarms you, call 911."

"I love Tiana like she is my own. I would protect her with my life."

Danika's eyes moistened. "I know you do. God blessed me when you entered my and Tiana's life. I wish you could have known Toby."

"If he was anything like you, I'd have loved him like a brother."

"One more thing." Danika glanced out of the window facing the backyard in bloom with yellow lantanas, orange marigolds, and deep pink pentas. A pair of hummingbirds darted about the feeder on the patio. "Do not answer the door to Jacob."

Sandra's eyes widened. "Has the problem gotten worse between Jacob and Barbara?"

"Nadine has not been found, and Jacob is not acting like himself."

"I'll pray for them too."

"Good. I knew I could depend on you." Danika pulled her

hand back to her coffee. "I have an errand to run before going to work."

"I'd planned to take Tiana to the park after Mass. Is that okay?"

How Danika wished she had the answers. "I'd say make sure there are lots of people around. If anyone looks suspicious, snatch up our little girl and leave. In fact, go straight to the police station."

Tiana still slept when Danika readied to leave for the day. Planting a kiss on her child's forehead and brushing a lock of dark hair from her face, she tiptoed from the bedroom and regretted all the hours spent away from home. Danika grabbed her uniform and drove to the McAllen Medical Center.

When Alex had left his message on her cell phone last night, he indicated he had an early morning and asked for her to call. The conversation she planned to have with him needed to be conducted in person, and she counted on the hospital's being quiet this morning.

The receptionist summoned him, and she waited. Too nervous to sit, Danika paced the ER waiting room. She must have been crazy to think she could establish a friendship with Alex. Too many problems stalked her life, and putting a good doctor in harm's way was a mistake. She'd been selfish, and regret had sunk in deep.

Then she saw him walking down the hospital corridor, smiling and waving. What a difficult conversation to have with such a great guy.

"Good morning," he said. He looked far too appealing for what she needed to convey to him. "Sorry I called so late last night."

"No problem. I did get your message."

"I'm one lucky man to have you pay a personal visit."

She failed to stop her smile. A relationship with him might

be in the future, but not until life settled down. "Got a minute? I need to talk."

"Sure." His gaze swept the ER waiting room. An elderly couple and a young woman with a baby were the only occupants. "Is the left-hand corner okay?"

She led the way, just like she needed to lead the conversation. Once they were seated, she found herself momentarily lost in his blue eyes. Not a good start. "Some things have come up, and I have to end our friendship before we continue."

Alex peered into her face. No emotion, and she wished she could read his thoughts. "Why? I thought we both agreed to give a relationship a try."

"Things have changed."

"Job related?"

"Yes."

"Not another man?"

Her stomach did a flip. "Not at all."

"The dangers of your job?"

How truthful could she be? "As a matter of fact, you're right. There are serious problems at work, and it's not fair to you."

Alex crossed his legs and rested his hand on his knee. "That excuse won't work. What's the real reason?"

She contemplated feigning anger and leaving him, but honesty had always played a vital role in everything she did. "What if my job came between us? What if I were in a perilous position and you were thrown in the middle?"

"Do you want to guess the number of times I've been threatened? Do I need to remind you of McAllen Medical Center's policy of treating all those who need care, without question? innocent people who want care for their children as well as tattooed gang members filled with bullet holes?"

She moistened her lips. Her situation was not the same. "I don't want you hurt . . . physically . . . for befriending a border agent."

He leaned closer. "I'll deal with it."

"You're not taking no for an answer, are you?"

"And you don't really want to stop seeing me. Nor do I want to end our friendship when it's barely begun."

Could he read her thoughts? "Do you understand some people play for keeps?"

His brows narrowed. "Precisely my point."

His loyalty endeared him to her. "But—"

Alex's pager buzzed like a bell during a prizefight. "I'm being summoned." He patted her arm. "And you have places to go too."

She'd accomplished nothing. Or had she?

CHAPTER 25

**Whoever stubbornly refuses to accept criticism will
suddenly be destroyed beyond recovery.
PROVERBS 29:1**

JACOB HADN'T RESTED well in days. Even when his stomach
retched from the flu, he had been able to sleep for an hour or so
at a time. But lost sleep was nothing compared to an evil more
perverse than anything he'd ever dreamed lurking at his family's
door.

He studied the forms on his desk from last night's processing.
Nameless faces. They meant nothing to him unless he'd been
riding the line and apprehended them himself or participated
in the talk generated during and after a shift. He'd been isolated
from the one thing that had given him purpose.

His mind fixed on the same problem attacking his family for
days. He'd chosen not to tell Barbara about the ringed finger.
Why upset her until more facts were uncovered? He wrestled
with the hope that Nadine was alive. Then he struggled with
how someone managed to steal her ring. Or had she willingly
given it up? The thought of his daughter collaborating with
criminals warred against what he believed about her. The other
devastating side of the dilemma was Nadine could have been
abducted. No one had seen or heard from her.

Jacob's insides burned. He wanted to reach out and touch his
Naddie, hear her laughter, and watch her grow into a beautiful
woman. Their petty differences meant nothing. Barbara accused

him of running her off, claimed he'd been too hard on her. Jacob still denied any wrongdoing. Nadine's life was school and church, not friends who had the potential of leading her astray. He swallowed the horror threatening to overtake his mind. Nadine's friends, ones Barbara sanctioned, may have already led her down a path of briars.

Jimenez stuck his head inside Jacob's office. "Any new developments with your daughter?"

"No, sir. Nothing's changed." When Jacob considered the number of years he'd been with the Border Patrol, he should have Jimenez's job. The chief patrol agent should be calling Jacob "sir."

"Did you tell your wife about the incident this week?"

That is none of your business. "No, sir."

"How's the counseling going?"

Jacob sensed fury raging through him. "I've gone once."

Jimenez slammed the door shut behind him. He leaned over the desk, his face the color of ripe tomatoes. "Do you want to be dismissed? Because if that is what your refusal for help is all about, I can take care of it right now."

Fury sped through Jacob's veins like a fire raging out of control. "I don't know what I want or need or should be doing."

"Then why aren't you in counseling?" Jimenez's voice bounced off the walls of the office. "If you aren't strong for your family, who's going to be there for them?" He picked up the desk phone. "Call now and get another appointment scheduled today, or you definitely won't have a job by the end of your shift."

CHAPTER 26

The world becomes a strange, mad, painful place, and life in it a disappointing and unpleasant business, for those who do not know about God.
J. I. PACKER

SANDRA SIGNED for Tiana to put away her toys before lunch. The little girl glowered, and Sandra raised a brow.

Tiana sighed. Her little shoulders slumped, and Sandra stifled a smile. "Yes, ma'am," she signed.

Sandra kissed her cheek and made her way to the kitchen. The little girl loved chicken salad and apples, certainly a treat for her obedience. Not that she believed in bribing children, but she did believe in reward.

As she reached for an apple from the bowl of fruit on the kitchen table, she heard a light rap on the door. It was Jose. She hadn't told Danika about him to obtain permission for him to visit. With her own sigh, she answered the door.

"I can't come in," he said and gave her a dimpled grin. "You're working, and I don't want to get you in trouble."

Thank you. "How are you?"

"Great. I made arrangements with Lucy to work out the cost of the documentation papers, and I'll start doing the yard here on Wednesday. If I can get a few yards more, I can soon pay her back."

Her heart raced, but not for Jose's benefit. "Be careful. Lucy can be difficult."

"Oh, I will. Gotta go and get to my next job. Aren't you going to say congratulations? I'll get to see you every week. Maybe more if Mrs. Morales has extra work for me."

She'd have to light a candle for him at church, just as she did for Danika and Tiana. "Oh, I'm excited for you—for us."

He disappeared to his dented and paint-scraped truck, and she closed the door. How did she really feel about Jose working for Lucy? What if she treated him unfairly as she did Sandra?

Lies and more lies. Tears streamed down her face, and she didn't wipe them away. Sometimes the thought occurred to her of running away rather than continuing to deceive Danika. It would be the loving thing to do, and she did love her. Instead she'd assisted Jose in misleading Danika even more.

Life had become a merry-go-round. Sandra wanted off, but it was spinning out of control.

★ ★ ★

For Danika, Monday had been an exceptionally long day. She second-guessed every vehicle behind her, as though an assailant tailed her. A little action and excitement would have kept her mind off the junk in her life. Phoning Barbara on the way to work this morning was like peeling a scab off a wound. Her sister-in-law stood on the brink of a mental breakdown. When Jacob was at home, he alienated himself from her and the other children by brooding and sleeping in his office. Where was he spending his off-hours? Too many options poised on the forefront of Danika's thoughts: hiding from his family, another woman, illegal activities. All seemed possible.

Her cell phone rang. The caller ID read *Felipe*. She could use a friendly voice.

"What are you up to?" she said.

He was laughing so hard that he couldn't answer.

"Let me in on the joke. I could use a good laugh."

"You would not believe what just happened at the Progresso Bridge."

"You're right. I have no clue."

"Get this. A woman crossing into the U.S. was arrested for smuggling chorizo."

Danika must have been totally out of it. "That's stupid, not funny."

"She had it stashed in her kid's diaper."

Danika laughed until tears rolled down her cheeks. "So what causes an agent to investigate a diaper?"

"Beats me. The smell, I guess."

She laughed about the sausage-stuffed diaper all morning. After her shift, she changed clothes and headed home, then pulled into a convenience store near the McAllen station for a Diet Coke. Although she was in jeans and a T-shirt, she lived and breathed her job. It was her habit to scan every face and interpret body language wherever she ventured.

She opened the refrigerator compartment inside the store and wrapped her hand around the drink. She chuckled at the huge stock of Red Bull, guaranteed to keep the buyer wired for hours. A sure sign of illegal activity was a trail of empty Red Bull cans and the familiar beeps of Nextel phones, which had service on both sides of the border.

A Hispanic woman with a small boy caught her attention at the register. Danika held her breath, afraid to breathe for fear the woman would run. It was *her*. The woman Danika had been trying to find for two years. She had to talk to her, ask her how she knew Toby.

"*Perdón,*" Danika said once she'd made her way to the checkout. She trembled, not her usual style when on the job. But this was different. "Can I talk to you for a moment?"

The woman whipped her attention in Danika's direction.

Recognition settled in her eyes, then panic. She swung the little boy into her arms and left her purchases at the register.

Danika hurried after her. "Wait, please. I only want to talk."

Too late. The woman snatched open the passenger-side door of an old dusty Toyota, and the driver, an elderly man, sped away, kicking up dirt and stones. Danika saw the Mexican license plates. A lot of good that did. The old suspicions and doubts about Toby's possible infidelity crept into her mind.

At Toby's funeral, this woman had sat in the back of the church. When the crowd was dismissed, she lagged behind, weeping and holding a baby. Danika remembered the intense grief. She attempted to talk to her, but the woman had rushed from the church, rooting the fears of Toby's possible unfaithfulness.

Days later the doubts still bedeviled her, and she confided in Becca one evening while her friend visited. "Did you see the woman at the funeral who was so upset—the one with the baby?"

Becca hesitated, and Danika realized the woman had caught her friend's interest too. "Are you referring to the woman who left in a hurry?"

"The same." Danika tried to hide the misery over what she feared. "Did you see the baby?"

"Yes. Cute little guy." Becca rose from the sofa with an empty glass in her hand.

Danika touched her arm. "Sit down, please. Do you think Toby could have been unfaithful?"

"I . . . I have no idea."

"Which tells me you're thinking the same thing."

Becca eased onto the sofa. "What are you saying? The baby did not look like Toby, if that's what you're asking. . . . I looked."

Danika realized she needed to know why the woman had attended the funeral. None of his family recognized her either. Toby obviously led a second life with his pro-immigration activities. Could he have deceived her in other ways too?

Her cell phone rang, jarring her to the present. There were times she'd like to pitch that thing out a window. Alex's name and number popped up on the caller ID. She toyed with not responding, but maybe a break from all the garbage running through her head was a good thing.

"Hi, Alex."

"What wears a mask, wields a knife, and smells like oregano?" Was he talking about Zorro in the kitchen? "I have no idea."

"A doctor standing at your door with an extra-large pizza. The problem is Sandra won't let me in, says she has orders from you not to open the door to strangers."

Danika laughed until her sides ached. "You poor, helpless delivery boy. I'll call her right now. How very nice of you to bring dinner, especially when I'm starved. I suppose you'd like to stay?"

"Oh, can I? That sounds better than a tip."

★ ★ ★

Alex, Danika, and Tiana ate pizza and played board games on the living room floor. He pushed a red checker into Tiana's path.

The little girl wriggled her nose and jumped it. "You're too easy," she signed.

"You're too good," he signed back. "Since you're the winner, you get to go with me to the rodeo—if Mom says it's okay." Oh no. He should have asked Danika first. His gaze flew to her, but she smiled back. Whew. "The next one is Saturday night. But I'm not riding. It's spectator only."

"I've already made plans for Saturday," she signed. "Maybe a rain check?"

"Sure. Sorry for jumping in and not checking with you first." He rolled over onto his back and rubbed his stomach. "That sure was good pizza," he signed.

Tiana giggled. "You ate the most."

"And I'm ready for dessert."

Tiana peered at Danika. "Can we, Mommy?"

"Dessert is a special treat," Danika signed to Alex. "But it sounds great to me. Want to go for Italian ice cream? Tiana loves the mint chocolate chip."

Although Danika gave all indications of enjoying the evening, Alex sensed her preoccupation. No wonder. He wouldn't be able to hide his worries nearly as well as she did.

Today he'd overheard a conversation in the ER that he passed on to Ed. The condensed version was the Border Patrol had met its match, and they'd never find the traitor. They were looking in the wrong place. *The wrong place.* Did the clue mean Jacob Morales wasn't involved?

Ed hadn't commented, and Alex had been too swamped to pursue an answer. Later he'd contemplate the information. Right now he was driving two beautiful ladies for gelato. Sandra chose to stay home. He knew the woman feared he'd tell the truth about her undocumented status. But for now, tonight anyway, he'd keep the information to himself.

Within the half hour, the three scooted around a small round table with their bowls of gelato. Each had selected two flavors and then set the bowls in the middle so all could sample the mint chocolate chip, peanut butter and chocolate, tangerine, hazelnut, chocolate cookie dough, and rainbow fruit. It amazed him how Tiana acted so much like a normal four-year-old. That was due to Danika's taking appropriate steps to help her daughter communicate in a silent world.

Alex inwardly chuckled. Years ago while in college, his church started a deaf ministry, and he'd learned sign language. Once in a while he used signing at the hospital, but not until he was introduced to Tiana had he been able to put it to good use.

Tiana dipped her spoon into his hazelnut.

"You are going to pop," he signed.

"I have lots of tummies like a cow," she responded and retrieved a second spoonful.

Danika laughed. Alex liked making her happy, making both of them happy. If Danika couldn't open up to him, at least he could add a little sunshine.

"You talk a lot," he signed to Tiana.

"That's 'cause I have fast fingers."

"She got you there," Danika said audibly. "Thanks for dinner tonight. It's been a diversion I needed."

"I took a gamble after our conversation this morning."

She pushed her bowl in Tiana's direction. "Why are you pursuing me? I mean, let's be honest here."

"I could ask the same of you. After all, you phoned Sandra to unlock the door."

She took a moment to answer and wiped a dribble of sticky gelato from Tiana's chin. "I don't know for sure."

He captured her gaze. He read sincerity, but he also knew part of the story behind her and Toby's relationship. A lot of hurt lay behind those blue-gray eyes, and one day soon Alex would have to tell her about his friendship with Toby and his views about immigration.

"I know you're talking," Tiana signed. "Is it about me?"

"Typical female," Alex responded. "Always about you."

"I think you like talking to my mommy. Do you think she's pretty?"

"Tiana," Danika's fingers flew, "that's not appropriate."

"But true," Alex signed. He turned to the little girl. "You and your mommy are the most beautiful women in the world."

Tiana beamed. Danika blushed. Tonight he was once more a lucky man.

CHAPTER 27

**I doubt one could live in the darkness,
but one could probably survive.
NATHANIEL LETONNERRE**

Alex stood at the ER receptionist desk and joked with the orderlies and the security guard. He faced the parking lot and drank in the peace of an empty waiting room. For a Friday afternoon, the city seemed quiet—no accidents and no outbreaks of illnesses, other than a much-needed afternoon rain that now soaked into the dry ground and continued to steadily fall.

A white Lexus sped across the back section of the parking area and stopped at the concrete post encasing the emergency call button. Immediately Alex was alerted to a possible serious situation. The passenger door of the car opened, and a woman stumbled out, nearly falling to the pavement.

Alex started for the door. The woman needed emergency care and was obviously incapable of making it inside the hospital. Usually that meant the one dropping off the ill or injured person didn't want to be identified. He raced through the ER doors into the afternoon rain.

The woman reached for the emergency call button and slid down, still grasping the concrete pole. The alarm sounded through the security guards' radios all over the hospital, alerting them to an urgent situation.

The driver reached across the seat and yanked the door shut, wasting no time in escaping the scrutiny of the security guards and orderlies rushing to help the fallen woman. Alex rushed ahead of the others. Not only did he hurry to aid the woman, but he also wanted the Lexus's license plate number.

The fallen woman glanced up, then closed her eyes. She looked to be in her early twenties. Hard to tell with her swollen face. One look at the way she held her arm, and he could tell it was broken.

The Lexus sped away, and he hadn't been able to read all of the license plate numbers. Somebody with money dumping off a young woman who'd been beaten. The driver must have known what direction the camera was pointed and avoided the tags being seen. Didn't take a detective's mind to figure out some sex-crazed guy thought he'd have a few hours of fun, then lost his cool.

At the station, Jacob took a call on his cell phone, thinking it was Barbara. He'd left a message at her office during the lunch hour, and she hadn't responded. Last night he'd leased a one-bedroom apartment and planned to move in after work today. A decision had been made. A divorce was imminent, and the church's opinion no longer held any weight. He'd fight for custody of his children and keep them away from their mother. Father Cornell had encouraged him to seek reconciliation with Barbara and to work on the source of his anger. Brainwashing, if you asked him.

"Agent Morales," a man said with a heavy Hispanic accent.

"Speaking."

"I'm thinking you'd like information about your daughter."

Jacob stiffened. He sensed his blood pressure skyrocketing. "Where is she?"

The man chuckled, a low tone that grated at Jacob's nerves.

"I can see her pretty brown eyes from here. Want to know what I'm thinking?"

"Touch her and you're a dead man. I'll find you." Jacob stood from the desk and glanced up and down the empty hallway. Where was Herrera or Jimenez when he needed them? "I want my daughter returned now."

"For a price."

Jacob understood his kind. He'd apprehended enough low-lifes to recognize greed. But he feared what would come next. "What do you have in mind?"

"First of all, this conversation stays between us, or Naddie is a dead girl. No running to the supes or the cops or Barbara."

The use of the family's pet name for Nadine twisted at his heart. "What else?"

"I want you to update the list of sensors, and I'll instruct you where to leave it."

The gravity of what the man suggested translated into exchanging Nadine's life for some of the agents'. "You have no idea what you're asking."

"I'm not finished. We want your cooperation in planting decoys so shipments of our goods are able to make it safely across the border and to our suppliers."

I don't have a choice. "If I do these things, when will you release my daughter?"

"When we're satisfied you're willing to uphold your end of the bargain, we'll talk about it."

Jacob expected no less. "Can I talk to her?"

"Maybe next time. And, Jacob, keep your nose clean. If the board decides to fire you, that's a signature on Nadine's death certificate. The supes can't hold your hand through this. Looks like you need to beg for your job so you can beg to keep Naddie alive."

The call disconnected.

Jacob leaned against the doorjamb, fighting the urge to throw his phone across the room. For the first time he contemplated betraying all he believed in . . . the Border Patrol and his country. He had no choice but to comply with the caller's demands. The rogue that Homeland Security was looking for had done a thorough job. Herrera or Jimenez could be the traitor . . . or Danika. The latter made sense since Toby had been pro-immigration.

Jacob couldn't trust anyone, and God had let him down too many times.

CHAPTER 28

My friends scorn me, but I pour out my tears to God.
JOB 16:20

SUNDAY AFTERNOON, Sandra sat at the kitchen table and read a Beth Moore book while Tiana colored at the kitchen table in her favorite princess coloring book. The little girl's behavior had greatly improved since she'd asked why her daddy was not available.

Tiana liked Alex, and that frightened Sandra. Last night when Danika and Tiana had attended Saturday evening worship, the little girl wanted Alex to join them. Danika suggested they ask him another time. Sandra hoped "another time" never happened.

For Sandra, seeing the doctor again would be terrifying, but she doubted if she had much choice. How would she answer his questions about her illegal status, and what about the consequences if the Border Patrol discovered the truth? Worse yet, what about her relationship with Danika and losing the company of her dear friend and little girl. She'd like to think Danika wouldn't turn her in, but Sandra knew better. Danika could lose her job and face prosecution for harboring an illegal. But Sandra had so much more to worry about. She had higher stakes. Her father needed surgery, and his procedure required money her parents didn't have.

Her phone rang, and the ID read *Lucy*. Sandra ignored it, but the call came through again. Then a third time. She'd turn the phone off except Danika might need her.

What if the call was about Jose? Knowing Lucy, she'd drive to the house. When the phone rang a fourth time, Sandra answered it.

"About time." Lucy swore. "I have things to do."

"So do I."

"Hey, I did you a favor with your boyfriend."

So now she owed Lucy for Jose? "He's not my boyfriend."

"How about an extra two hundred dollars a week?"

"Not interested."

"Think about it, Sandra. Wouldn't you rather have a few extra dollars to send to Mexico instead of worrying about medical expenses?"

"I can take care of things myself. Whatever you want is wrong."

Lucy laughed. "Who are you to challenge what is right or wrong? Two hundred extra dollars a week for supplying information."

"I said not interested."

"I have my ways, and it looks like I'll have to use them."

Sandra disconnected the call and put her cell phone on vibrate, something she should have done in the beginning. All she could do was live each day and hope Lucy ceased with her demands. *Un pensamiento loco.* A crazy thought. Lucy's ceasing to manipulate her was as unrealistic as the fairy princesses in Tiana's coloring book.

Tuesday afternoon, Danika took advantage of Tiana's nap to pay a visit to Barbara at work and to see Shannon for an afternoon counseling appointment. Alex had invited her and Tiana to dinner, and she'd accepted without hesitation. She should have weighed the consequences of too much too soon before accepting, but her heart overruled her good sense. Establishing a relationship with Alex scared her, as though past encounters with drug smugglers were easier, and yet she wanted to step into uncharted waters.

Walking up the steps to Barbara's office in the four-story, glass-encased office building, Danika realized she hadn't been checking on her sister-in-law enough. Families and responsibility partnered in good times and bad. Calls needed to be placed every day, and visits made to the kids on her days off. Nadine had not been found, and the inability to locate her ripped fear through Danika's heart. But reality was not a viable excuse. Barbara deserved a listening ear to vent her grief and a shoulder to cry on. The longer Nadine was missing, the more it increased the likelihood of her not being found alive. First Toby and now possibly Nadine. Tragedy was no respecter of persons.

To add even more trouble, yesterday morning Jacob had been dismissed from the Border Patrol. As much as she despised rumors, it seemed Jacob was the suspected rogue, and she'd heard charges had also been filed against him for the mistreatment of the illegal.

Danika took the stairs to the second-floor office. The extra few minutes gave her time to contemplate what to say to Barbara. But at the top of the staircase, she had no more idea of what to say than before. A long hallway loomed ahead. *Paste on a smile, girl, and pray up.*

The receptionist phoned Barbara and sent Danika to her office. Taking a deep breath, she opened the door. Barbara stared into the computer screen, and when she turned to Danika, hollow, reddened eyes told a grief-filled story.

Barbara stood and Danika embraced her. "Hey, sweetie. What can I do?"

Barbara slumped back into the chair. Besides being pale, she'd lost weight and she didn't have any to lose. "I keep thinking things cannot get worse, but then they do."

"No word from Nadine?" Danika slid into a chair across from Barbara's desk.

Barbara reached for her hand. "I'm afraid something horrible has happened to her. I know my Naddie. She was angry, but with time she always comes to me."

"How are the other kids?"

"Sad. Yesterday Amber asked if she'd ever see her sister again. I honestly didn't know how to comfort her except to lie."

"Do you want me to take them for the night?" Danika had no problem canceling tonight's dinner with Alex.

"I couldn't stand having them gone." She hesitated. "Maybe a movie or something would divert them—but not tonight."

"I'll swing by in the morning, pick them up for breakfast, and spend the day with them. Do they need school supplies?"

Barbara took a deep breath. "As a matter of fact, I haven't bought a thing for school."

"If you and Jacob approve, I could do a little clothes shopping with them."

Fresh tears dripped from Barbara's eyes. "Jacob moved out. Said he filed for divorce."

Danika chose not to discuss his dismissal from work. "I'm so sorry."

"Maybe it's for the best. I don't know. He says he'll fight me for custody."

"On what grounds? Never mind. He'd never win."

"I want to believe that. The priest told me God and the courts are on the mother's side."

Danika believed the same in this case. "I want to be more of a help. I've neglected you."

"You have your own hands full. All this time I've admired you for the way you are raising Tiana and managing your career. Now I must do the same thing, and I'm frightened." Barbara reached for a tissue. "If only my Naddie would come home. I want to hold her and tell her I love her."

"Have you been talking to Lucy?"

"Sometimes twice a day. She has a way of making me feel better."

"Good. Support during a crisis is so important, and I know you two are close. I don't want to stay too long and have your boss upset with me. I'll pick up the kids in the morning about eight thirty and return them when you get home. I'll call about eight to make sure they're up and ready."

"That's wonderful. They will be excited to be away from the problems for a little while. I love you, my sister."

Danika blinked to keep from shedding her own tears. They embraced again, and Danika left the office for her counseling appointment. Her prayers circled around the Morales family. So many needs, so many broken hearts. Where was Nadine, and was she alive?

An eerie sensation swirled through her. Could someone be out to destroy the Morales family—one by one? Could the same person who killed Toby also have snatched Nadine? Worse yet . . . The thought sickened her.

Danika shoved aside the nightmarish thoughts the moment Shannon ushered her into the small office and began their session with prayer.

"I see oppression in your eyes," Shannon said. "Tell me what's going on."

And begin she did, crawling through the horrendous situation with Nadine's disappearance, Jacob's deserting his family, the threats against her, and wondering if she was nuts to welcome a relationship with Alex. Not to mention Toby's unsolved murder. The enormity of stating all the garbage smelling up her life depressed her.

"Do I need to remind you that worry solves nothing; it only

proves our lack of trust in God?" Shannon offered Danika a bottle of Diet Coke.

"I understand the principle. What throws me off balance is the application."

"You tell me you're taking safety precautions with the threats. You're dedicated to supporting your sister-in-law in single parenthood and walking with her through a divorce and the high probability of losing a daughter."

"Jacob and Barbara haven't gotten along since Toby's death. I could kick myself for not noticing how badly it had affected Nadine." Danika shrugged. "I'm beginning to think the telephone threat was meaningless. No illegal wants to be questioned by a Border Patrol agent."

"Don't discard it. I understand you live with this, but be careful." Shannon took a sip of her own Diet Coke.

"I'm trained, and I trust my instincts, my supervisors, and God." Danika hesitated. "I should have listed God first."

Shannon laughed lightly. "Good save. What about the new man in your life who is saying and doing the right things?"

"Doesn't sound like much of a love potion, does it? I've tossed the odds of a relationship working back and forth with no solution."

"What do you want to do?"

Danika preferred to keep the comments and suggestions light, but this was a haven for honest emotions. "I'm torn, but I like Alex. Perhaps caution is the key word here."

"I agree. Let's keep this an open dialogue. Look for areas that are positive as well as negative. Remember what our moms told us? Trust has to be earned."

Maybe Shannon's mother, but Danika's mother expected her to already know life's lessons from watching the mistakes in their church. "I saw the Hispanic woman who was at Toby's funeral, the one who didn't want to talk to me. Not sure if you remember, but she ran when I approached her."

Shannon nodded, and Danika continued. "When I tried to talk to her this time, she took off again. She climbed into a car, but I was able to get the license plate numbers and trace it to a Geraldo Romas. Nothing's been done with it. I just want to know if she has any idea who killed Toby."

"So you feel like you're juggling slippery bottles of nitro."

"Several of them."

"Don't try to do this all alone. In the time we have left today, let's make a list of priorities and talk about how God wants us to rely on Him. We're going to list feelings and emotions as well as how you best handle stress." Shannon walked to her desk and grabbed a legal-size notebook. She handed the notebook and a pen to Danika. "God gave us a left and a right side of the brain to understand and interpret our world. You can make it through this crisis, and you can distinguish what active roles you are to be involved in."

"One of the things to toss aside is pursuing a relationship." Danika didn't have to list Alex as a priority. It was ludicrous.

"Have you and God talked about him?"

Danika gripped the armrests of the plush chair. "In fact, I have."

"And?"

"I can't tell if what I want is the same as what God is telling me."

Shannon nodded. "I suggest you keep asking for direction. God has a habit of giving us what we need when we least expect it or when we feel we least deserve it."

CHAPTER 29

**A truth that's told with bad intent
beats all the lies you can invent.
WILLIAM BLAKE**

ALEX PULLED UP in front of Danika's house. He looked forward to an evening with the two charmers who had quickly
snatched up his heart, but not the inevitable conversation about
his and Toby's friendship. He should have told her about knowing Toby from the start. Trust. How would she feel about the
doctor who had deliberately kept important information from
her? And if by some miracle their relationship proceeded after
tonight's conversation, he should venture to the topic of his previous marriage. Hmm. No, he'd save that for another time. His
blood pressure might not take it.

Had anyone written a book about twenty-first-century dating? What about a book dealing with the relationship between a
Border Patrol agent who'd been widowed by a killer and a doctor
who believed the U.S. immigration laws had room for improve-
ment? He was not a policy maker. Neither did he have a solution. He simply believed the laws warranted examination.

Danika met him at the door, wearing a lime green sundress.
"You're stuck with just me tonight. Tiana has a runny nose, and
I think it's best she stay in."

"I'm sorry. Can I see her? And by the way, you look gorgeous."

"Thanks." She smiled and didn't seem quite as nervous as the last time they were together. He wished he could say the same about himself.

After a brief visit with Tiana to confirm the little girl didn't have a fever, the two left for dinner—and conversation. Once he opened the door to the passenger side of his truck, he realized he needed a topic that would lead up to *the* subject. He closed the door and struggled with what to say. After buckling his seat belt and starting the engine, he led in with the obvious.

"Do you like seafood?"

"Love it. Especially if I don't have to catch it."

"I have a great place in mind. Afterward, I thought we could spend a little time at Barnes & Noble and have dessert at the café."

She turned to face him. "You've guessed my weaknesses—coffee and books."

"I was hoping it was this certain doctor." This might not be so difficult after all.

"You mean Tiana's pediatrician?"

"Wrong answer. But we'll work on changing your mind. How's work?"

She turned to face the street. Not a good topic. "It's been hectic. Lots of things going on."

"Do you need to talk?"

"I can't. You know, protocol and all that."

He pulled away from the curb. "I should have known better than to ask." He'd find a neutral subject. "Tell me about your parents."

"They live in LA."

"I bet they spoil Tiana. Probably wish you two lived closer."

"They've never seen her."

Great. He'd tripped onto another sore subject. "I'm sorry."

She smiled. "No, I'm the one who's sorry. I can't discuss work, and you didn't know about the situation with my parents."

He was striking out, and he had his own grim topic to discuss. He'd try something else. "What caused you to choose the Border Patrol?"

She grinned. "Are you thinking there might be a vaccine for it?"

Good comeback. "Possibly. I know different agents have various motivations for dedicating their lives to protecting our borders. Just curious about yours."

She glanced out the side window as though forming her words. "I'd always been interested in law. Did my undergraduate work at UCLA in political science and planned to go on to law school. But while volunteering at a mission that served a huge Hispanic population, I began to think seriously about law enforcement."

"What happened?"

"Are you sure you want to hear this?"

"I'm sure."

"I'd been tutoring a young woman in English, and I became very attached to her. Then one night she was killed in cross fire between two gangs. The arrested gang members were illegal. So was she. Another young man was killed, and he was a citizen."

Too much tragedy had happened in Danika's life, and he hoped his news didn't add to it. "So the loss of your friend caused you to apply to the Border Patrol?"

"Eventually. Up to that time, I advocated open immigration— let them all come in from south of the border so they could have a better life. The more I looked into the situation, the more my views changed. If we were to allow everyone into our country with no restrictions, we would be inviting gangs and drug smugglers and those who have an agenda against the U.S."

Alex nodded. He'd heard this argument before, and he had to agree it made some sense. There was also a flip side, of course. If the government set up a reasonable legal procedure for people to enter the country, only those with something to hide would take the risk of entering illegally. The Border Patrol's job would be much easier, in his opinion. They'd only have to watch for the lowlifes. But this was not the time to get into those particulars with this particular Border Patrol agent.

Danika went on. "I still had—and *have*—compassion for hardworking, decent people who are struggling just to provide for their families, and I hope our government makes some changes in our laws to help the poor have a better life. After all, that's how our country was formed. But in the meantime, the senseless killings of my friend and the other young man gave me a new awareness that led to a strong sense of truth and justice. I decided to serve my country and its citizens by doing my part to enforce the immigration law."

"Sounds noble to me."

"My father thought it sounded stupid. But that's another topic. Another day."

"Ever thought of getting out?"

"You mean when my husband was killed?" Danika turned on the radio, and when a male singer strummed his guitar to Spanish lyrics, she switched it off. "At first I drowned my grief in my work. Then two things shook me back to reality—I had a daughter who needed me, and I needed to find who killed her daddy."

"Why don't you leave the latter to the authorities?"

"They've written him off. Human beings deserve more dignity than *unsolved* stamped across a death certificate."

Jacob unlocked the door to his apartment, a furnished one-bedroom where his only company was cockroaches—a miserable hole, much like his life. On the balcony, children played and a mother scolded them in Spanish. A motorcycle revved up its engine, then sped through the parking lot to the street. The driver probably didn't pay taxes or have a valid driver's license. It scraped at his gut to think of the billions of tax dollars spent to educate and take care of illegals.

The stench of garbage permeated the air, and the grit of desperation clung to his fingertips. He knew that with the setting sun, those inside the apartments would be out looking for something to steal, a dealer to feed their habits, and a hundred other ways to raise the crime rate.

And now he lived among them. Probably the only legal citizen in the bunch.

With a newspaper in hand and a stack of mail that he'd picked up from the house, he tried to tell himself life would get better. But hope had disappeared, leaving nothing but perpetual heartache in its wake.

The silence produced an offensive ringing in his ears, not like riding the line alone at night or during the late hours when everyone in the house was asleep. This was different, a terrifying solitude that nearly paralyzed him. He no longer had a career or a home or a family. At forty-eight years old, his life had fallen into quicksand. His means of support was now constructing furniture, what he'd depended on to put Nadine and her sisters and brother through college.

Powerless to save his daughter.

Powerless to salvage his career.

Powerless to restore his marriage.

Powerless to bring Toby's killer to justice.

Where had it all gone wrong? Had Danika and Toby worked together to undermine the work of the Border Patrol and shift the blame to him?

He tossed the paper and mail onto the bed and sat down on the lumpy mattress.

"If the board decides to fire you, that's a signature on Nadine's death certificate."

Jacob buried his face in his hands and cried. His body shuddered. A vise seemed to squeeze his heart, and for a moment he willed the pressure to end his life.

God, if I can't make any of this right, let me die now.

CHAPTER 30

The greatest homage to truth is to use it.
RALPH WALDO EMERSON

ALEX PARKED HIS TRUCK at one of McAllen's finest steak and seafood restaurants. He needed a thick prime rib to boost his courage. All through the appetizer, salad, and entrée, they talked about his college rodeo days and more about Danika's decision to enter the Border Patrol academy instead of practicing law.

"Once on the job as an agent, I realized I had to prove my mettle. My goal was for the male agents not to look at me like a woman but as a capable agent who could handle herself on their level."

"You succeeded." He lifted his water glass.

"I think so. Hope so." She paused, and in an instant, sadness passed over her face.

Alex understood the meaning, but he was bound by his word to Ed and the trust Homeland Security had placed in him. "I have to tell you something. Should have told you right from the beginning."

She lifted a brow. "This sounds like serious stuff."

"It is. Toby and I were good friends."

Danika stiffened and paled. "He never mentioned you."

He saw the hostility in her eyes. "Most likely because of the nature of his—"

"Pro-immigration activities."

Alex took a deep breath and silently prayed for help. "He often brought people to the hospital for treatment."

Her now-emotionless face left him scrambling for words. "We talked about his wife and daughter and how much he loved them."

Danika placed her napkin on her plate. "Oh yes. He loved us so much that he went behind my back to help illegals." She peered into Alex's face. "I didn't see you at the funeral."

"I had emergency surgery, a car crash."

She continued to study him. This was a side of her he hadn't seen, a side that reflected her profession. "Are you an activist, Alex?"

"Not at all. You've asked me the question before. I'm a doctor who believes in the sanctity of life. Every human being has the right to medical care."

"As Toby's friend, did you assist illegals to find safe houses? give them food and water?"

"No."

"What did you do in addition to treating their medical problems?"

He'd sure hate to be on the wrong side of an interrogation with this BP agent. "Nothing. But if I had known someone was hungry or thirsty, I'd have made sure those needs were met."

She glanced down, then back at him. "I can't go through this again."

Alex leaned over the table. "If you were standing on the banks of the Rio Grande and you saw someone drowning, what would you do?"

She said nothing. He'd taken a gamble in posing that question, knowing many agents would not enter the toxic waters amid the waste and strongly rooted hydrilla for anyone—except maybe a child or another agent. To complicate matters more, an agent who jumped in to save a drowning individual was weighted

down by her own heavy equipment. But Alex wanted Danika to
see his commitment to saving lives was not much different from
hers. They both had muddy situations in their lives.

"I once watched two men drown," she said. "They were mid-
river and called for help. People on the Mexican side threw an
inner tube. I thought the two were okay, but they were washed
downstream. I never forgot it. Toby would have gone in after
them without hesitation."

"My immigration convictions focus on the people who are in
desperate need of medical help. I'm convinced the current laws
are in need of reform . . . but I have no solution. Like you, I have
compassion for those who are misled and taken advantage of.
But I am not an immigration activist. Neither do I agree with
those who take the law into their own hands."

"Did Toby believe in violence?"

Didn't she know her own husband? "I really don't know. Are
you saying you two didn't have this discussion?"

"No." She dabbed her mouth with the napkin and grabbed
her purse. "I had no idea about his activities until the day he
died. I'd like to go home now."

Her revelation sank in deeper. She'd been betrayed. How
could Toby have kept his beliefs from her? "Our thoughts about
immigration are not that far apart."

"I think they're at opposite ends of the spectrum. You kept
vital information from me. You befriended me and my daughter
as though we were a curiosity. And because of your deceit, I can't
trust you." She stood from the table. "I can call a taxi."

"I'll take you home. But you have never been a curiosity. I was
attracted to you before I knew who you were."

"I'm supposed to believe you? Did Toby tell you I was stupid,
or did you assume my ignorance?"

He needed to let her cool off. Imagine her anger if she knew
he'd agreed to help Ed and Homeland Security find the rogue

agent through his contacts at the hospital. More mortar to the bricks would be his awareness of her threatening phone call. Add his knowledge about Sandra's undocumented status and Jacob's job loss, and Alex stood on a flimsy foundation of truth. He wouldn't trust himself either.

After paying the check, they stepped into the night air as hot as the fire leaping from Danika.

"Don't write me off until you think about it," he said, breaking the silence between them. "I'd like to think we could discuss this."

"Fat chance, Dr. Price."

He had it coming.

"What else haven't you told me?"

Great. "Like you, some things involve my job."

Danika stared straight ahead. "I'm angry, and I've been betrayed. A relationship with you is not feasible."

Unfortunately he agreed with her. The evening had been a total disaster, and it was his fault.

A late-model Ford sped around the end of the parking lot, seizing Alex's attention. It slowed several feet in front of him and Danika. He studied the car, noting the many dents and scratches as though it had been in its share of accidents. The Hispanic man on the passenger side glared, as if Alex had done something to offend him. He didn't look like anyone Alex had ever treated at the hospital.

Time seemed to move in slow motion. Alex shivered, questioning his reaction to seemingly nothing.

The man lifted a gun to the open window.

"Watch out!" Danika tugged on Alex's arm.

The screams of women and children roared in his ears and flipped the switch to his adrenaline. Grabbing Danika by the waist, he pulled her behind the shooter's car and across the parking lot toward a line of parked cars. A shot cracked the air, and a piercing sting tore through his right calf. He started to stumble and braced his fall. For a brief moment, he caught a glimpse of the license plate numbers.

Ignoring the pain, he urged Danika on, hoping and praying she hadn't been hit. Another bullet ripped the flesh of his right thigh, and he fell between a pickup and an SUV, a shield between Danika and the shooter.

The car sped off, leaving bedlam in its wake.

"Alex. Oh no. You've been shot. I'm calling for help."

He listened to her 911 call, noting she was amazingly calm. But she was trained for emergencies. He was trained to treat them.

He glanced at his leg. Blood seeped onto the pavement, and the pain increased. Being tossed by a bull or a horse seemed like child's play next to this. "Are you okay?"

"I'm fine, thanks to a hero."

He attempted a smile. "So you've accepted my apology?"

"I'm thinking about it." Her sad voice relayed her apprehension. Was it about them or the shooting?

"Hey, I'm good. Just a scratch." He clamped his teeth down on his lower lip to cover the agony tearing through his leg. Later he'd think through all the happenings tonight from what he'd confessed at dinner to the drive-by shooting. "Do you know those guys?"

"Couldn't get a good enough look to place them."

"I got part of the license plate number." He moistened his lips. Lately his expertise had been partial numbers. He'd never make it in police work. "Can you write it down before I forget it?"

She pulled a pen from her purse and opened her palm. While she jotted the first three digits of the number on the inside of her hand, he caught sight of folks gathering around them. A woman handed Danika a package of tissues. A teen offered a bottle of water. A man knelt beside them and prayed. Alex wondered if he might be hurt worse than he thought.

"Promise me you'll call Ed Jimenez," he whispered.

She took his hand. "Sure—after you're at the hospital."

An ambulance wailed in the distance. Alex fought the dizziness threatening to envelop him, but he wanted to see whether the wounds were a graze or required surgery.

"Lie still." Danika's tone implied he'd better obey.

The siren grew louder. What if this had been Danika?

CHAPTER 31

A hero is someone who has given his or her life
to something bigger than oneself.
JOSEPH CAMPBELL

DANIKA PACED the surgical waiting room. How long did it take to remove two bullets? Had the doctor run into complications? With her fledgling relationship with Alex, she had no idea about his medical history. Her mind was bombarded with urgent questions. Who were the shooters? The same people who had threatened her must have been following her. Her mind continued to spin with who, what, and why.

In all the pandemonium, she forgot to make the requested call to the chief until long after Alex was wheeled into surgery. Granted, Alex and Chief Jimenez were friends, but it seemed strange Alex preferred a friend to be notified before a family member.

"I'm on my way," Jimenez had said. "How bad is he?"

"He's lost a lot of blood. The good news is the bullets are not near a vital organ or artery."

Closing her eyes, she prayed again for Alex's recovery and the doctor's wisdom. He'd taken those bullets for her. She'd been the target, not him. The evening had been a conundrum of events; the beginnings of a pleasant dinner, then Alex's confession, and finally the shooting all bewildered her. How did she really feel about him?

Reality hit hard—a wicked punch to her heart and mind.

Someone was stalking her, someone who wanted her dead. She replayed the conversation with the man who had threatened her. He claimed Jacob was the rogue agent giving confidential information to drug smugglers. He'd gone on to say Jacob had killed Toby and was out to kill her for supposedly going to the supervisors about his alliance with drug smugglers. To make matters worse, the caller said Jacob blamed her for wrecking his marriage.

Tiana. How could she ensure her daughter's safety? Where could Danika send her? She had no siblings or friends outside of McAllen who would take in a four-year-old. Neither could Mama and Papa Morales, who were ill and struggled to care for themselves. Neither would Danika want to put their lives in jeopardy. Somehow this had to be linked to Toby's death— some intricate labyrinth of treachery that she'd not been able to untangle. Tomorrow night after Tiana went to bed, she'd resume searching through police records, newspaper reporting, court records, and the coroner's finding. The clues were there. She simply had to find them.

She glanced at her watch and contemplated a way to keep Tiana safe. Her parents were night owls, and they'd still be up. She still remembered the number, but she needed courage to call them. This was for Tiana, not her. Surely they'd want to help.

Danika slid into a chair in a corner of the waiting room. Reaching into her purse, she pulled out her cell phone and stared at it for several seconds before pressing in the old but familiar number.

Her heart pounded in time with her rolling stomach. Perhaps the years had melted the differences separating them. They'd never gotten along well, but adults should be able to work out their problems for the sake of a child. She was willing—oh, so very willing.

On the third ring, Dad answered.

"Dad, this is Danika."

Silence met her ears.

"Dad."

"Yes. What do you want?" His tone proved reminiscent of years gone by.

"I need a place for my daughter to stay for a few weeks."

"Is this the daughter who's deaf?"

Rejection swirled through her. "Yes, it is. She's a sweet little girl and—"

"What kind of trouble are you wanting to bring us? First you leave law school for some grandiose dream of having a purpose with the Border Patrol. You disgrace us by marrying a wetback, and when he's killed, you're left to raise a deaf kid. What have you done now?"

Dad's words spit like venom and with such force that she didn't have an opportunity to explain. She couldn't send Tiana there, even if Dad and Mom agreed. "Never mind. I see nothing's changed."

"What did you expect with all you've done?"

"I don't know, Dad. Compassion? A desire to see your granddaughter? A relationship? Isn't that what you preach on Sunday mornings?"

He hung up, and she slipped her phone into her purse. Fresh tears pooled in her eyes, but she refused to give in to them. She and Dad always managed to bring out the worst in each other.

The doctor exited the surgical doors. "Miss Morales?"

She stood and hurried into the hallway. "Is Alex going to be all right?"

"He's in recovery. In about twenty minutes, you can see him, but just for a few minutes."

Praise God. No matter what she'd learned about him tonight, he'd saved her life . . . and she did care. Must be her destiny.

Her first glimpse of Alex's pale face and the assortment of

monitors attached to his body reminded her of Jon Barnett's ordeal. Although Barnett had been worse, he hadn't taken the bullets for her. Alex would not see her cry, especially when she hadn't figured out where he fit—if anywhere—in her life.

"I wanted to make sure you were really okay," he whispered.

"That's my line." She reached for his hand. She'd offer compassion for any man who'd been shot while protecting her. "How are you feeling?"

"Pain free for now. And sleepy. "

"Good. Who else can I call?"

"I hate to bother you."

"It's already on my list."

He closed his eyes. "In my contact file on my phone, you'll find my mother's information—Karen Price. Make sure she understands it's a flesh wound, nothing more."

"Can I expound on your supernatural abilities to save a damsel in distress? hint of a Purple Heart?"

"Hardly." He was pale and fighting to keep his eyes open.

"Consider it done. I can stay for only a few minutes, so I'll make the call when I leave."

He smiled but didn't open his eyes. "Oh, the ways of a woman when she's in the company of her hero."

"Something tells me you're never going to let me forget this."

"That's right. Did it convince you of my sincerity?" His response triggered the memories of earlier in the evening.

"Not now, Alex. Let's get you on the road to recovery first."

Danika sensed another person in the room. She turned to see Chief Jimenez beside her. She seldom saw him in street clothes. He looked . . . nearly human.

Worry lines creased his eyes. "How's our resident doctor?"

"After the surgeon pulled two bullets from my leg, I'd say I'm ready to do the rodeo circuit."

"Did either of you recognize the shooter or driver?"

She opened her palm. "Alex caught this much of the license plate numbers."

Jimenez flipped out a small pad of paper and jotted down the numbers. "I sure would like to know where Jacob was tonight."

Danika attempted to respond, but the words failed her. Although Jacob wasn't in the shooter's car, the same question had been planted in her thoughts too.

Alex opened his eyes. "Hey, Ed. I bet you wondered which one of us was the target."

Danika's gaze flew to Jimenez's face. What did Alex mean by that remark?

Sandra read Tiana one more bedtime story, an increasing chore as the little girl's interest in longer books grew and the signing became more difficult. But all too soon, Tiana would be able to read herself, and the cherished time with the dark-eyed beauty would be gone forever except in memories.

Tiana lifted Sandra's chin. "Where is Mommy?"

"At the hospital with a sick friend."

"Who? Mr. Barnett?"

"No, honey. He's fine and at home getting better every day."

"Did Dr. Alex get sick at dinner?"

Sandra toyed with what to say. "I'm not sure. Mommy will tell us when she gets home."

"Can I wait up for her?"

"What if I ask her to wake you up when she comes home?"

Tiana tilted her head, her hands in her lap, her typical pose for thinking before signing. "Okay. Can you read me one more story after this?"

Sandra kissed her cheek. "One more, then off to bed."

An hour later, Sandra sat in the living room with the TV

muted, no sound, just the picture. It merely offered her company. When she first came to live with Danika and Tiana, she watched TV this way to gain a connection into the child's world. Tonight was different. Suspicions had crept into Sandra's mind about Toby's death, Nadine's disappearance, and tonight's shooting, and she craved answers like Tiana craved stories.

The idea happened upon her this afternoon while Tiana climbed on her gym set. The little girl struggled to reach the top rung of a ladder. Tiana was afraid of heights, and the only way for her to reach the top was to close her eyes and take one step at a time.

The scene reminded Sandra of Lucy—determined to reach the top, even if her eyes were closed. Sandra would catch Tiana if she fell, but no one would catch Lucy. She made sure those under her power knew she was in control, and they all hated her for it. The evil in the woman made Sandra cringe. The women who worked for Lucy, especially those who were illegal and paid only half fare to cross the border, were often beaten into submission.

That's when Sandra's thoughts turned to Nadine. Did Lucy know anything about the girl's disappearance? Would she use Barbara's daughter for her own selfish purposes?

Sandra's stomach tightened. She had no proof that Lucy had been involved, and she refused to think about it a moment longer . . . but it made sense. And if Lucy was connected to Nadine's disappearance, did that mean she had her dirty fingers in the other tragedies of the Morales family?

Danika sat with Chief Jimenez in the surgical waiting room. No one was around, and she took advantage of the opportunity to settle some work matters. With all the happenings tonight, she wanted a few things cleared up.

"I need to be frank with you," she began.

Chief Jimenez looked tired, and rightfully so. His job seemed to deepen the lines on his face. In the dim lighting, he didn't look as formidable as she'd often found him. "Go ahead."

"I'm tired of being under suspicion for whoever has sold out the Border Patrol. My record is clean. Eight years I've been there, and I've never been reprimanded or done anything against the rules and regulations of my job."

"I agree with your record."

"Have I been exonerated?"

"Unofficially, yes."

Frustrated, she probed deeper. "Was Jacob dismissed because of the abuse incident or because you suspect him of being the rogue?"

Jimenez took a deep breath, blew it out, and leaned forward. "Do you really think I can answer that?"

She'd been pushing her luck, and she knew it. "I believe you did. Is there proof?"

"Are you in contact with him?"

"Just his wife. He moved out."

"You need to be more careful. Your daughter needs a parent to rear her."

Her thoughts exactly. "Are we talking about Jacob or the shooting tonight?"

"You have a way of bringing your point back around to the present."

"I want to know if you suspect Jacob is behind the shooting."

"I don't know."

Yes, you do, and I deserve an answer. "What did Alex mean when he asked if you wondered which one of us had been the target?"

"He's on pain medication—delirious."

Jimenez's evasive attitude frustrated her. "Does that mean you won't tell me or you can't?"

"Both."

"Would you like my resignation?"

"Don't even consider it, because I'd refuse."

Anger surfaced, leaving her body trembling. "I believe that's my choice."

He stood. "We need to talk in private. Do you need a ride home?"

Every bit of her wanted to call a taxi, but he obviously had more to say, and information was what she craved. They exited the hospital and walked toward Jimenez's truck. She'd heard he hired, fired, and made his biggest decisions in that truck. Where did she fit since he refused her resignation?

She slid into the passenger side and watched him walk around the front. If she read his body language correctly, he was about to deliver a lecture.

He started up the engine and drove out of the hospital parking lot. "Danika, if you quit, then they've won."

"Who's won?"

"Those who are threatening you." They stopped at a red light. "Look at it this way. If someone wants you dead bad enough, do you think it matters if you're working for the Border Patrol or not?"

"I get your point." She steepled her fingers and tapped them together. "I want to take a polygraph."

"We can do that. And for the record, I'm working to keep you safe."

His tone bothered her, as though he hid more information than he was revealing. "Do you have agents trailing me and watching my house?"

Jimenez eased through the green light. "Something along those lines. I'm glad you're friends with Alex Price."

"We ended it." One journey down the road with a deceptive man had been enough. Granted, she was grateful for his protection and felt horrible about his being shot. But a personal relationship was out of the question. It had to be no matter how she felt.

Whatever he had going on with Jimenez could be their little secret. Those two could play their games with someone else. But Alex's question still burned in her mind. Why would he be a target?

CHAPTER 32

A man's character is his fate.
HERACLEITUS

FRIDAY MORNING, Danika woke before dawn and began reading and rereading all of the information she had compiled after Toby's death. The police reports and newspaper accounts spread across her bed should offer clues, but no matter how many times she read them, nothing new surfaced. His fellow teachers at the high school had been equally shocked at the senseless murder. She'd spent time contacting parents and students to see if any of them could offer a lead. But they were either afraid to get involved or illegal and feared deportation.

Like a tenacious detective, she played the game of what-if. Toby had been murdered and his body found on a trail used by illegals to avoid the checkpoint. No suspects. No motive. No clues. A dead end.

From the threatening phone calls, she believed the shooters were connected to Toby, but how? Was he killed because he held pro-immigration ideals or because he'd been caught up in something out of his control? And if Toby's killer was after her, why wait two years?

Until her conversation with Chief Jimenez, she thought perhaps she was overreacting. But Jimenez convinced her that the happenings were serious—and she should be careful. And if she should be watchful, how safe was her little girl? Tiana needed to be moved to a safe place. Her father had refused, which left her with no one to turn to.

Danika leaned back on her pillow and closed her eyes. Her father could preach like a white-haired prophet and call hundreds to repentance, but he didn't know how to show love. How sad. His hypocrisy had nearly driven her away from God until she met her husband. Toby's contagious love for the Lord had drawn her back into a right relationship. Even now, with unanswered questions and mounting bitterness aimed at Him for taking Toby, she understood that only God could restore her faith and keep her daughter safe.

Alex. According to the nurses' station, he'd be released today. She'd phoned earlier in the week to check on his recovery, but she didn't leave a message. Three days, and she missed him. Ludicrous. They'd shared only two dates, and all he'd done was mess up her mind and break her heart.

Glancing at the time, she shoved the file about Toby from her lap and lifted the heap onto her dresser. This morning she needed extra-strong coffee—more like a triple espresso.

Sandra had finished grinding coffee beans when she entered the kitchen. It smelled heavenly.

"Bad night?" Sandra asked.

"How'd you guess?"

"Dark circles under your eyes, and I heard you in the kitchen at two thirty." Sandra measured coffee into the filter. "Have the police caught the men who shot at you and Dr. Alex?"

"No. Probably won't either. The shooters' car was found abandoned—and listed as stolen. You know my cynicism about the local police finding criminals ever since they gave up on finding who killed Toby."

"Some bad people are smart enough not to get caught."

"I'd rather think they are cocky and will one day make a mistake."

Sandra measured water and poured it into the coffeemaker. "Maybe so. I'm taking the precautions like you told me."

"Good. I wish I had a place to send Tiana until this is over. I'd rather err on being overprotective than make a serious mistake about her safety."

"I think you're right." Sandra stared out the window to the backyard. "Isn't there anyone? an aunt or a cousin?"

"No, but I'm thinking. If I don't come up with someone by tonight, then I'll look into hiring a bodyguard."

Danika reached into the cupboard for two cups, aligning herself with staying positive and trusting God for the outcome of all that beset her life. Alex had seemed like a blessing. . . .

"Are you missing him?" Count on Sandra to read her thoughts.

"I'll get over it. Silly, don't you think? A couple of dates, and I'm hooked like a fish."

"Do you want to tell me what he did?"

Danika had already decided to move on with her life—and her emotions. "No point. He should have revealed a few things about himself before asking me out."

"Honesty is always the best way."

"The only way. I can't tolerate deceit. He knew Toby and chose not to tell me."

Sandra tapped her chin. "Did he tell you why?"

"No. Just confession and an apology. He claimed there were things he couldn't tell me, just like there were things I couldn't tell him."

"Maybe you should forgive but not be his girlfriend."

Danika hugged Sandra's shoulders. "You're right. It's too soon after Toby to be thinking about another man. Thanks for helping me see things clearer."

"I wanted you to weigh your options."

Danika smiled at the cliché. If only her dilemma could be

weighed on a balance, one side measuring decisions made and the other mysteries solved. The Border Patrol and Homeland Security dealt with safety issues for families. She'd talk to Chief Jimenez at the end of her shift to see if he could suggest a safe place for Tiana. But that meant strangers would be taking care of her, possibly people who didn't know how to sign.

What if those who'd tried to kill Danika weren't apprehended quickly? She hated the thought of Tiana miserable and alone. But what choice did she have?

A new thought swept through her. She could send Sandra with Tiana.

Alex didn't know which was worse—staring at the ceiling at the hospital or staring at the ceiling in his house. Both bored him to near insanity. Mom had insisted on coming for a visit, and he'd given in. She planned to arrive midafternoon. Unlike most moms, she'd defied aging. At sixty-eight, she walked five miles a day, pumped iron, and believed in holistic medicine. She kept up-to-date with politics and fashion and had a definite opinion about everything, along with a fearless faith. She'd be entertainment for sure, even if he had to eat tofu and soy yogurt.

Regret once again smacked him in the face. If only he'd been up-front with Danika and hadn't destroyed his relationship with her before it really began. Strange how he met her and was immediately attracted to her. A lot of good that did now. At least Ed thought it was only a matter of time before the authorities had the evidence to prosecute Jacob as the rogue agent.

His cell phone rang, alerting him to a call from the hospital. How nice to be needed, even when he was high on pain meds and waiting for his mother to arrive.

He recognized the nurse's voice from the ER. Indispensable,

as far as he was concerned. Elaine would break every rule in the book to ensure a patient's care. Just like he would.

"Sorry to bother you, Dr. Price, but a woman is here with a little boy. Says only you can look at him. Won't talk to any of the other doctors."

"That's because I'm the best."

"I see your surgery didn't do a thing for your humility." Elaine's sarcasm came with her sense of humor.

"Sorry, the pain meds have me a bit crazy."

"You sound normal to me."

He chuckled. "Guess I had that coming."

"You did. Can you take this number? It's her cell phone. She's waiting outside for your call."

The two bantered a few more minutes before Elaine claimed she had work to do.

Alex disconnected the call and turned his attention to the patient who needed help. He pressed in the numbers.

A woman answered in Spanish, and he replied in her native language. "This is Dr. Price. Can I help you?"

"This is Cira Ramos."

Alex hadn't heard from Cira since shortly after Toby's death. At the time, she planned to take her infant son and flee to Houston, far away from a woman who had fronted half of the money Cira needed to cross the border and then abused her by forcing her into slavelike labor. "Yes, Cira. I thought you left McAllen?"

"My grandfather became ill and needed me to care for him."

"Are you safe?"

"I don't know. I'm working and being careful."

"Good. Are you sick?"

"No, it's Mickey. He's very hot and has a horrible cough, and his chest rattles. Can you see him?"

"I'm not doing so well either. There are other doctors at the clinic who can help you."

"I'm afraid. Can you come just to check Mickey?" She wept, the sobs evident in every word.

Alex hesitated. Already his leg had started to throb, and he couldn't take the pain meds for another hour. What a wimp. Hadn't he dedicated his life to helping the sick? He could call a taxi and ask the driver to wait while he examined Cira's little boy. Maybe this time she would tell him who had provided her front money. If Jacob Morales was involved somehow, then Ed's case was closed and Danika no longer had to worry about someone stalking her. "Wait for me there. It will take about thirty minutes."

"Thank you, Dr. Alex. God bless you."

Alex smiled and reached for his crutches. He'd sneak into the hospital, treat Mickey, and sneak back out.

When Alex's taxi arrived at the hospital, Cira stood outside the ER doors holding the sick toddler, her anchor baby. Mickey was born in the United States, but his mother could be deported if caught.

Cira's gaze darted about as though the woman who had held her captive might suddenly emerge from the many cars moving in and out of the parking lot. Poor girl. She had nowhere to turn with only fear in her path. Perhaps he could convince her to take her grandfather to Houston.

Climbing out of the taxi sapped his energy level. The driver assisted him and offered him a tissue to wipe the perspiration dripping down his face.

"I'm a doctor here," Alex said, once he caught his breath. "I have one patient to see; then I'll need a ride home. Can you wait?"

The driver—a short, round man—pointed to Alex's leg. "You're the one who should see a doctor."

"Already did."

"What did you do, man? I know you weren't skiing. Must have

been a woman. What she'd do, shoot you?" The man grinned broadly revealing several missing teeth.

"Would you believe a drive-by?"

The man shook his head. "Not in your neighborhood. Now, mine is different."

"The kind with safe houses?"

The driver handed Alex his crutches. "That's a good one. I'll have to remember it."

Cira's face was pulled taut, no doubt from worry. She saw him and gasped. "What happened to you? You . . . you are very hurt."

"Just a little surgery on my leg."

"I had no idea. I'm so selfish."

Mickey started to whimper, and she soothed him with soft whispers.

A hot arrow of pain shot up his leg. "Let's get this little guy fixed up."

She followed him inside, and he hoped no one saw him.

"Dr. Price—" Elaine rounded the ER desk, hands on her full hips, reminding Alex of a prison guard—"do you have pea soup for brains?"

He winced. "I'm here for one patient. You know; duty calls."

"Right." She looked at Cira and greeted her in Spanish. "I had a bet you wouldn't stay at home one afternoon. Looks like I won ten bucks."

Elaine took care of Cira's paperwork while Alex examined Mickey. His fever spiked at 104 degrees, and his chest rattled like a baby's toy.

"Cira, I need to admit Mickey. I don't need a chest X-ray to diagnose him with pneumonia."

"Admit him? Can't you give him medicine?"

How many times had he heard this question from mothers who couldn't bear to leave their children in the hospital? "I can, but he needs breathing treatments, an IV, and the care of nurses to get better. He's very sick."

Alex understood her hesitation on another level. He'd treated her when she'd been beaten. "If your son isn't hospitalized with special medicines, he might die."

She swiped at the tears dripping onto her cheeks. "I don't know what to do."

Alex took a deep breath. An idea occurred to him. "We won't use your name or Mickey's."

She nodded. "She wouldn't be able to find me."

If only he could secure the woman's name. "That's right. Both you and Mickey would be safe. Are you ready to tell me the woman's name?"

"I can't tell you."

Alex pressed his lips together to keep from asking more questions and upsetting Cira. "I'll make the arrangements." He remembered Rita and realized her beating and death might have a connection to Cira.

CHAPTER 33

Marvelous Truth, confront us at every turn, in every guise.
DENISE LEVERTOV

"So my problem is finding a home for Tiana until the shooter's found," Danika concluded. She'd spent time all day rehearsing how to tell the chief about her problem. Of course the shooter and Toby's killer could all be related to Jacob.

Jimenez and his unreadable face. Drove her nuts. His scrutiny had a way of boring a hole through her, as though he could analyze her thoughts. "I'll make a few calls to see if we can find a solution. A bodyguard may be the best idea."

"Finding the shooters has my vote."

"I agree, but until then we need to be realistic. You said your nanny could accompany her. What about putting them in an apartment in Houston or Austin?"

That idea hadn't occurred to her. Must be why he was the chief and she rode the line. "Let me think about it. You may be on to something."

He smiled. "I'm trying my best to keep you and your daughter safe. I know how I'd feel if my wife and sons were in danger. Someone would have to scrape the blood and guts off the walls once I was finished with them." He shook his head. "Right now I'm furious at an elementary school."

She lifted a brow.

"My youngest son—the one in first grade—was placed in a bilingual class because he couldn't speak Spanish. This is an

English-speaking country. I won't tolerate having my child forced to learn Spanish because that's all the other kids can speak."

"Ouch." She felt sorry for the school system.

"I phoned them earlier, and my wife is there now." He picked up his pen and tapped it on the desk. "I wanted to take care of it, but she talked me out of it. Anyway, my point is, I know how you feel when it comes to protecting kids. Are you keeping your weapon with you?"

"Yes, sir."

"Good. Any contact from Jacob, or has his daughter been found?"

"Nothing."

"I'm sorry to hear that. He was a good agent before all the tragedy hit."

All of Jacob's good and bad qualities had been said. She'd stopped concerning herself with his problems and instead concentrated on Barbara and the need to find Nadine. Children were always a priority over adults. Jacob didn't want help, or he'd have stayed in counseling and not gotten involved with the wrong people.

Guess I do believe he's guilty. But could he have killed Toby too? The mere thought left her running for the Lord, not knowing whether to ask for forgiveness or help to accept the truth.

"I'm flipping shifts to nights soon, and the thought of Tiana alone with her nanny during those hours really bothers me."

"We'll have the situation handled soon." He cleared his throat. "I appreciate your taking the polygraph."

"I don't want any doubts about my integrity, sir. I hate the sense of helplessness that has filled me for two years. I've looked everywhere for more clues about who killed Toby, and it's been nothing but dead ends. I refuse to sit back and allow the same nightmare to destroy me." She leaned forward. "It's not happening. My daughter will have a mother. I deserve to be part of the solution. Do you believe Jacob is the rogue?"

"I can't give you classified information, especially in an ongoing investigation. You know that."

"Whoever is out to get me is banking on my resignation or my death, and he's throwing enough obstacles in my way for it to happen. Toby is dead, my niece is missing, I've been threatened, Alex is in the hospital, and I'm sick with worry about my daughter."

"You're not alone, Morales. We all want this ended."

Sandra carried an armload of light blue towels to her bathroom and set them inside the linen closet. While Tiana slept, she'd tossed in the last load of dirty clothes and vacuumed the living room. Jose had come by to clean out the flower beds. He said Danika had requested it, but she hadn't said anything to her. No matter. Jose was here and Sandra enjoyed taking a peek out the window at him working.

All the past came rolling back—her feelings for him and how they'd gotten along so well until Linda stole him away. Maybe she and Jose had needed distance to come back together in a stronger relationship.

She heard a thump and glanced at her watch. Tiana had not slept long, and she'd played hard outside all morning. Sandra pulled on the dust ruffle of her bed and made her way toward the other side of the house.

The noise captured her attention again, but it was coming from Danika's room. She must be home early—hopefully not sick. But her dear friend had been through so much lately, and having it all make her sick would not be a surprise.

Jose emerged from Danika's bedroom.

Sandra's heart sped past shock to anger. "What were you doing in there?"

A dimpled grin met her. "I was looking for you."

"You can't ever come in the house. Didn't Lucy give you instructions?"

"No. I'm sorry."

"We both could lose our jobs." She took his arm. "Please, if Tiana wakens and finds you here, she could tell her mother."

"I thought she was deaf."

"She is, but she talks with her hands." Sandra hurried him down the hallway to the kitchen. Then she recalled the sounds coming from Danika's bedroom. "What were you doing in there?"

He shrugged. "Just looking. I've never been in a nice house like this and wanted to see what it looked like."

Sandra sensed the blood leaving her face. "If I lost my job, Lucy would destroy my documentation papers—and any chance of getting them for you."

"Oh, I promise I'll never come inside again without your or Mrs. Morales's permission." He picked up his pace and hurried outside.

Sandra caught her breath. She trembled while fear refused to leave her. What if he'd stolen something? She'd check for tracked-in dirt and grass—and for anything missing.

★ ★ ★

"I've already been to the grocery," Mom said from Alex's kitchen. "And the supply of organic vegetables was fairly decent."

"I'm starved." Alex could only imagine what she'd concoct for him to eat while she was there. "I skipped lunch to see a patient."

She joined him in the living room. "What were you doing seeing a patient in your condition?"

"I wondered about that at the time. Anyway, I'm hungry now."

"Son, skipping meals does not lead to good nutrition. Don't you have PowerBars for those times when you need an energy boost?"

Pushing Mom's buttons was good for a laugh. "Snickers bars are pretty good."

She wagged a finger at him. "While I'm here, you will eat nutritious meals. We've got to get you on your feet—so to speak. Dinner will be salmon and steamed veggies."

"Don't forget the white bread and apple pie."

She tossed him one of her menacing mom scowls, but it didn't work. He blew her a kiss, and they both laughed.

She sat on the sofa beside him, which he'd crowned the official couch potato site for the evening. "Are you seeing anybody?"

Typical mom. "I thought I was, but I blew it."

"How's that? Working too many hours to suit her?"

"Not at all. She works as much as I do. She's a Border Patrol agent."

"Sounds dangerous."

"It is, which is how I blew the relationship."

"Tell me about it." Her tone softened.

He was far too old to bring his love life to Mama. But his testosterone-pumped friends didn't need to hear about his wounded heart. "Are you going to bribe me with chocolate chip cookies and cold milk?"

She tossed him a grin. "Organic graham crackers and soy?"

He laughed, a dose he needed after the last couple of days. Running his fingers through his hair, he deliberated how much to tell her. "She's a widow. Her husband and I were friends, and he was murdered two years ago. Problem is, I neglected to tell her about the friendship."

"Alex, that doesn't sound like such a crime to me." She tilted her head. "Knowing you, there's more."

"Oh, there is." Alex proceeded to spill his guts about Toby, his pro-immigration activism, the threat made to Danika, and the shooting. He didn't mention any association with Ed or Homeland Security.

Mom buried her face in her hands. Drama was her specialty. "Did you leave anything out?"

He grinned. "Probably. But you have the gist of it. I'm not an activist, but at this point, I doubt if she'd believe anything I said."

"Why is someone out to shoot her?"

"My personal thoughts are it has something to do with her husband's murder or the fact that the Border Patrol suspects a rogue agent."

Panic seared her eyes. "You didn't tell me about a rogue agent. I think I need to pack you up and take you home with me."

"Things will settle down soon."

"At whose expense?" Mom pointed to his leg. "His aim might be better the next time."

"I—" Alex's cell phone rang before he could finish his statement.

It was Ed, wanting to know about his recovery process.

"My mom's here. Going to be the cook and nurse for a few days."

"Does she like kids?"

Weird question. "She's a retired pediatric nurse. What's up?"

"Danika talked to me before she ended her shift. She's looking for someplace to send her little girl until things cool down here, possibly the child's nanny too. She doesn't have any family who could take her daughter."

Alex thought about Danika's reaction when he brought up her parents. Their relationship must have been worse than he guessed. "Danika is not speaking to me."

Ed blew out an exasperated sigh. "I'm not playing matchmaker."

"Who asked you to?"

"Do you need a pain pill?"

"As a matter of fact I do."

"Thought so. Guess I was out of line. Got a boatload of work to do and was trying to help Danika get her daughter out of the city."

Alex glanced at his mom, who pretended interest in a magazine. No one could read pages that were turned that fast. "Her little girl is a sweet kid. Maybe I can approach Danika as a friend."

"In terms of your mother?"

"In terms of a little girl who needs a safe place to stay. Danika and I may not be an item, but I do care about their safety."

"Let me know."

"I will."

"And, Alex?"

"Yeah?"

"Take a pain pill." Ed chuckled, but Alex didn't find it a bit amusing.

Mom closed the magazine as soon as he disconnected the call. "Who needs a babysitter?"

CHAPTER 34

**For every man who lives without freedom,
the rest of us must face the guilt.**
LILLIAN HELLMAN

JACOB WIPED THE SAWDUST from his jeans at the cabinet shop. The bench was completed, a custom piece for an interior decorator, rough finished to look like it had come from an eighteenth-century mission.

"Every piece you construct is superb quality. Are you ready to go full-time?" Harv clasped him on the shoulder. "Sure could use you."

Jacob studied the bench, proud of what he'd accomplished. The store's owner, a bald man long past the age of retirement, had been pressuring him for the past few days. "I never thought I'd like to build furniture full-time, but this is a lot easier on my blood pressure than riding the line for the Border Patrol."

"I have an order for custom kitchen cabinetry for an upscale house. It's yours if you want it."

Jacob crossed his arms over his chest. He didn't have to think long about the offer. "I'll take it. My grandfather was a craftsman too. He built beautiful pieces of furniture. Used to watch him for hours."

"You've got a gift. That's for sure." Harv stuck out a veined hand scarred with his profession. Jacob grasped it, and he felt good.

Jacob left the shop without the usual depression weighing

on him. He enjoyed taking pieces of wood and forming them into something beautiful and useful. Father Cornell was right—working with his hands could calm his spirit and reshape his heart.

He'd started meeting with Father Cornell the day he'd been let go from the Border Patrol and learned they suspected him as the rogue. In the beginning it looked like a good way to show his innocence and get custody of his kids. But he'd actually started to feel better.

For a few minutes he'd shoved aside the losses in his life. Would he ever see his Naddie again? His throat tightened.

★ ★ ★

Karen Price delivered a cup of herbal tea to Alex. "Son, you have a heart for people in need. It doesn't matter whether the problem is physical, mental, or spiritual, you're ready to help. God wired you that way."

Alex inhaled the apple cinnamon tea. "I inherited the trait from you."

"Remember when you called me about those nineteen undocumented people who died in the back of a truck transporting them to a city near Houston? It was all over the news."

May 2003. The memory still haunted him. He knew the relatives of one of the men who had perished in the suffocating heat. A child was among them too. All those people wanted was to reach Houston and find work—start their lives with hope for the future. "A sad situation. Senseless deaths."

"From what I can tell, the situation with the border is a mess, and I certainly don't have a solution. But all the authorities can do, like your friend, is enforce the laws of our country."

"The agents I've met are concerned about the welfare of those who cross the border. They don't hesitate to bring them to the hospital for treatment."

"How appropriate if the media reported those cases instead of the dirt."

"Exactly. I do think the media has been doing a better job since the drug cartels have been threatening our borders." He studied her. This was leading to something.

She stood and lifted her chin. "Grab your crutches. We're taking a ride."

"Where?"

"To get a dozen roses and a sweet card for your friend. Then we're going to talk to her about having her little girl come home with me until this is all over."

He should have known. "How's your signing?"

She tossed him a puzzled look.

"Tiana is deaf, and so the nanny would need to come along." *Except she's undocumented. What a mess.*

Mom lifted her chin. "I have plenty of room, and I'd enjoy the company. Maybe I could learn to sign too. My fingers aren't eaten up with arthritis yet and won't be for years."

Alex wanted to think about Mom's proposal. Dragging her into this gave a whole new meaning to uncomfortable. "Are you certain this is what you want to do?"

One look told him there was no changing her mind. "Absolutely."

He glanced at the clock on the fireplace mantel. "Her shift ends at six." He worried his lip. "Sometimes she goes to church on Saturday nights. I think the service begins at seven thirty."

"Then let's get going. Do we need to bring dinner?"

Alex laughed. "I've already done that once."

For a woman who should be planning the next senior club event, his mom sure had energy. They'd always been close. After Dad left them for a younger woman, she'd jumped in and played both parental roles. They went camping, played football, took piano lessons, learned how to take care of the house inside and out, and everyone attended church on Sunday morning and Wednesday night. When she made a mistake, she owned up to it. When she was right, she didn't let you forget it. All three of the kids had gone beyond college education and were firmly rooted in their relationship with God. Not a bad life when he considered the statistics of what usually happened to kids from broken homes.

He struggled to his feet, dread nipping at his heels. He anticipated Danika would not be happy when she opened the door and saw him and his mother. The pain meds had definitely knocked loose any good sense that might have taken residence in his brain.

Danika smelled dinner the moment she opened the front door at home. Chicken noodle soup and homemade bread. She could use a little comfort food. Driving home from work, she'd realized the best solution to finding a haven for Tiana was to send her and Sandra to another city. Paying rent along with her mortgage payment would be a stretch, but she could do it until those threatening Danika were brought to justice. It also occurred to her that she wouldn't be able to visit Tiana and Sandra for fear she'd be followed.

She searched her mind again for suspects, but nothing surfaced, leaving her feeling frustrated and stupid. It was as though she'd pulled into a one-way cul-de-sac. In two years she'd failed to find Toby's killer, and now someone had set out to get her, too. What battered her senses was *why now?* This person or persons had two years to come after her. Something had triggered the stalking . . . but what? She arrested people every day for crimes. Any of them could hold a grudge. Any of them could have murdered Toby. Oh, the depths of reality.

I'm not going to sit back and be the hunted. If they want me, they'd better be prepared for a fight.

Danika set her backpack in her bedroom closet and sought out Tiana and Sandra in the backyard. Roses climbed the fence and crepe myrtles in bright pink added color to the otherwise-green area. With Tiana's jungle gym, there wasn't much room for anything else. A ceiling fan on the enclosed patio circulated the air, and Sandra and Tiana were involved in a paint-by-number book—in Spanish.

No sooner had Danika hugged her daughter and greeted Sandra than the doorbell rang. "I'll get it," Danika signed. "You two finish up your masterpieces."

"Dinner's ready," Sandra said. "All I have to do is spoon it into the bowls."

"Wonderful, because I'm starved."

Danika took a precautionary glance at the street. Alex's truck sat parked at the curb. What was he thinking? Did she now have more than one stalker?

Swinging open the door, she considered a thousand and one retorts. Alex stood beside an older woman with short blonde hair and a wide smile. She held a bouquet of red roses. All it took was one cursory look into the woman's eyes, and Danika saw the resemblance.

"Hi, I'm Karen Price. I thought you could use a few roses to brighten your day." She extended the green-wrapped bouquet, forcing Danika to take them.

"Uh, thank you." Danika breathed in the roses. Some were open, and others hadn't yet made their grand entrance. They smelled sweet, and the ones Alex had previously given her had withered and died. How apropos. She glared at him. "I thought we had an agreement."

"We do." He offered a thin-lipped smile that immediately faded. "Mom, this is Danika Morales."

"What a pleasure," Karen said. "May I come in? Alex can stay in the truck if you like." Alex's mother looked quite the fashion statement with her white jeans and purple and blue silk blouse.

Startled, Danika questioned Alex's motivation in this silly, immature setup. Well, she could play the same game. Maybe Dr. Price and his crutch didn't understand the word *no*. "Please come in, but Alex can wait outside." She smiled at him, silently letting him know she wasn't a pushover for any man who had the nerve to bring his mother to the door to plead his case.

Then guilt assaulted her. He *had* taken two bullets for her. "I'm sorry. That's rude, and you just got out of the hospital. Come on in."

"Actually, I think I'd better wait in the truck." He looked a little pale. He turned and made his way back to the vehicle, painfully, if his hunched shoulders and grimace were any clues.

She wanted to call him back.

Once Karen was seated and the roses placed in the kitchen until they could be arranged, Danika offered the woman a cup of coffee.

"No thanks. I don't drink the stuff. Do you have any idea what coffee does to your stomach lining and your colon?" Her shoulders lifted and fell. "But that's not why I'm here."

"I didn't think so." Danika leaned back in the chair.

The back door opened and closed, and Sandra entered the kitchen with Tiana. The little girl ran to her mother. Danika signed for her to help Sandra set the table for dinner.

"She's a very pretty little girl."

"Thank you."

"I understand you need a safe place for her and her nanny to stay until some undesirables are found?"

Danika hesitated before answering. How did she know this?

For that matter, how did Alex know? "I'm not sure I'm following you."

Karen clasped her hands in her lap. "One of Alex's friends called to check on him while I was there. He said you were looking for help with your daughter. I think his name is Ed Jimenez. So here I am."

Danika didn't appreciate Chief Jimenez sharing their conversation with Alex. She'd handle that on her next shift. "Why would you want to burden yourself with Tiana? You don't know her, and she has special needs."

The woman scooted to the front of the sofa cushion. "I'll give you my qualifications. I'm a retired pediatric nurse, I raised three children, I teach third-grade Sunday school, and I have a house far too big for me."

"Alex put you up to this?"

"No. He's embarrassed. I know all about the stupid thing he did. That man was not brought up to keep the truth from people. He's a doctor, for heaven's sake. What has gotten into him is beyond me." Karen leaned toward Danika. "I was a single mom. I understand the issues and problems of carrying the load. Let me help you, sweetie. I promise to take good care of your little girl and her nanny."

Danika drank in every word. She didn't know if the peculiar, yet likable, woman before her was an answer to prayer or a distraction. "I'm not sure what to say." She massaged the back of her neck.

"Long day?"

"The longest."

"And then you still have to play mom and dad."

Danika lifted her head and smiled. "I love it. Tiana is why I get up in the morning, why I work hard at keeping our borders safe. But it's tiring."

Karen stood and stepped behind Danika's chair. She began kneading the muscles in Danika's neck.

"You don't have to do that."

"True. But a massage feels good, doesn't it?"

Danika laughed softly. Alex's quirkiness came honestly.

"Why don't you think about my offer? This has nothing to do with my son. He did a jerky thing, so let him pay the toll. He's a good man and a fabulous doctor, but still a man. Multitasking emotions is not a part of their operational database. Anyway, I wrote down about ten references, and those are in my pocket. Check them out. Run a criminal check—I would—and let me know. From what I hear, you have a lot of stress right now. I'd like to help, and it would fill my hours."

Danika let all the information sink in. *Numb* best described her. "Thank you. I will think about it. How long will you be in McAllen?"

"Until early Wednesday morning." Karen pulled a piece of paper from her jean pocket and handed it to Danika.

She could pray about this and talk to Shannon and Becca about the possibility—as absurd as it sounded. "Can I let you know on Tuesday?"

"Oh, sure. I drove from San Antonio, so I'm flexible." Karen continued the massage, and it felt good. "I had a thought the moment we pulled up in front of your house. I could park my car in your garage before sunup on Wednesday morning, load up Tiana and all of her things with her nanny, and leave while it's dark. No one would have a clue."

Did this family think of everything?

CHAPTER 35

Everyone thinks of changing the world, but
no one thinks of changing himself.
LEO TOLSTOY

SUNDAY MORNING, Alex swung his crutches down the hospital corridor. He was well aware the patients could hear the dull thuds of his approach.

No word existed in human language that touched how Alex felt about his mother's intrusion into his private life. *Mortified* was a good beginning. He tried to tell himself his mom meant well, and yes, her plan provided a safe place for Tiana. But he felt like a junior high kid whose mommy had marched to school to defend him against the bullies. Except Danika was far from a bully. She had every right to be furious after his failure to be honest with her. But he was a man, and he had his pride, and he sensed there would never be reconciliation with her. He'd rather she envision him as a caveman protector who'd fight to his death defending her. Nothing in medical school prepared him for a mother who took life's problems head-on or a Border Patrol agent who had stolen his heart or a pint-size angel who had him in the palm of her hand.

Women. This went far beyond textbook bedside manner.

Still dressed in a shirt and tie from church, Alex continued to hobble through his patient visits with a determination to nix his frustrations. He enjoyed checking on his patients after worship.

High on Jesus and high on the gift of healing, why not reach out to see if he could make a difference in someone's life?

Cira's little boy, Mickey, had responded to the treatment and medication for the pneumonia, but not as quickly as Alex desired. He'd explained to Cira that her son was very ill. She'd delayed seeking medical care and sacrificed the strength he needed to fight the fever and illness. Alex had little tolerance for parents who allowed children to suffer, especially when the care at McAllen Medical Center was free.

Alex stepped into the pediatric section to find Mickey sleeping and Cira's face pinched with concern.

"Shouldn't he be better by now?" She adjusted the light coverlet around his body.

"He *is* better." Alex studied the chart one more time, then the IV level. "Remember, Cira, we talked about this. Your son will be fine, but it'll take a little while."

"I understand." She looked pale, thin, and exhausted.

"Are you working, taking care of your grandfather, and attempting to spend every possible moment at the hospital?"

She nodded and fingered a small cross around her neck. "He is my life, my heart. I wonder if I'm not praying right."

Alex leaned his crutches against the back of Mickey's bed and eased into a chair next to her. "You're carrying far too many burdens. God hears your prayers. Be sure of that." He gestured toward Mickey. "And your son is making progress. In a few days, he'll be scrambling to get out of that bed and play."

She smiled through damp lashes. "I pray so."

"Me too." Alex took a breath. Another matter needed to be discussed. "Cira, the police are looking for the woman who fronted your money to cross the border. They have enough evidence to bring her in for questioning, specifically for running an illegal operation and abusing other women."

"I can't risk being sent back. Someone might take my son since he's a citizen."

An anchor child . . . at the heart of the problem for so many undocumented immigrants. "If you were escorted back across the border, Mickey would go with you. He'd still retain his citizenship so that when he was old enough, he could return to the U.S."

"I want to raise him here." She set her lips, but Alex refused to give up.

"I've treated young women who've been beaten and then dropped off here at the hospital. One had lost a finger. None will name their abuser. They hadn't been raped, and there were no signs of drugs in their system. Is this a part of the same operation?"

Cira sighed. "Possibly. But that's all I can tell you. She's a mean woman, a devil. I don't care about myself, but she'd hurt my son."

Mickey stirred, and she glanced his way. Love filled her face with a special light that only a mother possessed. "You see, when we agreed to have her front half of our money, we were told that if we got pregnant, the baby would be aborted. No argument. I've seen what she has done to other women who didn't obey her."

"Don't you want it stopped so she can go to jail?"

"What is worse, Dr. Alex? Running from her or being deported? As far as the other women trapped here, they have to stay put until their debt is paid. Here we have a chance to provide a better life for our families. They know one day it will be over. No one wants to risk being caught by the Border Patrol."

"I think one young woman died because of her," he finally said. "But she'd been raped."

Her face paled. "I'm not surprised. Before Toby was killed, he . . . "

"What? Did Toby know this woman you won't identify?"

"I'm not saying anything else. It's too dangerous."

Alex reluctantly stood to examine Mickey. Later he'd process what little information Cira had given him. A name, if only she'd give him a name. For the first time, Alex realized that Toby might have met the woman Cira feared. But the murder hadn't been solved, and Cira might be the one to supply the missing link. She may already know who murdered Toby.

But first Alex had to convince her to trust him. Like another female he knew.

CHAPTER 36

Too long a sacrifice
Can make a stone of the heart.
O when may it suffice?
WILLIAM BUTLER YEATS

SANDRA WATCHED Tiana splash in a small, blue plastic pool under a covered area in the backyard. Danika had thought of everything when she hired a landscaper to turn the oversize yard into a play area that shielded the little girl from the sun. Every piece of equipment was in the shade or under a constructed overhang. Hanging plants, flowering shrubbery, and trees also invited adults to relax. This was what Sandra needed today.

She never imagined leaving Danika and Tiana, but Lucy's continual demands for Border Patrol information had not given her much choice. The guilt of how she'd lied to Danika seemed to mount daily. In the wee hours of the morning, she realized that even her friendship and love for Danika and Tiana were based on lies. The fact made her a user, as though she were hooked on cocaine.

No, I'm a better person than that. Love is what God calls us to do, and I love this country and my adopted family. If only her documents were legitimate.

"I have information for you," Lucy had said. "Something that will persuade you to do what I ask. My messenger will arrive in about thirty minutes."

Sandra wanted to take Tiana and leave the house, but what

good would that do? Lucy had spies, and she always learned things. In times like these, Sandra wished someone would find a way to rid them all of Lucy.

The moments ticked by while she rocked back and forth on the glider. Tiana's laughter usually calmed Sandra's troubled spirit, but not today. Uneasiness slithered up her spine with a chill at her nape that scoffed at her apprehension. She guessed Danika would agree to Karen Price's offer, which meant Sandra would accompany Tiana to San Antonio on Wednesday morning. Oh, time played the advocate in balancing her devotion to Danika and Tiana with Lucy's demands.

A black Ford pickup pulled into the driveway, a new truck. Each wheel probably cost the same as what she earned in a month. A young Hispanic man exited the vehicle and looked around.

She gasped. Jose was her messenger? He must have sold his soul to Lucy for that truck. Surely not. She swallowed hard. Maybe he agreed to do whatever she asked without knowing what Lucy would expect of him. Her messengers did all of her dirty work, whatever it took to keep Lucy's girls in line . . . whatever it took to get the job done.

Tiana squealed, capturing Jose's attention. He walked toward the gate and spotted Sandra. When she failed to move his way, he let himself in and joined her on the glider. Tiana appeared oblivious to him as she continued pouring water over a small paddleboat.

"You weren't expecting me." Not a trace of a smile laced his words.

"Is this how you're getting your documentation papers?" Sandra hoped he couldn't hear her heart hammer against her chest.

"It's my chance to have everything I want."

"At what price?"

"Whatever it takes."

Sandra rubbed her arms and remembered, the truth making her ill. "You were working for Lucy when you came to see me the first time."

"Did you think I'd really want you? I can have any woman I want."

She tried to ignore the knife twisting in her heart. No, her very soul. "You were looking for information when I found you in Danika's room."

"Right, and I couldn't find a thing. Lucy has a couple of messages for you." His whisper came out more like a hiss.

"So I heard. Why don't you say what you came for and leave?"

He clutched her arm. "If you weren't living here, you'd get a beating."

"And I suppose that's your job now?"

He chuckled. The lure of Jose turned to disgust—his dimpled grin and handsome face meant she'd been a fool. "Whatever it takes."

"So you enjoy licking Lucy's feet?"

He pulled a knife from his jean pocket. "I'd like nothing better than to cut your face into bite-size pieces, but Lucy needs what only you can provide. The moment she's finished with you, I'll track you down."

She trembled, and his grasp on her arm tightened. "Get it over with," she said, her words sounding more courageous than she felt.

Jose's smile twisted into a sneer. "Don't tempt me. I came on an errand, remember? Have you heard the latest news from near Barranquillas?"

Blood drained from Sandra's face, and horror captured her.

"A fire destroyed the home of an elderly couple," he said. "Perhaps you know them, Estella and Pedro Rodriguez? Unfortunately they died in the blaze. I hear the church can't find a thing but charred bones to bury." He flipped open the cover to his cell phone and showed her a picture of the charred remains of her parents and their home.

Acid rose to her throat, and her stomach churned. She knew every inch of her parents' home, a shack to some, but it was where laughter and love had lived. Jose had captured it all on his phone—in ashes.

"Oh, and here's another one so you don't think I'm lying." He displayed a second picture, showing the neighbor's house.

Unfathomable grief attached its claws to her body. Lucy had threatened her parents, but murder? Paralyzed, she struggled to respond to him. "Both of you are animals."

He lifted a brow. "Are we? Lucy thinks they won't be needing medicine any longer. She thought this might persuade you to get what she needs."

The sensors' locations. Sandra shivered. "I'll do what I can and have it for you on Thursday morning. She's off on Tuesday and Wednesday, but I don't know if she carries the information with her."

"You better hope she does." He slipped the knife back into his pocket and released her arm. "Don't be putting us off, or I'll let you personally witness what we plan to do next."

"I'll do my best."

Jose stood from the glider and watched Tiana, who had yet to be interrupted in her water play. "I've been thinking. The kid can't hear, so she doesn't need one of those ears." He left Sandra sitting on the glider and Tiana playing in the water.

The little girl watched him leave and waved as though he were a friend.

Emotion bubbled in Sandra's throat and unleashed in grief she didn't know existed. Memories of a little girl who adored her father and cherished her mother surfaced and faded one after another. Her parents hadn't done anything to deserve this horrible death but wish her a good life and pray for her.

Sandra glanced at her precious Tiana. She'd persuade Danika to send Tiana with Karen Price on Wednesday—away from this madness. And if that didn't work, she'd tell Danika the truth . . . all of it. Even what she knew about Toby's death. Then she'd run to where Lucy or Jose or the Border Patrol would never find her.

She couldn't even attend her own parents' funeral.

Danika pulled into the parking lot at the Hidalgo station for her quarterly weapons qualification. Today she'd recertify the use of her assigned HK handgun, a shotgun, and an M4 assault rifle, and she'd need to pass all three. As usual, she was nervous, and she'd been an agent for over eight years. The latest news report along the border told of Mexican police seizing a machine gun that had the ability to pierce steel up to a mile away—U.S.-made, of course. Citizens and undocumented immigrants alike worried about the cartel marching into border states with their limitless supply of money and weaponry.

Positioning earplugs in her ears, she stepped up to the target with the handgun. Fortunately she'd never killed a man. Came close a few times with drug smugglers. They didn't have much to lose by gunning down a Border Patrol agent, and gang leaders scored extra points for killing agents.

Taking a deep breath, she cleared her mind of everything but the task before her. Concentration and determination took precedence. Her senses numbed except for focusing on the target, Danika took aim and squeezed the trigger.

Several minutes later, she removed the earplugs, satisfied with the results in all three weapons.

With the pressure gone, she relaxed and headed to her

assigned truck. A huge decision needled her, and she needed to call Karen Price one way or the other. If Tiana and Sandra left on Wednesday with Karen, then her little girl deserved to know the changes about to occur in her life. Another meeting should be arranged with Karen so Tiana would feel comfortable. She'd always been a sociable child, but this was a stretch. And what about Sandra? Danika chose not to think of her refusing to go. The mere thought of coming home to an empty house each day was overwhelming.

Oh, God, Tiana is my light. Tell me what to do. I want her safe, but sending her to San Antonio frightens me.

Danika wanted to know what God advised now, and the drive home would offer a bit of quiet for His response.

"Hey, Crack Shot, you did good out there."

Danika recognized Felipe's voice behind her. What a great guy, and just what she needed today. Grinning, she stopped until he caught up. "Did it scare you enough to stop teasing me about my softball finesse?"

"For sure. I'm writing my apology tonight."

"Sign it in blood. I want to post it for the rest of the guys who are still laughing."

"I'll think about it." He sobered. "Are you okay?"

Did she wear her anxiety like a shoulder patch? "Most of the time."

"That's a good, honest answer. I mean, with Jacob gone and the shooting and the wondering if the chief is finished with his investigation."

Danika didn't believe in signs—except for footprints and empty Red Bull cans—but the dilemma with Tiana was making her crazy. She desperately craved advice. Karen had checked out to be everything she claimed. "You're my friend, right?"

"For the five years I've been here. And you introduced me to Becca."

She hesitated, then drew in a breath. "I'm thinking about sending Tiana and Sandra away for a little while. The shooting scared me."

He nodded. "Do it."

Could she trust him? "No questions or an advantage and disadvantage list?"

"Nope. Someone tried to kill you. Your husband was murdered two years ago. Jacob's been fired, and he's mad at the world. His daughter's missing. I don't know what's going on in your life, but I'd have already hidden Tiana someplace far away from this mess."

She had her answer.

CHAPTER 37

In a dark time, the eye begins to see.
THEODORE ROETHKE

ALEX WATCHED his mom poke carrots and celery and then an apple into a juicer. The machine buzzed like a chain saw. If she thought he was going to drink that muddy mess, she was wrong. So much for allowing her to drop him off at the hospital and leave her with idle time to shop.

"You'll love this," she called from the kitchen. "And it's so good for you."

"Wonderful, Mom."

"Do I denote sarcasm?"

"Absolutely. I'm a doctor, and I know all about proper nutrition. But I'm a firm believer that food is supposed to taste good."

"Which is why I purchased you this magnificent juicer."

Before he could think of another remark, his cell phone rang. Danika. Did he dare hope she wanted to talk to him?

"Hi, Alex. How are you feeling?"

"Actually, pretty good. Working helps."

"Is your mother spoiling you?"

When he considered the disgusting brew in the juicer, *spoiled* rang true. "Guess you could say that." He wanted to talk to her about Cira and his suspicions about Toby's murderer, but not over the phone. "Have you made a decision about Tiana and my mother teaming up?"

"I have. Is Karen around?"

"She is. Hold on; I have to grab my crutches and take her the phone." He hesitated. "It's been good talking to you."

She laughed softly as though she detected his nervousness. "Thank you."

Alex hobbled into the kitchen and handed his mother the phone.

"Must be Danika," she mouthed and smiled—that mom thing that a grown man never outgrew.

Mom took the phone and walked outside. He glanced at the counter where she'd poured her health drink into a glass. The nondescript, rather greenish, thick mess reminded him of gummy bears after a whirl in the food processor. Or the mess he'd made of his and Danika's relationship.

Oh, Danika, you've tormented my heart. I can't undo the damage, and I can't seem to shake what I feel.

His thoughts turned to a few of his patients. With his limited mobility and the time taken off for his leg to heal, he had to rely on other trusted doctors to help him. Those arrangements bothered him. His patients deserved their own doctor, and he was finished with making excuses for himself.

Danika chatted to Karen about McAllen and listened to how the woman enjoyed the city. She'd shopped and taken note of all the new construction since she'd last visited Alex three years prior. All the while Danika's pulse raced with what she was about to do. She barely knew this woman, and in less than thirty-six hours, she'd have Danika's most precious treasure. Granted, Sandra would be with Tiana, but a nanny was not a mommy.

"I've made a decision," Danika said. "If you're still willing to keep my daughter for a little while, I . . . I'll have her ready on Wednesday morning."

"Oh, honey, I know this has been a tough few days while you contemplated handing over your Tiana to a stranger."

The angst was only beginning. "A lot of prayers and tears have gone into this, but it's the best solution. I'll have my attorney draw up the papers in the morning giving you temporary guardianship. I'll bring them to you in the afternoon."

"Does she know yet?"

"I'm telling her in a little bit. But I need your word—and Alex's—that no one learns about this. I'll let Chief Jimenez know."

"I promise. Alex had mentioned the same thing. Would you like for me to stop by later?"

Relief helped ease the lump in Danika's throat. "Yes. Very much."

"Is about an hour and a half okay?"

Karen wanted to help keep Tiana safe, and now Danika must continue—or she'd fall apart. "I want to say how very much I appreciate what you're doing."

"Children have to be protected. It's our role as women to nurture. It's how God wired us."

Danika whisked away the tears. "You are an angel."

"Tell that to Alex."

She laughed. "As long as he's not at the hospital, Tiana would like to see him."

"I'll have him tag along."

She disconnected the call. The insufferable task before her swirled with the feeling of loss. But she had no choice. Let whoever despised her come. Tiana would be safe, and Danika was not afraid to fight.

Sandra had overheard enough of Danika and Karen Price's conversation to confirm that she would be accompanying Tiana to

San Antonio. Relief flooded her, but with it came a mixture of fear and guilt for all she knew and kept secret. The most important thing was Tiana, and she would be safe. The little girl had been Sandra's baby, the child she'd never had. Might never have. She breathed a prayer of thanks, more for Tiana than for herself. But she'd taken another step deeper in betraying Danika.

Danika walked into the kitchen. Her listless eyes gave away the burden shadowing her soul. "If you would consider going to San Antonio with Tiana and Karen Price, I will continue to pay Lucy for your services as though you were here."

The official request was like manna from heaven, a solution she'd only dreamed about. "Of course I'll go."

"Thank you so much. If you are with Tiana, I know she'll be happy."

"She'll miss her mother, but I'll do my best."

"I have another favor," Danika said. "Please don't tell anyone where you're going. I have no idea who is after me."

Not even a consideration on Sandra's part. "I understand."

"The only people in McAllen who will know your and Tiana's whereabouts are Alex and the station's chief."

Sandra relaxed slightly. She'd be safe with her *niña preciosa*— precious little girl. Neither Lucy nor Jose would find them in San Antonio. "I know this will be very hard for you."

"It's hard already. I'm not sure I can risk driving to San Antonio to see you."

"I think you're right."

Danika nodded, and for a moment Sandra feared both of them might cry. Guilt continued to assault her. She could put an end to Danika's misery by confessing the truth about Lucy and the role the woman may have played in Toby's murder. Lucy had no conscience and was capable of anything.

Sandra still couldn't believe Lucy had ordered the deaths of her parents as though they were nothing. But she'd seen the pictures, and she knew how far Lucy had gone before. Sandra had slept fitfully last night with the memory of her parents haunting her. In one dream, her father accused her of lighting a match to their home. In essence, she had. The grief felt raw, as though her heart had been severed from her body. She hated Lucy for condemning her parents to such a merciless death. The woman should pay, but whom would Sandra tell? Going to the authorities meant facing deportation. She must bear the tragedy alone, mask her feelings so Danika wouldn't question her. Someday Lucy would pay for those she'd beaten and killed.

What am I to do? The idea of searching through Danika's backpack for sensor locations had made her feel dirty, the same low caliber as Lucy. But now she didn't have to. She wouldn't be anywhere near McAllen.

For a moment, terror seemed to swallow her up. Sandra realized she'd be spending the entire time in San Antonio looking over her shoulder. Where could she find peace and safety?

CHAPTER 38

Walk softly and carry a big faith.
ANONYMOUS

ALEX GRABBED HIS CRUTCHES from the bed of his truck and swung his way up Danika's driveway behind Mom. He muffled a groan, determined to portray the cowboy role. But with each step came a needlelike sensation that pierced his leg. This might officially end his rodeo days.

Gazing at the flowers and neatly kept yard that belonged to Danika Morales, he recalled another time he'd been there. The evening had ended like a nightmare: lost his potential girl-friend and gained two bullets in his leg. Both had added some character.

What a surprise to learn she'd invited him this evening—for Tiana's sake, of course. That made little sense since she'd been concerned about Tiana forming an attachment to him and then the relationship going sour. Danika didn't present herself as a woman who made rash decisions or tossed out invitations at a whim. He'd rather believe Danika was taking the first step toward mending their differences. Or she might have found a soft spot in her heart to forgive him, since he'd arranged a safe place for her daughter and Sandra. His musings sounded selfish and full of self-pity, and they were. If only they could take sand-paper to the past and start all over.

"Don't you two get into an argument," Mom said when they reached the door.

Alex bit his tongue. He loved his mother, but his patience had become a stretched rubber band. "This is an emotional time for her, and I'm not about to make things unpleasant."

Sandra answered the door, and as usual she avoided eye contact with him. He had weighed whether or not to tell Mom about Sandra's undocumented status, but he couldn't very well tell her and not Danika. The secrets needed to stop. He'd never been a man of pretense, but lately he considered carrying a pocket recorder so he'd remember what he'd told whom. No better time than the present to rectify his mistakes.

Once he entered the Morales home, Tiana ran to him. He hugged her, but he couldn't bend to her level.

"Is your leg better?"

At least she didn't ask him how he'd hurt it. "Yes, thank you."

"What happened?"

Oops. "I had surgery."

Alex saw Danika had a game in her hand. He smiled at her, and she returned the expression. That was headway.

"Would you like to join us?" Danika lifted the box to show it was Candy Land.

Tempting, very tempting. "I would, but first I'd like to talk to Sandra."

The woman's round face paled, and he noted the dark circles under her eyes. "I have a pie in the oven."

"Five minutes." He did his best to convey friendship without frightening her. Urging Sandra to tell the truth had to be presented as a way of her showing love for Danika and Tiana and not an opportunity for the woman to do something irrational— like run off, leaving Danika wondering what happened.

In glum resignation, Sandra opened the front door. He followed her outside and closed it behind him.

"I'm not afraid of you," she said barely above a whisper.

"No reason to be. I'm not the enemy. I simply want to look out for the welfare of Danika and Tiana."

"You're not Tiana's father. Why should you care?" Hostility dripped from Sandra's words. "Danika doesn't even like you."

Alex sighed. Although his past actions deserved some animosity, he'd protected this woman from deportation. "Unless your situation has changed in the past two years, you're keeping vital information from Danika."

She wrapped her arms around her stomach. "Are you planning to tell her?"

"Not tonight."

"So this is a threat? What do you want me to do, Dr. Price, persuade her to give you another chance?"

Anger took root, but he refused to let it surface. This woman lived in fear of being discovered. "My point in this conversation is that Danika has enough problems right now without learning from someone else that an undocumented worker lives under her roof. So I'm urging you to tell her before you leave for San Antonio."

"You think about this, Dr. Alex: I make it possible for Danika to work. I love Tiana and take care of her as if she were my own daughter. No one wins if I tell her the truth. Unless you think you'll look honorable."

"Do you think the Border Patrol would keep an agent who houses someone who is undocumented? Danika's a smart woman. I don't care how you managed to falsify papers in order to work for a legitimate business. It doesn't really matter. Danika cares for you, and I can see you care for her and Tiana. But one day she *will* learn the truth, and it had better be before Wednesday morning."

Sandra moistened her lips. "I thought you had sympathy for hardworking people who'd do anything for a better life."

"I haven't changed."

"Yes, you have. Because of how you feel about Danika, you no longer want to help us."

"Don't give me your helpless and defenseless attitude. You knew what you were doing when you crossed the border illegally. You took a chance, and you're still taking it. My help has always been to administer medical aid. Nothing more."

"But you were Toby's friend."

He had no intention of explaining his observations about the U.S. immigration policy. "Not all of our views were the same. In my opinion, it's Mexico's fault for encouraging illegal entry. They distribute brochures showing how and where to cross the border. They even tell you what to bring. The money the undocumented immigrants send back to Mexico aids their economy—substantially."

"You're an American. Fix it."

"Sandra, sarcasm is not going to remedy the situation." Alex had one more question. What did he have to lose? "Do you know who killed Toby? Because I think you do. I think the woman who fronted your money is responsible."

"I don't know who could have done such evil." Sandra glanced at her watch. "My pie is done."

Just as he had thought. "Again, I'm not the enemy. I'm simply warning you that working for a Border Patrol agent when you have a fake ID is playing with fire. You need to come clean with her."

"And be deported? I need this job. I'm not hurting anyone. I pay my taxes like any good American."

"Wednesday morning, Sandra. It's either you or me."

Sandra whirled around and entered the house without another word, and he followed her inside. He hadn't accomplished a thing. Or had he? He'd heard the arguments before, and he did have sympathy for the immigrants who simply wanted to work.

His cell phone rang, alerting him to a call from the hospital. He snatched it up, welcoming a reprieve.

"Dr. Price, one of your patients, Jimmy Padilla, has a fever of 104 and has had what looks to be a febrile seizure."

Cira's son, the assumed name given to the boy to ease his mother's fears. "Go ahead and administer an acetaminophen suppository, 120 milligrams stat. I'm on my way. If he seizes again, give him ten milligrams of diazepam gel rectally." Alex could only imagine Cira's panic. Seizures were scary but usually benign. His history with the woman had shown her to be strong but fearful of strangers. He'd treated her when someone had beaten and raped her. He'd been the one to tell her she was pregnant from the rape, and he'd delivered her son into this world. Alex's stake in Cira's and her son's lives took priority over any personal problems.

"Please tell the mother that I'll be right there." He slipped the phone back into his pocket and glanced about the room. Mom, Danika, and Tiana were sitting on the floor. "Hey, ladies, I'm sorry. You'll have to continue your game without me. I have an emergency at the hospital."

"Would you like for me to take you?" Mom offered. "Oh, of course I need to take you."

"I can do it," Danika said—but not with much enthusiasm.

"Both of you have business here, and I can drive just as well with my left foot as my right. I'll call when I leave the hospital." Without giving either woman an opportunity to oppose his plans, he exited the house. Dumb move. He should have asked one of them to drive him.

Once at the hospital, he'd run some tests to see why Mickey's fever had spiked. Maybe a urinary tract infection. Perhaps an infection around an IV line. He'd order a urine culture, change the IV site, culture the needle that was removed, and change the antibiotic.

Someday soon he and Danika would have to talk. No more secrets on his part. For now he'd keep his silence about Sandra and hope the woman confessed the truth—soon.

★ ★ ★

"There's no room for God to work in a family where the husband insists upon control."

Father Cornell's words repeated in Jacob's mind and would not let him go. He continued to sand the tabletop without protecting his nose and mouth. Let the sawdust settle in his lungs; he didn't care. The counseling session earlier in the day had left him confused, frustrated.

"The Bible says a man is the head of the household." Jacob had sensed his blood pressure escalating.

"Scripture also says a man is to love his wife as Christ loved the church." Father Cornell spoke as if he had a clue about what it was like to live with a woman who had turned his children against him and caused his daughter to run away.

"I'd give my life for my family. Haven't I worked hard all these years to provide for them?"

"Providing and loving are two different topics."

"Have you been talking to Barbara?"

"No. She has sought the counsel of another priest."

Jacob hated the man's calmness while his own pulse increased. "Our differences can never be resolved. She's betrayed me and not allowed me to lead my family."

"How do you lead, Jacob?"

"The way Scripture says. I know what is best for them, and I tell them. I expect them to obey."

"Is this the way you've always led your family or just since Toby's death?"

Jacob leaned forward, and his throat seemed to squeeze shut.

"My brother died because the Border Patrol failed to stop those who enter our country illegally. I vowed then to protect my family at all costs. Criminals seek out Border Patrol families and prey on them like rabid animals."

Father Cornell nodded. "I know you love your family. I know you feel responsible for Toby's death. I also think if you'd give yourself a moment to face the truth, you'd realize you blame yourself for Nadine's disappearance. You cannot shield the world or even your family from evil. It's there. It can't be avoided. We all do our best to keep our loved ones safe, but those people cannot be smothered, because then they begin to despise us. We lead by example in love—and prayer."

"You don't know what you're talking about." Jacob fought the hot tears threatening to spill. "I do all those things."

"There's no room for God to work in a family where the husband insists upon control."

Five hours later, Jacob still ached with those words. And why did he feel such physical agony? Shouldn't he instead feel the winds of anger toward the priest who didn't even have a family? Instead he wanted to run and hide, pretend the last two years didn't exist. Perhaps he could empathize with Nadine after all. It had been four and a half weeks since he'd seen his baby girl. The authorities claimed they were still looking, but Jacob believed otherwise. They'd written his daughter off like a lost puppy until they found her hiding or her decomposed body.

He closed his eyes and waited for the weight bearing on his chest to subside.

CHAPTER 39

Farmers who wait for perfect weather never plant.
If they watch every cloud, they never harvest.
ECCLESIASTES 11:4

DANIKA CARRIED HER SLEEPING DAUGHTER through the kitchen and into the attached garage, where Karen's car sat ready to leave McAllen. She toyed with waking Tiana, but her motives were purely selfish. They'd said their good-byes last night, and Danika's strength waned this morning. She'd cry buckets of tears, making the departure more difficult for all of them.

"You and Sandra are going to have a vacation with Mrs. Price," Danika had signed. "You will have a wonderful time at her house."

"Without you?"

"Yes. This is a special big girl and Sandra time. Just think of the fun you will have swimming in Mrs. Price's pool, going to the park, and playing with the cat and dog."

"I wish you were going." The look on Tiana's face nearly broke Danika's resolve.

Danika realized the strength to tell Tiana about the trip to San Antonio came from God. On her own, she'd be a flood of emotion. Packing her clothes and toys had been a mixture of relief and sadness. But Danika had found Toby's Bible in the process. At the time when she'd placed it at the top of her daughter's closet, she intended to give it to Tiana one day. Now it sat on her own dresser. Perhaps reading his notes and what he'd underlined would help Danika gain closure to that part of her life.

"I'll come to get you as soon as I can. Mommy has to start nights soon, and we wouldn't see each other anyway."

Tiana nodded. The night shift was hard on both of them.

With only the dome light of the car on, Karen opened the door for Danika to buckle her little girl safely inside. Two pillows had been propped so Tiana could sleep. Sandra sat in the front.

"Good-bye, my sweet girl," Danika whispered, thankful that the darkness concealed her tears.

Sandra reached to the backseat and grasped Danika's hand. "I will watch out for her."

Karen wrapped her arm around Danika's shoulder. "I promise to take good care of both of them. Now you can work to find who has caused all this trouble."

"Thank you. I pray it's today."

"Me too, Danika. Alex said he'd show you how to set up a video call on his computer so you and Tiana can communicate. He said it might not be safe to use your PC."

She brushed the salty tears from her face. "He's right, and I appreciate that."

"He's not a bad character."

"Character says it all." She laughed despite the sad situation. She couldn't trust him, but he'd saved her life and possibly Tiana's too.

"Oh, honey. That's true of all men. Now give me a hug, and we're out of here."

How good of God to give her a true friend in a time of crisis. As the car backed out of the garage in the predawn shadows, Danika realized nothing stood in her way to find who wanted her dead and who had ended Toby's life.

★ ★ ★

Sandra stared at the gray highway ahead—empty, endless. She despised herself for all the lies, and deep down she realized that all of this could have been prevented if she'd been honest. When Dr. Price asked her if she knew who'd killed Toby, the reality about Lucy's depraved mind wrapped its recognition around her heart. *Lucy could have ordered Toby's death.* The woman hated him for helping Cira and the others escape.

Before Sandra's parents were murdered, she wanted to believe Lucy would not resort to murder. But now . . . Where would it end? She should have been nicer to Dr. Price. Maybe he would have postponed or even chosen not to tell Danika about her. Now all she could do was pray.

★ ★ ★

Thursday morning Danika couldn't bear the empty house one more minute and drove to work early in hopes of catching a few moments with Chief Jimenez before morning muster. She found him in his office reading the previous shift's report. He glanced up.

"My daughter and nanny left for San Antonio before five yesterday morning."

Steam swirled off the top of his coffee cup. "Good. No one knows but Alex, right?"

"Yes, sir."

"When you call to check on her, use a public phone."

"I've already taken precautions." She understood the danger of the wrong people getting their hands on her cell phone, whether it was a call to trace or a text message. It also occurred to her that she couldn't send e-mail to Karen from her own PC.

The chief must have heard the determination in her voice

because he set his coffee cup down and studied her. "I want to do everything I can to find the evidence necessary to make an arrest."

Jacob must be at the top of their list of suspects. "Me too. I'm determined."

"Let the professionals track down this guy," he said. "You can't afford to take chances."

"Which is another reason why I can't confide in anyone."

"Off the record, have you patched up things with Alex?"

She started to make a none-of-your-business comment but instead thought she'd probe deeper. "What is it with you and Alex?"

"Longtime friends, that's all."

"I haven't forgotten the comment he made in the hospital." She heard Alex's voice again: *"I bet you wondered which one of us was the target."*

"Chalk it up to drugs."

"If I asked him about it, what would he say?"

"Under the influence of pain medication."

She didn't believe him and added Alex's comment to her long list of things to investigate.

Morning muster revealed nothing out of the ordinary. Twenty-five illegals had been caught during the night, but no drugs seized. The checkpoint had stopped a van carrying eight Chinese nationals on their way to Houston for work. Flying into Mexico and stealing across the border was a cheaper option than the legal route.

Agents greeted Jon Barnett, back from his medical leave. He looked good, minus about twenty pounds. Fire-Eater had recovered well and had stepped back into duty with his handler.

On the road, she tried to clear her mind of personal matters and watch for signs while listening for the radio. For once she wished she rode with someone else to keep her mind off the separation from Tiana. Her cell rang, and she responded to Felipe.

"Are you doing okay?"

"Sure. Why?" She had to do a better job concealing her separation anxiety.

"You looked sad this morning. Becca said you and Alex were no longer seeing each other, and I wondered if you wanted me to fix you up with someone."

The last thing she needed was another man. "No thanks."

"I don't know what the guy did to make you mad, but taking two bullets has to say something."

Felipe meant well, but she'd heard all of this before. "Let's talk about something else."

He laughed. "I get the message. I heard checkpoint found another body yesterday."

Another reminder of Toby. "Whenever I'm there, the vultures are always circling." Much like her life. "What's the count now, seven since January?"

"Nine. Desperation breeds bigger risks."

If she were in an illegal's shoes, with no other options to provide for her family, what risks would she take?

"One more thing, then I'll let you go."

"Fire away." As long as it wasn't about Alex.

"We're all watching your back."

This was her real family, and the warmth his words generated would keep her spirits up all day. "Thanks. One minute I can shake off the fact someone tried to kill me, and the next minute my knees are like rubber. I keep trying to connect the dots. You know, look for links to Toby's murder. But nothing turns up."

"We're right here until it's ended."

The radio blared, indicating four hits on a sensor in Danika's watch area. Her foot pressed on the gas pedal.

★ ★ ★

Alex couldn't believe it. Fifteen hours after Cira's son had experienced a seizure, she fled the hospital with him. Who or what had she seen to put her son's life in jeopardy? She had no medicine, and the boy was weak.

Alex kept looking around the ER hoping she'd come to her senses. But Cira's fright came honestly. When Toby had brought her to him a few years ago, Alex witnessed true terror. The horror of what she'd experienced had given her living nightmares. If and when he did see her again, he'd urge her to get out of McAllen. She'd be safer in Mexico.

When he wasn't concerned about Cira and Mickey, his thoughts swerved into another train wreck. This time about Danika parting with Tiana and Sandra. Sure glad he had God to carry this burden. Alone, he'd be buying stock in Tums.

His desk phone buzzed. "A woman is asking for you at the ER desk."

Elated with the prospect of Cira returning with Mickey, he snatched up his crutches and hurried toward the ER. Instead of Cira Ramos, he found Danika leaning against the counter.

"Hey." Her eyes testified to her nervousness. "Since your mom has left, I wondered if you needed a ride home."

"I took a taxi this morning. I do a lousy job driving with my left foot. Hadn't thought much about it since."

"How late do you plan to be here?"

He glanced at the clock on the ER wall and the patients waiting to be seen. Sure, another doctor had taken his place, but he hated to leave him with such a load. "Can you give me another hour?"

"You got it."

He took a deep breath. "Have you eaten?"

Their gazes met, and he no longer saw the animosity. But he

didn't see trust either. "Not yet." Sandra must have told her the truth, and she needed to talk.

"I'll buy."

She hesitated, and he could almost hear the wheels grinding in her head—or rather her heart. "Okay."

CHAPTER 40

There is no witness so dreadful, no accuser so terrible as the
conscience that dwells in the heart of every man.
POLYBIUS

ALEX CHOSE A LITTLE Italian café with good lighting and
sensational food. Not too busy and not too noisy. The perfect
site for a confessional. *Cordial* best described Danika's attitude.
But she'd agreed to let Alex buy her dinner, and to him, that
meant progress.

She ordered eggplant parmesan, and he opted for lasagna.
When the waiter disappeared, Alex braved forward. One look
into Danika's sad eyes, and he nearly faltered.

"Have you heard from my mother?"

A faint smile graced her lips. "Yes. I called her from a pay
phone. And the trip to San Antonio went well. Sandra and Tiana
are unpacked, and everyone is getting to know each other."

Sandra must not have told her the truth. "Mom's a great gal.
She'll do her best to make things pleasant for Tiana. Ed called to
reinforce that no one is to learn where Sandra and Tiana are."

She nodded. "I keep thinking he has more information that
he's not passing on. Specifically about Jacob."

He probably did. "I have no idea." Would this conversation
ever get past the stiff formalities?

She studied him, and from the way she tilted her head and
gave continuous eye contact, he realized she didn't believe him.

"Danika, I do not have any more information about this case that I can give you." *Lord, help me to tell her about Sandra.*

"I'd like to believe you."

Guilt assaulted him. He could be protecting valuable evidence. "I'm hoping the things I have to tell you tonight will build a little trust."

Her gaze pierced him, and he now understood what it felt like to be on the other side of a Border Patrol agent. She lifted her water glass to her lips. "Karen said you could hook up a video call so I can communicate with Tiana. She also said it shouldn't be done from my computer."

"Right. You can use mine."

"I wish there were another way, but thanks. I appreciate all you've done for us."

"No problem." He squirmed in his chair like an eight-year-old, and his leg had started to bother him. "Danika, I want to start all over by telling you a few things about me."

Her brows narrowed. "This conversation is a little post-mortem, don't you think?"

Ouch. "I'd like to think you might want to give me a second chance."

Before she had an opportunity to respond, the salads came, but his appetite had slid south. Danika toyed with her fork but stayed focused on him. Why ask for permission when he could simply tell it all?

"First of all, I was married for four years. Divorced. My fault. Renee claimed I loved my job better than I did her and left me for a banker. Truth is, if I'd given her a little more attention, she might not have had to look for it from another man."

"Is that supposed to garner sympathy?"

He tucked his frustration into his pocket and continued. "If it does, good for me. But my purpose is to lay out the truth. Renee and I had no children—her choice."

"I'm sorry about your failed marriage, and I can see you love children." She paused and glanced down at her hands in her lap, then back to him. "Your friendship has already been established with Toby. What I don't understand is Ed Jimenez. Your friends are pro-immigration and Border Patrol supervisors? Looks like different sides of the coin to me."

She picked up her fork, and he picked up his. Both salads were smothered in balsamic vinaigrette dressing. The vinegar tasted as sour as their conversation.

"Ed and I go to the same church and occasionally play golf. He has great kids, and his wife's a fabulous cook. I think I told you before that we're accountability partners."

She laid her fork across her plate. "When you'd been shot and he came to the hospital, why did you ask him if he wondered which one of us had been the target?"

Did this need to come so early in the conversation? "This is one of the things I wanted to tell you. Please let me finish with all of it before you comment." Forget the food. He needed to come clean. "Ed asked me to help out the Border Patrol and Homeland Security by keeping my eyes open for anything said at the hospital that might lead them to the rogue agent. He had information that led him to believe a rash of abused undocumented women may have something to do with the case. The request had nothing to do with patient confidentiality, but direct comments pertaining to the safety of our country and its people."

"Did he ask you to spy on me?"

Another hurdle to cross. "He mentioned that you were one of the agents being investigated. However, I told him you were dedicated to your job."

Her gaze softened—a fraction. "Thanks. Have you learned anything to help him find this agent?"

"Possibly. I've also encouraged the women who've been beaten to talk to the Border Patrol or the police—like Rita. But that's done little good."

She rubbed her palms together as though each word was carefully calculated. "I still don't understand why you questioned who the target was."

This time he hesitated to give himself time to form his words. "I saw a car drop off a young woman by the emergency call button. I tried to get the license plate number, but I only got the first three digits. I'm sure the driver saw me. Anyway, the authorities haven't been able to track it down, and they suspect the driver changed plates."

"Sounds like gang involvement."

"Possibly. Probably. I'm a doctor, not a detective. I do know I've treated too many women in the past couple of years who've been beaten, and they all refuse to name their abductor. None of them had drugs in their system, but they could have been forced to smuggle them."

Her shoulders relaxed slightly, which told him her anger had subsided. "Do Chief Jimenez or the McAllen police suspect a prostitution ring?"

"Most of the women were not sexually active. Rita was a different case and may not be connected at all." He leaned across the table. "The latest victim left the hospital on foot after I talked to her about going to the Border Patrol. I didn't think she had the strength to walk, but fear can do strange things to a person."

She nodded. "You and the chief talk quite a bit. Of course, if you're helping him and Homeland Security, it would warrant open discussion. Looks to me like I'm back at zero. The same end-of-the-road syndrome that has plagued me for two years. I still believe Toby's death is connected. Looks like the shooter could have been after either of us."

The server brought their entrées. He cautioned about the hot plates and shredded parmesan cheese on both dishes. Although the food smelled delicious, both of them seemed to have lost their appetites.

"I used to spend my time trying to find clues to solve Toby's murder, but now I'm spending time trying to stay alive. I keep wondering about Jacob." She took a deep breath. "All my doubts and fears and suspicions point to him. He's changed, and none for the good."

Alex realized he did have more to tell her than Sandra's deceit. "It can't be Jacob."

Danika unlocked her dark house after ten o'clock. She reset the alarm and checked the system to make sure no one had tampered with it. Silence greeted her like an evil omen. Emptiness, so much like her heart.

Alex's news about Jacob's receiving a finger sickened her. Pity ran through her veins for the man who obviously had emotional problems—and the roller coaster of events attacking him. Barbara must not know, or Danika would have been told. *A finger, a ghastly finger wearing the ring Jacob had given Nadine for her sixteenth birthday.*

Danika remembered the preparations that went into Nadine's celebration. It was a special birthday. Although the situation between father and daughter had started to deteriorate, he'd planned a grand family celebration and crowned it with the presentation of the ring. For a while Nadine and Jacob had gotten along as they bathed in the afterglow of the birthday gift. Then it all began to fall apart again, and both father and daughter slipped deeper into depression and farther apart.

But Jacob could have been blackmailed. . . .

Danika walked into the kitchen and turned on the lights for company. The finger sent to Jacob would not leave her alone, especially since Alex said he had treated a young woman with a missing ring finger.

Danika put aside the gruesome event for now and glanced about. The house looked as though Sandra were there, merely sleeping. But as she made her way into the living room, there were no toys or books. If ever she had motivation to find who was causing the agony in her life, it was now.

Perhaps a cup of chamomile tea would soothe her ragged nerves. As Alex suggested, she wanted to make a list of all those people close to her. As much as she didn't want to admit it, one of them was leaking information to the enemy. Back in the kitchen, she opened the cabinet door for a tea bag and saw a flashing light on the phone indicating a message. She pushed the Play button, anticipating a sales call.

"Hi, Danika. This is Lucy. I've been trying to reach Sandra all day. She isn't answering her cell phone, and I'm a little concerned. Would you have her call me? I don't care what time it is when she calls. I'll be up. Thanks."

Could it be that Sandra's cell phone was out of range? That didn't sound right. Maybe Karen lived in an area with poor coverage or Sandra's phone needed to be charged. Or maybe Sandra didn't want to be bothered with Lucy. That seemed the most believable. That way she didn't have to lie about where she was.

Danika picked up the phone and pressed in Lucy's number while grabbing a mug and filling it with water.

"Hi, Danika," Lucy sounded perky. "Is Sandra available?"

Danika sensed a catch in her stomach. "No, she's not."

"Is she okay?"

"I believe so. What's up?"

"I'm worried about her. The last time I talked to her, she seemed down."

Since when did Lucy care if Sandra was down? "I'm sorry.

I have no idea when you can get in contact with her. She and Tiana took a much-deserved vacation."

"Where are they?"

Danika took a breath. "I promised not to reveal where they were going."

"I'm her employer, and I have a right to know where she is."

This insistent side of Lucy irritated her. "And since she works for me as my maid and nanny, I have the right to protect her privacy. Did you receive my check for what she owes you to complete her contract?"

"I gave it to my attorney. Sandra did not have permission to take a vacation."

"Since I ultimately pay her salary, I can send her wherever I want. Good night, Lucy. I'll tell her you called."

CHAPTER 41

**Nothing ever becomes real till it is experienced—even a proverb
is no proverb to you till your life has illustrated it.**
JOHN KEATS

THURSDAY AFTERNOON Jacob walked up the sidewalk of his
home feeling more like a stranger than the owner of the two-
story home. Father Cornell had encouraged him to see his children, to form a new relationship with them. Armed with the
affirmations of "this is not your fault," "I love you," and "I'm
here for you," he rang the doorbell. The act angered him, especially when he made the mortgage payments and paid the utili-
ties, but he shook it off. Nothing, absolutely nothing, would
stand as a barrier between him and his children. For the next
couple of hours, he needed to undo the harm Barbara had done
to alienate him from all he treasured.

Jake Jr. answered the door. His son looked like he'd grown
a foot, and when had he shed the little boy look for that of a
twelve-year-old?

"Hi, Dad." Jake shifted from one foot to the other.

"Can I come in?"

Jake's face reddened and he widened the door. "Oh yeah.
Sorry. This just seems strange."

Jacob blew out a *humph*. "I agree, but we'll talk about our
relationship with your sisters." He walked into the living room,
the place for guests. Thank goodness Barbara was at work. The
familiar smells sent an ache through him. He wanted what he

used to call his own, but not at the cost of losing his dignity and respect.

Kaitlyn and Amber came bounding down the stairs. They stood at a distance on the landing—Kaitlyn twirling a long strand of dark hair around her finger, and Amber looking everywhere around the room except at him.

"How about a hug for your dear old dad?" Jacob opened his arms.

Jake gave him a limp hug, and the girls barely touched him. He didn't hear a single "I love you" or "we missed you." He started to ask them why the cold treatment, but they'd been deceived, and it was up to him to right the situation.

"So how's the first week of school?"

"Not fun," Jake said. "Already the work's hard, and my teacher likes to give homework."

"That's how you learn, Son. Stick with it, and one day you'll see the payoff." He smiled at Amber, who was still avoiding him. "How's second grade?"

"Third. It's okay. Better than sitting around here."

"Sounds like you were starting to get bored," Jacob said. "Now you'll have something to keep you busy."

Her face darkened, and her eyes held distrust. Jacob expected this; she'd always been a mama's girl. "And you, Kaitlyn?"

"All right," Kaitlyn said. "Feels weird being in high school without Nadine. I expected to see her."

"She'll come home soon." Jacob wanted to believe she'd soon be home instead of what he feared. . . .

"When?" Amber's voice rose to near hysteria. "She's dead. I'm sure of it. Why wouldn't she come home since you're gone?"

Silence kicked at the corners of the room. Jacob vowed not to lose his temper. He counted to ten like the priest had suggested and attempted to put himself in her shoes. "I'm sorry you feel this way. What can I do to make things better?"

"Find my sister and make Mommy stop crying."

"Amber," Kaitlyn whispered. She put her arms around her sister's trembling shoulders.

Amber's sobs were typical of her drama-queen personality, but Jacob could not come up with a single response. Father Cornell said the Holy Spirit would guide him through troubled times. So where was He now?

"I'm doing all I can to find Nadine," Jacob said. "I want you to know I love you, and just because Mommy and I aren't getting along doesn't mean I'm not your dad."

"Daddy," Kaitlyn began, "this is hard for us. I want to be respectful, but are we supposed to forget about all those months when you yelled and screamed at us until Nadine ran away?"

She'd turned against him too. What could he do or say to fix the situation? "Is this what your mother said?"

Kaitlyn's stare bored into his. Her young eyes revealed hurt and anguish, the very things he'd vowed to make sure she never saw. Had he caused this? "No, Daddy. Mom has never said anything bad about you."

"Could we start all over? Let's go get some ice cream and just talk."

"My friend at school says his parents are divorced. His dad comes over sometimes, and they do fun stuff. Then his dad goes home, and my friend is all alone again with his mom."

"I don't want any ice cream," Amber said through her sobs. "I want things the way they were a long time ago when we were happy." She shook off her sister's arm and raced up the stairs.

Kaitlyn watched her sister disappear. "Maybe this is enough of a visit for the first time."

"Yeah," Jake said. "Besides, I don't want ice cream either. I need to be here when Mom comes home. I don't like her to be alone without us. She needs us."

I don't like being alone either.

★ ★ ★

Alex's day had been nonstop patients, and it wasn't until after four that he had a break to grab a sandwich . . . and think. He'd realized the night before how badly he wanted to help Danika end the nightmare in her life. He had no clue who could have killed Toby or who was behind the threats made to her. Last night he'd lain in bed and thought about how strong the possibility was that it was he, not Danika, the shooter really wanted dead.

Or they could both be targets. Alex had a connection to Toby, Danika, the undocumented immigrants who sought medical care, and the Border Patrol. What was the missing link? Moreover, what was the motivation?

Danika had agreed to dinner on Friday night, and then they'd drive to his house to try the video call again. He hadn't been able to get the connection to work earlier and had to call customer support. Fit his mood. Maybe on Friday their food wouldn't go home in a carryout box, and Danika could communicate with Tiana. He still hadn't told her about Sandra, and obviously Sandra hadn't admitted her undocumented status.

They decided to compile a list of people who were close to them in their work and personal lives. Then they'd compare the lists to see which people were common to both of them for possible suspects.

Alex pounded his fist into his hand. Doctors weren't supposed to solve crimes. He didn't have the tools to read body language or discover motives. All he had was a deep affection for Danika and a perpetual prayer to see her safe.

CHAPTER 42

Time discovers truth.
LUCIUS ANNAEUS SENECA

DANIKA LOOKED FORWARD to seeing Alex tonight, actually anticipated seeing his face and hearing his voice. She'd abandoned—for now—her irritation over his not being up-front with her, especially with the knowledge of what he was doing for the Border Patrol. The rogue agent had to be found soon so everyone could focus on their own lives—or the evidence to convict Jacob. Agents double-checked everything they said and evaluated what everyone else said until the investigation was completed. Most of them believed the gangs working both sides of the border were involved, and others audibly accused Jacob of selling them out. The Mexican drug cartels were working hard to infiltrate the country, but the Border Patrol was working even harder to stop the smugglers with their thousands of pounds of illegal drugs—not to mention the weapons. Work went on as usual at the station. But the tension could be cut with a knife.

She waved at Alex across the restaurant. His smile caused a ripple to her insides. Tonight it was Tex-Mex, and the lively sounds of a Friday celebration usually put her in a good mood. He was trying hard to make up for the past, and she wanted to give him a chance, despite her tendency to mistrust.

"It's going to be hard to talk tonight with all the noise," he said once she was seated in a booth across from him. His crutches leaned against the booth behind him.

"Do you want to go somewhere else?" She wrestled with being alone with him all evening instead of during the video call to Tiana.

"Not really. The food is great, and we could postpone discussing our lists until later. I was thinking we could talk at the library before heading to my place."

Stunned at his unusual choice, as though they were kids and needed a quiet place to talk without the temptation of being alone, she shook her head. A good choice. "That will do. Not too late, though. Tiana will need to go to bed." She hesitated. "But it's Friday night, and I usually let my little night owl stay up later."

Conversation flowed much easier than on Wednesday. Alex had talked to his mother and signed with Tiana earlier in the evening, and Danika had talked to Sandra at the station. Jealousy seared her heart when Alex conveyed his conversation with her little girl, but soon she'd be able to do the same. Oh, how she missed Tiana.

On Sunday, Danika faced the dreaded double shift when she would finish at six in the evening, then return to the station at midnight to begin three months of working nights. More action took place between the hours of midnight and eight, and her body already took a beating as she adjusted to the work schedule.

Danika glanced at a young woman clearing a table beside them. It was her—the young woman who had attended Toby's funeral, the same woman who had run from her at the convenience store. Alex saw her too.

"Cira," Alex said when she looked his way.

He knew her? Danika's insides twisted, cementing what she'd always feared about the woman and Toby.

The woman smiled.

"*Cómo está Mickey?*" Alex asked.

"Está mejor."

"Taking him from the hospital was a foolish thing. He needed to be there until the pneumonia had cleared his lungs."

"I saw someone I knew, and I was afraid she might tell." Cira looked at Danika, and her face paled. "You . . . you are Toby's wife?"

Danika nodded while questions flooded her mind. She didn't want to frighten Cira again. "I'm sorry your little boy has been sick."

"*Gracias.* Your husband was a good man."

Danika refused to dwell on her statement. "What did he do for you?"

Cira whirled around and grabbed the plastic container of dirty dishes. She hurried through the restaurant to the kitchen.

Danika rushed to her feet and followed her, but an olive-skinned waiter stopped her at the door.

"Customers are not allowed in the kitchen."

Danika's pulse raced through her veins. "But I need to talk to one of the workers, a woman named Cira."

"Ma'am, she could lose her job. Come back when her shift is over."

"When will that be?"

He shrugged. "Midnight or so. It depends on when the kitchen is clean."

Danika wanted to cry. Every time she ventured close to the woman, she seemed to slip away. Tonight Danika would wait in the parking lot until Cira finished her shift, no matter how long it took.

She walked back to the table and slid into the booth. "They won't let me talk to her until after her shift."

Alex nodded. "We both know Cira," he said. "And she's not on my list."

"I didn't know her name to have her on mine. So her son is one of your patients?"

"Toby brought her to me after she'd been beaten. Her fee to get across the border had been partially paid by a woman who said she could work off the front money. I gathered the beatings were a common occurrence. The woman took advantage of illegal women and made them work much longer than the agreed period in payment for the debt. When Cira attempted to escape, the woman had her beaten by a man who also raped her. Later she learned she was pregnant, and I delivered her son."

Danika leaned against the seat, literally sick at what she had believed for the past two years about Toby. "I made a terrible mistake."

"What do you mean?"

"She came to the funeral with the baby. When I tried to speak with her, she ran away. I thought . . . I assumed Toby had been unfaithful, and the baby was his."

Alex's face filled with compassion. "Danika, one thing I can tell you about Toby is he loved you very much."

She desperately needed to hear those words. "Thank you. If only she hadn't been afraid of me, I could have learned the truth long ago."

Alex pushed his plate back. "Fear of being deported and of the woman who would most likely beat or kill her keeps Cira on the run. She left McAllen shortly after Toby's death, but her grandfather became ill and needed her here to take care of him."

"Life keeps getting more complicated. So you met up with her again when her little boy got sick?"

"Right. She doesn't trust any of the other doctors. Remember the night I brought Mom over and had to leave for an emergency?"

She'd been so angry with him and was glad he left. "What a

way to live." Their order hadn't arrived, and she'd once again lost her appetite.

"Did you and Sandra have a long talk before they left?"

"Oh yes. She wanted to assure this pitiful mom that her little girl would be in good hands. Sandra loves Tiana. I don't worry when she is with my little girl."

He frowned. "Want to get the food to go, and we can eat later at my house? I'd like to head to the library where it's quiet."

So he'd picked up on her loss of appetite. Alex read her pretty well. Scary, but true.

Alex suspected something so vile that the thought made him furious just considering it. Sandra and Cira had been friends. Both had tasted the repercussions of angering a greedy woman who worked them like animals. Sandra worked out her debt and went on to work at a reputable maid and nanny service, but Cira escaped. Perhaps Cira had seen Sandra at the funeral and that was why she ran. Sandra wouldn't tell Danika about the woman being undocumented, but she could turn Cira over to the same people who had beaten her.

He searched the library to ensure their privacy. An older couple sat at the next table over, and a teen worked at a computer.

Alex looked at his list and compared it to Danika's. They weren't getting anywhere. The only common names were Toby and Sandra and now Cira.

"You deserve to know something," he said.

Her eyes revealed the sadness. "This is not good, is it?"

"Nope." He stared into her face, wanting to spare her the hurt and betrayal. She deserved to know the truth about Sandra, and he should have told her on Wednesday night. This information had the potential to change the course of the investigation.

"I don't think you're the only person whom Cira ran from at the funeral. She and Sandra were friends."

Danika nodded, as though she understood. "Are you saying she was afraid Sandra would tell me about her illegal status?"

"Or Sandra would tell the people who were after her. What's important here is Sandra is undocumented."

She paled. "But the service said she's a citizen, and her papers are in their file." She rubbed her palms and said nothing for several moments. "I can't believe this. She deceived the service and me. My baby. This can't be happening. Is that why she acted strangely the first time she saw you? Were you two talking about her illegal status the other night?"

"What do you think? She admitted her false documents. I gave her an ultimatum to either tell you before Wednesday, or I would."

Danika buried her face in her hands. "She's been so loyal. She learned sign language for Tiana, and she loves her so very much. She's been a faithful friend."

Compassion filled him. Danika was indeed the strongest woman he'd ever known, but how much could she take? "I don't doubt her caring for both of you."

"She's in San Antonio with my daughter." She gasped and started to stand. "I need to talk to your mother now. Make sure Sandra doesn't leave the house with Tiana."

"My guess is she's banking on me not telling you." Alex grabbed his crutches. "Let's step outside to make the call. And use my phone."

They made their way to the lobby. As soon as Danika alerted Karen to Sandra's illegal status and returned Alex's cell phone, he began to voice the rest of his suspicions. "Would Sandra have access to any confidential information about the Border Patrol?"

The blood drained from Danika's face. "I don't bring any work information home or discuss what's going on. Some agents carry secure items back and forth in their backpacks, but not me."

"Good. I needed to ask."

"Alex, I have to report her status now. How does this look to the Border Patrol? I could lose my job." She pulled her cell from her purse. "I'm calling the chief." She punched in the number and met Alex's gaze. "How long were you planning to wait until you told me about this?"

"At first I wanted to give her the opportunity to tell you. Then I started to tell you on Wednesday. But when you connect her and Cira, it's possible there's much more at stake."

Before Danika could answer, she had Chief Jimenez on the phone.

"I've just discovered my nanny has false documentation or immigration papers." She studied Alex's face. One more time their relationship was on the line, and he had no excuse for not telling her about Sandra except to give the illegal an opportunity to be honest.

"She works for me through a large, reputable service. I was told the papers are on file there," Danika continued. "Right, she's in San Antonio with Tiana at Alex's mother's home." She moistened her lips. "Alex suspected it and confronted her. He recognized her from the hospital." Danika closed her eyes. "Yes, sir. We'll talk in the morning."

She dropped the phone back into her purse. "What else are you thinking of keeping from me?" Fury burned from her eyes.

No holding back now. "I'm wondering if Sandra has contact with Jacob."

"Sure." Danika crossed her arms over her chest. Misery had left its mark in the tiny lines fanning from her eyes. "She accompanies me to Jacob and Barbara's—at least we used to. She's like family." Danika hesitated. "Jacob used to bring sensor location sheets home in his backpack."

"What if Jacob was giving Sandra the sensor locations? What if she gave or sold the information to those transporting undocumented immigrants?"

"If that's true, then Jacob most likely knows who killed Toby and who wants me dead. No wonder Sandra doesn't like her boss. She was afraid the service would learn about her falsified papers."

"Where's Jacob living?"

"I have no idea. Barbara said he refused to tell her. I also wonder if a gang has Nadine and he's being blackmailed."

"He certainly isn't able to obtain sensor locations in his current situation. Are you up to another call to Ed and a trip to the police station?"

CHAPTER 43

The strongest of all warriors are these two—Time and Patience.
LEO TOLSTOY

DANIKA BREATHED a little easier after she and Alex talked again to Chief Jimenez. The police issued separate warrants for Jacob and Sandra, and the chief expressed a possible end to all the chaos. A call to Karen assured Danika that Tiana was asleep and would not see Sandra's arrest. At last, Danika would have some answers about the mystery of Toby's death and the rogue agent. *Jacob and Sandra.* Who ever would have thought the veteran agent, whose file was once laden with commendations, had turned rogue—and possibly killed his own brother? And Sandra . . . She'd lied not only to Danika but also to Lucy. First thing in the morning Lucy had to be notified. So much now made sense.

Surely the questioning would clear up the discrepancies about Jacob. But Sandra would be sent back across the border unless she was detained for criminal activity.

The moment Danika and Alex walked out of the police department headquarters, the night's revelations slammed against her heart. She shivered despite the sultry night, her thoughts sinking to depths she wanted to leave alone.

"Why don't we sit in my truck and talk through this?" Danika's car sat beside Alex's truck, and he must have sensed her state of mind.

"I didn't get to talk with Tiana. She will think her mommy has deserted her."

"We'll spend hours on the computer tomorrow to make up for it. I don't want you to go home with all this junk on your mind."

Danika sighed. "It's late, Alex. Are you sure I won't be dipping into your beauty rest?"

"Not at all. The beauty fairy gave up on me about ten years ago." He limped toward their cars.

"Have you considered the crutch Olympics? You move at a good clip."

"It might help pass the time while I'm healing for the rodeo."

She laughed, the first time in a long time. Then she felt guilty for it.

Once they were inside his truck, the bantering from a few minutes before vanished. The weight of tonight hit her again.

"Talk to me," he said. "I have a great ear."

Where did she begin when two people she cared for could be involved with deceit and possibly murder? And Tiana was so attached to Sandra. "As much as I want Toby's murder solved and the killer brought to justice, the thought of Jacob's involvement is hard—real hard. I never had a brother, and Jacob filled the role. Before Toby's death, we had wonderful family times together. He was a great husband and dad. And the best agent— a bit of a maverick in his methods and highly respected."

Memories about Jacob's legendary days rolled through her mind. "He used to hide in the brush at night with nothing but a flashlight, his assigned weapon, and a can of mosquito repellent in order to catch illegals floating across on inner tubes. He was happy then, no scowls and fits of temper."

"Did he and Toby grow up in this area?"

"Arizona. They lived in a small border town. When it seemed like their area filled with illegals overnight, their dad grew wary. He called it 'like bindweed.'"

"You mean the weeds that pop up overnight?"

"Exactly. And it's difficult to get rid of. If you take a hoe to them, it seems to stimulate more growth."

"Great analogy."

"Right. When Papa Morales saw a trailer was rented to a single man and within a week fifteen men between the ages of seventeen and thirty were living there, he packed up his family and moved to McAllen. Jacob joined the Border Patrol, and Toby became a teacher and track coach.

"Then Toby died, and you know the rest." She looked at Alex. This was all wrong. She knew Jacob, the real Jacob. "I'm having a difficult time believing Jacob could have killed Toby or had a hand in it. And I've seen a lot of bad blood between families when drugs are involved. Oh, I know I wanted to think he could lead us to solid answers earlier this evening, but he loved his brother. The arguments they had never lasted long. Certainly nothing that would have caused Jacob to think murderous thoughts."

"Are you thinking he may have turned rogue after his brother died?"

Did she really want to consider Jacob had turned against the Border Patrol? "That makes more sense than his direct involvement before Toby's death. He changed so much during the last two years. I watched his wife try to help him, but he refused to admit he was the source of any problems, always blaming her for his unhappiness." She shook her head. "Unless he was being threatened."

"That makes more sense."

"The thought of Sandra living in my home and caring for my daughter is a little overwhelming. Tiana loves Sandra just as I do. Toby betrayed me with his pro-immigration activities, and Sandra has done the same thing. I feel stupid, weak, duped, and incredibly angry."

Alex reached across the truck and took her hand. The firm

grasp gave her silent strength, and she needed something tangible to hold on to. "She fooled the maid and nanny service too," he said.

"But my job is detecting illegal immigrants. Now I fear what the chief will say—or if I will be given disciplinary action. I know the business Sandra worked for is liable for her illegal status, but . . . this seems to be a nightmare with no end."

"When I think of the shots fired at us and the threatening phone call made to you, I realize there is something bigger going on. But the whys and hows are still out there."

The finger . . . the ghastly finger. Danika's mind refused to shut down. "Hear me out on this. What if Sandra's illegal status has nothing to do with Toby's killer or the rogue agent? What if Jacob is being blackmailed by someone responsible for Nadine's disappearance? and that someone also killed Toby and is after you and me?"

"Why wait two years? If that's the case, what did Toby, you, and Jacob know or have that would cause someone to come after you?"

"I only wish I knew."

CHAPTER 44

Deeds, and not fine speeches, are the proof of love.
SPANISH PROVERB

DANGER HAD NEVER been a pothole that Alex deliberately drove over, yet a nagging thought persisted. If he went to the grass roots of the problem surrounding Danika, someone there might tell him what he needed to know. Undocumented immigrants feared the Border Patrol and any authoritative figures who represented deportation, but a doctor symbolized healing and compassion. At least that's what Alex chose to believe. Toby had indicated where a few safe houses were located, but that was over two years ago. Alex decided to pay one of them a visit and hope it was filled with people.

Late in the afternoon, after placing two cases of water on the bed of his truck—rather awkwardly while balancing on crutches—and grabbing the same load of supplies that he'd used for the free vaccinations at the elementary school, Alex drove to a spot near Hidalgo. He doubted if Danika and Ed would approve of his methods, but he was fresh out of ideas. This was what Toby used to do, and his friend had been an activist. The thought persisted, and Alex questioned if his means of helping Danika were also a way to alienate her.

Who knows. In one breath he felt good about what he was doing, and in the next guilt assaulted him for using the needs of these poor people to gather information. Never mind how Danika and Ed might react.

★ ★ ★

Thirty minutes later, he pulled into the gravel driveway of a modest frame home. Nothing about it appeared out of the ordinary. No broken windows, and the trim had been freshly painted. A scraggly dog lumbered down from the front porch. It stretched and wagged his tail. Could this be the right place?

Alex grabbed his keys and straightened his white lab jacket. Instead of his heart thumping like a scared rabbit, he sensed the same excitement as he always felt in the rodeo ring. He refused to take the time to consider the difference between getting thrown from a bronc and getting shot—again. His limp served as a reminder.

The dog sniffed him and continued to wag its tail. Alex patted its head. Hopefully the reception inside would be as friendly. He scanned the area and saw no one. Two years ago, Toby claimed this safe house did the best job because of its neat and clean appearance.

Once on the porch, he rang the doorbell. Not a sound, and the closed blinds of the windows revealed nothing. He knocked. The same reception.

"My name is Dr. Alex Price from the McAllen Medical Center. I was told that someone here needed a doctor. I'm by myself with a few medical supplies. And I have a couple of cases of water on the truck bed."

He waited and bent to pat the dog again, his body language and every gesture aimed at setting an observer at ease.

"All right," Alex continued. "I imagine you are nervous and maybe a bit fearful of me. But I have water, and I assure you I'm a doctor, and if you need medical assistance, my services are free. If anyone needs a hospital, the McAllen Medical Center treats everyone without question."

Frustrated with the lack of response, he turned to leave. The moment his boot hit the well-worn path to the driveway, the door squeaked open, and Alex viewed a round-faced man who looked to be in his fifties.

"Sir, we could use the water."

Alex smiled. No doubt they had a long journey ahead. "I'll bring it right up."

"We have a woman who cut her leg."

If she had injured her leg crossing the river, infection had most likely set in. The river was a wasteland of disease. "I'll take a look at it."

Alex walked to his truck with optimism in his footsteps. He opened the truck gate and scooted out the box of first aid supplies. Balancing it atop the case of water, he lifted both from the truck bed, a crazy balancing act that might cause him to fall. A pinpoint of guilt niggled his insides again for what he was about to do. Most likely these were hardworking people, frightened and waiting to move on to a safer destination.

Fifteen men, women, and children gathered together in clumps of twos and threes in the living room and kitchen of the house. The odors of river-bathed bodies mingled with sweat and desperation and yanked at his senses. If any of them had drugs, they were well concealed.

Alex knelt at the side of a pretty young woman seated on a broken and slashed sofa. Her jean leg had been cut, exposing a three-inch gash. "How did you cut your leg?"

She wiped at the blood dripping down to her mud-soaked tennis shoe. "Something in the river."

"I see. I'm going to clean it up, apply medicine to stop the infection, and then bandage it."

She nodded. "*Gracias*. I can't let it slow me down."

"I understand." He worked quickly, weighing each question and comment that entered his head. The others watched, no doubt curious and welcoming a diversion from the day. "Do you have food here?"

"Soup and crackers," a man beside him said. "We're lucky."

"That you are. Do you have jobs waiting for you?"

A couple of men grunted, and a woman replied positively. A young woman joined them from the kitchen. She looked to be about fifteen. "I have a job waiting for me in McAllen."

Alex searched through the bandages for the correct size. "I know a couple of women who had part of the cost paid to get here by someone who allowed them to work off the money owed."

"That's where I'm going," she said. "I'll work off the rest of my fee; then I can get my own job."

"I wonder if it's the same person." Alex crumpled the paper that encased the bandage.

"I don't know her name, but she'll have someone pick me up later this afternoon."

This could be the real thing. Alex stood from the injured woman's leg. "Anyone else need to see me?"

No one answered. More patients would have helped him cement more information from the young woman destined to work in McAllen. He'd have to conceal his truck down the road until she was picked up.

Three hours passed with mosquitoes swarming around him, despite the insect repellent. Alex hid around a bend in the road, armed with a fishing pole and binoculars. His white jacket had been tossed onto the seat, leaving him wearing a T-shirt and jeans. What a ridiculous idea. To think he'd taken off this afternoon from the hospital to attempt to find out where the undocumented young women were being held. This might not be the same person, but the young woman did refer to a "she."

He was about to give up when he took another look at the safe house. A truck slowed and pulled into the driveway. A man of about twenty-five wearing a baseball cap got out and entered the house, but all Alex could see in his binoculars was a side view. Less than five minutes later, the man and the young woman who had indicated she had a job in McAllen climbed into the truck and sped away.

Alex hurried back to his vehicle, adrenaline pumping. Finally he had an opportunity to help Danika and all of those poor, abused women.

"Sir, what are you doing out here?" A Border Patrol agent leaned against Alex's truck.

"What were you thinking?" Ed had looked happier after Alex had beaten him on the golf course.

"I wanted to help Danika."

"By getting yourself killed?"

"I was about to find a few answers until your agent interrupted me."

"Had it occurred to you that he could have followed the truck?"

Alex didn't want to admit he hadn't thought of it. "How rich. Do you think the driver would have taken the girl to where he was going with the Border Patrol on his rear?"

"Agents are trained to pursue illegals and to handle the situation in an appropriate manner."

"None of your men could have gained the confidence of those people to find out where the women are being held."

"How did you know where to look?"

Alex crossed his arms over his chest.

"Are you protecting a rogue?"

A surge of anger lit a fire in Alex's veins. He stood, his fists clenched and his nerves singed. "I'm done here." He turned to the door.

"Wait a minute—"

Alex spun around. "You wait a minute. You're so determined to find this agent that you're destroying an agent who'd give her life for the cause. Jacob is the rogue, remember? Someone is out to kill Danika. Are you an idiot? How could she be trading secrets?"

"Sounds a bit dramatic to me."

"Maybe so. But I'd rather be a little over-the-top than attend a funeral."

CHAPTER 45

**A million things can happen which are not the will of God
. . . [but] nothing that is allowed to happen has within
itself the power finally and ultimately to defeat God.**
LESLIE D. WEATHERHEAD

DANIKA HAD WAITED long enough to call Lucy and tell her
the truth about Sandra. She also owed Lucy an apology. For two
years she'd believed Sandra disliked Lucy because the owner of
McAllen's largest maid and nanny service was a difficult person
to work for. But Danika must have been mistaken. Sandra's illegal documentation papers explained why she kept her distance
from Lucy. And befriended Danika. Sandra had given a grand
performance. The treachery cut deep, and Danika wanted to
believe on some level it hadn't all been a lie.

Sandra had been picked up for questioning, which was also
her one-way ticket out of the country. Danika asked the chief for
the opportunity to speak with her and hoped he would honor
her request. A desperate yearning for answers plagued her about
why Sandra had chosen to deceive her. Was it for a better way
of life—or did she have information not only about who was
behind the tragedies in the Morales households but also about
the rogue BP agent? The eerie sensation caused Danika to wonder if a demon hid in the shadows of her life.

She snatched up the landline in her kitchen and pressed in Lucy's number. One ring. Two rings . . .

"Danika. What can I do for you?"

She dragged her tongue across dry lips. "I have some bad news for you."

"What? Has something happened to Barbara? Has Nadine been found?"

"Nothing like that. It's Sandra. She's illegal. The papers you have on file are false. I'm not even sure Sandra Rodriguez is her real name."

Silence met Danika on the other end.

"Lucy?"

"I'm here. Just in shock, I guess. I'll be audited, but then I have nothing to hide."

"Of course. She's been taken into custody."

"Here in McAllen?"

"Soon. I plan to talk to her. She may even know something about Toby's death."

"Danika, you deserve an explanation for all the lies. She deceived us both."

"I understand that desperate people will do anything to protect themselves." Danika sighed. "I owe you an apology for all the times I stood up for her."

"Don't give it another thought. I'm simply glad we both now have the truth. Is your little girl okay?"

How could Danika know for sure? "Yes, she's fine."

"I'll be looking for someone to take Sandra's place. It will be hard, though."

"Probably impossible. Let's talk in a couple of days. Good night." She hung up the phone and walked into her bedroom. The tears came, gently at first, then harder as the enormity of Sandra's betrayal washed over her.

★ ★ ★

Danika had managed two-and-a-half hours' sleep before heading back to the station for the night shift. Yawning, she took another gulp of hot coffee and sputtered it onto the steering wheel and her jeans. At least the newly formed blisters in her mouth would help keep her awake tonight.

She glanced into the rearview mirror. Truck headlights bored into her vision. She despised tailgaters. They were poster children for accidents and a nightmare for insurance adjusters. But apprehension slithered from her fingertips to her toes. Was she being followed?

She swerved into the left lane and turned at the next stop sign. The truck barely stopped at the intersection and followed close behind. If night had not settled around her, she'd have tapped her brakes.

A half mile down, she swung a left and sped onto the expressway. The truck trailed behind her.

Danika's mind switched to control mode, and she pressed the gas pedal to the floor. Let the jerk behind her tail her right up to the security fence of McAllen's station.

The truck inched closer, and she pushed aside the thought of a bullet shattering the rear window.

Seventy-five miles an hour. Eighty. Eighty-five.

The truck did not ease up.

Gunfire ripped into the mirror on the driver's side, and she instinctively sped ahead. No time to call for help.

A tire popped with the distinct sound of a .45-caliber handgun. Another tire blew, swinging the car out of control. It leaned to the right, and the sound of it skidding down the road roared in her ears. The truck tipped, then flipped to the right. The air bag exploded into her chest just before the car rolled again, sending her into a world of darkness.

★ ★ ★

Alex was jarred from the depths of his dream world. *The phone.* With the next ring from his cell phone came the acknowledgment of a serious situation at the hospital. He snatched it up.

"Alex, this is Ed."

Their last conversation had been like two enemies instead of two friends. "What's going on?"

"There's been an accident."

"Who?"

"Danika. Someone blew out her tires while she was on her way to the station."

His heart shifted into overdrive, and he threw back the sheet covering him, momentarily forgetting his wounded leg until his foot touched the floor. "How bad?"

"Not good. They've resuscitated her twice. She's headed into surgery. Internal injuries. Regional Hospital."

Alex reached for his jeans. "Do you know the doctor's name?"

"No. I'm real sorry."

Alex knew Ed's apology was not all about Danika's condition but included their previous argument. "I'm on my way."

"I'm here for you, bud. If you have any problem getting to the surgery wing, have them call me. I have guards posted. No one is to find out about this."

Alex rushed, grabbing the rest of his clothes and fumbling for his keys, dropping them and groping to find them. *Help her.* His leg throbbed, but he didn't have time or the inclination to swallow a couple of Tylenol. Repeatedly he prayed for God to give Danika the breath of life.

CHAPTER 46

I'll come to thee by moonlight, though hell should bar the way.
ALFRED NOYES

ALEX FOCUSED on the monitor above Danika's head. *Keep beating. Stay strong.* As if by his staring at the numbers and EKG lines, they would continue to read normal. Her blood pressure was stable. But he knew how quickly that could plummet. Her body's oxygen saturation was good. Yet the question that pounded against his brain was whether Danika could hold on to life once the automatic supports were gone. Prayer permeated every breath—even to the point of thinking he could bargain with God for her life.

The problem twisting his heart was his knowledge of what the sights and sounds of the monitors meant. For once he wished he weren't a doctor. He didn't want to know what the equipment meant or how closely she teetered toward death.

Danika lay on a precipice, and only the great Healer could pull her back from the edge.

"How does it all look to you?" Ed whispered, as though his voice would disturb her.

Alex hesitated. "I'll feel better when she wakes up. However, she's in a medically induced coma for the next forty-eight to sixty hours."

"You hadn't told me how much she meant to you. But I should have guessed."

Alex brushed a curl from Danika's forehead. Her left eye looked like a black hole. "I didn't really understand until now. It hasn't been long. The chemistry's there for me anyway." *No, it's more. So much more.*

"That's the way I felt about Susie. No logic as to why she was the one for me. Scared me to death. I'd been more in control as a sniper for the Marines. Truth was I'd have rather faced two dozen armed illegals hoisting cocaine. By the way, I called our pastor, and he's got a whole team of prayer warriors doing their thing. All he knows is that someone I care about is critically ill."

"Thanks. Any lead on who did this?"

Ed pointed to the hallway, where two policeman stood guard. "That should answer your question. All we know is a .45 was used to blow out the tires."

Could be any number of handguns. The thought sickened Alex. How long before the experts could identify the weapon? "Who is this guy?"

"If we could figure out why someone wants her dead, then we could better nail him." Ed walked to the window and stared out at the sunlit day, contrary to the turmoil in all of them. "The police are working on it, but who knows?"

"She and I have talked about the people she knows and a possible tie to Toby's death. We've even debated whether or not the person is also after me. Did Sandra give you any information?"

Ed's pinched face revealed his disgust. "She says she'll talk to Danika but no one else. I think she has critical evidence, but I imagine she wants a plea bargain."

Alex had mixed feelings about it, but it wasn't up to him. "Can you oblige her?"

"Think about it. If she knows who murdered Toby and who is trying to kill Danika, do you want her living legally in the States? The best she can hope for is not to be charged as an accomplice."

They both looked at Danika's pale face. Alex hoped she recovered soon to talk to Sandra and end this nightmare. He needed to call his mother. Not that Tiana should be told about Danika's accident. It was Alex's prayer the child would not have to be told about any of the tragedy stalking her family. Mom had found someone through her church to sign for Tiana, and Mom was learning too. But who wanted the responsibility of telling a child she no longer had a mother?

It would be me.

He hated what had happened to Danika, and the thought of Sandra being a part of it made him furious.

Sandra's body refused to respond to her brain's commands. She'd heard lies. Nothing but lies to trick her. The words forming in her mind suspended like a church bell with no clapper. The hands and fingers that she'd exercised faithfully in communicating with Tiana lay in her lap like weights. Dr. Alex Price had sold her out.

She studied the face of the ICE officer. *U.S. Immigration and Customs Enforcement.* Their Web site boasted of the over ten thousand gang members arrested throughout the country. One could click on the latest business shut down for employing undocumented immigrants or the number of illegals arrested in California or someone involved in child exploitation and human trafficking. Sandra had made it her business to educate herself about everything affecting her life. But what good did her accumulation of knowledge do her now? She'd lived with fear of so many things, and now life could not get worse.

She hadn't uttered a word to the police, and she wouldn't. Why did this grim-faced man with his impressive uniform and ICE insignia think he could accomplish any more?

"You stated to the police that you would only speak to Border Patrol Agent Danika Morales. But as I said previously, she's been critically injured in a tragic accident—an accident in which some-one blew out the tires of her vehicle." The ceiling light shining on his bald head cast a yellowish hue, as though he were the one under interrogation. Whether it was hysteria or panic, she nearly laughed. The only difference between him and a gang member was the colors.

What a clever ploy to draw out a confession. The official had lied to her about an accident. Danika knew how to take care of herself. The good doctor should be the one facing death. He'd told Danika about her illegal status and deserved the worst punishment. To think he called himself a friend—a healer—to those who were in need. He'd taken that information and thrown it in her face.

After several deep breaths, she willed the stone in her throat to be crushed into digestible pebbles so she could plan her way out of this mess. "I don't believe you. My friend Danika is a trained Border Patrol agent."

His folded hands didn't budge. "Miss Rodriguez, I assure you, Agent Morales is in critical condition. The person who tried to kill her needs to be stopped before others are hurt or killed. We need your information."

For a few seconds, he had nearly convinced her. "Bring me the newspaper report."

Mr. ICE pressed his lips together. "The media has been denied access to the accident's details. Our discussion has to remain pri-vate. Per the Border Patrol."

"Then you won't hear anything from me." She rubbed the chill bumps on her arms. Lucy wouldn't try to hurt Danika without the information she wanted. Would she?

Danika floated in a delicious sleep. High above the world in a weightless freedom, she willed the sensation to fill her and carry her on to a mass of light beckoning to her in the distance. In a sea of smiling faces and waving hands, she heard her name, a musical sound that soothed and lulled her simultaneously.

"Join us," the voices harmonized.

She wanted so much to reach out and grasp the beauty, the warmth of love embodying the liberation of senses. "Yes," she breathed, or was it merely a thought?

"Not yet," came from all directions—not a sound as much as a feeling, an embrace. "I'm not finished with you."

A loud whoosh sucked her into a vacuum that forfeited time and matter. Again she heard her name, but she recognized the voice. Oh, the pain. She moaned. What happened to the world she'd left behind?

"Danika, if you can hear me, lift your hand." The voice calling to her was Alex's.

She could do this; she concentrated on raising her hand, but all she managed was to wiggle her fingers.

"Good. Can you open your eyes?"

They were glued shut. She was certain.

"Keep trying."

She forced her lids to flutter. At last, blurred images appeared; a mass of color and sound etched in her mind. It was getting easier. There, she could focus. Her breath came in a short gasp.

"Good morning, beautiful," Alex said.

Despite the pain, she forced a smile. "I've felt better."

"I imagine you have."

"What day is this?"

"Wednesday."

Her day off. How appropriate. Maybe Alex could hook up the video feed so she could talk to Tiana again. Then she remembered the accident.

Someone had tried to kill her.

CHAPTER 47

You gain strength, courage, and confidence by every experience in which you really stop to look fear in the face. You are able to say to yourself, "I lived through this horror. I can take the next thing that comes along."
ELEANOR ROOSEVELT

"Do you have any idea who did this to you?" Chief Jimenez said.

Danika allowed the ice chip to dissolve on her tongue. In the last half hour, the chief had revealed a compassionate side that she'd rarely seen. Oh, he always seemed sweet to his wife and kids, but in his capacity of chief patrol agent, he was all business. Perhaps she'd be the same in his role.

"I never saw a face. It was a truck—a Ford. I could tell by the grille." Speaking sapped her energy, and she paused to drink in precious oxygen.

"I'm sorry," he said. "But I want this guy stopped."

"I . . . I want to help." She determined not to fade away into the sleep tugging at her eyelids. "Can't remember anything but the bullets hitting the tires."

"Well, you beat the odds last Sunday night."

She lifted a brow.

"You flipped your car twice."

She shook her head. "Call me a tiger cat."

Alex chuckled. "Glad to hear you haven't lost your sense of humor." His voice soothed her. Later she'd thank him.

"Some . . . sometimes I think we're no closer to ending this than the day Toby died."

The chief cleared his throat. She smiled despite the pain in her abdomen. That was his "clearing the room for a speech" prep. "The police received a call from an unidentified teen from Nadine Morales's school who believed he saw her in a Ford truck in the southeast part of town. The windows were tinted, so I'm not sure if he could have made a positive identification."

That meant Nadine could be alive. Something despicable crept through Danika's thoughts. "Are you thinking if she's alive—"

"Save your strength," Jimenez said. "My guess is you're wondering if she's playing a part in all this."

She nodded. If true, the knowledge would kill Jacob and Barbara.

"Ed, is this enough for now?" Alex said. "Danika needs her rest."

"Sure." Jimenez leaned over the bed. "We'll be in touch. Do what the doctor says. I need you on the line. No one knows about this, and we've got to keep it that way." He picked up a copy of the McAllen *Monitor*.

"Leave it," she said.

"Why do you want the paper? Get some rest like Alex suggested."

"Wrong." She closed her eyes. "I might be stitched up like a kid's wounded teddy bear, but I'm smart enough to see you're keeping the media from me." Her last words stole her breath. She forced herself to raise an IV-loaded arm and open her eyes. "I want to know what's going on."

Jimenez exchanged a glance with Alex.

She understood the silent communication. "You don't . . . need Alex's permission. I'll . . . see this to the end."

He laid the paper at the foot of her bed and jammed his hands into his pants pockets. "The Border Patrol doesn't hand out Purple Hearts."

"Yeah, but . . . it doesn't stop me from carrying the flag."

Once Chief Jimenez left, Danika turned her attention to Alex. He should be tending to his own patients at the medical center, not babysitting her. Two guards stood outside her door. Obviously someone wanted her alive—and someone wanted her dead.

Alex lifted the cup of ice chips to her lips. The richest delicacy to the human palate. They melted and soothed her parched throat. Once she finished, he pulled a chair closer to her bed.

"Read it to me," she whispered.

"Why?" He reached for her hand, and she did not resist.

"I can't do anything here but think. If I know what's happening—" An explosion of pain rippled from her head to her abdomen. "Do I have a head injury?"

"A concussion. As Ed said, you are extremely lucky. But you need to sleep and regain your strength. How can I hook up the video feed with you here?"

Poor Tiana. She blinked. Her precious baby didn't have her mommy or Sandra. Danika had to get better soon. "Has Tiana been told anything?"

He kissed her hand, and she didn't mind. "Mom has found a woman in her church to sign. Tiana believes you're sick. She knows you have to rest and will talk to her as soon as you're feeling better."

Not too far from the truth. "Thank you." She gave in to the sandlike sensation and closed her eyes. "I'll rest after you read to me."

His sigh seemed to come from his toes. The paper crinkled and snapped open. "Guess it won't do me any good to read the *Monitor*'s world news. Or the funnies. At least the authorities were successful in keeping the accident from the media. Here

DiANN MILLS

goes. 'Border Patrol Suspects Rogue Agent in McAllen. Border Patrol and Homeland Security are joining forces to find the agent who's trading policies and procedures with those threatening U.S. borders. One agent has been dismissed, but no charges have been filed. . . .'"

Danika groaned, but not from pain. At least Jacob's name had not been mentioned. But would evidence surface and he be charged? For the first time, she wondered if Nadine had the key to unlock it all.

CHAPTER 48

Only the brave know how to forgive.
LAURENCE STERNE

JACOB STOOD in the lobby of the four-story office building where Barbara worked. He stared out the glass wall to an impressive landscape of flowering bushes and trees. A long time ago, his lawn had looked manicured. But then, so did his life. With sawdust beneath his fingernails, caking his T-shirt, and splattering his jeans, he looked like a down-on-his-luck blue-collar worker. Most of that description fit.

A young man in dress slacks and a white shirt stared at him as he walked by. Illegal immigration had become such a problem that every Hispanic American was viewed with a generous share of doubt.

The BP had actually done him a favor. He'd grown cynical and bitter toward the illegals instead of respecting them as human beings. His attitude hadn't improved, but at least he wasn't actively abusing anyone. The other day, he waited in line at the grocery to pay for bread and lunch meat while an illegal in front of him unloaded two carts of groceries and paid for them with food stamps. He'd escorted the woman across the bridge a couple of years ago, and now she was eating his tax dollars.

Jacob needed to see Barbara before he lost his nerve. Three hours ago, Father Cornell had called a face-to-face with her imminent—a spiritual prescription for healing.

"I'm beginning to wonder if I'm the one to blame for what

has happened to my family." Jacob had spent the past few days trying to figure out what kind of a man he'd become. Most of his findings were loathsome.

"Why's that?" The priest walked with him down the church hallway to his private office. He opened the door and gestured Jacob inside.

Jacob wrestled with his thoughts and the right words to communicate them. Over the weekend, he'd begun to remember what life was like before Toby died. Jacob had loved life and his family. God was a priority, and he valued his career as a Border Patrol agent. With those memories came the realization he wanted back what he'd lost.

"I want to be the man I used to be. Problem is I don't think I'd recognize him if I met him on the street."

"The first step is to confess your sin and ask for forgiveness."

"Until yesterday, I didn't think I had any." Jacob slumped into a chair. "But everything's gone. All the things I once felt were important. And I'm beginning to wonder if it's my fault."

"Jacob, what do you want the most?"

"My family." His voice trembled.

Father Cornell sighed. "Jacob, as long as your desires are about what pleases you, your heart will ache for all that is missing in your life."

Jacob sensed the angst rising in him, souring any hope for a fulfilled life. "Are you saying it's wrong to want my wife and children? And what about Nadine? Do you have any idea what it's like knowing you may never see your daughter again? She might be dead."

"You're right. I have no clue about what you feel. But God does. His heart breaks every time we sin and deny Him. He wants us back, just like you want Nadine safe and your family beside you. Until you want your relationship with God restored, life is going to be a living hell."

Jacob hated what the priest was saying. It burned in a deep part of him where he couldn't reach. He wanted out of his tragedy, but he wanted someone else to carry the blame. "I can't go on like this. Most days I have to fight to keep from putting a gun to my head." He stood and walked across Father Cornell's office. "I even tried and didn't have the guts to pull the trigger."

"There's only one answer. Are you man enough to reclaim your relationship with God?"

Jacob sensed the despair spreading through his heart. "I have no choice."

Father Cornell's words still echoed across Jacob's mind. He wrung his damp hands and climbed the marble steps to the second floor of Barbara's office—to his wife—and, if it wasn't too late, to his family.

With fear of rejection nipping at his heels, he opened the door. Barbara looked pale, her eyes hollow, and she'd lost too much weight. Her frame had always been small, bouncing back into a tiny shape after the birth of each child. But she looked weary. Jacob had caused her misery, and if Father Cornell was right, he had to take the first step in reconciliation.

"Barbara," he heard his shaky voice say. His anger had fled like a thief in the night. Tenderness replaced the guilt and bitterness he once felt, and a sincere desire to make things right filled him.

Her brown eyes lifted, at first in surprise and then in sadness.

"Can we talk?" Should he have apologized first? "I mean, before you throw me out of here, can I have a minute?"

"Why?" Her lips quivered.

"Because I made horrible mistakes. I hurt you and our children. Because of me, Nadine is lost and alone somewhere. I've begged God to forgive me, and now I'm asking you. I'm begging you to forgive me. I . . . I don't want to think of another day without you."

★ ★ ★

Danika sensed her body was healing. Medication managed the pain and forced her into many sleeping hours. However, she hated to numb her body and brain. She denied the pain relievers until agony forced her to use the pump attached to her hand. Even going to the bathroom required assistance from the nurses' station.

She desperately needed to get back to work. The nightmare stalking her weeks ago had generated intense anger in her, and she wanted the shooter found. The idea of Jacob betraying the Border Patrol and having a hand in Toby's demise continued to punctuate her waking and sleeping thoughts. Many dreadful things had happened to Jacob too, but did he cause it all? Nadine's disappearance was the most critical. Could she be working against her own family, or was this a tragedy that Jacob caused by mixing with the wrong people? Nadine had not been a rebellious teenager until after Toby's death, and nothing in her past indicated she would willingly embrace breaking the law.

Danika's thoughts went full circle. She had no answers to any of it. All she could do was stare at the ceiling of the hospital room and weigh the possibilities. Someone wanted Jacob and Danika destroyed. But why? What had the two of them done to warrant the repeated attacks? The Border Patrol and Homeland Security believed a disgruntled agent was responsible. But Danika didn't think so. She sensed the answers were so obvious that she'd ignored the clues. Sandra had information, or she wouldn't have refused to talk to anyone but Danika. She had to get out of the hospital and back on track.

Noting it was time for the noon news, she clicked on the TV. She watched an interview with a local high school football coach and another news piece about senior citizens volunteering at schools in a mentoring program for at-risk elementary students.

"Here is the latest on the fire at the home of a local resident. Barbara Morales woke at two this morning to the sound of an explosion in her garage. . . ."

Danika gasped and increased the volume. Surely she'd not heard correctly.

"Mrs. Morales rushed her three children outside to safety. The fire was contained to her garage, originating from an explosion inside her SUV. A watch belonging to her husband was found near the scene. Jacob Morales has been separated from his wife and family for several weeks. He's the Border Patrol agent recently dismissed from his position due to abusing an undocumented immigrant. Morales is also under investigation as a possible suspect in the ongoing search for a Border Patrol insider who's sharing secrets and procedures with those threatening U.S. borders. He's been charged with arson and attempted murder and is being held on a $250,000 bond. More at five."

Danika clicked off the TV. Stunned, she allowed the news report to wash through her. All of the evidence that caused her to once suspect Jacob surfaced again.

Dear God, be with Barbara. She needs You. Danika couldn't call her. The police and Jimenez had ordered her not to contact anyone. When would this end?

Alex heard the news about Jacob's arrest in between his rounds at the medical center. But the time slipped by until after lunch before he could squeeze out a few minutes to call Danika. He hoped she hadn't seen the news report. The moment she answered the phone, he heard the despondency and realized she'd learned of the latest twist of events. "Have you had your TV on today?"

"Oh yeah. I saw the photos of what's left of Barbara's garage and heard Jacob was arrested." Her voice no longer held any emotion, and it bothered him.

"How are you doing?"

"I want out of here. I want to see Barbara and help her through all of this. I miss my daughter, and I'm grieving for what I know about Sandra and how Jacob's insanity has nearly killed his family." She took a deep breath, and the mournful sound tugged at Alex's heart. "I want to get back to work."

"Honey, I know you want all of this to end, but the most important thing for you to do now is rest and heal."

"Are you patronizing me?"

Great, he'd bumped her into a worse mood than before he phoned. Calling her "honey" hadn't sat well either. "Not at all. I'm simply telling you the truth. You can't help anyone until you're healed from the surgery. Your goal right now is to grow stronger."

Silence greeted him.

"I'm being a pain," she finally said. "I'm sorry. This bed and the guards outside my door and the suspicions about Jacob—and Nadine—are making me whine like a two-year-old. I'm writing down names and attempting to connect dots. The problem is I'm a Border Patrol agent, not a detective."

"Could you use a little company later on this evening?"

"I have a poor attitude about everything."

"Try a nap." Humor might help her surly mood.

"If I thought all of this would disappear, I'd sleep for the next three days."

"Dr. Price has another prescription."

"What's that?"

"Prayer. I know you've prayed for the case to be solved, and I have too. But we haven't prayed together."

She didn't respond, and he wished he could see her face.

"You have a powerful suggestion, Alex. Let's do it." She

paused. "I appreciate you. Don't imagine I've said those words enough."

The three words he wanted to hear rang through his head. Yet it was too soon to say them with all that was happening. But if he realized the beginnings of love, felt it, and whispered it, then they must be real.

CHAPTER 49

You need not be afraid of sudden disaster or the destruction
that comes upon the wicked, for the Lord is your security.
He will keep your foot from being caught in a trap.
PROVERBS 3:25-26

DANIKA HAD TO talk to Barbara. The horror of her sister-in-law's home set on fire and Jacob's arrest compounded with Nadine's disappearance sounded like a prescription for a mental breakdown. Barbara had to wonder why Danika had not contacted her.

With the door to her hospital room closed, she reached into her nightstand and pulled out her cell phone. Chief Jimenez and the police authorities would not approve of this call, but too bad. Barbara should be at work, but with all the tragedy, she might be tending to estimates for her house repairs. She answered her cell phone on the second ring.

"Barbara, I just saw the news. I'm so sorry. Are you okay? What about the kids?"

Her sister-in-law sighed, a mixture of grief and despair. "We're doing the best we can. *Shock* best describes all of us. I can't believe half of my house is destroyed. If I hadn't wakened, we'd all be dead."

Danika struggled for the right words, knowing advice was not what Barbara needed. "I don't know what to say except to cry with you."

"And I love you for your tears. What has happened to our family?" The morose tone of her voice caused Danika to shiver.

"It seems that we're being beaten, but we have to stay strong. We have children who depend on us. I think all we can do is believe the authorities will soon solve these crimes. I wish I was in a situation where I could visit you."

"Are you out of town with Sandra and Tiana?"

Danika had promised to keep her whereabouts a secret, although she questioned whether she was any less a criminal by lying. "No. But I'm not in McAllen. Doesn't look like I picked a good time to take a few days off."

"What could you do?"

"Be there for you. Do you have a place to stay?" The moment Danika posed the statement, she regretted it. If Barbara and the kids needed her home, where would Danika go once she was released from the hospital?

"We're at my mother's. Thanks anyway."

"Have you talked to Jacob?"

"I'm driving to the jail after work. Something's not right about the fire and his arrest. We talked yesterday afternoon—about the mistakes he's made. He's been meeting with a priest from our church and wants to put our family back together. That's not a man who blows up his wife's vehicle and sets his family's house on fire."

Stunned, Danika no longer knew what to believe. That sounded like the man she remembered, the gentle giant who gave unselfishly to his family. "You're certain he wouldn't have done this?"

"No matter how angry Jacob was with me in the past, he'd never try to hurt his children."

"He does love those kids." *And I hope his words to you were sincere.*

"You're my role model right now, and Lucy is my encourager.

You made it through Toby's death and all of the investigation. With God, I can handle the damage done to our home and what the future holds for Jacob—and all of us." Muffled sounds of weeping filled the phone line. "The police say Nadine's fingerprints are on Jacob's watch. But they are not letting anyone else know until they talk more with Jacob."

How should Danika respond to that bomb? She heard a buzz. "Do you have to go?"

"Yes. Got another call. I appreciate your encouragement during all of this. I'd like to see you when you're back in town. I desperately need your support."

"I'm praying, Barbara. I have my cell phone, so don't hesitate to contact me."

Danika slipped her phone back into the nightstand drawer. Nadine's fingerprints on Jacob's watch? That aspect sickened her. Danika didn't want to believe her niece would resort to attempted murder any more than she believed Jacob was capable of the same thing. The fire made no sense if Jacob had reached out in reconciliation. He was overprotective and stubborn, but not an arsonist. Or had Jacob and Nadine gone completely insane?

She pulled out her notebook with all the scribblings about her life over the past two years. Making a list of everything that had happened might expose a piece of evidence.

1. Toby's murder, yet to be solved. He was supposedly killed by an illegal while administering care to the person.
2. Jacob's decline into bitterness and depression.
3. Nadine's rebellion against her dad's rules; subsequent drug use.
4. Rita found in safe house and taken to hospital. Did this have anything to do with what was happening?
5. Arrested illegal threatens me.
6. Nadine runs away from home.

7. Jacob disciplined for abusing an illegal.
8. Chief Jimenez questions me about Toby's death. Station suspects rogue agent.
9. Rita is murdered in the hospital, and the station receives a call that I'm next.
10. Jacob receives a finger wearing Nadine's ring.
11. I receive a threatening call to my private cell phone.
12. I see the woman who attended Toby's funeral, and she runs away.
13. Jacob is fired from the BP.
14. I learn about Toby and Alex's relationship.
15. Alex is shot outside the restaurant while protecting me.
16. Jimenez refuses my resignation. Jacob is suspected as a rogue agent.
17. I find out from Alex that Toby helped Cira escape from a woman who fronts money for illegals. He was not unfaithful. Connection?
18. Alex tells me that Sandra is illegal. Connection to Cira and Jacob? Is Nadine involved?
19. Someone tries to kill me.
20. Sandra's arrest; she refuses to talk to anyone but me.
21. Jacob arrested for setting Barbara's house on fire. Nadine's fingerprints found.

Twenty-one events and no substantial clues. But her suspicions fluctuated between Jacob, Nadine, and Sandra. Perhaps all three?

Alex stepped into the hospital with a dozen red roses, a box of Ghirardelli chocolates, and a CD by Andrea Bocelli. Every time he considered how he'd nearly lost Danika, he wanted to tell her what he truly felt. Was it too soon to tell a woman he was falling in love with her? Possibly, especially when he understood Danika and Tiana's world needed to be safe before taking on any commitments.

Tomorrow the authorities would transport Danika to talk to Sandra. If the woman offered any clues—and the outlook for that looked optimistic—then arrests could be made.

Alex nodded at the policemen outside Danika's door. He offered his driver's license, and they checked his information against a list of approved visitors before allowing him to enter her room.

"Hey, gorgeous."

The flowers were no match for the brief sparkle in her eyes. "Are those for me or the cops posted outside the door?"

He glanced at the roses. "I intended to use these as a bribe, but since they let me in, you can have them." He set the pewter vase on the windowsill beside an equally large summer arrangement.

"Between you and Chief Jimenez, I'm keeping the florists in business." She lifted her chin. "Are those chocolates?"

"Absolutely." He handed her the candy and the CD.

She inhaled the package of candy. "Not sure what smells the best, the flowers or the chocolates." She tilted her head. "Have you come courting, Dr. Price?" The moment the words left her mouth, she reddened. "I don't believe I said that. The pain medication has given me loose lips."

He laughed. "It's most likely the truth. At least in a hospital, I feel comfortable courting in my own environment. Something we can talk about when this is over."

She rested her head on the pillow. Aside from blushing, she still lacked good color. "I want to apologize for all the times I've been rude."

"No problem. Remember, I kept information from you."

"Doesn't excuse the way I behaved." She reached up with her

free hand, the one not attached to an IV, and he grasped it. "I'm sorry."

"Me too." What a moment to kiss a beautiful lady, but he'd wait until she wasn't numb from pain medication. "This whole immigration issue is tough to figure out. My church has Spanish services. They bring others and sing the loudest. I'm sure most of those attending are undocumented."

"My church has Spanish services too. We also offer classes in English. I've been asked to teach, but I can't. Not with what I do, but those asking don't know I'm a Border Patrol agent. Christians all along the border face controversial issues when it comes to our faith and our laws."

"The situation with Sandra has to break your heart."

She pressed her lips together. "We were like family . . . but obviously not when it mattered the most."

"We've got to get you out of here so you can make a video call to San Antonio."

"Have you talked to Tiana?"

"I did. She says for you to get better, and she loves you."

Danika brushed away tears. "Thank you. Did she ask about Sandra?"

Alex hated telling Danika things that would upset her. "Yes, and I told her Sandra was needed here with important people. I didn't want to lie to her. Neither did I want to tell her the truth."

"I couldn't have done any better. Poor little thing. When this is over, I'll make it up to her." She released his hand and pulled a tissue from a box on her bed. "I'm sort of weepy this afternoon— with the news about the fire and Jacob's arrest. The police told Barbara that Nadine's fingerprints were on Jacob's watch. No one is to know that part of it."

Frustration crept through him. He wished Danika hadn't phoned Barbara, although he understood why. The whole unsolved murder and continued threat against Danika and her family had to end soon. "Do you think either of them tried to burn down the house with their family in it?"

Her eyes narrowed. "I don't want to. Barbara believes Jacob is innocent. Says he wants to put the family back together. I didn't pry about Nadine."

Alex moaned. The situation with the Morales family seemed to get more and more complicated. "I understand he was questioned about where he was the night of your accident."

"Chief Jimenez didn't reveal any of that. I imagine Jacob was in his apartment asleep."

"Right."

"I tried to get Sandra to agree to a phone call, but she insists our conversation has to be in person, which makes no sense. I think she's being stubborn, maybe holding out to see if I have any clout that would stop her deportation."

Alex remembered earlier in the day when they had agreed to pray. "What do you say we pray and ask God for wisdom and guidance?"

"Perfect." She touched his hand, and he held it firmly. "Not so very long ago, I was so angry with God that I couldn't pray or attend church. He'd taken Toby, and I wanted to know why. The tough realization came when I realized the *why* didn't matter. People have free will to choose evil things, and I must forgive them. God didn't stop Toby's murderer, and I have to accept the reason is beyond my understanding. Rough realization, but true. Those nearly two years I spent away from God didn't accomplish a thing but make me empty and bitter. I still want the killer found and brought to justice. Don't think I've given up. I'm determined to find who is behind this nightmare and stop them before someone else is killed."

The blue-gray pools of her eyes brimmed with tears. "See what happens when I'm on pain pills? I spill my guts."

Alex leaned over and brushed a kiss against her lips. "You are such a blessing to me." His whispered words connected to his heart, and the look he received from her said she understood.

"Heavenly Father," he began. "We don't know which way to turn with all the problems around us. But we're trusting You to bring the darkness to light. Give us wisdom and guidance and strength to see this through to the end. We're scared, Lord. . . ."

CHAPTER 50

If a man hasn't discovered something that
he will die for, he isn't fit to live.
MARTIN LUTHER KING JR.

SANDRA HATED being in jail even though she knew she'd broken the law. She wanted to believe she had a right to live in
this country, even if her documentation papers were false. The
thought of deportation churned her stomach. It would be different if she smuggled drugs or helped terrorists. After all, she paid
taxes. She'd learned to read and write English before leaving her
time of indenture to Lucy. Actually, forcing her to read was the
best thing Lucy had ever done for her. Sandra consumed every
book, magazine, and newspaper she could get her hands on. She
worked hard to increase her vocabulary and keep up to date on
current affairs, and she probably knew more about the politics
in this country than the average American.

Without Sandra, Danika would not have been able to work
and provide for her daughter. . . . Without Danika, Sandra
wouldn't have a home or a purpose or a dear friend.

Danika had given her so much love and devotion, and Sandra
gladly returned it. But life and its complications were terribly
unfair, and now the U.S. wanted to send her back to Mexico
because she hadn't entered the country legally? She'd do anything to stay in this country.

Sandra buried her face in her hands. She missed Tiana, the
precious baby she'd never had. What did she have in Mexico

without Tiana, without her parents? She should have left McAllen months ago—like Cira had fled with her son. Then Danika would never have had to face the disappointment of her maid and nanny living a lie.

Sandra's one hope rested in Danika. After all, she was a Border Patrol agent, and she had access to those higher-up people who enforced U.S. laws. Besides, Sandra had valuable information about Lucy. Bargaining for her freedom seemed wrong, but Sandra had no choice.

What Sandra knew about Lucy could send the evil woman to death row. She'd killed and beaten women who attempted to escape her abuse. Lucy dabbled in drug dealing and worked with gangs on both sides of the river. Yes, Lucy was her ace. Sandra would tell all she knew about the supposedly legal maid and nanny business and fill up pages of information for the police or Border Patrol or ICE or Homeland Security or whoever wanted it. But first she had to tell Danika the truth. Her friend deserved to know why Sandra had betrayed her, not just a confession. Only Danika knew how loyal Sandra had been.

Sandra had suspected for a long time that Lucy was involved with Toby's murder, and now she was certain of it. Especially after Lucy had Sandra's parents killed. If Danika wanted Toby's murder solved and all the terrible things happening to her and her brother-in-law's family to end, then she'd have to ensure that Sandra never set foot in Mexico again.

I don't know what is right anymore. I'm afraid, and maybe Danika can help. But am I using my love and friendship like a selfish child?

Sandra allowed the tears of regret to freely flow. As soon as she talked to Danika, she needed to request an audience with an attorney and a representative of the Mexican embassy. This was all going to work out just fine. Important people needed her and would make sure she wasn't sent back to Mexico.

Then why did fear stamp terror across her heart?

★ ★ ★

Alex wanted his relationship with Danika to deepen, but it would never happen until they confronted the elephant in the room. Oh, they could discuss Jacob and the fire, the missing niece, Sandra, and whoever had tried to kill them, but none of that was what should be—must be—talked through. Undocumented immigrants. Or as Danika would call them, *illegals*.

He glanced at her, hooked up to IVs and monitors, her face pale and her body bruised. But she was out of danger, and he knew her mind raced as fast as his.

"Do you think it's time to stop dancing around the one topic that stands between us?" Alex wasn't sure where it would lead them, but honesty was the only road to understanding.

She blinked. "Why is it you seem to know exactly what I'm thinking?"

"I work at it." He chuckled and took her hand.

She glanced away, then looked at him. "Okay. I'll start. First of all, let me say that I grew up in church, and over the years I've examined every piece of Scripture about helping the alien and the poor and needy, and additional Scriptures about not moving our borders and obeying laws."

"Where do you hold your ground?"

"I believe the laws are in place to protect our country. I'm against anyone stealing their way across the border for any reason. My heart goes out to those who risk everything they have—or don't have—to get here. I know most of them are decent human beings, and I agree that they're entitled to medical care and compassion before they're returned to their own country. When I'm responsible for those being escorted across the bridge, I pray their lives will be better. I pray their country will become a safer and healthier place for them to live. And I pray for an end to gangs and drug cartels on both sides of the border. But

I still maintain that immigrants need to enter through lawful means."

He lightly squeezed her hand. "We're very close in our beliefs. Despite what you might think, I'm not an immigration activist." He winced as he realized that might hit close to home with her memories of her husband. But he couldn't stop to worry about that right now. "My calling is to administer healing. I'm committed to that every bit as much as you are committed to the Border Patrol. I don't ask for citizenship papers or green cards when I treat patients. I believe in understanding and respect. I hope we can come up with a way to reform the laws that will allow more compassionate treatment of the poor and needy who deserve it. But until that happens, my allegiance lies with the current laws."

She nodded, her gaze never trailing from his face. "Considering that there are those in my own church who hold vastly differing views on these issues, I'd say we *are* very close."

"Close enough to keep seeing each other?" Alex waited. He was determined not to say another word, despite his inclination to beg her on bended knee to give him a chance.

"If we're to remain friends—or more—we have to be able to talk. So many times I've thought back over that last morning with Toby. I drove off in a rage when he wanted me to stay and talk to him. I was furious. Couldn't get away from him fast enough. If I had stayed and allowed him to express his feelings, he'd be alive today, and Tiana would have her daddy." She shook her head. "Eventually I figured out he was just doing his best to follow Christ. I know he wasn't setting out to undermine everything I stood for."

She glanced out the window. "In answer to your question, maybe we can keep seeing each other. I need a little time—time for the turmoil around me to subside."

Time he could give, if it meant a lifetime with her.

CHAPTER 51

You will know the truth, and the truth will set you free.
JOHN 8:32

DANIKA REALIZED TWO THINGS this morning: today she would be released from the hospital and see Sandra, hopefully resolving the tragic mysteries plaguing her life. Both made opening her eyes in a hospital bed a little easier. No more IVs. No more lab-coated technicians drawing blood—and reminding her of Rita's killer—and no more open-ended gowns. After today, the turmoil would end.

She'd miss Alex's visits to the hospital, but she wanted to continue seeing him. In him, she saw a strength and an enduring faith that moved her to be a better person, to be more considerate of others, and to try harder. Soon, tonight even, she'd be able to see her sweet Tiana and talk to her via Alex's computer.

A pair of policemen would be posted inside her home 24-7 until the authorities arrested the shooter. What she honestly wanted to do was get back to work. The doctor said two more weeks before he'd consider it. Two long weeks of boring TV and reading months-old magazines. Maybe she could do paperwork at the station. . . .

A knock on her door alerted her to Chief Jimenez's noon visit. He'd been to see her every day since the accident, which had boosted his popularity rating with her. The flowers helped too.

"Come on in. Is my escort ready? I'm so anxious to talk to Sandra and get this mess cleared up."

One look at Jimenez, and her enthusiasm plummeted. His forehead held the rutted lines of worry.

"What's wrong?" A hundred scenarios rolled across her mind, and none were optimistic.

"There won't be an escort to the jail."

"Why? Did Sandra change her mind?"

He grabbed the back of a chair and pulled it to her bedside. He sat down, his shoulders carrying the weight of what she knew she didn't want to hear.

She'd shaken hands with disappointment before, and she could do so again. "Has something happened to Jacob?"

"No." He rubbed his hand over his face. "Bad news, Danika. Sandra Rodriguez is dead."

Danika's ears hammered pain. She must have misunderstood. "Sandra's gone? Was . . . was she killed?"

Jimenez's eyes narrowed. "Someone got to her inside the jail. A guard found her body in her cell."

Danika covered her mouth, the news too shocking, the grief overwhelming. Sandra was her friend, her sister. *We are like sisters in our hearts.* "Wasn't she under special protection?"

Jimenez frowned. "I asked the same thing. Looks like you and I weren't the only ones who believed she was critical to the case."

Had it been such a short time ago when they stood in the kitchen and laughed over Sandra's concerns about Danika not needing her? But later on, Danika realized Sandra's fears that night were about Alex revealing her illegal status. The animosity for her deceit had mixed with pity and compassion for all she'd done for Tiana and Danika.

This wasn't supposed to happen. Toby had been killed. Jacob's family terrorized. Nadine gone. Someone had tried to kill her. *Now Sandra* . . . Who would be next, Tiana? Was there any way to protect her from an evil being who seemed to know Danika's every move?

★ ★ ★

Jacob wondered why his life continued to be miserable when he'd made his peace with God. How could anything get worse? Yesterday he believed he and Barbara had a fighting chance of putting their marriage and family back together. They had cried and prayed together. Then in the wee hours of the morning, someone had blown up the SUV inside the garage, nearly destroying what he wanted to preserve.

He glanced around the small cell. Reality had numbed him. Who could have set his home on fire and planted his watch? Why had Nadine's fingerprints been on it? He remembered missing the watch at work and assuming it was on the kitchen counter of his small apartment.

Today he stood before a judge and pleaded not guilty. A snot-nosed public defender fresh out of law school had been assigned as his lawyer. While the kid took notes, Jacob saw he couldn't spell *arson*. How about spelling *life*?

The light in the day came when he discovered Barbara sitting in the back of the courtroom. She rushed to him when the officer escorted him out.

"I know you didn't do this." She sobbed. "I love you, and we'll find out who is doing these terrible things to our family."

Jacob blinked away the tears. If he hadn't been handcuffed, he'd have taken her into his arms. "Pray for me, Barbara. Pray for us and our children. I love you." As he was led away, he swung back around to find her watching him. "Tell Kaitlyn, Amber, and Jake I love them with all my heart."

The look in her eyes had kept him from shattering today. Father Cornell had come by the jail later in the afternoon. Together they talked, and he offered to find a lawyer who could represent him better than a kid who mispronounced law terms instead of practicing them.

★ ★ ★

Danika's house did not seem like her own. Oh, the furniture rested in its proper place, and the pictures on the wall were ones she'd selected, and the photos of Tiana smiled back at her. But the quiet had a voice—a voice of loss.

One of the police officers carried her bag of belongings to the kitchen and set it on the table. She followed him. Sandra's presence was everywhere. She'd loved roosters, and they were on the counter, the windowsill, on top of the refrigerator, and even on salt and pepper shakers by the stove. Danika wanted to hurl them all through the window. Instead, she determined to move them as soon as she had the strength. She opened the door to her garage and remembered her car had been totaled.

Danika turned to the officers, a man in his late forties and a woman in her midthirties. "Would you like some coffee?"

"That sounds wonderful," the woman said. "My name is Angie, and if you'll just tell me where things are, I'll be glad to take over."

Danika pointed to what Angie needed, then walked into the living room. Coming home had worn her out. Or was it the stress? If only Tiana would come running from her room and beg Danika to play a game. If only the smell of coffee came from Sandra's handiwork.

She was ready to quit. Leave McAllen. Change her and Tiana's name and start life all over again. She paused for a moment and let the thought of running sink in. She had a child to think about, a child who deserved to grow up without fear.

"Mrs. Morales, do you drink your coffee with sugar and cream?" The voice came from the other officer. She couldn't remember his name—*oh yes, Walt.* "Just black, thank you."

He delivered hers, and the pair took their cups and stood by her exterior doors, one at the front and one at the back. Danika had been reduced to being a prisoner in her home. What had happened to dignity and the ability to grieve in privacy?

"Officers, could I have a word with you, please?"

"Can you speak to us from there? Our shifts have rolled into place." Walt spoke with authority, reminding her of Jimenez. But she'd started to like the chief.

"I'd like for you to leave my home. I can't live like this."

"Pardon me, ma'am, but from what we've been told, you might not live if we don't stay to protect you."

She trembled, but she must stand her ground. The pain in her abdomen was a reality, but so were her capabilities. "I really would like for you to go. I'll call the police station and explain to them I don't need protection."

"Mrs. Morales," Angie began, "think about your health. You've just been released from the hospital, and there is substantial evidence that someone wants you killed."

From deep inside, Danika drew up the courage needed to dismiss the officers. "Angie, I'm a crack shot. My life is in danger every minute I'm riding the line for the Border Patrol. I don't need protection. I need to be alone."

CHAPTER 52

Excel in all that you do; bring no stain upon your honor.
SIRACH 33:22 (RSV)

ONE MORE TIME, Danika examined the series of events plaguing her life and those she loved. For the past three hours, she'd
sat in her living room and rethought every event that had vexed
her. Evening shadows had crept across the room like the preda-
tors who wanted her dead. She snapped on the light. The notion
of being in the dark affected her physically and emotionally, and
she dare not enter that abyss. The notebook she'd started in the
hospital remained at her fingertips, as though the answers were
a mere thought away. She repeated the conversation with Barbara about Jacob and Nadine's involvement in the fire, and it
settled uneasily in the pit of her stomach. She needed to check
on things herself—talk to Jacob and search deeper for Nadine.

Whoever was after all of them had grown bolder, and with
boldness came a chance of error. They had to be stopped, and
she had to be ready to accept the truth. Sandra had evidently
known whom to blame, but she'd refused to give the information to anyone but Danika, and now she was gone. Obviously
the killer feared her confession. Who had connections with both
households besides Sandra?

She considered Jacob and Toby's common friends, some of
whom were Border Patrol agents. No one seemed to fit. Jacob
didn't care for Toby's teacher friends, and the two men had never
accompanied each other to church functions.

Danika's heart hammered against her chest as realization nearly choked her. There was one person connected to both her and Jacob.

Lucy.

Barbara's best friend. Sandra's employer and a woman Sandra despised. But Danika had never learned why Sandra disliked her, and Lucy knew Sandra had been arrested. The possibilities floating through her mind ranged from Lucy's having discovered Sandra's illegal entry to Lucy's having masterminded the plot to destroy the Morales family. But the question was still why. Without motivation, Danika had nothing but a frail supposition.

But what if Lucy was behind all of this? She had access to Jacob's house, and Barbara shared personal and family matters with her.

Had Toby suspected Lucy? A chill crept over her. If he had, wouldn't he have said something to Danika or Jacob—unless he didn't have proof?

She struggled to stand. *Water.* Danika needed water to quench the dryness in her throat. She walked slowly into the kitchen, opened the fridge, and selected a bottle. Her suspicions were unwarranted. If Toby suspected Lucy, he wouldn't have kept the information to himself. He cared too much for those who were being abused.

What if he had discovered the truth just before he was killed? What if *that* was the reason he'd been killed? Danika drank deeply of the cold water. Had her thoughts run crazy under the influence of her medication? Still, she wondered if she'd stumbled onto the truth. For a moment she pondered where Toby could have noted what he'd been doing in aiding the illegals. He neither kept a journal nor had a confidant.

For the next several minutes, she dug through his personal items in the bottom of her closet for a clue or a lead. Greeting cards and photographs brought tears to her eyes, but nothing indicated his work with illegals.

Toby's Bible . . . There were slips of paper and church bulletins tucked inside. Would he have referenced anything about his possible killer?

She picked up his Bible and eased onto her bed. A prayer for truth left her trembling, as though whatever she learned would shatter her frail belief in Toby's integrity. One by one she opened the paper inserts in his Bible. A piece of paper had been slipped into the book of John, where Toby had underlined verse thirty-two of the eighth chapter. "And you will know the truth, and the truth will set you free." She opened the folded paper and read:

> I find this hard to believe, but I've stumbled onto something that disturbs me greatly. Cira slipped and said the name "Lucy" the other day when I was taking her to Alex for her prenatal appointment. The longer I think and pray about it, the more I realize Lucy— Barbara's best friend—could be the one who is taking advantage of desperate young women who will do anything to get across the border. I'm going to follow her. Find out the truth.

Danika gasped. It was Lucy. Tears flowed and she did nothing to stop them. Dear Toby had searched out the truth, and it appeared that it may have killed him. The happenings over the past several weeks all made sense, and she held in her hands enough suspicion to have Lucy brought in for questioning and her business investigated.

She closed the Bible and walked into the kitchen for more water. All the while her thoughts raced. She snatched up the landline and pressed in Alex's number in hopes he was available. A horrible car crash had detained him at work.

The phone rang once, twice, three times . . .

"Hey, are you all right? Ed text-messaged me about Sandra." His voice grounded her to the truth.

"I'm in shock and grieving. I loved Sandra, and like a child, I wanted to believe there had been a mistake about her legal documentation."

"When I stop by tonight, we'll talk. You loved her, and she played an important part in your life and Tiana's."

Danika appreciated him not mentioning the lies, but instead the good things. "I have an idea who could be behind this." Her breathless voice caused her to swallow and begin again. "Barbara's best friend is Sandra's boss." Thinking about Sandra in the past tense cut deep. "Or rather, the woman *was* Sandra's boss. She has access to and knowledge of both households because of the cleaning service."

"What makes you think she's our mastermind? Doesn't she own the largest maid and nanny service in McAllen? And didn't you tell me that Jacob helped her get started?"

"Yes, he did. But Sandra disliked Lucy. I never knew why. Until a few minutes ago, I assumed it was because of her lack of documentation. Now my mind is spinning with what could be the answer to all of this."

"Are you thinking she's the one fronting the money for the women?"

"I'm fairly certain of it. I found a piece of paper in Toby's Bible in which he states his suspicions about Lucy. He was going to follow her and find out the truth."

"Is it dated?"

"Oh, how I wish it was. I'm thinking she could have easily gone through Jacob's backpack for sensor information since she has a key to Jacob and Barbara's house."

"Yours too?"

"No. Only Sandra had an extra key. Besides I have nothing here anyone could use."

"But if Barbara and Lucy are good friends—"

"Barbara talks to her about everything, and Lucy has always been close to Nadine." She swallowed the emotion threatening to surface again. "I'm thinking she could have ordered Toby's death—and possibly Sandra's—or she knows who did."

"Have you called Ed or the police?"

"Not yet. I wanted to make sure my conclusions made sense to you, and my suspicions weren't an overreaction to all of this medication." She closed her eyes, fighting fatigue.

"I don't think it's far-fetched at all."

"Some investigators—and understand that's not my job description—want to know what motivates a perp, while others try to find the person by following a criminal pattern. But for me, it's both. I know why people cross the border, and I also know how to follow the signs to track them down. The paths they take are fairly predictable." She paused. "Yet this is different. Too many variables. But the more I think about it, Lucy Pinion seems like someone the authorities would want to question."

"If she's fronting money for undocumented immigrants, then I see the tie-in even to me." Alex's tone softened, as though his mind churned with each word. "Lucy's reputation is impeccable. She gives money to charitable events at the medical center and offers jobs to those who are legally cleared to work. I've met her— sociable, caring, a respectable member of our community."

Danika hesitated. The final conclusion of over two years of wondering who could be behind Toby's death and the turmoil surrounding her family caused her to shiver. "She advertises as bonded and licensed. When Jacob first hired her, he went through every letter of her paperwork." Was her heart going to burst from her chest? "If she's behind all of this, why is she after Jacob and me?"

"Danika, the key is Toby." Alex's words were sobering.

She rubbed her arms. "You're right. If Toby followed her to

learn the truth and he's dead, then Jacob and I are involved by who we are."

"He pulled women out of her business and not only got them medical care but also encouraged them to run. I never considered Sandra's former creditor—whoever helped her across the border—to still be involved in her life today."

The pieces were beginning to fit. "Toby's interference cut into her profits."

Alex continued. "It would make the puzzle pieces fit. And it explains why Sandra is dead—why she refused to talk to anyone but you."

"Why would Lucy be out for revenge against me and Jacob when Toby's no longer in the picture?"

"I don't know."

She rubbed her weary eyes. "If Lucy is the key, then all the questions rolling around in my head have answers—except why now. Whom do we call first, Chief Jimenez or the police?"

"I'll call Ed and let him make the next move. But Barbara is in a scary position. If we're right, she could be in danger."

"Like Nadine." Her precious niece may very well be dead too.

"Yes, honey."

"I'll call Barbara." Danika stood and began to pace until the pain in her abdomen reminded her of why she was at home.

"Take a breath. The end is near, and it could be today. Thank goodness you have the police there to protect you."

She'd been very foolish. "I sent them home."

"Danika, have you lost your mind?" His tone alarmed her. "I'm calling Ed and having him send someone to guard you now."

"Lucy doesn't know I'm here because Barbara thinks I'm out of town."

"Lucy didn't get to where she's at because she's stupid. She wasn't supposed to find out about Sandra either."

He was right, and she'd been the stupid one. Anyone could

have watched her leave the hospital or arrive home. "I know better, Alex. I'm sorry. I have my assigned weapon in my bedroom."

"Go get it, and keep it on you."

Danika disconnected the call. She heard the doorbell but refused to answer it. Again, it sounded like a pipe organ ringing through the house. She crept to the dining room window and with her finger lifted a slat of the blinds. Her breath caught in her throat. Nadine stood on the porch, her small frame looking so much like her mother's.

Danika's heart pounded painfully against her chest. How many times had she feared her niece was dead or caught up in drugs and a gang? Relief and anger wove confusion. In one breath she wanted to shake Nadine, and in the next kiss her. Yet there she stood looking every bit like the sweet little girl who used to crawl on Danika's lap for a story, the sweet little girl who wanted Danika to take her to a movie, to help her convince Barbara that she was old enough to wear mascara.

She had to answer the door. Nadine would not have come to her if she didn't need help. Talking to her would dispel all of the doubts plaguing Danika about the teen's involvement in Jacob's blackmail. Barbara would have her daughter back, and maybe she'd gather information about Lucy.

Danika didn't need to weigh her decision about opening the door any longer. She'd deal with the police, Jimenez, and Alex later. With a prayer of thanks for Nadine's safety, she unbolted the door and opened it just enough to talk. Nadine looked healthy but definitely thinner, and she'd always been tiny.

"Nadine, I don't know what to say. We've all been so worried about you."

The girl's lips quivered, and she held her hands in front of her. "I'm sorry. I've been hiding, afraid to contact my parents because of all the trouble I'd caused." Tears pooled in her eyes. "The longer I stayed away, the harder it was to go home. And then I read about how Daddy lost his job, and then how he tried to kill Mom, Kaitlyn, Jake, and Amber."

Compassion swept over Danika. Caution nudged her, but she shoved it away, blaming it on the medication. The teen had come to her for help, and Danika could not deny it. "Your mother and I believe he's innocent of the explosion and fire. Come in. Let's talk about this."

"I was hoping you'd help me. I knew I could depend on you. Can I ask my friend in too? He's the one who convinced me to come here."

Danika glanced at a pickup parked a little farther down the street. All she could see was the outline of the truck bed. She couldn't tell the make or read the license plates in the dark. But Nadine had come to her for help.

"Please, Aunt Danika. I want to make this all right with my family."

How could she refuse? If Nadine did know what was going on, Danika could learn the truth. "I guess so. I'm not supposed to be letting anyone in the house."

"Why?"

"It's not important. Sure, invite him in."

Nadine motioned to someone in the truck.

A man exited the truck and walked up the driveway. In the shadows, she didn't recognize him, and Danika didn't want to turn on the porch light. Nadine introduced them and called him Joe. Danika shoved aside her apprehensions, but she didn't forget them. This could be an opportunity to help her niece reunite with her family.

Once in the living room, Nadine glanced about. "Where's Tiana?"

"Out of town visiting with a friend of mine."

"Sandra too?"

"She's gone too." Danika nearly choked on the lie, but she

needed to be careful. She studied the man Nadine had introduced as Joe. His eyes held a wild glint in them, and not that of a
man who lusted after a young woman. He looked familiar. . . .

And then she placed him.

He's the one who murdered Rita.

Danika hid her recognition. Surely Nadine was not a part of
this killer's life.

Nadine's eyes widened. "What's been going on?"

"Too much. Please sit down, and we'll work through getting
you reunited with your family. And I do have some questions."
Danika turned to Joe. "Can I get you something?"

"No, ma'am." He sat on the sofa beside Nadine. The girl
cringed.

Danika smiled. "If you'll excuse me for a moment, I—"

Joe whipped out a .45. "The only place you're going is with us."

Had Nadine been reduced to this? to planning the demise of
her own family? The thought sickened Danika, but the proof
was before her.

Nadine stood and took a step back from Joe.

"It's only a matter of time before the authorities discover who
you are," Danika said. "The volunteer who saw you at the hospital has given the police your description. My guess is you're the
one who blew out my tires."

He laughed and waved the firearm in her face. "Maybe so, but
by the time I'm across the border, no one will find me."

Danika watched Nadine draw a .380 automatic from the
back of her jeans, where it had been covered by an oversize shirt.
What was she about to do? Nadine trembled and pointed the
gun at Joe's back. "Jose, drop the gun before I kill you."

His eyes narrowed, and he lifted his weapon to Danika's face.
"I thought you and I could get something going here. But you
played me."

"I'll send a bullet through you for every woman you beat, for setting my house on fire, for sending that finger to my dad, for trying to kill my aunt."

He sneered. "Got us a stand-off, Nadine. What's it going to—"

Pop. Nadine sent a bullet into Jose's back. Then again.

His eyes went wide, and Danika slapped away his arm before he fired at her. His limp body fell against her, the weight forcing her to the floor. Her gaze darted to Nadine, who shook with the gun in her hand.

"I had to make them believe I didn't care about what they did." Her voice broke into sobs. "Lucy and Jose have hurt and murdered so many people. You have no idea what they've done. She's behind all of it."

"It's all over." Danika struggled to shove the body from her. She grabbed the sofa for support and forced herself to stand, the agony in her abdomen nearly taking away her breath. Nadine had drifted into shock, her eyes glazed and her body seemingly paralyzed. "Give me the gun, and I'll call the police."

The front door opened and shut with a crash that shook the house. Danika's attention flew to the entranceway, where Lucy aimed a gun at Nadine. "Toss that piece over here, Nadine. You thought you could outsmart me? Jose wasn't the only one listenin' in."

Nadine did as she was told, still trembling and ashen. Danika stepped in front of the girl. "I'm the one you're after. Leave her alone."

"Brave talk for an unarmed agent." Lucy shook her head. "And so soon after surgery. By the way, I don't have a problem killing you both."

"Take my advice and get out of here. The police are on their way."

"How's that? The pair guarding you left hours ago."

Danika wondered how quickly Jimenez contacted the police.

The time neared ten thirty. If not for an emergency at the medical center, Alex would have been there hours ago. Now he'd be walking into a hornet's nest. "Chief Jimenez wasn't happy with me dismissing the cops, so he's sending more."

"Now's as good a time as any to leave. Both of you are to walk through the kitchen to the garage, where Danika will pull my car inside. Either of you try anything, and Nadine gets the first bullet. In fact, Nadine, you are to laugh, talk about all of us going to dinner. We want the neighbors to think this is a good time. Do not use any names. Understand?"

The teen merely nodded, obviously too frightened to speak.

Danika had to stall for time. "Where are we going?"

"None of your business. But the McAllen station will receive at least one body tonight. Move. Now. You two have a date in the trunk of my car."

Danika and Nadine moved toward the door. Lucy took a step back, just out of Danika's reach. "Why, Lucy? What have we done to you?"

"Nadine hasn't done a thing but play into my hands. You, on the other hand, have stood in my way for a long time."

"How?" Danika studied Lucy's face. The woman would not see fear. "Are you going to tell me why I'm your target?"

"Toby."

Danika had to confirm what she'd read in his Bible. "He discovered what you were doing?"

"Shut up." Lucy opened the door and motioned them into the garage. The hot air mimicked the ordeal. She handed Danika the keys.

Lucy pushed her into the garage while pulling Nadine along. She pressed the garage door button, and it hummed into action. The ceiling light cast a jagged path across the garage floor, illuminating some things and concealing others. The pain in Danika's abdomen made her dizzy. She didn't want to think about the lack of air and the heat in the trunk of Lucy's car.

A 1992 Dodge Dynasty sat in the driveway. *Think, Danika.* She refused to allow meds and fear to dissolve her into a pool of inaction. Perhaps a cell phone had been left in Lucy's car. Fat chance, but a hope. Normally Lucy drove a Lexus.

Danika slid into the car and started the engine. Nothing lay on the bench seat. Lucy knew how to cover her tracks. Danika drove the rattletrap with Texas plates into the garage, and the door buzzed back down.

She scooted out—with no more idea of how to free Nadine and herself than she had before, except to get close enough for hand-to-hand combat. Still the questions assaulting her for two years begged for answers, and that meant precious time. As soon as she climbed out, Lucy demanded the keys.

Danika slapped them into her palm. If Lucy pointed the gun away from Nadine's face for two seconds, she'd use her martial arts skills and hope the lack of physical strength wasn't their demise. She calculated Lucy's reaction time to a blow against her arm while the garage door closed. Yet the pain made her dizzy.

According to Sandra, Lucy loved to talk about herself.

"Why did you have Toby killed?"

"*I* killed him. Put the gun to his head and pulled the trigger."

The news of Lucy murdering Toby staggered her, but she refused to dwell on it now. Later . . . "He didn't tell any of us what he suspected."

She popped the trunk open and motioned for Nadine to get inside. "Toby tried to ruin my business, and I had to eliminate him. But he was stupid. Claimed you and Jacob had evidence against me." She sneered. "He either lied or it's in your house somewhere. I'm tired of looking for it at Barbara's."

Danika shoved aside the fury pelting her and willed it to subside. Toby had chosen the law and his love for her and Tiana that day, and the result killed him. "If I had proof, it would have been used a long time ago."

"Unless Toby hid it."

"Search my house. Or is that what you had Sandra doing?"

Lucy laughed. "Sandra's refusal killed her."

Oh, Sandra. "Is that why you set up Jacob?"

"He ticked me off when he got in bad standing with the Border Patrol. See, I used the sensor info in his backpack before he got fired."

Keep stalling her. "Why did you wait two years to come after me?"

"It's more complicated than you think, dear Danika. Business expansion required it. I always had a scapegoat if you or Jacob found the evidence. But Naddie just shot him."

"If you're going to kill me, I deserve to know why."

With her gun aimed at Nadine, Lucy motioned Danika to crawl into the trunk beside the girl. As she did, a staggering burst of pain spread across her lower body, and she grabbed the bumper to steady herself.

"You think you hurt now? Wait till later. How's that old song go? 'By the light of the silvery moon'?"

"I deserve to know why."

"You? You've cost me money just like all Border Patrol agents. Six months ago, you and Jon Barnett stopped an oil tanker at the checkpoint carrying 784 pounds of marijuana in the bottom of oil drums. Over $625,000. At the time I wanted to poison every K-9 and handler on the Border Patrol payroll. Less than a year before, you and Jacob stopped an 18-wheeler carrying 20,000 pounds of marijuana. I was supposed to get a cut off of that. Sixteen million dollars gone up in smoke. Is that reason enough?"

She slammed the trunk shut. A moment later, the garage door opened and the car backed out. Did Lucy have the rest of her plans as carefully laid out?

CHAPTER 53

While there's life, there's hope.
TERENCE

ALEX'S MIND SPUN. Why wouldn't Danika answer the front door or her phones? He pounded on the door with his fist, ready to kick it in. Maybe she'd fallen asleep.

"Sir, what's the problem here?" A police officer walked up the sidewalk behind him.

"Are you the officer sent to check on Danika Morales?"

"Let's start with your name." The young officer had a radio in his hand.

"I'm a friend of Ms. Morales and Chief Jimenez at the McAllen Border Patrol Operation. She's been expecting me, but she's not answering the door."

Two police cruisers sped into the driveway, lights flashing. A truck whipped to the curb, and Alex recognized it as Ed's. Two other cruisers joined them.

Officers jogged to the front door. "Thanks for the license plate numbers, Warner," an officer named Montoya said. "How long ago did the car leave?"

"Six minutes at the most."

"Who? What car?" Alex had long since lost his patience. He wanted an explanation now.

"Sir, we have no idea who you are," Officer Warner said. "If you'd kindly step aside, we need to talk to Ms. Morales."

Alex's nerves shot into panic. "And I'm telling you she's not answering the door."

"Sir, you are interfering in police business. Your name and purpose?" Officer Warner was about to be on the receiving end of Alex's temper.

"Alex Price. Dr. Alex Price." He spotted Ed. "Would you tell these officers who I am?"

"Officers, I'm Chief Ed Jimenez of the McAllen station. This man is with me. He has clearance. What's the problem?"

Alex took a moment to regain his composure as Officer Warner began to explain. "I received the call and got here first in time to see a '92 Dodge Dynasty pull away from the house. I jotted down the license plate numbers and learned the car was registered to Jose Aznar. He's wanted for armed robbery."

"Did you see who was driving?" Officer Montoya said.

"No. The car looked suspicious for this neighborhood." He banged on the door, then turned the knob. It opened. "Ms. Morales, this is the police. Are you all right?"

Nothing. A lamp glowed in the living room, and the kitchen light was on. Alex followed the officers into the house. A Hispanic male sprawled on the floor in the living room with gunshot wounds in his back. Blood soaked the carpet.

Alex bent clumsily and felt for his pulse. "He's dead."

"Dr. Price, please do not touch anything until the area can be swept for fingerprints." Officer Warner radioed for an ambulance.

The officers and Ed conducted a search and found Danika's purse, cell phone, and weapon in her bedroom. No sign of a struggle. Each room, each closet held the possibility of containing Danika's body.

Alex stood in the living room with Ed and Officer Montoya while they waited for the ambulance. He leaned on his crutch. "What happens next?"

Officer Montoya pointed to the body. "Do you know this man?"

Alex shook his head. He hesitated. "You might want to see if he's the one who murdered a young woman at McAllen Medical. A volunteer gave the police department a rough sketch."

Ed whipped his attention to Alex. "You and Danika suspected Lucy Pinion. I called the police chief, and he's having her brought in for questioning."

A lot of good that would do if Lucy had taken Danika. "Earlier, Danika and I realized the Pinion woman may have had access to both homes and may also employ undocumented immigrants in her maid and nanny service. Danika was to call Barbara Morales with questions—and to warn her—while I contacted you. She would not have left willingly with Lucy."

"We need to assume Danika left in the car. Did she get ahold of Barbara?"

"I have no idea."

Ed yanked his cell phone from his belt. "I'll call her now." He walked outside the front door.

Alex detested waiting for any purpose, and he desperately needed to do something. The question of Danika's whereabouts slammed against his brain. He hobbled to the garage, where Officer Warner bent to the concrete floor and examined a faint indication of liquid.

Warner glanced up. "Looks like condensation from the car, and it's fresh. Can't tell anything else." He unclipped his radio. "We need to find that car."

Ed appeared in the doorway. "Barbara hasn't heard from Danika. She put me on hold and called Lucy but didn't receive an answer. She also relayed a strange conversation they'd had earlier. Said she came to see Barbara and mentioned Nadine's fingerprints on Jacob's watch. Lucy had no way of knowing about that piece of evidence. Barbara was getting ready to call me. She suspects Lucy is involved."

Alex sensed the blood draining from his face.

Officer Warner's radio alerted him. He answered it and glanced at Ed. "We're on it." With the radio replaced on his belt, he took long strides to the door. "The car's been spotted on Old Military Highway. Possibly heading toward the Hidalgo Bridge."

★ ★ ★

In the blackness of Lucy's trunk, Danika maneuvered her body to tear away the carpetlike material and the vinyl protecting the taillight. She hadn't been able to locate a tire iron; Lucy had probably removed it a long time ago.

"Pull on the other side," she said to Nadine.

They both tugged on the covering until it broke free. With only flip-flops on her feet, Danika kicked against one taillight until it shattered. The plastic shards cut into the side of her foot and heel.

"Do you have anything we can wave through the hole?" Danika said.

"My shoe," Nadine said. The teen was amazingly calm. No doubt she'd seen and heard worse happenings while captive with Lucy. "Here." She twisted her body to hand a sandal to Danika. "I can manage this easier than you."

In the cramped quarters with her stomach crying out in pain, Danika breathed out thanks. "I'm going to do the same with the other taillight. If a vehicle is behind us, they might be able to see. Of course, now Lucy's taillights are out."

A few minutes later, another hole offered air and provided means to show their imprisonment. Both of them waved their shoes through the jagged holes. But how could anyone see unless they were right on the rear bumper?

"Lucy hired guys to kill your friend. A doctor, I think."

So Alex had been the target, just like he suspected. "He's alive."

"Good. Aunt Danika . . . I killed Jose."

How could she comfort Nadine? Certainly not by telling her it was okay. The girl had always been analytical and extremely bright. "You killed him to protect me and yourself."

"God says do not kill."

"It was self-defense, honey. Like a soldier who has committed himself to keeping others safe from the enemy."

"I've been praying for Lucy and Jose to be stopped, but I hadn't counted on me pulling a trigger. Lucy is working with a drug cartel. I heard her say it took nearly two years to gain their trust. She told me to run away. Said I could stay with her. Then she kept me prisoner."

Before Danika had a chance to respond, Lucy hit a pothole and jarred the car.

"Are we going to get out of this alive?" Nadine's voice had softened to that of a child.

"I won't lie to you and say we're not in serious trouble, but good people are looking and praying for us. The police were on their way when you arrived." Danika sounded more encouraging than she felt. All she could do was trust God. "Do you know where she's taking us?"

"I'm afraid so. It's an exchange with a drug lord at the river. I heard her call a man by the name of Carlos to meet her there. You were to be an exchange for something Lucy wanted."

"Carlos Galvan?" He led one of the largest drug cartels and operated from Reynosa. His business had spread into South America. Last year he beheaded two opposing gang members and dumped their heads near a church in the city. She didn't want to think what he'd do with them. And if Nadine knew, she wasn't saying.

"I only heard his name. Nothing else."

Danika refused to tell her any more.

CHAPTER 54

You'll find us rough, sir, but you'll find us ready.
CHARLES DICKENS

ALEX RODE IN ED'S TRUCK in pursuit of Lucy's car. Humidity hung in the air, and clouds drowned the stars and moon. The combination did nothing to boost Alex's hope for Danika's rescue. He prayed and fretted. Prayed and fretted. *O ye of little faith.*

"They have at least a fifteen-minute head start," Alex said.

"But the Border Patrol is waiting for them on the U.S. side and the Mexican police on the other." Ed pressed the gas pedal. "And we've called for a helicopter to assist."

Alex's worst fears rose to the surface. "I'm concerned about a shoot-out in Reynosa between the Mexican police and one of the drug gangs."

Ed didn't respond.

How could Danika survive? Reynosa was a constant bloodbath. They weren't going to make it in time. Lucy would drive into a barricade, and that would be the end of one courageous Border Patrol agent. And Alex hadn't told Danika he was falling in love.

From the jostle inside the trunk, Danika realized Lucy had turned off onto a dirt road—which could be anywhere.

"Toss your shoe on the road," she said to Nadine. "In fact, let's leave anything we can."

In the next few minutes, both pairs of shoes were tossed out, hopefully leaving a trail. Danika didn't want to think it would be a path to their bodies. No car followed them or they would have seen the headlights. The car sped along, hitting all the potholes and bouncing them all over the trunk. Nadine squirmed against her.

"What are you doing?"

"My bra," Nadine said. "Never liked it anyway, and I don't have much to fill it."

Any other time, Danika would have laughed. Now she wondered if she could wiggle out of hers. No matter how hard she strained her ears for the pulsating *whew-whew* of a police car, all that greeted her was silence.

"My parents will never find out how much I love them," Nadine whispered. "They will forever believe I helped Lucy commit horrible crimes."

"Don't believe that for an instant. Jacob and Barbara know you, their daughter."

"I lay awake at night and dreamed about how we used to laugh and have good times before Uncle Toby died."

Danika yearned for the same thing. "We'll have them again. I found out your parents are working out their differences. Your dad's been meeting with Father Cornell again."

"That's worth dying for."

Nadine had grown up. Too bad it had taken this. "I'm not giving up, and neither should you." Danika hugged her stomach. She feared passing out. "Are you praying?"

"All the time."

The car slowed, turned, and rolled to a stop.

This is it. She wanted to think like the apostle Paul and tell herself that she won either way in whatever happened next, but she couldn't bring herself to be resigned to a bullet.

Not yet.

Lucy's car door slammed, her footsteps clapping against a gravel and dirt road.

"*Estoy aquí,*" she said, "near the point we discussed." Silence. "I've got the car hidden in the *carrizo.*" Silence. "How soon?" Silence. "*Bueno.* I'll be waiting. I kept my word. Now you need to keep yours."

Whoever Lucy was talking to on the phone would be there shortly.

"Do you think it's ransom money?" Nadine whispered.

Danika refused to tell her it was most likely their executioners. The image of beheaded victims burst through her mind.

Lucy knocked on the trunk. "You two are in for a special treat tonight. Memorable."

So they waited.

CHAPTER 55

Great deeds are usually wrought at great risks.
HERODOTUS

ALEX REFUSED to give up hope, but Lucy's car had disappeared.

"They aren't at the bridge." Ed snapped shut his cell phone. "I have an idea."

He spun his truck around in the middle of the highway while downshifting, then hit the accelerator, squealing tires that could be heard a mile away.

Alex grasped the hand grip above the truck door but said nothing. Ed had a handle on what he was doing, and hopefully God guided the truck. "Where are we going?"

"Near the riverbank. I bet there's going to be an exchange, and it's taking place in the blackest, thickest part." Ed whipped the truck onto a dirt road at the intersection where a convenience store often held illegals who mixed in with the other customers. He flipped open the phone again and dialed. "See where I turned off? Right. I need backup with no lights or sound and a couple of good shooters." Without waiting for an answer, he disconnected the call. Good thing the Border Patrol and police worked together. He doused the lights and swung a glance toward Alex. "Okay, rodeo star, I need you to take over the wheel."

Alex shoved aside the thought of his wounded leg to size up Ed's request. "I could grab the steering wheel, while you scoot out from underneath it. Then I'll take over."

"I don't intend to slow down much."

No point in wasting time and energy to argue. "Let's do it."

Alex slid next to him and took the wheel. The gearshift on the floor would be the next obstacle. "Why are we doing this?"

"So I can get a clear shot."

Alex guided the truck with one hand and positioned himself to straddle the gearshift. "Aren't you taking a risk?"

"Don't think we have much choice. Get your foot on the gas now."

With both eyes on the road, Alex managed to steer and swing his leg over to the accelerator. Fire raced through his right leg, and he still had to drag it over the gearshift. Ed drew his feet up onto the seat and maneuvered to the passenger side. For a big man, he moved quickly.

Alex gritted his teeth and pulled his right leg over the gearshift. He eased down onto the seat, his leg throbbing while he blinked back the blinding pain. "That was impossible."

"Not for two old cowboys." Ed chuckled and pointed to the right. "There, slow down a bit and follow the road. I'll tell you where to stop."

Ed grabbed his backpack from the floorboard and pulled out his night vision goggles. He reached under the seat and wrapped his hand around a rifle. Alex had seen this jewel before, a M40A1 sniper rifle.

Danika listened to the distant sound of Spanish-speaking voices—two, possibly three men. Obviously the men didn't trust Lucy and wanted her to bring the women to them. Danika heard the word *decapitar*. Nadine heard her fate, but she no longer sobbed. Maybe they'd see youth and beauty and spare the girl. But that alternative sounded almost as grim. Nadine needed the courage that had kept her strong for the past several days. More importantly, she needed God's grace. They both did.

The trunk popped open. In the darkness, Danika made out Lucy's shadowy form. The woman stood back to avoid a kick or a punch, knowing Danika would have welcomed an opportunity to send her sprawling on the dirt road.

"Get out," Lucy said. "Slowly. You don't have anywhere to run."

That was her opinion. As soon as Danika climbed from the trunk, a man stepped from the side of the car and jerked her hands behind her, tying them with a cord. Nadine followed behind her.

"The girl shot Jose," Lucy said. "Should bring you a good price."

The man laughed. "If she doesn't slit a man's throat."

Lucy swore. "What she's about to see will take care of her fight."

Dread washed over Danika, not for herself but for Nadine.

"We're taking them back with us," another man said. "We got plans."

"What about mine?" Lucy's voice tightened. "I've thought about this for two years."

"What's more important to you: revenge or money?"

Lucy paused. "Okay, Carlos, take them with you."

The men laughed, drowning out the dirge of insects in the surrounding brush. Two of them grabbed Danika and Nadine.

"Wait a minute. I want my money for the girl." Lucy's exasperation wouldn't go down well with these men. They'd chew her up and use her for fish bait.

"When we're back, I'll send it to you," Carlos sounded confident, his mocking words no doubt aimed to frustrate her.

"Neither of them go until I have the cash."

"You don't know who you're talking to." Carlos's tone edged beyond menacing.

"I'll kill them right here." Lucy raised her gun and aimed straight at Danika's face.

This is it. Is this how Toby felt? I wish I hadn't argued with him that day. . . . I wish I'd gotten to know Alex better . . . been a better friend. Trusted more. Jesus, take care of my baby.

Danika stared into the dark outline of Lucy's face. *I'm ready.*

Rifle fire cracked and Lucy fell as the shot echoed across the night. Two more rapid shots, and the men holding Danika and Nadine fell. Only Carlos remained.

"U.S. Border Patrol. Raise your hands." Chief Patrol Agent Edwardo Jimenez's booming voice sounded like sweet music as four vehicles swarmed the riverbank drop point.

It was over. Finally over.

Danika peered at Nadine and the two leaned into each other. Words failed both of them, for none existed to claim the joy of life and the sadness of death in one breath. Nadine did not sob. She was made of the same sturdy stock as her dad and uncle.

"Danika." Alex's voice rang out in the darkness. She heard the thud of boots and the thump of his crutch and craved his arms around her.

Helicopter blades whirled above them. Vehicle headlights ahead flashed on, and then she saw them—the dynamic duo of the chief and Alex. Her superheroes. Alex limped faster, and her eyes pooled. Shaken, she refused to give in to a complete breakdown. Alex reached for her at the same time that the chief reached for Nadine.

"You all right?" Jimenez asked as he untied the young girl and Alex untied Danika.

Nadine nodded and sniffed. "Thank you, sir. I was so scared. I just knew they were going to kill us."

"They're dead or in custody," he said. "This whole thing is finished."

"I'd like to see my dad," Nadine said. "Can we do that? I have to tell him I'm sorry and ask him to forgive me."

"I'll take you myself."

While Danika listened to the conversation and the scuffle of men handling the bodies and handcuffing Carlos, she basked in the arms of a man who meant more to her than she could imagine.

"I was afraid I'd lost you," he said, "that Ed might be wrong."

"Was he the one who killed Lucy?"

"Sure thing."

Danika turned to Chief Jimenez. "I take back all of the things I ever said about you. You saved my life."

"Why do I think all those things weren't good?"

"Maybe the other agents need to get to know you better."

"Ruin my image? Hey, there's something you can do for me."

She breathed in and fought the pain tearing through her body. "What's that?"

"Take the supervisor position. Chasing you down is making an old man out of me. Besides, I think you have a lot to teach the new guys."

"Deal." She nestled into Alex's embrace. Deep inside, she realized they'd been placed together for a purpose. "Thank you," she whispered.

"For what?"

"For not giving up on me. For being here. For finding a place for Tiana. For helping to solve this whole thing. For—"

"Agent Morales, hush and let me kiss you."

And she did.

Jacob woke in the wee hours of the morning. A police officer rattled Jacob's cell, startling, then annoying him. He snapped his attention toward the cop.

"You're out of here, Morales," the officer said. "Free to go."

Barbara must have paid his bail. She shouldn't have gone

into her savings for him. She'd get it back, for sure. "Is my wife waiting?"

"I have no idea. Let's go get your belongings, and you can see for yourself."

The fluorescent lights immediately wakened him, and he followed the officer down the hall and through two locked doors. He hoped he never saw the inside of a cell again. A clerk who talked through his mustache shoved discharge paperwork Jacob's way and had him sign a receipt for his personal belongings. Odd, there wasn't a bondsman or paperwork to complete for the bail.

The officer opened the door to the front office and bade him good night. Jacob hoped so. He stepped across the threshold and saw Nadine. He blinked, wondering if he was still asleep.

She hurried across the waiting area. "Dad, oh, Daddy."

The sound of her voice awakened a part of him that he thought he'd never find again. She rushed into his arms like the little toddler who used to greet him after work. He could die this very minute and be one happy man.

"It's over," she sobbed. "I'm sorry for running away and causing all of this trouble. It was Lucy who killed Uncle Toby, and she wanted to kill Aunt Danika and you too. She made me ride along and hold your watch when Jose put a bomb in the truck."

"Go ahead and cry, Naddie girl." He stroked her silky black hair. Never would he let anything come between him and his family again. God might have to bridle his tongue, but it would happen.

He glanced up to see Barbara standing with a small group—Danika, Alex Price, Chief Jimenez, and a handful of Border Patrol agents. They all looked beat. Must have been a hard night on the line. Later he'd find out what all had happened. Right now, he wanted to hold his daughter and his wife. Blinking back the tears, Jacob beckoned Barbara to join him and Nadine.

CHAPTER 56

**O Lord, you have examined my heart
and know everything about me.**
PSALM 139:1

Six weeks later

"HEY, HONEY. The coals are about ready for the meat," Alex called from the door leading to the patio.

"I'll bring the burgers." Danika dried her hands on a dish towel and stole a moment to watch Alex through the window. He must have sensed her staring at him and turned to wave.

She blew him a kiss and felt a tingle clear to her toes. Their relationship kept getting better and better. And even though she'd not admit it this quickly, Alex was a keeper and she had no intentions of letting him go. He'd mentioned the big *M* word, and she'd suggested they wait until after the first of the year. But all it would take was a weak moment and one of his kisses, and she'd be saying yes to becoming Mrs. Alex Price.

"Here, I'll take those." Jacob took the tray of meat and grinned. "If we wait on you and Alex to stop making eyes at each other, we'll all starve." He nodded toward the kids in the living room. "Listen to that. If we don't feed them soon, we'll have mutiny."

Danika wrinkled her nose at him. "You're one to talk. I heard your kids say you and Barbara act like newlyweds."

"We are," Jacob said as he headed for the patio.

Danika whirled around to Barbara. "Do you know how wonderful it is to see Jacob happy and your marriage rock solid?"

Barbara nodded. "Every day I thank God for my family. I never dreamed my husband would be content building furniture. His blood pressure is back to normal without medication, and he's home with us every night."

"I'm so happy for you." Danika hugged her.

"Mom, we're starved," Jake called from the other room.

"You're only hungry because I'm beating you at Monopoly," Nadine said. "Little brother, you're bankrupt."

The doorbell rang, and Danika hurried to answer it. "Must be Felipe and Becca. They're bringing the dessert."

She glanced out the window. The media had ceased to follow her around like the paparazzi, but they were clever. She'd insulted enough reporters to last a lifetime, but sufficient time had passed for them to move on to something else. A black taxi was parked at the curb.

Curious, she opened the door and started. The blood seemed to drain from her face, and she couldn't utter a word. Mom and Dad stood before her. They were older, Dad's hair a little whiter and a few more lines around Mom's eyes. They looked as anxious as she felt.

"I know you're shocked." Dad shifted from one foot to another. "We didn't know how else to do this. Can't blame you if you slam the door in our faces."

Danika stood in the doorway numb—hot and cold at the same time. A part of her wanted to cry. Another part of her *did* want to slam the door in their faces. The biggest part of her wanted everything to be right.

Tiana patted her leg. "Who is this?" she signed.

"Can I tell her?" Mom asked. Danika had forgotten how soft her mother's voice was and how she always dressed in fashion.

"I . . . I suppose it's all right."

"Danika, who's at the door?" Alex called from the kitchen. She hadn't even heard the back door close.

"My parents."

Mom bent to one knee, visibly nervous. "Tiana, I am your grandmother. Your mommy's mommy," she signed.

Mom had learned sign language? Danika attempted to stop the flow of tears, but they swept over her cheeks. She was angry. She was happy. She didn't know what to feel.

In an instant, Alex's arm slipped around her waist. He stuck out his hand to Dad. "Alex Price."

Dad grasped his hand. "Good to meet you. William Cutchner." He sounded like he was greeting church members.

"Danika looks like you," Alex said.

"Prettier than her dad. She gets her stubborn streak from me," Dad said. "I have the dominant gene."

"Is this my grandfather?" Tiana signed.

Dad stiffened. He took a deep breath and nodded.

"Is this true, Mommy?"

The lump in Danika's throat thickened. For the first time she was glad to sign her response instead of speaking it. "Yes."

"Can they come in?" Tiana's dark eyes sparkled. She clapped her hands.

Mom's gaze peered into Danika's face, tears brimming her eyes. "I've missed my daughter."

Dad cleared his throat, his normal habit before delivering a sermon. "I feel like I'm the Prodigal Son asking for forgiveness." He shook his head. "I regret the years I tried to dictate your life. Our last conversation was . . . my fault. You reached out for help, and I smacked you in the face with it. And then when what happened to you hit the news, I realized I had to get my girl back. I'm so sorry. I can't even imagine what the past two years have been like—how dangerous your job and the enormity of responsibility."

Danika stared into the faces of two people whom she'd never stopped loving. Her own tears fell unchecked for all the years of misunderstanding. "Please, come in," she finally said. "I want you to meet the rest of my family."

Danika walked through her home, stepping around children and toys and listening to the sounds of what real love was all about.

The Rio Grande was not just murky. It was toxic. Danika Morales respected the river's temperament—lazy and rushing, crystal and muddy, breathtaking and devastating. To many illegal immigrants, its flowing water signified hope and an opportunity for a better tomorrow. Others viewed the river crossing as a means of smuggling drugs or spreading terrorism. But for Danika, the depths had brought back life and love.

A NOTE FROM THE AUTHOR

Dear reader,

When I started writing *Sworn to Protect*, I believed I had an understanding of the immigration problem. After all, I know people who are undocumented immigrants, and I know people who are Border Patrol agents. Their situation and plight are familiar to most of us living in southern Texas.

Then Danika and Alex's story began to unfold. As I looked into their hearts and those of the people around them, I discovered I really didn't know much at all about the emotional, physical, mental, and spiritual stresses of our neighbors south of the Rio Grande or the brave men and women who protect our borders. Learning along with my characters proved to be a challenging and enjoyable journey.

While conducting research, I was fortunate to ride the line with a couple of Border Patrol agents. I hope I have been able to portray these courageous people accurately. I remember how hot the days, how muddy the Rio Grande, and how desperate the people. The Border Patrol agents' compassion and respect for undocumented immigrants impressed me. I also became aware of the dangers the agents face. Can you imagine not wearing your uniform to and from work for fear of endangering your family's lives?

Without a doubt, *Sworn to Protect* does not attempt to address all the complex issues surrounding immigration in the United States. It would be difficult to do that within the pages of a novel. If you'd like to learn more about the Border Patrol and undocumented immigrants, I invite you to read *Patrolling Chaos: The U.S. Border Patrol in Deep South Texas* by Robert Lee Maril (Texas Tech University Press, 2006). For a distinctly Christian perspective, you may want to read *Welcoming the Stranger* by Matthew Soerens and Jenny Hwang (InterVarsity Press, 2009).

I hope you enjoyed *Sworn to Protect*. I left a piece of my heart with the characters. It's been said that if a writer doesn't change and grow in writing a novel, then she can't expect the reader to change and grow either. I hope this novel has made you more aware of our immigration issues, and may we pray together for a resolution.

Expect an Adventure
DiAnn Mills
www.diannmills.com

ABOUT THE AUTHOR

AWARD-WINNING AUTHOR DiAnn Mills is a fiction writer who combines an adventuresome spirit with unforgettable characters to create action-packed novels. DiAnn's first book was published in 1998. She currently has more than forty books in print, which have sold more than a million and a half copies.

Six of her books have appeared on the CBA best-seller list. Eight of her books have been nominated for the American Christian Fiction Writers' Book of the Year contest, and she is the recipient of the Inspirational Reader's Choice award for 2005 and 2007. *Lightning and Lace* was a 2008 Christy Award finalist.

DiAnn is a founding board member for American Christian Fiction Writers and a member of Inspirational Writers Alive; Romance Writers of America's Faith, Hope and Love chapter; and the Advanced Writers and Speakers Association. She speaks to various groups and teaches writing workshops around the country. DiAnn is also a mentor for the Jerry B. Jenkins Christian Writers Guild.

Her latest releases are *Awaken My Heart* and *Breach of Trust*.

DISCUSSION QUESTIONS

1. Have you ever considered taking a job that might put you or your family in danger?

2. How far would you go to protect a family member?

3. Grief is often a formidable monster. How well does Danika handle the second anniversary of her husband's death? How do you handle reminders of loss or grief in your life?

4. Jacob is bitter about his brother's death, and it affects his relationship with his family. How might you react in a similar situation?

5. If you were Danika's friend, would you encourage her to seek out a relationship with Alex? Why or why not?

6. Should Alex have told Danika from the beginning about his friendship with Toby? How might his doing so have changed the trajectory of their relationship?

7. Alex has his own personal views about undocumented immigrants. How are they different from Danika's?

8. It's been said that desperate people do desperate things. What particular desperation motivates Sandra? Lucy? Jose?

9. How do you feel about Sandra's deceit? Was she justified in what she did?

10. Jacob made a renewed commitment to God and his family. Do you think he will be able to keep his word? Why or why not?

11. At the end of the story, Danika and Alex pledge their love to each other. What have they learned from past relationships? Where does their faith in Christ fit?

12. Before reading this novel, what was your opinion of the Border Patrol and the immigration debate? Has it changed, and if so, in what ways? Do you have any ideas for a solution to the situation with our borders?

Turn the page for a preview of book
three in the Call of Duty series.
AVAILABLE FALL 2010.

THE MOMENT BELLA accepted the reassignment to the FBI's field office in Houston, she realized the past had stalked her to the present. And she was ready, or at least she told herself she was. Her training and experience had sharpened her skills and provided the tools she needed to solve crimes the average American deemed unspeakable.

Fear and memories had climbed into her luggage when she relocated to Houston, but she defied their strangling hold. Bella was determined to work hard to build her credentials and help curtail the endless barrage of crime, especially within a city that contained more people than Chicago.

Her BlackBerry interrupted her thoughts and her drive to work with its musical rendition of "That'll Be the Day." A quick glance showed the caller was Frank.

No way, super agent. I don't have a thing to tell you. She answered on the third ring. "Morning, Frank. What can I do for you?"

"Lunch?"

She laughed. "You heard I have an appointment with Swartzer, and curiosity is killing you."

"Me? I wanted to talk about spending the weekend in Galveston."

"Right. Frank, it's been nine months since we dated."

"Nine months, huh? As in giving birth to a new relationship?"

She envisioned a slight smile spreading over his face—a good-looking one, but one that was not for her. "No thanks. Remember, we tried and it didn't work. I don't want to put my heart in that place again. See you later."

"But—"

"Bye, Frank."

Bella tossed the phone into her purse. Regret over the failed relationship with Frank settled like a day harboring poor air quality. She'd known from the start a relationship with him wouldn't work. He wanted a wife who'd stay home and raise kids. She refused to give up the bureau, no matter how much she cared for him. The only thing she'd ever formed a lasting attachment to was the FBI, and mistakes in the name of love were not in her playbook.

A promotion had been within her grasp for the past few months, and she desperately wanted it. Ambition always ruled over her logic, but she didn't view her objectives as selfish. The meeting this morning with her supervisor might be a jump in her career. A coveted opportunity to prove her mettle sounded almost too good to be true, and like a kid at Christmas on this early June morning, she drove toward the field office to see if she had a gift marked "promotion."

Bella moved into the right lane of 290 to take the exit off the highway. For certain, battling traffic at seven in the morning had hardened her for criminal activity—or destroyed any trace of patience. Her mind raced with anticipation over her meeting with Swartzer. This meeting could be about a number of ongoing investigations—or possibly a new one. No matter, she'd take the assignment and keep climbing the ladder.

She swung into the parking lot of the eight-story, glass and steel building and stopped in front of the guard shack. After displaying her creds, she eased into the covered parking area and hurried inside. Her heart pounded against her chest, and she sensed the familiar excitement of a new challenge. She scanned her badge and keyed in her security code at each door, making her way to the floor housing the violent crimes task force team and the office of Larry Swartzer, her supervisor. While his secretary informed him of her arrival, Bella took several deep breaths in an effort to settle her nerves and will away the anxiety making her feel like a kid sent to the principal's office.

Swartzer opened the door. "Mornin', Bella. Come on in."

Her heavy shoulder bag shifted and slipped from her arm to the floor. Thank goodness it was zipped. She cringed at the idea of her Glock, handcuffs, and all of her other equipment, including her makeup bag and wallet, dropping at her feet.

"Little nervous, are we?" He chuckled, and her confidence suddenly fell to somewhere between diffused and lack-of.

She laughed and hoisted her bag. "Add curious to the mix."

He ushered her into his office, and she took a seat across from his desk. The wall behind him intimidated her with its framed certificates and honors earned over his twenty-year career. Most likely his wife refused to have them all displayed at home. Bella attempted to read his face, but Swartzer prided himself in being unreadable, and this morning was no exception. Although short and stocky, her supervisor had the neck and shoulders of a man who must bench nearly 275 pounds. He removed his signature black-framed glasses and turned to retrieve a couple of files from atop his credenza. She hadn't seen him without his glasses. *Must be farsighted.* Swartzer's military haircut and polyester pants still made him look nerdish, but then superintelligent people usually were.

Where did that leave her? Shoving aside the bazillion thoughts darting in and out of her mind like mosquitoes over a stagnant pond, she realigned her focus and attempted to give the impression of professional calmness.

"I have an assignment for you." He tapped the file and eased back in the chair that was made for a much taller man, at least physically.

"What kind?"

"Murder. Three bodies were found Monday afternoon on a ranch in west Texas." His calculated gaze met hers. "Sixty miles southwest of Abilene."

He had her attention, and he knew it. "Runnels County?"

"Ballinger area."

She nodded and forced aside the implications of what the location meant to her. "Why the FBI?"

"It's linked to a man on our fugitive list."

Suspicion flared, and she opened the file, complete with photos of the victims. She pressed her fingertips into her palms. "Who?" But she already knew the answer.

"Brandt Richardson."

"Murder for hire." She stated the fact while memories slammed against her mind in apocalyptic proportions. "Also obsessed with finding the so-called Spider Rock treasure."

"The victims were hunting for this treasure and believed their clues led them to the High Butte Ranch, owned by Carr Sullivan. They sought permission to dig, and he refused. Ran them off. One of the victims wrote 'Spider Rock' in the dirt before he died."

"Runnels County doesn't fall within the triangle of where the gold was supposedly hidden."

"You know more about it than I do."

"What were the victims' names?"

"Forrest Miller, a history professor at The University of Texas. Daniel Kegley, a geologist from Austin, and Walt Higgins, retired oil man from Waco."

She didn't recognize any of them. "Family?"

"Miller has a wife and three teenage girls. Kegley was engaged, and Higgins was divorced. The families have all been interviewed. Professor Miller's wife said a fourth man was in the mix, but that's all she knew. Nothing else at this point." Swartzer slipped on his glasses and steepled his fingers. "You know why I want *you* on the assignment. Or would you rather I brief Frank Benson?"

Not on her life. Both of them were up for the same promotion. "I'll take it."